EMORY

Wordly Press

EMORY

DERIN ATTWOOD

ROB BURT

ALISON DAVIE

TERESA HERLETH

KAMALA JACKSON

CLARE MATRAVERS

ANNA WILLIAMS

Emory

A Wordly Press Publication
Ashhurst, New Zealand
Phone 64 6 326 8066

First published by Wordly Press in 2017

Set in 12/14/18/24 Adobe Garamond Pro
This text uses English (UK) spelling.

ISBN 978-0-9941108-7-9

A catalogue record for this book is available from the National Library of New Zealand.

Wordly Press

www.wordlypress.com

Dedication

Derin Attwood

To Ron, as always, for the usual encouragement. Also for my nephew, Steven, who is learning, as I have, that stepping out of our comfort zone can bring huge rewards.

Rob Burt

To my old friend Anand, who I have not seen for years, and who nurtured in me my fascination and love of India.

Alison Davie

To my family, especially my Mum and brother for all their continued support.

Teresa Herleth

To my Whangarei writing friends who have supported me in realising my dream of telling stories on paper, especially Derin, for Paul and Vicki who inspired that crucial first step of action, and for second-cousin Becs, who has listened enthusiastically and given valuable feedback to this particular story. I hope you all know how extremely grateful I am.

Kamala Jackson

In memory of Deborah Turner.

Clare Matravers

To all those who have encouraged me in my writing.

Anna Williams

To the people closest to me, who know first-hand how my Emory characters evolved.

NEW ZEALAND TERMINOLOGY

Because we wished to show this as a classically New Zealand story from the 1980's, we used terms that were common in New Zealand then. Because meanings and use changes over time and between countries, we have given their use as we remember them.

Aakronite	Vanity tops, basins etc.
Aye	New Zealand variation of eh.
Cheese	In the context of this story, 'Cheese' was a common saying, made famous in NZ by John Clarke in his TV series, Fred Dagg, with the saying "Cheese Trev". Adaptation of Jeeze.
Dunger	An old decrepit car.
Godzone	New Zealanders' name for their country. A shortened version of God's own country.
High School	For school students aged thirteen to eighteen in New Zealand.
Hottie	Hot water bottle.
Jug/Kettle	In the context of Emory, a kettle is heated on an Aga, while a jug is electric.
Kindy	Kindergarten. For pre-schoolers from ages three to five.
Kowhai	One of New Zealand's best known native trees. Has beautiful yellow flowers.

Plunket Nurse	Baby and Child Health Nurse. Plunket is an iconic name in NZ. The organisation was started by Dr Frederic Truby King in 1907. It got its name from an early patron Victoria Plunket, wife of the then Govenor of New Zealand, William Plunket.
Pounamu	Nephrite jade, also known generically as greenstone.
Ranchsliders	An external sliding door, made generally of glass and aluminium.
Raro	Tinned orange juice.
School C.	School Certificate. An exam passed by school children in their 5th form (year ten).
Silverbeet	Swiss chard or mangold.
Skite	To Brag.
Snax	Plain cracker biscuits, common in NZ.
Tui	Bird, endemic to New Zealand. They appear black, but have an iridescent blue and green sheen, especially on the head and wings, and a distinctive white tuft at its throat. Also known, for that reason, as a parson bird.
U.E.	University Entrance. The entrance exam for school students wanting to move on to university.
Weet-Bix	A New Zealand product, similar to England's Weetabix.
Whiteware	Stoves, fridges and other similar household electrical equipment, mostly coloured white prior to the nineteen eighties.
Windolene	Window cleaner.

PEN-ULTIMATE WRITING GROUP

In 2013, a small group of writers, undergoing various writing projects met to help each other. They named themselves Pen-Ultimate, Pen-U for short, and learned the art of gentle, but tough critiquing of their current work in progress. They met fortnightly, and utilised their personal strengths with the ultimate goal of publishing their books.

In late 2014, the idea of writing a joint book grew—an anthology—so they could all go through the actual experience of taking a novel from original concept to finished book. Again, they planned to rely on internal experience, but also endeavoured to use professionals where necessary.

With much laughter, the odd missed deadline, a bit of nagging, and a few tears, the story grew. The writing portion of Emory was finished.

Then the learning began. Editing, formatting, dealing with proof copies, and finally cover-creation, was a new experience for many of the writers. Each was managed well. The diverse writing styles melded together to allow Emory to appeal to all tastes.

Set in the early to mid-1980's, the stories of Oak Tree Lane grew to be more. It is about people, neighbours and friends. It is about life in a rural town, but it could be any suburban street in any town or city.

This is EMORY.

Oak Tree Lane, Emory

Oak Tree Lane, Emory, began life as a farm track, leading to two houses on land bought and farmed by Henry Thompson and Robert Romford. Worker houses, barns and other outbuildings were added over the years.

In 1895, Robert and Henry planted twenty oak trees along the side of the track to celebrate the birth of Henry's daughter, Charlotte. By 1898, Oak Tree track was known to everyone in the district.

In 1949, the City Council extended the city limit south past the track. The Council removed most of the oak trees, widened and paved the track to make it an official city road. Because the residents, led by Miss Charlotte Thompson, the only daughter of the original Henry, protested against removing the last oak tree from the end of the street, the Council circled the road around it, and the cul-de-sac was officially named Oak Tree Lane.

Part of the northern area of the farm was bought by the Council to use as a park. Over the next few years, many of the quarter-acre sections were sold, and most were built on. Never-the-less, the area continued its rural outlook, with extensive farm-land on the southern and western sides, as the then City of Emory concentrated its growth towards the north and east. Oak Tree Lane sat somewhat alone, just inside the fifty kph area.

In 1978, the whisper of change was in the air. Talk of new subdivisions opening up, south and west of Oak Tree Lane, got louder. The outgoing Mayor, Anthony Hunt denied the rumours, and the people of Oak Tree Lane continued to live their lives.

1

by Alison Davie

The sunlight breaking through the small gap in the curtains woke Edith. Her weary eyes opened slowly. It had been another bad night. She turned over to see the empty space next to her in the bed. She closed her eyes, and let out a long sigh. "Dammit!" she said, under her breath.

She dragged her aging body out of the bed and put on her housecoat. "Charles?" she called, but no reply. She put her feet half into her slippers and scuffled out of the bedroom.

"Charlie?" Still no reply. She walked into the living room and saw the front door open.

"Damn that man! He's going to drive me to an early grave," she grumbled to herself.

She went outside and down the path, checked the mail box, even though she knew it was too early for the mail.

"I saw him head that way, Edith," called Ginny, the neighbour from across the way, as she got into her car.

"Thanks," replied Edith.

"At least he's got his undies on today," laughed Ginny, "and his, not yours."

"God help us all," said Edith slightly embarrassed. "That day was a sight for sore eyes," she shouted as she headed in the direction Ginny had pointed.

Edith hadn't gone far when she heard the all too familiar neighbourly shriek. She headed towards Kirstin's but stopped in her path when she saw Kirstin walking Charles down the side path.

"Sorry about that."

Kirstin chortled, "Gave me such a scare. I bent down to pick up the laundry and when I came up, he was just staring at me through the window. At least he's got some underwear on today."

"Sorry for the bother, Kirstin."

"Oh, no harm done. There but for the grace of God, aye Edith."

Edith took Charles by the hand and led him back to the house. She was grateful she had such understanding neighbours.

Her oldest son Derek lived in Australia and insisted his dad belonged in a nursing home. He reckoned Charlie was too much for his mother to handle, and on nights and mornings like these, sometimes Edith would agree. But then she would see glimpses of the old Charles, and she couldn't let him go.

She guided Charles into the house and lead him straight to the bathroom. She sat him down in a chair and filled the sink up with warm water.

"You gave Kirstin a right old fright there."

She took a soapy flannel and began to wash him. The tenderness in her touch made Charles smile.

"I can do it myself, you know, Edie," he said.

She smiled. He remembered her name today.

"I know you can darling, but it's just faster if I do it."

"You're just an old fusspot," he muttered tenderly, and puckered his lips up for a kiss. She smiled and obliged.

"And you're still an old charmer, Charlie Stanwell."

She lifted up his arms one by one and washed under them.

"Do you remember our first kiss? We'd just come out Carnegie's dance hall. I was in my army uniform and was nervous as all to buggery and I said, Edie Harris, I'm gonna lay one on ya, and I leaned over and kissed you right there and then."

She smiled.

Wasn't the most romantic moment, but it was wonderful."

He laughed, "Good job I've learned a thing or two since then. We should go dancing again someday."

"Oh Charlie, we haven't been dancing for near fifty years."

"Then all the more reason to go."

He started to sing 'when we're out together dancing cheek to cheek,' and took hold of Edie and waltzed her around the bathroom, as she laughed at his antics.

This is the Charles she remembers. How can she let him go? She knows he still loves her. Some days he may not remember her, but she knows he loves her.

Charles woke. It was still dark as he glanced at the clock; 4.30 in the morning. He looked over at Edie who was fast asleep. A gentle purring snore escaped on every out breath which made him smile. He had teased her many times about her lady snores.

Charles slid out from under the covers figuring he could

get in a few hours of freedom before Edie was looking over his shoulder observing everything he did.

"Stop fussing," he would say, but she was always within earshot, which, at times he found very annoying.

He tottered quietly into the kitchen to make himself a cup of tea. He switched on the jug, and got out a cereal bowl. He turned to get a tea bag out the cupboard, but couldn't remember what he was actually going for. He looked in the cupboard and took out the bread. As he turned, the jug clicked off.

Oh, I was making tea. He turned, put the bread back and shut the cupboard door.

As Charles turned back, he saw the cereal bowl on the counter top and stood there looking at it for a moment. *Have I had cereal or was I going to get the cereal?* He checked the bowl and figuring it looked dry, he deduced he was going to get cereal. He went back into the cupboard and pulled out the bread. He turned, saw the cereal bowl and couldn't remember...*GODDAMMIT!* He threw the loaf of bread down on the counter.

He decided he may go for a walk so as not to disturb Edie. Wearing only his underpants he headed out the front door, leaving it slightly ajar as he left. It was a bit chilly out but Charles thought a brisk walk should warm him nicely. He wandered up Oak Tree Lane towards the big tree. He loved that big tree. The splendour as it stood guard over the street. It had provided a playground for the local kids and its sheer size and beauty had commanded many a street party and social gathering.

Feeling a bit lost, Charles looked around. The street was eerie, only lit by the street lighting and the full moon above, and the quietness was overwhelming. A cat ran out in front of him, meowed as it crossed his path, giving him a bit of a fright. "Get out of it, ya mongrel!" he shouted.

Charles wandered in and out of people's gardens, unknown by the sleeping bodies inside.

As the sun started to rise, he began to feel the chill and decided to head back home. He turned on his heels and headed back the way he had come. *Now what number is it? Ah, this house looks familiar.*

He walked up the path into the backyard and tried to open the back door, but it was locked. Charles tried again, giving it a bit more of a rattle. "Edie?" he shouted. "Open the door, Edie!"

Ginny appeared at the door and opened it. "Charles, what are you doing out? It's five in the morning, darling. You'll catch your death. Come inside and I'll make you a hot cuppa."

"You're not Edie. Where's my Edie?' he shouted. "What have you done with her?"

Ginny tried to take Charles by the arm and gently lead him inside, but he pushed her off.

"Help! Help!" he cried.

"Shhh! You'll wake Rebecca. C'mon, I'll take you home."

She shut the door behind her and led Charles over the road. Hesitantly, she knocked on the door that was already ajar. She slowly made her way in and made her way to the kitchen, the only room with a light on. She shouted in a loud whisper, "Edie? Edie?"

Edie soon appeared in the kitchen where she saw Ginny with Charles in tow. He stood there in his undies. *He looks so, so, lost* thought Edie.

"Oh thank you, Ginny. I'm so very sorry. I never even heard him get up. I hope he hasn't been a bother."

"Just gave me a bit of a fright," replied Ginny. "Anyway I'll go now, got some early meetings today. Take care, Edie."

"Thanks again, Ginny."

Edie led Charles back to bed and sat him on the side. She

got some pyjamas for him and put them on.

"You could have frozen out there. From now on you're sleeping in PJ's whether you like it or not!"

Once she got him dressed she quickly rubbed her hands up and down his arms trying to warm him up.

"Not tonight, Edie. I'm too tired!" With that he lay down in bed, pulled the warm duvet over him and closed his eyes.

Edie was stunned for a little bit, and then burst out laughing. *Not tonight, Edie!* The more she thought about it the more it made her chuckle. She got into bed, leaned over and kissed sleeping Charlie on the cheek. Another laugh escaped, that laugh where you feel sad at the sentiment, but it lightens your heart to think about whatever it is that is making you laugh. Like, at a funeral and someone tells you a funny story about the person who has died.

I'm too tired. She laughed out loud again. *Would never have said that in his heyday.*

Daniel visited at least once a month, even if it was just for the day. Today, he brought his teenage son, Matthew. Edie had been telling them about the garden and a few other small handyman fixes needing to be done.

Charlie heard the laughter and came in from outside.

"What's going on, Edie? Who's this?"

"It's me, Dad, Danny." Danny approached with caution. He had been on the end of a punch from Charles. His dad's mind may be fragile, but it belied his right hook, which landed Danny flat on his arse with a black eye last time. This time, Charlie gave his son a hug. "Good job you're here. Your mother's not much help in the garden

6

these days. Place is overrun. And who's this young lad?"
He stared warily at Matthew.

"It's Matthew, Pops. Your grandson."

Charles never remembered anyone past his own kids
so the grandkids always had to remind him. Fortunately,
they understood.

"Well, whoever you are, you look like a strapping young
lad. The grass needs mowing. Think you can do that?"

"Sure, Pops."

With that, Matthew and his father stripped down to tee-
shirts and headed into the garden with Charlie, while Edie
left for a few hours of leisure.

Edith treasured the few hours she got alone. She could catch
up with friends for coffee, or just go and sit in a café and do
a crossword. Today, she was off to get her hair done.

She sat in the chair ready for her cut and curl. Josie the
hairdresser came over. Edie's normal hairdresser was away
and Josie had come highly recommended by Carol, and Edie
trusted Carol's judgment.

"What can we do for you today, Mrs Stanwell?"

"Usual, cut and wave." Edie caught sight of her old tired
looking face in the mirror.

"Can you make me twenty years younger too?" she asked,
smiling.

"If I did that I wouldn't be able to cut your hair; that
would make me four," said Josie, laughing as she leaned
Edie back in the sink for her hair wash.

Edie wasn't amused at the gentle reminder she no longer
had her youth. *Young whippersnapper.*

"You know when I was about your age, I was married and

living on rations while my husband was away fighting in the war. And not even for our country really, for some other country. We had it much tougher then."

"Wow. Which war was that?" Josie asked, as she chewed on some gum.

Edie frowned at young Josie in the mirror with slight disgust.

Carol would not approve of the gum chewing.

"Didn't they teach you history at school?"

"Nah, I never paid much attention in history class. Boring, if you ask me. Who wants to learn about stuff that happened years ago?"

"It's that *stuff* that happened years ago, that shaped the country you live in today."

"Yeah, but history was probably more relevant in your day cos that's when it all happened aye?"

Edie never had much tolerance for ignorance! *If this is what our education system is spitting out, no wonder this country is in bad shape.*

Edith was a staunch Labour supporter who always believed they worked in the best interest of the people who were the backbone of this country. But since David Lange had introduced that new superannuation surcharge, she had her doubts.

"That conniving scoundrel," she had complained to Charlie. "As if things aren't tough enough. If I had known, well, he wouldn't have gotten my vote."

Edith didn't partake in much conversation with Josie after that but had to agree with Carol, Josie did do a fine job with her hair. Edith was very pleased with her refreshed hairdo and politely thanked Josie.

I wonder if Charles will even notice. She placed her scarf over her hair to protect it from the slight wind that was starting up. *When he was of sound mind he always noticed these little things.* Sometimes he would pretend not to, just to annoy her, but then he would let slip a small comment that would let her know he had indeed noticed, and she would lovingly scold his teasing ways.

Edith looked out the window. It had only been a few weeks since Danny, Matt and Charlie had done the garden and she thought it had looked beautiful. However, the grass and weeds were growing again like there was no tomorrow.

When she and Charlie had bought in the street many years ago now, they had been lucky enough to be able to purchase two sections of land and build on one. The second was for Charlie's garden. He loved to potter around and grow his own vegetables.

"Daylight bloody robbery!" he bellowed when Edith brought home the shopping one day. "I'll grow my own."

He had gone out and purchased a whole lot of seedlings and from that day on, they pretty much grew their own, and supplied the neighbours too, when there was an abundance.

One time when Charles was beginning to be unwell, he had set fire to the garden because Edith had been nagging him to cut the grass. She didn't realise he was unwell though and she felt a pang of guilt later when she did find out. Charles would never have let the garden get in such a state.

"I should have known," she had said to Danny.

Edith spied the beautiful large red pot. Kirstin's pot. The doorbell rang. Edith knew it would be her. She never knew who was more embarrassed in these moments; Edith, for having a magpie for a husband, or them, for actually having to come and ask for their own property. *I'm lucky to have neighbours who are so understanding about Charles's illness.*

Edith answered the door and smiled timidly. She didn't have to say anything. "Come in, Kirstin. I've just seen it. I'll fetch it for you. I'm ever so sorry."

"I wouldn't mind, Edith, but Tommy made the pot for us as an art project at school," replied Kirstin so apologetically, that Edith felt slightly ashamed.

Edith picked up the plant-pot, "I think that's why Charles likes it so much. It's so colourfully decorated." She handed Kirstin the pot plant.

"Thank you. He got an A for it. He's such a creative kid. Maybe I can ask him to make Charles one?"

"Oh no," replied Edith, "I don't want him to go to any trouble."

"Not at all. He won't mind. I'll ask him."

"Thank you. Charles would love it I'm sure."

Edith didn't really want it. The last thing she needed right now was more plants and pots. However, her father had always taught her to 'never refuse a kind offer, as it can offend.'

As she let Kirstin out, she heard Charlie's movements in the bedroom. Time to make breakfast.

"What's for breakfast, Edie? A man can't put in a hard day's work on air alone."

She turned and smiled. Today was a Charlie day. He was back. She was never sure for how long. It may be a few minutes or a few days.

He looked outside, "Jeez, Edie, whatever happened to the garden?"

"It's been raining all week, darling. Don't you remember?" she lied.

"No excuses today. Sun's out and I'm raring to go."

He turned and smiled at her. Edith loved Charlie days.

Edie let Charles sleep in this morning. Not only because he had been up all night agitated about something, but it also gave her an hour or so to herself where she could breathe easy, knowing he was safe in bed.

She sat with her toast and cup of tea and did the morning crossword, then gathered up the plates and placed them in the sink to wash later. She quickly tidied, putting things back in their place. As she picked Charles's book off the side table, she noticed the dust had collected again.

I just did that a few days ago she thought with slight frustration.

The phone rang. Shhh! She quickly went to answer it. It was Danny. He enquired after his father, and Edie explained about the rough night and that he was still asleep. Danny said he couldn't make it up this weekend as Matthew was bringing his new girlfriend over for dinner.

"Oh what happened to Susan?"

"Susan's long gone Ma. It's Tracey who's coming to dinner."

"Is he working his way through the alphabet?' laughed Edith, "Wasn't it Rosie before Susan."

Danny roared with laughter, 'I think you may be right. Anyway, I have to go to work. Give my love to Dad."

"Okay, will do. Love you, Dan."

"Love you, Mum. Bye."

With that she hung up the phone and took a peek into the bedroom. Charles was still asleep. She decided to chance a shower and hope he wouldn't escape if she were quick.

She was in and out and getting dressed before her body had time to get properly wet. As she dressed, she tried to remember the last time she had been able to relax under the beautiful warm water as it gently fell on her frail body and eased her aches and pains.

She remembered the old bath they had in their first house. It was a huge bath. She smiled to herself as she reminisced, feeling the warm bubbles lightly caress her young body.

Some time back when she and Charles had been married a few years, they had had a quarrel. Edie had taken herself off for a bath to give her some alone-time to calm down. She couldn't remember what the tiff was about, but as she lay in the bath reading a book, Charlie came in with a rose between his teeth.

Wearing only his jeans, and his blonde hair swept back like Gary Cooper's in his heyday, he attempted to dance the Flamenco. He turned his body as he clapped his hands above his head. She remembered how handsome he had looked, how full of mischief he was, and within minutes, she was laughing so loudly at his antics.

He spun round, landed on one knee and presented the rose to her.

"Let's not argue," he said.

She smiled and took the rose as he jumped in beside her, jeans and all. She laughed even louder as water and bubbles went everywhere. That was probably the night Derek was conceived. She blushed.

She laughed now at the memory. *The good old days.* She looked at the old reflection staring back at her from the mirror, and sighed. *Where had the time gone?*

She decided to wake Charles. If he slept too late he would be up all night again. She sat on the bed and gently ran her fingers through his thick grey hair. She gasped a little. She pulled the covers back from his face. He looked so peaceful.

Oh, my poor Charlie. Tears ran down her cheeks.

She sat for a moment and just watched him. She gently caressed his face, then lay down next to him and placed her arm around him.

"I'm going to miss you, you old bugger."

She lay for a while.

Eventually she got up and picked up the phone. Her fingers trembled as she dialled.

He answered. "Hello?"

"Daniel…"

That night Edie climbed into bed. She looked over at the empty space next to her, and smiled through some tears that escaped. She had never slept alone for near on fifty-three years.

The irony was that tonight for the first time in a long time, she could sleep soundly knowing she no longer had to worry.

But, for the first time…tonight, she didn't sleep at all.

2

by Alison Davie

Tommy Dawes pulled his pack of ten out of his trouser pocket, took one from the pack and lit it up. He sucked on that first hit and slowly blew the smoke out in rings. He managed a couple of fair-sized ones before they dissipated into minute wispy puffs of clouds, and then nothing.

Since he started at Emory High School a few months ago, he had stopped by the stream at the bottom of the park under the small bridge and smoked a couple before heading home. His parents never knew, and even though his father smoked, it was nothing Patrick Dawes wanted for his own kids.

"Terrible habit," he would tell them, "waste of money too."

Tommy thought about school and Grant Baker, the arsehole from Morning Point. Since Tommy started high school, for some unknown reason, he had been the target for Baker and his gang. Not that there had to be a reason, apart from the fact they were teenage boys. Grant looked down on Tommy and his friends, teasing that they were the slum-boys because they lived in South Emory.

They had done all the usual things boys did, from dunking his head in the toilet to tripping him up, and throwing his school books out the window seconds before the teacher came in. Tommy had trouble explaining that one, that his books 'fell' out the window when he took them out of his bag. This had landed him a punishment essay on top of his usual homework.

Today, in the playground at lunch-time, Tommy hadn't seen Duncan, one of Grant's mates kneel behind him, so when Grant came up and pushed Tommy, he fell with a thud onto his backside, much to the amusement of pretty much the whole school.

Tommy hated Grant, and at night would conjure up different ways for Grant's demise. It would end in a sword battle at dusk, where Tommy conquered the Prince of Evil, being regaled as the conquering hero of Morning Point and beyond.

Now, he sat in the park and puffed away his teen troubles. People rarely came this way, maybe a couple of cyclists cutting through the park on their way home, so he knew he probably wouldn't be caught.

He heard footsteps scuffing towards him, and quickly hid the cigarette, but it was only Brad.

"What the fuck are you doing creeping around like that?" asked Tommy.

He offered Brad a hit on his cig, but he shook his head.

Brothers, Kev and Paully appeared. They didn't live in Tommy's shit-de-sac. They lived over the other end of the stream in the newer houses, in one of the suburbs between Oak Tree Lane and Morning Point. But they were all in the same class at school.

"Give us one," said Paully.

"What? I'm not giving you one. Five cents each," Tommy demanded.

"You stole them from the fucking dairy!" said an animated Kev.

"So? Go steal your own fucking packet if you want one."

Kev and Paully glared at him.

"Five cents. Take it or leave it," said Tommy, smiling at his own business savvy.

Kev looked at Paully, who then hesitantly pulled out some change from his pocket and handed over the ten cents. Tommy lit their cigarettes with his own and handed them over.

He offered Brad a hit again, but once again he shook his head. He only ever talked the talk; one of those kids. But him and Tommy had been mates since kindergarten and Brad was pretty cool in other ways. And his mum was always baking cakes.

"Hey did you guys see peg-leg trying to run after that kid who swore at him?" Tommy asked. "He was rocking side to side like a ship in a fucking gale-force wind."

Tommy got up and demonstrated the run, much to the gang's amusement. Paully had this weird snorting laugh, and once he got going it set them all off. They rolled about with laughter.

Tommy was technically the leader of the gang, even though it was never voted on or anything. It just turned out that way. They did what he asked, most of the time.

Kev and Paully finished their cigarettes as Tommy was finishing his second. He offered Brad one final hit and he again refused, but they all egged him on.

"C'mon you fucking pussy," they teased.

"Just one puff," said Paully.

Nothing worked better than a little peer pressure, as Brad

relented and took a puff. He nearly coughed his lungs up. The boys laughed, and Paully snorted.

"Bradley Coup!"

Brad threw down the cigarette and jumped to his feet. No one could mistake the sound of shrieking Mrs Coup.

"You get straight home this instant."

Brad grabbed his bag, and ran as fast as his legs could carry him. The other boys stifled their laughter until Mrs Coup was out of earshot, then they let loose.

The smoking incident had Brad grounded for two weeks, but he never told on any of the others. That was the cool part of Brad that Tommy liked. They were best friends.

No sooner was Brad out of 'solitary confinement' as he described it, he was getting into more mischief, innocent though it was.

It was a Sunday afternoon, and Tommy and Brad sat up in the old oak tree that stood tall at the arch end of the cul-de-sac. They hid amongst the leaves, and as the occasional person went by below, they would call out their names, causing the people to look around, but see no one.

"Hey, Bella," Tommy shouted, in a low, gruff voice, trying to disguise his own.

Bella turned, but couldn't see anyone, so carried on her way.

The boys sniggered.

"What's the time, Bella?" shouted Brad. She looked around again.

"Hello? Who's there?" She looked irritated as she went on her way again.

The boys sat there for a few hours doing this, much to

their amusement. They occasionally threw acorn buds at unwitting passers-by.

"I'll tell your mother!" Mrs Smith shouted angrily, to no one in particular. As she turned back, she saw Jake and Abhi approach and glared at them.

Jake and Abhi walked past her and smiled. They stopped at the tree and saw Tommy in the branches.

"Hey, Tommy."

"Hey," replied Tommy, "Where you guys going?"

"Aw, Abhi has to be home for dinner soon. I'm just heading home too."

They were about to leave when Grant and his boys turned up. Abhi carried on walking, but Grant stepped in his way.

"Where do you think you're going, Punjab?" said Grant.

"I'm going for dinner. And my name is not Punjab!" said Abhi, defiantly, "You know fine well it is Abhi."

"Hahahaha, Punjabi Abhi!" Grant said, much to the amusement of his gang.

"Actually, I am Hindu," replied Abhi.

"Why are you going home for dinner? Can't you just eat out of the tree, monkey boy?" asked Grant. His boys laughed.

Brad jumped down, with Tommy right behind him.

"Leave him alone." Brad stepped between Grant and the others, so Abhi and Jake could leave, but not before one of Grant's boys pushed Abhi and punched him on the arm. "Run, you fucking curry muncher."

Grant got toe to toe with Brad.

"Did you want to fight me, slum boy?"

Brad tried to walk away, but Grant's boys stopped him. Brad looked at Tommy with his look, and Tommy knew what it meant.

Brad swiftly put one of his feet behind Grant's foot and pushed him, causing Grant to lose his balance. This was Brad's move. He did it to Tommy all the time when they were play fighting. While Grant was down, Tommy and Brad ran for it. They ran as fast as their legs could take them, until they reached Tommy's house at the corner of the street by the junction. They burst in through the door out of puff and laughing nervously. They startled his mum, Kirstin, and Tommy's little four-year-old sister, Laura, who were doing a puzzle at the dinner table. His other sister, seven-year-old Sammy, had her head down reading a book, as always.

"What's going on?" asked his mum.

Tommy laughed and looked at Brad.

"Nothing, Mrs Dawes. We were, ah, just having a race to see who was faster and I won."

"No you didn't," said Tommy, pushing him playfully.

"You better not be getting into any trouble, Tommy Dawes. I don't want the neighbours coming to my door for you."

"No, we weren't, Mum." He grabbed Brad by the arm and tugged him to follow. "We're just going to my room."

"Okay. But not for long. I'm going to start making dinner soon."

Tommy and Brad went into Tommy's room and looked out his window, which faced onto the street. Grant and his boys stood out there and Tommy and Brad gave him the fingers. Grant clenched his fist, and pummelled on his hand, symbolising what he was going to do to the boys the next time he saw them.

Brad sat on the bed, "I hope he's gone when I have to go home for dinner."

Tommy looked at Brad. They hadn't thought of that!

Tommy sat under the bridge after school, and puffed away at

his cigarette. He saw Grant walking across the bridge in his rugby gear. He was alone, as was Tommy.

He had managed to avoid a punch up with Grant so far, and stayed perfectly still and quiet. Grant saw him anyway. Grant hoicked and spat a large glob of snotty sputum, which landed on Tommy's shoulder.

Tommy jumped up, dropping his cigarette.

"Ewww..." He pulled up a handful of grass and tried to wipe it off.

"If it isn't Dumbo Dawes," said Grant.

Grant made his way down to where Tommy was, just at the edge of the bridge.

Tommy tried to leave, but Grant blocked his way.

"I'm talking to you, fuck-face."

"I need to get home."

Tommy again tried to get past, but Grant grabbed him by the shirt.

"Did I say you could go?"

Tommy tried to break free, they got into a bit of a scuffle, and Grant punched Tommy square in the face causing him to fall back.

"You leave when I say you can. Got it?"

Tommy rubbed his now throbbing jaw and slowly got to his feet. As they stood there on the slope, Tommy realised he was now towering over Grant.

He clenched his fist. Just do it, he told himself. Just do it, you fucking pussy. Punch him. Destroy the Prince of Evil. But Tommy couldn't.

Grant saw the clenched fist, and threw down the challenge.

"Oh you want to fight, aye? You think you can take me, you fucking weasel?"

He chucked his school bag down.

"C'mon then."

Again Tommy tried to leave, but Grant grabbed his school bag and tried to pull it off his shoulder.

Turning, Tommy pushed at Grant to get off. Grant lost his balance and stumbled backwards. Trying to keep his balance, his arms wind-milled in the air as he tumbled, smacking his head on a rock.

Tommy's heart raced. A sickening feeling came over him as he stared at Grant's inert body. He glanced around to see if anyone had seen him. He looked back at Grant, stared for what seemed like an eternity, before he turned on his heels and ran.

At home, Tommy tried to calm himself down before he entered the house.

"What's up with you, love? You look a bit pasty," said his mother.

Tommy looked at her. "What?"

"You. You look all pale." She went over and put her hand on his forehead. "You don't feel hot."

"I'm fine. I've got homework to do." With that, he headed to his room.

"Okay. Dinner will be ready in about an hour," shouted Mum.

Tommy went into his room at the end of the hallway and sat on his bed. He felt panicky inside. *Should I tell my mum? I should call an ambulance. I just won't give my name. It's not as if it was my fault. And everyone at school knows Grant's a bully.* Tommy's thoughts were like a steam train going full speed ahead.

Tommy tried to get on with his homework, but couldn't concentrate.

Soon, Tommy heard sirens approach and go down the back towards the park. His room was front-facing so he couldn't see anything. He ran into the bedroom his sisters shared at the back of the house and watched the ambulance. He felt better knowing Grant would get help. Ironically, the red and blue lights seemed calming to him.

"Mum! Tommy's in my room."

Tommy turned to see Sammy standing at the door entrance.

"Were you looking for a doll to play with?" she asked, with an impish smile.

"Shut up," he said as he pushed past her.

"Mum, Tommy pushed me," she screamed down the hallway.

"Tommy. Sammy. Dinner's ready," Mum shouted.

Tommy headed through to the kitchen.

His dad, Patrick, came in from work, and Laura greeted him as if she hadn't seen him for weeks.

"Daddeeeeeee," she squealed with excitement, as she ran and jumped into his arms. He caught her and lifted her over his shoulder so her head hung down his back.

"Where'd she go?" he asked.

She laughed with delight, "I'm round here," she shrieked.

Patrick swung around, "Where?"

"Round here."

The shrieks and giggles made Mum smile, even though this was their nightly ritual.

Patrick was an immigrant from Ireland and still spoke with that beautiful lilting voice. Tommy loved the way his father spoke and had tried to emulate it when he was younger. His parents would giggle as little three-year-old Tommy would run about shouting

"Beee Jeezuzhhhh."

Tommy and Sammy sat at the dinner table, her long blonde hair a tangled mess atop her head, as always. No matter how often Kirstin brushed it, it always ended up looking as if she had a tangled ball of wool on her head. Sammy swept away a stray strand as she read yet another book. Patrick would say she was a woman who was destined to change the way of the world for the better, a determined kid, and a fast learner, boasting to anyone who would listen that she had read her first book by the age of two.

"Have you heard the news?" Patrick asked Kirstin, as he kissed her.

"No. You mean the sirens?"

"Yeah. Apparently they found a body in the park under the bridge."

"A body?" asked Tommy.

"A dead body?" asked Sammy.

Tommy felt sick to his stomach as the reality of the situation rolled over him.

"Do you know who it was?" Kirstin asked.

"No, but I heard it was a kid. I think he goes to your school," he said to Tommy.

"Did you hear anything, son?" asked Kirstin.

Dead? Shit! I'm going to hell. I'm going to spend the rest of my life in prison.

"What? No. I didn't hear a thing. Can I go to my room? I'm not feeling well."

Kirstin went over and put her hand on his forehead again.

"Definitely no fever. You must have caught that bug going about school at the moment."

"Maybe it's just hunger. I know I'm starving," said Patrick, as he pulled Laura back upright and squidged up his nose at her, which she did in return. He put her down.

"No. I just want to go lie down," said Tommy.

"Bee Jeezuz, he must be sick. Not wanting some of that fine cookin' I can smell."

Kirstin ruffled Tommy's hair and kissed him on top of his head.

"Off to bed with you then. I'll come in soon and check on you."

Tommy went to his room and lay down on his bed. His thoughts were still panicked, but his body felt heavy, as if he couldn't move. He felt so alone and scared. *I don't want to go to jail.*

After dinner, his mum looked in on him, a glass of milk and a sandwich in her hand. He still lay on top of his bed.

"I brought you something in case you felt better."

She placed it on his bedside table and sat next to him on the bed.

"How are you feeling now?"

Tommy shook his head.

"Well, if you're not feeling better tomorrow, we'll take you up to see Doc Collins."

She lovingly stroked his head and smiled at him.

"What are you smiling at?' he asked.

"I'm just so glad you're safe. Some poor mother won't have her son come home tonight. I can't imagine how horrible that must feel." She looked at him, "I love you, kiddo."

"Love you too, Mum."

With that, he did something he hadn't done in such a long time. He sat up and hugged her. Kirstin looked pleasantly surprised.

She usually had to fight these days to get a hug. She held him tight until he let go and lay back down. She got up to leave, but Tommy asked her if she could stay a bit longer. She smiled. She lay down next to him and cradled him in her arms.

"Remember when we used to do this all the time when you were little?"

"And you'd tell me stories."

"I can tell you one now if you like?"

"Yeah okay," he said, feeling suddenly safe and protected and a sense of 'everything was going to be okay' came over him. Before long, he drifted into a peaceful sleep.

The next day, Tommy said he felt better and got ready for school.

As he walked past the park, he saw it was still closed off, so he had to walk the long way around. Brad ran to catch up with Tommy.

"Did you hear about Grant? He was found dead in the park."

"Yeah. My dad said something about it when he came in. Did you hear how it happened?"

"Nah. You?"

Tommy shook his head.

Paully and Kev met up with Tommy and Brad at the crossing between the two suburbs.

"Hey, did you hear about the kid murdered in the park?" asked Paully.

"It was Grant Baker," said Brad.

"Who said he was murdered?" asked Tommy.

"Wasn't he?" asked Paully.

"Not that I've heard," said Brad.

"Oh," replied Paully.

At school, Grant's death was the buzz of the playground.

"I heard creepy old Miss Thompson went crazy and came down from the hill and killed him," said Darlene Smith.

"I heard he was stabbed to death. Stabbed twelve times through the heart," another kid from Morning Point said. "It was that crazy old guy who lives at the end of your street. That's why he has all those big fences up around him. He's done it before."

Tommy sat silently until the school bell rang to signal time to go in,

The school held a special assembly that day and mourned the loss of Grant, who was described as a bright student and fine sportsman.

At home, Tommy saw Grant's death had made headline

news in the local newspaper. Tommy sneaked the paper to his room to read it.

The police reported, 'under the bridge is a common place for the teen smokers to hang.' They had found cigarette butts at the scene. Evidence suggested Grant had been smoking under the bridge and when he got up to leave, he slipped on the wet rock and fell backwards. Foul play wasn't suspected, and they weren't looking for anyone in connection with Grant's death.

It was a tragic accident, which had left one family mourning the loss of their son and they had asked that people respect their privacy for now, while they grieve.'

Tommy couldn't believe it. 'No foul play is suspected and we are not looking for anyone in connection with the death.' Tommy read it again...and again...and again. He felt a remorseful sense of relief.

A few months passed and a lot had happened. Paully was found to have enlarged adenoids, which caused his snorting laugh. He was taken for surgery but there had been complications post-operative. Paully passed away, aged fourteen. Kev strayed from the group, leaving only Tommy and Brad.

One Sunday morning they sat up the tree. They hadn't done this for a few weeks. Tommy still brooded about the time under the bridge with Grant, but when Brad shouted out to Bella as she walked past below, Tommy smiled to himself as he felt everything was getting back to some sense of ordinary, which gave him a feeling of peace—for now.

3

by Anna Williams

"Heeeere kitty, kitty, kitty! Heeeere kitty, kitty, kitty!"

Keith Varney turned and frowned in the direction of the house next door.

I'm only just home and the first thing I hear is that woman! Why does she always have to make such a racket?

He unloaded his luggage from the car and carried it down the pathway to the back porch, glancing sideways at the cellar door and the shiny new padlock on it. He had purchased a load of timber before going overseas, and the cellar was the obvious place for storage, being easy to secure.

A neighbour had left the mail piled up on the porch. He looked with distaste at a sparrow's corpse laying a few feet away. Going by the smell, it had been there a while. He had read somewhere that cats would often catch birds, mice, and other revolting specimens, and leave them for their humans as offerings.

"Bloody cats," he muttered. "Can't stand the things."

Keith unlocked the door, and allowed the silence to wash over him as he stood there. Back to peace, quiet and solitude. He had visited the town of Emory years ago, looking for somewhere to live. He liked Oak Tree Lane straight away, as it was a cul-de-sac, with no through traffic. Surrounded by trees, the house backed onto the bush and farmland, secluding it from the rest of the street. No one could look in on him. There was plenty of potential in the house for renovation and though the section needed better fencing, it had ticked many boxes for him, especially the privacy.

He now lived on his own. The thought of constantly sharing his space again with someone else had become abhorrent to him. Never again. Women were nothing but trouble. They swept you up, sucked you dry, and then spat out the bones.

She ruined everything, the stupid bitch!

Now and then he might choose to have some female company, but it would be on his terms. When it suited him, and for as long as it suited him.

The house smelt stuffy, so Keith opened the windows, letting the breeze waft in, carrying the scent of freesias from his garden. He had been away for just over two months, but it felt like forever.

His home was his sanctuary, and he fiercely resented having to go away. His brother and elderly father lived in Australia and neither of them were well, so Keith was expected to fly over several times a year, 'do his duty' visiting them, sorting out their finances and other affairs.

It was an onerous chore. His childhood held only dark memories of cold, unforgiving parents and an older brother who had bullied him mercilessly. Love and respect had been non-existent. Yet, responsibility seemed to have fallen on his shoulders now, to ensure their welfare, even though he lived an ocean away. He was sick to death of it. One day, he was going to turn around and just say 'NO MORE! You can go to hell.'

Keith rarely socialised, though his one concession was to join a tramping club. The outdoor life was his passion. He could walk for miles, had climbed mountains and was a keen swimmer. He could do these activities with a group if he chose, but he preferred the solitude.

As Keith began to unpack from his trip, he was already thinking about what needed to be done outside. The garden was rampant with weeds. He was only halfway through all the exterior painting on the house. The trellis beside the garage needed repair from that last storm before he went away, and some of the boundary trees needed a trim.

He was looking forward to trying out the chainsaw he had purchased before heading overseas.

Which reminded him—he needed to start work in the cellar. He planned to put a concrete floor down soon, as well as building shelves and cabinets with the timber he'd bought. It would be a perfect place to store his power tools and other garden equipment. So, plenty to do.

He jumped when the phone on the kitchen bench rang shrilly.

"Keith! You're back!" Brian from the tramping club yelled into the phone.

Keith grimaced, and held the receiver away from his ear.

Why does he always state the obvious?

"I am," he said. "I've only just walked in the door, actually, and I'm in the middle of unpacking."

"I'll only hold you up for a minute," Brian said. "Thought I'd see if you wanted a night out? Some of us are heading out for dinner and there are a couple of new, unattached women coming along. You up for it?"

Keith pulled a face. He couldn't think of anything worse than sitting in a noisy restaurant making small talk. And, as for the women, well, he didn't want to go through anything like that again. The last one had been a disaster.

"No thanks, Brian. I'm pretty tired. All I want right now is to have the evening to myself."

There was a short silence.

"Okay. Don't say we never invite you along." Brian paused. "By the way, did you manage to track down Janine, that ex-girlfriend of yours while you were away? We hoped you might have made contact with her."

"No, I didn't." Keith closed his eyes. He could feel a headache coming on.

I never should have bothered with the cheating bitch.

"Strange." Brian's voice sounded puzzled. "We had all come to know her through the tramping club, and she didn't seem the type to up and leave like that. I knew the two of you were having a few problems, but even so..."

Keith gritted his teeth. "It proves a point, doesn't it? Some women just aren't worth the trouble."

"Shame. We were all hoping you two were making a go of it, then she was suddenly out of the picture. Everyone's been concerned."

Keith stared unseeingly out the window. "I've got to go, Brian."

"Are you sure you don't want to join us tonight? You'll be missing out on a good time. I think these two women are looking for some fun as well, if you know what I mean?"

"I'm not interested!" Keith spoke more sharply than he'd intended. Brian was like a dog with a bone sometimes.

"Right. You've made that pretty clear." Brian's tone was cool. "Give me a call when you feel more sociable."

"I'm just really tired. What about—?"

But Brian had hung up.

Great. I've been home for half an hour and I'm already being pestered. I wish people would leave me in peace.

Keith's mood was worsening. His stomach muscles felt as

if they were tying themselves in knots and he was light-headed. He badly needed a cigarette, but was trying to quit. Unfortunately, his nicotine cravings were increasing, not diminishing. He often found himself reaching for that absent packet whenever he felt stressed, then felt even more uptight when he remembered he was quitting. There was a half-used pack of ciggies in the kitchen cupboard he'd been trying to ignore. Maybe he would just treat himself to one...

No! He needed to get busy outside and take in some fresh air. Perhaps he would open up the cellar and check everything was as he had left it. First, he needed to find the padlock key. What had he done with it?

Keith pulled open several drawers in the kitchen, rifling through their contents. No sign. Where the hell was it? His anger grew as he searched other drawers and cupboards, throwing books, papers and magazines onto the floor. Nothing! By now, his headache was raging. Keith lurched into the bathroom, opened the first-aid box and found some pain relief tablets. He filled a water glass and swallowed two of the tablets. As he was about to close the lid, he saw a key lying at the bottom of the box.

Bingo!

He went into his bedroom and sat on the bed. The headache had made him feel dizzy. He took some deep breaths, lay back and closed his eyes for a few minutes.

"Heeeere kitty, kitty, kitty! Heeeere kitty, kitty, kitty!" Annie McFarlane's voice from next door went higher and higher as she called for her cats. It was really getting on his nerves.

Keith shot off the bed, shoved his barely-unpacked suitcase aside, slammed the back door and headed outside to unlock the cellar. No time for cigarettes anyway!

It was time to rev up his big, new chainsaw.

"Oh no, not again. Please not again." Emily Petersen rolled over in her bed and looked at the time on her bedside clock radio. The numbers 2:10 were stark and white in the darkness of her bedroom. The sound of her baby son's crying had woken her from what felt like a drug-induced sleep. She was so tired! Joshua had been restless all night and she'd lost count of the number of times she'd got up to him. If only she could have one night—just one full night's sleep, what a difference it would make.

She lurched out of bed, and pulled her dressing gown on, then padded into her baby's small bedroom next to hers. It didn't matter that it was pitch black. She could find the way with her eyes closed. She'd done it that many times.

His sobbing increased as she picked him up.

"Ssshhh, ssshhh. Please be quiet, Josh. You'll wake everyone else."

Emily held him close as she whispered into his soft little ear, and felt his hot and sweaty body against hers. She thought of Annie and Derek, her aunt and uncle, who slept directly below them. Noise travelled, especially during the night. Emily hated the thought that they were both lying there, listening and probably discussing her inadequacy as a mother of a young baby. A teenage mother as well!

She sat in the chair next to Joshua's bassinette, unbuttoned her nightshirt, and put him to her breast. He latched on eagerly and within a few seconds, settled into a rhythmical sucking, one little hand kneading her skin and the other pressed in to his tummy. Emily sighed, put her head back and closed her eyes.

Her tiredness was overwhelming and nothing, absolutely

nothing, had prepared her for this. No amount of reading, advice, or information from ante-natal classes even came close to warning her how hard it would be. Never-ending feeding, nappies, and sleepless nights coping with him crying. It just went on and on. Her aunt and uncle had helped where they could, and given her somewhere to live, which Emily was grateful for, especially as her mum and dad...

Tears prickled her eyes. *Don't go there! Don't keep thinking about what happened. If only I could turn back time to that day and do things differently. Why can't I wave a magic wand and make everything right again?*

She had had so many plans. After flying through her School C. and U.E. exams, nursing was going to be her future. Emily had applied to three hospital boards, and been interviewed by two of them, receiving acceptance letters from both. Choices, choices, choices. She'd felt as if the world was at her feet. Mum and Dad had been so proud of her. Her friends took her out to celebrate on weekends. One particular night, they all had too much to drink and she slept with a guy she had only ever been friends with. No thought, no precautions taken.

Stupid, stupid, stupid.

Emily looked down at her little baby who had stopped feeding and was now snuggled in close to her. The love she felt for him and the feelings of frustration at her predicament were constantly doing a tug-of-war within her. The intensity of Joshua's birth had frightened her, along with the huge responsibility of being a mum. But she couldn't imagine life without him now. He was the centre of her world.

"Don't worry, Joshie," she whispered, kissing his soft, downy curls. "We'll be fine. You and me together—we'll take on the world. And we'll win."

She swaddled her sleepy baby and carefully tucked him down, as the Plunket nurse had shown her. Her aunt Annie had told her it was okay to tuck babies down on their tummies, but Emily didn't agree. It looked unsafe and uncomfortable. Emily absorbed every piece of information given to her when it came to being a parent, and wanted to do her absolute best for her baby. She shivered. If something happened to Josh, she would never forgive herself. After losing her mum and dad so suddenly...the tears threatened again as she stood there watching Joshua sleeping.

They would have loved him so much and it was all really unfair. She longed to have her parents around, to reassure her and give her a cuddle too. Josh got his share, but it was a while since anyone had given her a long deep hug. How she needed it! No one but her mum and dad could fill that gap. And they never would again.

"Night, night, my baby" Emily whispered. "See you next when the sun's up."

She got back into bed and despite her tiredness, had to focus on relaxing. A grief counsellor had taught her a breathing exercise to do, which calmed and soothed her. Sometimes it worked and sometimes it didn't. But after a few minutes she could feel herself drifting. Emily could tell when sleep was coming, as her thoughts started spiralling upwards and outwards.

Her breathing deepened, her body softened and as the tensions eased away, Emily drifted off to sleep.

"Derek!" Annie McFarlane dug her husband in the ribs. "Are you awake?"

"No."

She ignored the sarcasm. "I'm worried about Emily and Joshua."

Her husband sighed, burying his face in the pillow. "What's the matter?"

"Did you hear him crying? He seems to have been awake most of the night. Maybe I should go up and see if I can help."

Derek rolled over and looked blearily at Annie. "No. Leave it, Annie. Sorry to be blunt, but it's not as if you can offer to breastfeed him or anything. Just give her some space—especially at—" he propped himself up on one elbow and looked at the time, "—at two-thirty in the morning."

Annie groaned. "I'm wide awake now and feel I should do something. I have a responsibility."

"Then give the cats a cuddle. They've taken over our bed again as usual and they'll appreciate it more than Joshua and Emily would at the moment."

Annie lay still. Derek's comments stung and her eyes filled with tears. He could be so tactless and clueless as to how she was feeling, especially after her sister's death.

Sensing her distress, Derek rolled over and put his arms around her.

"Sorry, that was a bit hard. I know you want to be there for them. And we have been. We've given them a home and helped out with Josh during the day. Ultimately, he's Emily's responsibility. We've done our bit raising a family, and I think we're entitled to some freedom now we're retired."

"But I still miss being a mum and having the kids around. I miss all the hugs and the feeling of being needed." Annie's voice rose as she became more upset. "I'm trying so hard with Emily, but I know she'd rather have her mum and dad around and I don't blame her. We're poor substitutes for them!"

"Annie, we'll never be able to take Joanne and Terry's place—we shouldn't even try to. But we've at least been able to offer Emily some stability and a safe place to live with

Josh. Remember, she's not only coping with her parents' death, but she's also carrying around so much guilt. She's still blames herself for what happened."

"That's silly. She wasn't to know some idiot was going to run a red light that night. They were simply in the wrong place at the wrong moment."

"We know that. And in time, Emily will come to realise it too. She just feels so guilty that she begged them to come and see Josh that evening, instead of the next morning as they'd planned. Now—can I please go back to sleep?"

Derek pulled the covers over his head and rolled onto his other side.

Annie sighed, sat up in bed, propped the pillows behind her and reached out to stroke one of the cats. It was too dark to see which one was beside her, but from the loud purring, she knew it was Sabrina. There was something very soothing about stroking that soft silky fur. She'd heard it was therapeutic and calming to caress a cat and it could help lower blood pressure. She imagined she could feel her own heartbeat slowing and her thoughts becoming clearer.

The ache of loss for her sister was still acute, but Annie had been told time softened the impact. Six months had passed since that terrible late night phone call and the crushing realisation that Joanne and Terry were gone forever. They had become grandparents just a few days before, and Annie had never seen her sister so happy and excited. Emily's pregnancy had shocked everyone at first, but it had been decided quickly, there would be no intervention. Annie wondered sometimes whose decision it had been. Had Emily's parents placed a lot of pressure on her to keep the baby? Or had it been a mutual wish? One day, when the time was right, Annie would ask her. There was no rush.

She knew how much Emily had wanted to become a nurse and she would have been perfect for it. She was good with people, popular with her friends, mature, caring, academically skilled, and hard working. Her future looked so bright.

Maybe when Josh was a little older, Emily might consider applying again. Then she would have to find someone to care for her baby. Someone she knew and trusted...

Annie stared into the darkness of the bedroom. She thought of Emily's interrupted dreams for her future, and about her own 'empty nest'. She thought how much she loved to cuddle Josh when Emily needed a break, and how responsive he was with her and Derek, cooing and smiling at them. He'd even taken a bottle of expressed breast milk for her when Emily needed to rest. He was so easy to look after.

"Derek? Are you still awake?"

A soft snore answered her question. Annie snuggled back down and pulled the covers up to her chin. She was so alert now that sleep seemed impossible and her thoughts were racing. Maybe it was an age thing, but being awake at this time was common for her now and was often when she did her best thinking. And an idea suddenly occurred to her. It was simply, blindingly obvious.

Getting Derek to go along with it might not be so straightforward.

Ironically, the moment June and Peter Mansell's marriage hit a speed bump was when they were doing something together, which didn't often happen these days.

They were standing in the kitchen doing the dishes, as their old faithful dishwasher had turned up its toes and died on them the week before. Peter was leaning forward, his hands deep in the soapy water, then looked up and out of the window in front of him.

"I can't do this anymore," he said.

"Just leave the rest then, and I'll finish up," his wife said, as she stacked the pots away in the drawer.

"No. I didn't mean the dishes. I meant...all this. Our life. I'm bored out of my mind."

Peter turned away, dried his hands on the towel, went and sat down, his elbows on the dining table and his head in his hands.

June stood still, feeling a rush of indignation, then dread. She told herself to keep calm, left the tea towel on the bench and sat beside him at the table.

"How long have you been feeling like this?" she asked.

Peter looked at her. His eyes were reddened and she thought how tired he looked. He shrugged and looked down at his hands.

"A while now. I'm sorry."

June swallowed hard. "What is it you want to do? Can I help?"

Peter frowned and shook his head. "No. This is something I need to sort out myself."

He paused and glanced at his wife.

"You're taking this pretty calmly. Aren't you surprised?"

June stood, turning away from him and looked out the lounge window. It was a pretty view, especially in summertime, with the large, leafy oak tree at the end of the cul-de-sac. They had lived here in Oak Tree Lane in Emory for over thirty years. Their children had grown up here. They knew their neighbours. She and Peter had put so much time, energy and love into this place. June felt she had a spiritual link to it and could never imagine living anywhere else. Peter had become annoyed with her once when he suggested moving on, and she said she felt as if she could never leave.

"It's just a house," he'd said.

June had snapped back at him "No! It's not just a house. It's our home."

Now she sighed and turned to face him. "To be honest with you, I'm not surprised. Maybe it's the stage of life we're at. I've had days when I've thought, what now? There must be something more, but I've kept myself busy with the garden and other things I enjoy doing. Can't you do that too?"

Peter shook his head. "It's not that simple. I'm sorry."

June tensed. "Is there someone else? You need to tell me."

"No, no, no, of course not." Peter shook his head again. "Nothing like that. I just feel as if I'm on a treadmill every day, doing the same boring things over and over and over and never moving forward. I feel old and stale and some days I get really down."

June felt exasperated as she looked at him. "Hasn't it ever occurred to you that I do too? But maybe women are better at adapting to life changes as they grow older. We accept things as they are; we move on and find other interests. You need something new to focus on. I'd rather you did it with me though. We still have a life together. At least I think so."

Peter sighed. "Yes, you're right. Maybe I do need another project. Something to sink my teeth into. We've renovated the house to within an inch of its life and done everything we possibly can to the garden. I feel like a spare part. Perhaps I should start building another boat on the driveway. I can drive the neighbours crazy again with all the noise."

June laughed. "Remember what happened last time? A certain nosey neighbour came over to complain about the noisy power tools one day and caught us having it off in the cabin. We couldn't even wait till the boat was in the water!"

"He didn't hang around did he?" Peter grinned. "Come to think of it, we didn't see him again for months. And then he made sure we were both outside and fully dressed!"

"It's nice to see you smile," said June. "Our lives are pretty good really. We're comfortably off in our retirement, despite Rob Muldoon and his government's policies. We both keep fit and in good health and we don't have any dependants now. This should be the best time of our lives."

Peter nodded. "I know, I know. You're right." He stood and looked out the window, onto neighbouring farmland. He liked all the trees and the soft greenery that covered the lower slopes of the hill. It all looked so restful.

The only jarring note was the old house that stood near the top of the slope. Dilapidated and forbidding were two words that came to mind. Charlotte Thompson, the elderly woman who lived there, was now in her nineties and Peter reckoned she'd been there all her life. As far as he knew, she was on her own and becoming increasingly reclusive. He sometimes heard her yelling at the children in the neighbourhood when she saw them stealing fruit from her massive apple tree, which was probably as old as she was. She reminded him of a witch. He shuddered. There was no way he or June were going to end up like that. Poor old woman. What a way to spend her last years; rotting away in an ancient dump, on her own and probably very lonely as well.

He wondered what state the interior of the house was in. The exterior looked bad enough. It either needed a massive renovation, or a bomb underneath it, when the old lady passed on. A newer, more modern house up there would certainly improve the view. If only he was twenty years younger. He would have jumped at an opportunity to take on a huge renovation project like that, but he was in his mid-sixties and the idea was just too daunting.

Keith Varney, next door, was always renovating his house, and Peter had hoped he would be asked to do some interior work there. He'd dropped a few hints over time, but Keith never picked up on them, or had chosen not to. He was a sour, reclusive bugger, apart from the occasional woman friend. There seemed to be no family around either. Hardly surprising really, considering how anti-social he could be. And, to top it off, he was doing some extensive work in his cellar, using his power tools. Peter had no idea what, but Keith certainly knew how to make a lot of noise.

No. Peter needed to find himself a new project. Something like a...he looked around at June. She sat at the table, watching him, looking unbearably sad, and Peter felt contrite that he had upset her. He loved her dearly and treasured their years together. He simply needed a new focus. And he suddenly had an idea.

"What say we buy a second-hand caravan and do it up? I have the skills and the time. We have a big enough driveway for me to work on it. I still have all the tools needed. It's something I could really get my teeth into."

June considered it for a moment. Then she smiled.

"Hey! I like it! We could take short holidays away and not have to worry about booking hotels or motels anymore. Imagine just being able to turn up anywhere we fancy on a whim, and come home when it suits us."

Peter looked at her. The idea had taken root and was growing and expanding in his mind. June was receptive to the suggestion, so that was a good start. He'd let her go on believing they'd just be taking short holidays away, if that kept her happy.

But he suddenly had a more long-term plan in mind. Something rather more permanent.

"Emily? Do you want to bring Josh downstairs? We could have a coffee while he plays on his mat. I've done some baking too. Your favourite sultana cake!"

"Thanks, Aunt Annie. We'll be there soon."

Emily finished changing Josh's nappy, then put him in his cot while she washed her hands. She gazed out the bathroom window, which looked out onto Oak Tree Lane. She saw the twins, Jolene and Darlene, crossing the road, giggling their heads off. And there was that young boy, Tommy, from farther along the street, with his group of mates heading in the opposite direction, towards the park. She dried her hands while she leant against the windowsill, pressing her forehead against the cool glass.

I bet they're going for a sneaky smoke. It must be fun to just hang around with mates and not have to worry about anything—no responsibilities at all. They don't know how good they've got it!

Something moving next door caught her eye and she looked over. It was that creepy guy, Keith-someone-or-other. He was unlocking the cellar door, but as he did so, he glanced around, as though checking that no one was watching him. He wouldn't be able see Emily, due to the angle of the window she was looking through, but she still pulled back. He really gave her the creeps. She'd been lying in her bikini on the back deck a few weeks ago, getting some much needed sunshine, while Josh slept. Suddenly she had the feeling she was being watched. Emily had turned her head quickly and seen a flash of movement between the palings of the wooden fence. She had sat up straight away and covered herself with her towel. The garden was silent, yet she thought she could hear the soft rustle of clothing, then quiet footsteps on the path next door.

Ugh! I'm sure it was him. Dirty old pervert.

After that, she hadn't wanted to lie outside again, which was a shame. She'd loved being out in the sun.

Emily went back into Josh's room and gazed down at her little boy. He looked up at her, gave a huge gummy grin and blew a raspberry. She picked him up and cuddled him close, feeling guilty for envying a bunch of young kids.

"Oh my baby, I could eat you up! You're worth all the hard work and the broken nights. I love you SOOO much! What would I do without you?"

She put him on her hip and carried him downstairs, not really in the mood for coffee and a chat with her aunt Annie. It felt as if Annie was trying to take the place of her mum; doing all the stuff that her mum would've been doing if she had still been alive.

IF. IF. IF. So many IFS. No one would ever take the place of her mum. Ever.

She was fond of aunt Annie and uncle Derek. They had been so kind and tried hard to make things easier for her and Joshua. She would always be grateful to them. But the time was coming when she needed to be in her own place and telling her aunt and uncle wasn't going to be easy. Emily was already setting things in motion. She wouldn't say anything to them though, until her plans were finalised.

Annie gave a big smile as Emily and Joshua appeared at the doorway.

"Hello, Josh! You're growing so fast! Here, Emily, you sit down and relax. The coffee's made, so help yourself, honey. I'll hold Josh for you. I love to spend time with him. He's such a happy little baby."

Emily watched her aunt cuddling Josh. It was obvious Annie was becoming very attached to him. Too attached.

Maybe I should tell her now.

"Aunt Annie. There was something—"

"You two mean so much to us, honey." Annie carried on. "We know these last six months have been hard, especially for you, but we love having you here. The house feels much more like a family home again, especially with a baby around. I love every moment of it. Whenever you go out for the day, it suddenly becomes too quiet."

Emily gulped. She sipped her coffee. "You've been very good to us, Aunt Annie. I don't know how we would have managed without your and Uncle Derek's help. I'll always be grateful. But I did want to—"

"What say the three of us go shopping tomorrow?" Annie interrupted again. "There's a new baby store opened in town and I'd love to treat Josh to some outfits and maybe some more toys. Then perhaps we could have lunch somewhere. You choose where we go."

"Ummm, sorry, no. I'm taking Josh and going around to see a friend tomorrow. Jacqui only lives a little way across town and she's invited us over for the day."

"Oh." Annie's face fell, and then brightened again. "Why don't you leave Josh with me? I could look after him for the day so you could have a really good break. He takes expressed breast milk from the bottle and he's enjoying some solid food now, so the feeding isn't an issue. And I'm good at settling him off to sleep. I've been getting plenty of practice lately!"

"Thanks, Aunt Annie, but I want to take him. Jacqui has a little boy too and Josh needs to get used to having other kids around. We've already planned to go into town together."

"Oh." Annie went quiet for a moment. "It was just a thought. Anyway, here I am talking away and hardly letting you get a word in. What were you going to say before?"

Looking at her aunt with Josh, Emily's courage disappeared

and she couldn't say the words. It wasn't the right moment, and she didn't want to hurt her aunt's feelings.

I'm such a coward. I'll find the right time, but now is definitely not it.

Emily smiled. "You know what? I've forgotten, so it can't have been important. And we'd love to go into town with you another day, if that's okay? What about Friday?"

Annie nodded happily. "Absolutely. I have all the time in the world and who better to spend it with than you and our little Josh? We can really make a day of it, Emily, with shopping and then lunch somewhere special. Now, how about a piece of my sultana cake to go with that coffee?"

"Yes please. It looks delicious!"

There must be an easier way to tell them what I'm planning, but I have to do it soon.

Emily sat back and watched Annie and Joshua. Two of the most important people in her world were right in front of her. She would need to tread carefully as her decision would have far-reaching consequences.

Annie decided to run her idea past Derek a few days later. Emily and Joshua had gone to Jacqui's place for the weekend and weren't due back till the following morning. The timing was perfect. Annie knew when her husband was in a mellow mood. He'd been out fishing in his boat and come home tired and happy with a decent meal for the two of them. She'd cooked the fish just the way he liked it and they'd sat outside on their deck, eaten dinner and shared a bottle of wine. It was a beautiful evening, only spoilt by the sound of Keith next-door, hammering away in the cellar.

He's so selfish! Doesn't it occur to him that people are trying to relax at this time of day? I just don't think he gives a damn.

As if reading her mind, Derek said, "There he goes again, with no consideration for anyone else! I've a good mind to go over and say something shortly, if he doesn't stop!"

"I'm sure he will soon," said Annie, hurriedly. She didn't want Derek's good mood to disappear before she'd talked with him. "We can always turn our stereo up if his noise gets too much."

"Why should we have to do that?" Derek grumbled. "It's bloody well eight o'clock on a Sunday evening. No normal person would carry on as he does, and Keith obviously doesn't care how much he disturbs his neighbours. All we ever hear night and day is banging, scraping and crashing. It never stops!"

Annie could see Derek getting more and more agitated. She tried to inject a bit of humour.

"We can always put our Bruce Springsteen LP on at full blast. Or Blondie? Keith might be a closet fan."

"He's certainly a 'closet' something." Derek managed a grin. "We already know he has a fetish for certain women—when he's not too busy enjoying his own company. But I doubt our taste in music would coincide."

Derek paused. "So...what's for dessert, woman of mine?"

"Your favourite. Apple crumble with custard, then with your special coffee to finish. I'll bring it out now, if you're ready."

"Are you trying to soften me up?" Derek leaned back in his deck chair, folded his arms and gazed at his wife. "Why do I get the feeling you're up to something?"

Annie felt her face get warm. "I do have something I want to talk with you about. Let's just have dessert, then I'll tell you."

She went through to the kitchen. Her hands were shaking as she served up the crumble, then put it on a tray with cutlery. She switched the coffee percolator on, so it would be ready when they'd finished eating.

Please, please, please let him agree to this. I SO want to do it.

The apple crumble was cooked perfectly, and the cream literally topped it off. Annie had to admit, it tasted pretty good. It was her favourite dessert too. She and her husband were very alike in many ways.

Maybe that's what years of marriage have done. We're often on the same wavelength, so...fingers crossed.

"Thanks, honey. That was good." Derek moved his plate to the side and looked at Annie. "Now, come on. Spit it out. You're very jumpy tonight."

Annie took a deep breath. *Here goes.*

"It's about Emily and Joshua. I've had an absolutely brilliant idea. We know how much trauma Emily's been through, losing Joanne and Terry, especially just after having her baby. Thank goodness, we were able to look after them both. We all know she was planning to become a nurse, but has had to put that on hold, as she feels Josh is too young to go into a crèche. He knows us well, and this has become his home now. And you know how much I miss having children around? Well...I'd like to become his full-time carer, which would mean Emily could reapply for nursing training. She wouldn't even have to pay me anything. I'd do it just for the love of it. And Emily would be here on her days off, so could have quality time with Josh then. It would be the perfect solution for all of us and especially for..."

Annie had been looking everywhere but at her husband's face as the words tumbled out, then her rapid speech tailed off as she saw his expression. He was sitting very still, and wasn't smiling. Annie imagined she saw a flash of pity, then sadness in his eyes.

She swallowed hard. "Well? What do you think?"

Derek slowly shook his head. "I'm sorry, Annie. It's not going to happen."

"But why not? Don't you think I could do it?"

"Of course you could. I know you're an incredibly capable mother and one day we'll have our own grandchildren to spend time on, when our kids start their families. You're loving, caring, resourceful and still have an amazing amount of energy."

"Then why are you so against it? You must know it would mean the world to me!"

Derek sighed. "I do know, and that's what concerns me. We're in our sixties now. We've worked for the last forty-five years and raised a big family. Our mortgage is paid off. We're now entitled to superannuation, so this is the time to kick back and think about ourselves for a change. I don't want you taking on the huge responsibility of looking after Joshua. It wouldn't just be daytimes either. Have you thought about how much sleep Emily is going to need once she starts training? You'll end up doing the night shift as well. That's a huge ask and I think it's too much for you to take on at this stage. You'll run yourself into the ground and I don't want to see you making yourself ill."

"But I'll be able to have naps during the day when Josh sleeps. And perhaps we could look at getting a cleaner to come in to do some of the housework for me? You have to admit that would be a help."

Derek shook his head. "No, Annie. I'm sorry."

She turned and looked away. The moon was rising above the trees, but it was a blur, from the tears of frustration welling up in her eyes. The night was still and warm, but Annie suddenly shivered.

"So...that's it then. You don't want me to do it."

Derek hesitated.

"There is another reason too. You obviously haven't spoken

with Emily yet."

"What?" Annie turned back and looked at him.

"Emily had a talk with me the other day while you were out. She really appreciates everything we've done for her and Joshua and says you've been amazing. But she's leaving here as soon as the details are finalised on her parents' house. Her friend with the little boy is going to move in there with her and share expenses. Emily needs the company of someone her own age and Josh will have Jacqui's son to play with too."

Annie closed her eyes. "Why didn't she talk to me first? Why did she tell you instead?"

"Because she knew you'd be upset. She also told me you remind her so much of her mum, and while it's been a comfort in some ways, it hurts her too. Every time you laugh or say something, it's like an echo of Joanne. You're unwittingly a constant and sad reminder she'll never see her mum again. I think you need to let them go, Annie. Give them some space for a while."

Annie sat motionless while Derek stood and cleared away the dishes. He put his warm hand on her arm and squeezed it gently.

"They'll only be five minutes away, just across town. Emily said you'll still see plenty of them. She thinks the world of you, Annie."

The sound of his footsteps faded as he carried the dishes into the house. Annie remained sitting. The smell of freshly brewed coffee drifted out to her and she could hear Derek getting the mugs out of the cupboard, then milk from the fridge. Annie looked upwards. The moon was full tonight and cast a soft light down through the trees. All the noise had abruptly ceased next door.

Two dark feline shapes emerged from under the table. Max sat beside her and started daintily washing himself with his paws. Sabrina rubbed up against Annie's leg, and then jumped onto her lap, purring loudly. Annie wrapped her arms around her cat and pressed her face into the soft fur, soaking it with her quiet tears.

"Peter! I called out half an hour ago that breakfast was ready. What are you doing now?"

"Yeah, yeah, sorry. I'll be in soon." Peter's voice was muffled, as he lay on the floor, half inside a new bench unit.

June stood at the door of the caravan, watching her husband fitting a cupboard door under the stainless steel sink. She felt her annoyance ebbing away and had to admit he was doing an amazing job. They had seen the advertisement for the caravan two weeks ago, in the New Zealand Herald. It was under the heading 'As is—where is' which usually meant it was a total bomb. She had thought it was beyond repair when they viewed it in Auckland, but Peter had seen its potential. He was literally rubbing his hands together as they checked it out, and June could see a decision had already been made in his mind. His eyes were positively gleaming.

The caravan was sound structurally, but badly in need of a facelift. That was Peter's forte. He was a skilled craftsman. The exterior had been stripped down and repainted, the areas of rust on the chassis underneath treated, and the tyres replaced. Inside, he had repainted the walls and ceiling a soft cream colour, and was installing a custom built kitchen unit with warm, honey-coloured timber cupboards. He had built the base for the bed, with small units each side and added a toilet and shower cubicle.

June smiled. *It looks good enough to live in.*

"Okay, honey, but please come in soon. Your poached eggs are hard-boiled now, and I'll have to make more toast. You can't live on coffee you know."

Peter grunted something; he hoped his wife would take it as a yes, and leave him in peace for another half hour. Once he got into the swing of it, he just wanted to carry on working.

He eased himself out from under the new kitchen unit and pulled himself upright when he heard their back door to the house open, then close.

Surveying his work, he recognised the familiar glow of satisfaction had returned. It was so good to be using his hands and being creative again. He loved being busy and immersed in a project, which made the days fly and it would be only a few months till the warm summer weather was here. The realisation had suddenly hit him the other day that this was something he could turn into a small home business. Restoring the caravan had increased his self-confidence and zest for life, giving him more reason to get up in the mornings. Why not sell this one on at a nice little profit, after he and June had given it a few test runs, then start renovating another?

If his idea took off, they would remain living here. He knew how attached June was to their house and garden and wouldn't have liked the idea of a permanent road trip. He was glad now he'd kept that idea to himself.

Peter stepped outside, found some sandpaper and started rubbing down a couple of painted areas that needed extra attention. He was a bit of a perfectionist with his work. No point in doing a job if it wasn't done right.

He heard their neighbour Keith Varney's gate latch click open and the crunch of footsteps on the pathway. Peter glanced over. A young, attractive woman, with long dark hair, dressed in a skimpy outfit and black stilettos and carrying a small bag, was leaving Keith's place.

I know what you were up to last night, you dirty old bugger.

As if she felt his eyes on her, the young woman turned and smiled, waved to Peter and called out, "Good morning!"

Without thinking, Peter called back "Good night?"

She glanced back at him and frowned. "That'd be telling," then carried on walking.

Peter grinned. Wait until he told June about that one. Ladies of the night seemed to be Keith's thing lately, and brief flings obviously suited him more than a long term relationship. The last girlfriend had only been around a few months. She was there one day and gone the next.

One night with him is probably more than enough for anyone. He'd be a miserable old bastard to live with anyway. Too much time being single would make anyone narrow-minded and selfish. No wonder the girlfriend left.

Peter finished sanding the paintwork down. He looked up at the kitchen window and saw June beckoning him. He sighed, then smiled up at her. Time to go in, eat something, and stop her fussing. Not that he really minded. Better that, than going in to an empty house, with just himself for company, like old wannabe lover-boy next door.

As he packed his tools away, he heard the sound of a car coming slowly past the top of the driveway. Peter glanced over and saw a police car cruise past, followed by a dark-coloured van. Both vehicles turned at the end of the cul-de-sac, and then stopped outside Keith's gate.

What's he been up to, I wonder?

Peter was tempted to stay outside a little longer, but his hunger got the better of him. He was already late for breakfast with his wife.

Annie was up late-ish the next morning. She had tossed and turned all night, fretting over the news about Emily and Josh. It was almost impossible to imagine them not living here any longer. How she was going to miss them! Those quiet, cuddly moments with Josh when Emily was asleep. The soft smell of talcum powder that seemed to have permeated everything in the house. Rattles and toys lying on the floor. His throaty gurgles and giggles. That velvety baby skin against hers and his fine, silky hair under her fingers. And his dark eyes, full of sparkle and mischief, yet so knowing as well. She'd grown to love him, as if he was one of her own.

"That's my problem!" she muttered. "I've gotten too involved. I'm not Emily's mother, and Josh isn't my grandchild. I need to get real and gracefully accept that they're leaving. End of story!"

Yet her heart ached.

Annie had decided when Emily and Josh arrived back later that morning, she would put on a brave face and smile her way through it. She would tell Emily how much they'd loved having her and Josh to stay, but had always understood it was only temporary. She would congratulate Emily on how she was taking control of her life. Owning a house when only nineteen-years-old was a big responsibility, but Annie would say she knew Emily would rise to the challenge, as she had with everything in her young life. There had been so much heartache for her niece already. Annie was determined she wasn't going to add to it.

She heard the sound of a vehicle and looked out the window, thinking it must be Emily and Josh arriving back. Instead, there was a police car turning and parking outside Keith's place, followed closely by a dark-grey van. Annie stood and watched as two men got out of the car, one in plainclothes and the other in uniform. They stood talking for a minute, then the man in plainclothes opened Keith's gate and walked down the pathway.

Annie was transfixed, momentarily forgetting how upset she was feeling.

Wow! I wonder what's going on? With any luck, someone's made a complaint about all Keith's noise. Then again, the police would hardly be turning up to enforce noise control.

At that moment, Emily's car appeared and swung into their driveway. Annie watched, her eyes misting over as Emily lifted Josh out of his car seat and planted a big kiss on his chubby left cheek. He looked up at his mum and smiled, reaching out a hand and touching her face.

"She's such a good mum," Annie murmured to herself. "I would have been proud to call her my daughter."

She saw Emily turn and glance at the police car parked a few yards away on the roadside, then grab her bag out of the car and carry Josh towards the house and up the outside stairs.

Annie waited a few minutes, then took a deep breath. It was time. She went up to the flat via the internal stairs and knocked on the door.

"Emily, honey?"

The door swung open and Emily smiled uncertainly at her. A few seconds passed.

Annie broke the silence. "Can I come in, please?"

"Sure." Emily stepped back and held the door open wider. Josh was lying on his back on the play mat, holding a rattle. He looked over and gave Annie one of his gummy grins as she came into the lounge.

"Do you want to sit down, Aunt Annie, and let me make you a coffee for a change? I was just about to boil the jug."

"Wait a minute, please, Emily. I need to talk with you for a moment." Annie took another deep breath. "Derek told me your news last night. It's very exciting! And as much as we'll miss having you here, we totally understand you need to move on with your life. I'm sorry if I've been a bit–you know–pushy with you and Josh, but I so wanted to look after you both. And I've loved every minute of it. Truly."

"Oh, thank you! I'm sorry I didn't tell you earlier but I felt so bad, after everything you've done. You gave us a home during the worst time of my life. I don't know what I would've done without you and Uncle Derek being here for me and Josh."

"So...what's the plan? When will you be moving? We're here to help, if and when you need us."

"Thanks. That would be great. Not that I have a lot of gear, but extra hands are always welcome. I have all Mum and Dad's furniture in the house, so it's really only my clothes and books. Josh is only six months old, and he already owns more stuff than I do."

They laughed, which helped ease the awkwardness. She looked fondly at her niece.

"It's good to hear you'll be sharing the house with Jacqui and her son, and that Josh will have someone else to play with. I'd worry if I thought you two were there on your own, but it sounds as if Jacqui will be a good support for you, especially if you decide later on to reapply for your nursing training."

"She will. But I've decided to wait until Josh turns one, before I do that. I really want to have him to myself for his first year, then, once he's on his feet and hopefully sleeping through the night, I can try for nursing again."

"Oh Emily, you're amazing and I wish I'd had half your self-confidence when I was nineteen. I admire you. I really do!"

"Thank you." Emily's eyes filled with tears as Annie moved forward and enveloped her in a long, warm hug. Emily sighed and laid her head on her aunt's shoulder. It felt so good to have someone hold her close.

After a minute, Annie wiped her own eyes and gave Emily a kiss on the cheek. "So, what about that coffee you promised me?"

Emily laughed. "Sure. First though…there was something I wanted to ask you."

"Absolutely." Annie sat herself down next to Josh on the floor. "Fire away."

"Well…I'd love you to babysit Josh for me sometimes, especially while we get settled into the house. But once I start nursing training, I'll need more regular care for him. How would you feel about taking turns with Jacqui, looking after him some days? It would only be two to three days a week at the most, so it wouldn't be too much of a tie for you. Jacqui will be living with us, so she's okay to do evenings, and of course she'll be there when I'm doing night duty. We've already discussed finances and I'm going to charge her a low rent, in return for her help. I'd also like to pay you something. It won't be much, but I'd feel better about it if you agreed."

Emily stopped to take a breath. "Well, what do you think?"

Annie had been staring down at Josh. He reached out his chubby little hand and wrapped his warm fingers around Annie's, then smiled up at her as though to say, "See? Things are going to be okay after all."

Annie looked up at her niece through a mist of tears.

"There's nothing I'd love more, Emily. You'll never know how much it means to me. Thank you."

"Do you need to run it past Uncle Derek first? He might want to have a say."

Annie smiled. "Don't you worry about him. He'll be okay with the idea, especially as it's only a few days a week. I'll sort it."

"Cool! I'm so happy everything's falling into place. And it's wonderful that Josh will still have you around. You know I trust you with him more than anyone else in the world. Thanks, Aunt Annie."

Emily went into the kitchenette and put the electric jug on to boil.

"Now, let's finally have our coffee. And tell me…what the hell's going on next door?"

Keith rolled over, stretched and yawned, relishing having his bed to himself again. The woman was gone. She'd spent the night with him, then let herself out the back door a while ago. He could still smell the traces of her perfume she'd left behind on the sheets. She'd been young, but experienced. Even when he'd gotten rough with her, she'd catered to his every whim. That's how a woman should be. She didn't make small talk either. In fact, they'd done very little talking at all.

Keith smirked. He'd even surprised himself with his performance and his staying power last night. She'd been very attractive, which always helped. Next time he contacted the agency, he would ask for her again.

What was her name? Was it Helen? Hilary? Keith frowned. Not that it really mattered. She was just a woman with a nice body. He'd used her and enjoyed her. Nothing more.

Suddenly, and inexplicably, Janine's face came to mind.

She had asked to move in with him. He'd been reluctant at first, but she had pleaded and pleaded, which appealed to him, and eventually he had agreed. Janine had been anxious to please and very amenable. He'd called the shots in the relationship from the start and she'd complied, even when he could see she was reluctant at times. She'd had no immediate family living close to interfere. It all went okay for a while. Then she began to change, and the arguments crept in. Nag, nag, nag. She was never happy.

"I don't want to."

"Why, why, why?"

"I don't like this."

"I don't like that!"

"I hate it when you behave that way."

Her complaints went on and on, and Keith found the only way to shut her up was to get rough with her. It had worked well for a while too.

Then, he began to suspect she was seeing someone else behind his back. She had gone out several times without telling him where she was going, and who she was meeting. And there were the phone calls. He didn't believe her when she said it was her parents on the phone and he especially didn't like the way she would end the conversation abruptly when he walked into the room. Something was going on.

His suspicions and accusations escalated, and in return, Janine became more defiant. Their rows became more heated, and one night she'd screamed at him that she hated the way he was trying to control her whole life.

That did it. He lost it and hit her. Hard.

That's when it ended.

Keith closed his eyes, took a deep breath, put his hands behind his head and listened.

It was so peaceful outside. All he could hear were the birds.

The neighbours on either side of him were retired and kept to themselves. They would wave and say hello, but that was all. They could be noisy though. Peter Mansell was always hammering and sawing, either building something or renovating the house. Now it looked as if he was doing up an old caravan. The man didn't know when to stop! Keith guessed Peter was a good craftsman, but he wouldn't be asking him to come over and do any work here. He didn't want anyone poking around.

Then, there was Annie McFarlane. She nearly drove him up the wall, always calling out for her cats. Early mornings, middle of the day, late at night. She even had conversations with them for God's sake!

Talk about the mad cat-lady.

Bloody things were a pain too—he'd caught them crapping in his garden several times, and even though he'd thrown rocks at them, they still hung around. He'd even found a cat in his kitchen once and had placed a well-aimed kick. Annie McFarlane didn't know how close she'd been to having one cat less.

Keith reached up and pulled the curtains open to let the sunshine in. After breakfast, he'd do some more work in the cellar, then get his chainsaw into action again. Nothing like a Sunday morning to get things done.

He hauled himself out of bed and changed into some overalls he'd pushed to the back of the wardrobe before he went away. They were covered in dark brown stains and the sour smell made his nose wrinkle.

Keith remained staring downwards, then sat abruptly on the bed and closed his eyes.

Bloody woman. Why did she have to spoil it all?

He put his head in his hands and waited for the rage to subside; made himself take deep breaths.

It was over and done with. Life went on.

Keith went into the kitchen and started to make breakfast, and then realised there was no milk. He'd forgotten to put the bottles and tokens out at his gate again, so he'd have to walk up to the dairy. The two men who ran the shop were bloody nosey, and always asked questions. Keith gave short, abrupt answers, so they soon got the hint and shut up. He had no time for small talk.

He grabbed his wallet and house keys and was heading for the back porch, when there was a knock on the door. Keith froze. He wasn't expecting anyone. He fervently hoped it wasn't Brian from the tramping club, come to pester him again.

I won't answer the door. Whoever it is will think I'm still asleep and go away.

Keith waited, not moving a muscle. This time the doorbell rang, then footsteps sounded along the porch. He saw a man, with hands cupped around his eyes, face against the glass, peering into his lounge. Keith flattened himself against the wall, breathing hard and fast, his heart thumping. After another couple of minutes, he heard the footsteps descend his back stairs and walk along the pathway towards the road.

He edged to the window and peered out. No sign of anyone. He'd stay out of sight a little longer.

Some minutes later, Keith locked the back door and walked up the path. He opened the gate and latched it behind him, only vaguely aware of the sound of car doors opening and the crackling static of a car radio.

"Excuse me, sir?"

Keith jumped and turned around. "Yes?"

"Are you Keith Varney?" The man addressing him was tall, sandy-haired and well dressed, in grey trousers and a dark jacket. A uniformed policeman stood beside him. Keith could see some other men sitting in the van parked behind the police car.

"I am. Who are you?"

The man flipped open a wallet, showing a silver badge. "I'm Senior Sergeant Tennant and this is Sergeant Williams. Is there somewhere we can talk in private?"

Keith pursed his lips, then shook his head. "Not a good

time. I'm going out."

The officer frowned. "I'm sorry sir. I need to speak with you now. Can we go inside please?"

Keith sighed. "Can't we talk out here?"

The police officers exchanged glances, then Tennant's gaze flickered up and down, over Keith's stained work clothes.

"We need to ask you some questions, Mr Varney. Inside. It won't take too long."

Reluctantly, Keith turned, acutely aware of eyes boring into the back of his head as the two men followed him. He unlocked the door and sat himself at the kitchen table. Sergeant Williams stayed near the door and Tennant also remained standing.

Keith leaned back in his chair, stretched his legs out and folded his arms, staring out the window. Both police officers regarded him silently.

"Well? Can you make it quick? I've got plans today."

"This will take as long as we need it to take, Mr Varney." Tennant leant back against the bench and folded his arms, mirroring Keith. "What were your plans, by the way?"

"Why?" Keith smirked. "I'm sure they'd be of no interest to you."

"Perhaps not. Then again..." Tennant shifted his position. "I'll get straight to the point. We're following up on a report of a missing person."

"So? What's that got to do with me?"

"Quite a lot, possibly. We believe you know the person in question."

Keith shrugged. "I've no idea who you're talking about."

"Does the name Janine Ellis jog your memory?"

"Yes, I know her." Keith grinned. "Intimately, in fact. She lived here for a while, then left."

"Is that so? Did she give you a forwarding address by any chance?"

"Why would she do that?" Keith's expression became thoughtful. "We hardly parted on the best of terms."

"Tell me more." Tennant straightened and walked slowly around the kitchen, pausing to stand behind Keith's chair. He could see an angry red flush spreading up the back of the man's neck. "What made her leave so abruptly?"

"I threw her out. She was cheating on me and lying through her teeth. I didn't want her living here anymore. That's not against the law is it?" Keith turned in his chair and glanced briefly at Tennant, who remained silent. "Why all these questions anyway? I can't help you. Maybe you should talk to some of the other men in our tramping club. It wouldn't surprise me at all if she was having it off with one of them. Have you questioned Brian Burroughs yet? I'm sure he would've liked to move in on her. He had plenty of time to do it while I was away overseas."

"We've already talked with Mr Burroughs and his wife. In fact, that's why we're here. He raised concerns about the nature of your relationship with Miss Ellis."

Bloody Brian! Shooting his mouth off again.

"Ha! He's got a cheek. He was jealous as hell because he had his eye on Janine. Sour grapes, I'd say. I bet he didn't tell you about all his nights out with the boys. I know for a fact he played around. His wife hasn't got a clue what he gets up to, and it's just as well. Who knows what else he's capable of?"

"We'll be talking with Mr Burroughs again, I can assure you. He was a mine of information, in fact."

Keith didn't respond. He tapped his foot impatiently and looked pointedly at his watch.

Tennant resumed his position against the bench, and folded his arms again.

"However, Janine's family in Australia are extremely concerned. They haven't heard from her in some time. Several months, in fact. They said it's most unusual. Normally, she rings her parents often. Apparently she sounded very unhappy the last time they talked."

Keith shrugged again. "She was never happy, no matter what I did for her. She cheated on me and she lied constantly. I didn't want her here anymore."

Tennant regarded Keith with narrowed eyes.

"We've also made enquiries with Brian from the tramping club she belonged to. We believe you met her when you became a member."

"Yes." Keith gave a rueful smile. "Unluckily for me. You can't win 'em all."

"And Janine moved in here, not long after you'd met. Is that correct?"

"Yes. A few weeks later. Everyone thought we were rushing into it, but we felt sure about what we were doing."

Tennant paused.

"And again...it's been mentioned by someone else that your relationship was...shall we say...difficult?"

Aren't they all?

Another shrug. "It started off okay. We had a few rows early on, but then who doesn't?"

"You're right there, Mr Varney." Tennant smiled, trying to catch Keith's eye. "Mind you, there are rows—and then there are rows. When you've always lived on your own, and you find yourself sharing your personal space with someone else, tensions can surface. A small disagreement can escalate quickly into something else."

Tennant paused. "Did you ever hit Miss Ellis?"

"No!" Keith sounded outraged .

"We've obtained a statement from Miss Ellis' doctor. She was examined at the surgery not long before she disappeared. According to his report, she had some severe bruising on her back, around her stomach and ribcage. He expressed concern, but she assured him she'd had a fall—"

"Yes! She did!" Keith cut in. "We were away tramping and she slipped and rolled down a rocky bank before I could grab her. No wonder she was black and blue."

Tennant hesitated.

"That's odd, Mr Varney. "She told her doctor she'd had a fall in the garden. In this garden, actually."

"Ha! That proves what a liar she was. No wonder I couldn't trust her. She didn't even tell me she'd been to see a doctor. She was always supposed to say where she was going—."

"I wonder why she didn't. Was she afraid, perhaps?"

"Afraid? Why would she be afraid?" Keith looked directly at Tennant as he spoke and the detective felt a chill run down his spine. Keith's eyes were like obsidian; dark, glassy and expressionless. Then his voice lowered and softened.

"I don't know why you'd say that. I gave her a home. I gave her money. I fed her. She should have been grateful, but she wasn't. She used me, cheated on me, told me lies, so I threw her out. She's probably left the country."

Tennant shook his head. "That's already been discounted. There's no record of her passport being presented anywhere. And it's even more of a concern that her bank account hasn't been touched for weeks. Don't you think that's unusual?"

Keith shrugged. "Not really. Knowing her, she'll be shacked up with someone else she's bludging off. She does that. She uses people. She's a lying, cheating bitch!" His voice rose, as he spat out the words. Then he took a deep breath, leaned back again and looked at Tennant, speaking more calmly.

"I get very emotional about the way she treated me. I really loved her you know, and I thought she felt the same, but I was wrong. Now she's someone else's problem. That's it. End of story."

Tennant stared at Keith. He was picking up some bad vibes from this terse man, with his smooth and ready answers.

Something wasn't right. Tennant could feel it in his gut.

"We'll have a look around while we're here, Mr Varney. Any objections?"

"Yes. I happen to value my privacy and my time, which you continue to waste. You'll also need to obtain a search warrant." Keith grinned smugly.

"Already done." Tennant reached inside the front of his jacket, removed an official form, and showed it to Keith. "Let's begin outside, shall we?"

Keith sighed. "As long as you're quick. I have work to do in the garden this morning."

He stood, and the officers followed him outside. Tennant stopped and looked up the pathway at the padlocked cellar door.

"What do you keep in there?"

"Just garden tools and my chainsaw. And I'm building cabinets and shelving to keep equipment on. That's all. Nothing very interesting."

"We'll start there, then. Can you open up please?"

Keith sighed again. "Oh dear. I can't remember what I've done with the key."

Tennant gazed at him. "Then you'll have difficulty working in your garden without your tools, won't you?"

Something flared in Keith's eyes for a second, then it was gone. He stared impassively at the detective, then smiled.

"I've been away, remember? I'll bet you can't always recall where you put something several months ago? Go on, admit it!"

Tennant waited. He signalled to the sergeant, then turned back to Keith.

"Sir, we have a search team waiting to enter the property, and I'm about to call them in. We'll use force if we have to, to break the door down."

"There's no need for that. I don't want you lot causing any

more disruption than you already have. Give me a minute. I think I know where it is."

Keith spun around and walked towards the back door. Tennant signalled to the sergeant to go with him. While he waited, Tennant's eyes scanned the garden and the high fencing encompassing the whole property. It reminded him of a fortress.

It's as if Keith Varney is shutting the whole world out.

The only possible vantage point for any of the neighbours to see in, was the house immediately next door. One of the windows angled in such a way that anyone looking out would have a prime view of Keith's pathway and the door to the cellar. Tennant made a mental note to talk with the residents later.

He turned as he heard footsteps approaching. Keith was back, accompanied by Sergeant Williams.

"Here. I'd put it away with my cigarettes. Been trying to give up, but it hasn't been easy." Keith forced another smile, which didn't reach his eyes. They were expressionless.

Tennant stood aside. "I'd prefer you to open the door for me, please"

Keith nodded, his face impassive, and his lips compressed in a straight line. He inserted the key and turned it. The padlock sprang open and he removed it and pushed the door ajar.

"Make it quick. The morning's half-gone already."

Tennant stepped inside. There was just enough visibility for him to see a light switch to the left of the door. He flicked it on and looked around, blinking in the sudden glare.

Timber was stacked in neat piles to one side of the cellar and on the opposite side, a workbench was set up, with wood shavings beneath it.

Power tools and garden equipment hung on evenly

spaced wall brackets, in meticulously straight rows. Bags of concrete mix had been stacked against a wall. A set of partially completed wooden shelves sat on a large sheet of black polythene. Tennant could see the soil around the edges of the polythene was dry, but loose, as if it had been recently disturbed. He scuffed it with his shoe.

He closed his eyes and allowed his other senses take over. The air in the cellar was damp, still, and cold against his face. He could hear the faint buzz of a blowfly nearby. And he could smell something almost indefinable. His nostrils flared as he inhaled deeply. The smell wasn't from the sawn timber. It wasn't the oily fumes from the chainsaw hung nearby and it wasn't the earthiness of freshly turned soil. It was a faint sour-sweet odour, one he recognised from years of work in the police force. He had encountered it many times before, and would never forget it. The smell of decay.

Tennant's eyes moved over the sheet of black polythene, weighted down with concrete blocks along each edge.

He figured it was as good a place as any, to begin the search.

Time for his team to move in.

He exited the cellar. Keith was standing still, arms stiffly at his sides.

"Mr Varney, I'm calling my men in now. Your property will remain secure, with officers in attendance. Sergeant Williams and I will escort you to the police station, where you will be read your rights, before further questioning. Do you understand me?"

Keith stared at Tennant. His eyes remained flat and dark.

"I keep telling you and telling you, you're wasting your time. You won't find anything in there. Nothing that's worth looking for anyway. Especially a slut like her!"

He then turned, looked out over his garden and the trees surrounding it, as if seeing everything for a final time.

Tennant could hear a woman calling for her cat, and the bang-bang-bang of someone hammering. There was the sound of laughter, then a baby's happy squeal from an open window next door. He could hear the birds in the trees and the hum of vehicles out on the main road. It was all so normal. Unlike the horror he knew awaited the search team in that cold, dark cellar.

"Mr Varney? Do you wish to ask anything before we leave?"

Keith turned back and faced the two officers in front of him.

He spoke in a monotone.

"Why couldn't everyone have just left me alone? All I've *ever* wanted, was to be left alone."

4

by Clare Matravers

"Big news. It looks as though the house next door has sold," Sheryl Croft called through the screen door, as she shook the raindrops off her umbrella. "I just saw the agent taking down the For Sale sign."

"It's about time," Herbert said, as he opened the door for his wife. "Scoot, Kerfluffle." Their elderly cat was doing his best rug impersonation in the middle of the kitchen floor and Herbert pushed him out of the way.

"How long has it been on the market for, now?" Sheryl bustled past him, carrying a paper bag of groceries.

"At least six months. I thought it would never sell."

"How exciting. I wonder who'll move in there?" At the sound of the fridge opening, the cat was instantly alert. Sheryl warded him off with her foot as she stowed the milk and butter away, and narrowly missed slamming his nose in the door.

Herbert put the bread in the cupboard. "Probably a family

with six kids—all noisy, yelling and screaming the whole day long," he muttered, ever the pessimist.

He couldn't have been more wrong. The new occupant seemed to move in overnight. One day the house was empty and lifeless, the next, pretty net curtains were hanging in the kitchen window—much to Sheryl's annoyance as it made it impossible for her to see in. Apart from that, there were no other signs of life.

After two days of not spotting the inhabitant or any activity, Sheryl had had enough.

"I'm going over there," she informed her husband.

He looked up from the newspaper he was perusing at the kitchen table. "Is that wise?" He knew better than to argue with his determined wife.

"I'll take some of my baking—it'll be a nice neighbourly thing to do—and see what's what."

"Any excuse to poke your nose in," Herbert murmured. She glared at him, but he had already turned back to his paper.

On her way over, Sheryl paused and gazed at the oak tree standing in the middle of the cul-de-sac. It was quiet now the children were at school. Later on, it would be full of youngsters clambering around in the branches, yelling and laughing. Her two, when they were young, had practically lived in that tree, until Steve had fallen out and broken his arm.

"Were you practising to be an acorn?" his father had asked, unhelpfully. After that incident, neither child had been quite so enthusiastic about climbing it.

Another time, Kerfluffle had climbed up and yowled he was stuck. When poor old Herbert clambered up to rescue him, the silly cat raked his arm with freshly sharpened claws and scampered down without assistance. It was just as well Herbert was so good-natured, or the cat would probably have lost all nine of its lives that day.

There was no response to her initial knock so Sheryl pounded on the door and stood back. There was a twitch of the curtains and then muffled footsteps. The door cracked open.

"Allo?" The heavily accented voice sounded cautious.

"Hello, I'm Sheryl. I live next door." She peered in, trying without success to make out a face in the gloomy interior. "I've brought you a house-warming present."

"You are too kind." A woman's arm appeared, slender wrist encircled by a silver bracelet, and hand held out to receive. With reluctance, Sheryl placed the covered plate of scones in the outstretched palm and watched it disappear in dismay.

"Merci."

"Can I have my plate…"

But the door had closed, leaving behind only a faint trace of delicate perfume. "Well, of all the nerve," she muttered to herself.

Back home, she huffed into the kitchen and slammed the screen door. Herbert, apparently still engrossed in the newspaper, didn't flinch. She had to stomp around for a full minute before he finally noticed her temper.

"So what did you find out?"

"A woman lives there and she has at least one arm!"

When Herbert failed to stifle a chuckle, she looked daggers at him.

"And not a word of thanks either. She just said 'mercy'..." Sheryl frowned as she remembered. She had been so busy being annoyed with the woman at the time, she hadn't taken much notice of what had been said. "At least that's what it sounded like—her accent was so strong; she was hard to understand. Do you think she could be in trouble?"

"Perhaps she's heard about your baking," Herbert murmured, teasing. "Ouch!" Sheryl had swatted him with the rolled up newspaper, and threatened never to bake for him again. "Your baking is fantastic," he exclaimed, cowering under a hail of mock blows, "and 'merci' is French for thank you!"

Marie Beauchamp squinted at the lines on the drawing board. She would have to turn the light on soon. She was nearly done anyway. There. She leaned back and admired her work. It looked good, even if she said so herself. The client should be impressed.

She couldn't be bothered cooking anything more substantial than boiled eggs and toast for dinner tonight. Not that there was much food in the house anyway—just what she'd found in the local dairy. She hadn't had the chance to do a proper shop yet; another item on her extensive to-do list.

With the light fading, she moved over to the window to close the curtains. Through the nets, she could see Sheryl standing in her well-lit kitchen, looking this way. Unlikely as it was the woman could see her, Marie still shrank back into the shadows, not prepared to risk tearing the shroud of mystery she had wrapped around herself.

Fancy the Crofts still living in the same house for all these years. Would they remember her parents from when they resided here? Dear old Herbert and Sheryl—she couldn't remember them herself, of course, being only a few months old when her mother had taken her to France, but Maman had spoken of them often.

Apparently, there had been two Croft children, a girl and a boy—who must be in their thirties by now. The Crofts had sounded like good neighbours to have, considerate, kind and generous, yet Sheryl had had the reputation of being a bit of a busybody.

Judging by Sheryl's visit today, not a lot had changed. But Marie could forgive the woman's nosiness with that sort of neighbourly gesture—those scones of Sheryl's—superb! As good as any produced by a French bakery, they were so light, they were in danger of floating off the plate. Marie was going to get fat at this rate, not to mention malnourished, if she lived on the neighbour's baking and didn't buy fruit and vegetables. Perhaps she could start a garden. There was certainly enough space for one out the back. But gardening wasn't really her thing. She was more of an indoors person and didn't like getting her hands dirty. Herbert appeared to have a fine vegetable patch in their back section. Maybe he would bring over some produce. It would be a lot better for her than home baking.

What was that bizarre noise? Oh, of course it was the tui in the kowhai tree next door, still chortling away even though the sun had gone down.

She was wasting time standing here. Feeling like a secret agent, she had another furtive glance out the window. To her relief, Sheryl was nowhere in sight so Marie hastily drew the curtains before the neighbour returned, and began to prepare her simple meal.

Would the Crofts remember her papa? He was something of a mystery, even to her, as her mother had seldom mentioned him, and on the odd occasion when Marie had asked about him, Maman had clammed up.

After her darling mother's tragic death five years earlier, curiosity had gotten the better of Marie regarding her New Zealand father, and she had decided to track him down in the country of her birth.

She finished her contract with the French modelling agency and applied to do a graphic design course at Auckland Technical Institute in New Zealand. To her delight, her portfolio had been accepted, and she had moved to the 'ends of the earth'.

Once settled in the country, she had started her search. At long last, and with considerable effort, she had managed to find her father. However, to her bewilderment, instead of welcoming her with open arms as she had expected, he hadn't seemed keen to see her. In fact, to her sorrow, he had said he didn't want to have anything to do with her and she wasn't his daughter. But he didn't explain, just shut the door in her face, leaving her confused and devastated as part of her identity shattered into tiny pieces on the floor.

What with having graduated and landed a job she could do from home, her father's painful rejection and the void it left—and of course the other reason—but she didn't want to think about that right now, she could see no point in staying in Auckland. The place of her birth, the obscure little town of Emory, was as good a place to be as any.

By an amazing coincidence, the house where she had lived as a baby was on the market, just at the time she was house hunting. Her mother had left her a sum of money, which she used to make a rather insubstantial offer. To her surprise, it had been accepted. And what a bonus—the seller had been prepared to throw in some furniture he didn't need, so she was able to move in with the minimum of fuss.

What was that clatter? Her heart pounded. She was so jumpy. Not surprising really after what she had been through. But it was only the milk truck doing its rounds. Checking that the nosey neighbours weren't watching, she slipped out into the gathering dusk to snatch up her one bottle of milk. On her return, she froze as a grey shape silently crossed the path in front of her, but it was only the neighbour's fluffy cat. With her nerves frazzled, she scurried back inside, locking the door firmly behind her.

While the eggs were boiling, she buttered toast. After arranging it all neatly on a tray, she switched on the TV and settled down to watch the news. A floorboard creaked behind her and she jumped, nearly sending her dinner flying. She turned to see what had caused it. Of course there was nothing there. It was just the house settling down for the night.

There was not much of interest on TV tonight. She was bored, a little bit restless and lonely. It would be nice to have someone to talk to, but she didn't dare go over to any of the neighbours for a chat. And she knew no one else in this wee town. Which was probably just as well, as the fewer people who knew her whereabouts, the better.

Perhaps she could ring up some of her Auckland friends. She headed to the phone. No, it would cost a bomb. Maybe she could write to them instead. And to her father in case he had changed his mind and wanted to contact her after all. She found some paper and envelopes but no stamps. Surely the corner dairy would sell them? If she wrote the letters now, she could send them off tomorrow, when she posted the work back to the client.

The following day, Sheryl was all set to go next door to retrieve her plate, but when she stepped out onto the back porch, she discovered a brown paper bag on the bench. She opened it with caution. Inside was the plate, the cloth neatly folded on top and a note upon which was simply printed 'Thanks'. A hint of perfume wafted up—French, no doubt.

So there went her excuse to further investigate the mystery woman. It was almost more than Sheryl could cope with. She put on her jacket and stalked over to Wanda's, glaring at their mutual neighbour's house as she went past, but her filthy looks were wasted as there was no sign of life.

At least she could be sure of hospitality at her friend's place. Wanda Summers had lived two doors down now for a good number of years. Although the two had become firm friends over time, Sheryl had never quite managed to find out Wanda's past. Like the new neighbour, she had just blown into town overnight, in a Mary Poppins kind of way. Oh, Sheryl had tried to find out, had asked many questions over the years, some subtle and some downright nosey. But each time, with a slight shudder, Wanda would answer, "The past is in the past, and it's better to leave it there." Then she would deftly change the subject. Which had piqued Sheryl's curiosity even more, but to no avail.

There was friendly rivalry going on between them regarding neighbourhood gossip. Sheryl loved to have the upper hand but Wanda didn't seem that bothered, which annoyed Sheryl intensely. Especially aggravating was the casual way Wanda would drop some juicy piece of information into the conversation.

"So have you seen our new neighbour?" Sheryl asked,

as they sipped tea. She reached out to stroke her cat, who spent his days lying on Wanda's armchair. Kerfluffle opened one yellow eye to glare at her and then went back to dozing again.

"Oh yes," Wanda replied, airily, "I saw her arrive in the taxi the other night—very quiet she was. And I've seen her walk past several times."

Sheryl fumed silently to herself. How dare Wanda have something over her? "But you haven't actually met her?"

"No, but I greeted her one day when I was out at the letterbox getting the paper. She didn't even look in my direction, the snob."

That was a relief—at least she was one up on Wanda there.

"I took some baking over to her yesterday and discovered she's French, so maybe she didn't understand you," Sheryl said, trying to impress her friend with her insider knowledge.

Her hope was in vain, as Wanda simply gave her a bland smile and offered her more tea.

Sheryl fumed for a minute, before her curiosity got the better of her. "I didn't get a good look at her." That was an understatement. "So what's she like?"

Wanda appeared to think for a moment. "It's hard to say, because each time I've seen her, she's been wearing a head scarf, dark glasses and a coat. Even when it's quite warm. Sort of like a disguise. She seems a bit twitchy, like a little bird, nervous about something."

"That sounds intriguing. Ooh, you don't think she's somebody famous, do you, hiding from publicity?" In her excitement, Sheryl quite forgot her grudge against Wanda. "Maybe she's a movie star?"

Wanda gave her a withering look. "What would a star be doing in this backwater?"

Sheryl deflated. "Maybe she's had enough of being famous

and needs some time out," she said, getting defensive. "Why else would a body be furtive like that?" Ha! Wanda didn't have an answer for that. They drank tea in silence for a minute.

"Perhaps she's hiding from a lover?" Wanda said, her eyes glowing with excitement. "I haven't seen any signs of a male there—I wonder if she's single?"

Sheryl may have been the busybody, but Wanda was most definitely the matchmaker. Her reputation for trying to pair up every single in the neighbourhood was legendary—and ridiculous.

Once, with well-meaning intentions, she had tried to match up a woman with her own nephew by mistake. And another time it was a pair of siblings. She obviously hadn't learnt, because so far the matchmaking had been fruitless, not one union had come from any of her attempts.

Sheryl groaned. "She's been here less than a week, and already you want to match her up with someone?"

"I didn't say that," Wanda said, sounding defensive. "But now you mention it...when does Steve come to visit next? He'd be just the right age for her, I reckon."

"You leave my poor son out of it," Sheryl said, then noticed the twinkle in Wanda's eye. "I'm sure that's one of the reasons why he left Emory, because you kept trying to match make him!" She grinned at her friend, teasing her back. "And leave her next-door alone too."

"You can't talk!" Wanda said. "You're the one who's been sticking your beak in at her front door!"

It was true, but Sheryl refused to be chastened. "Besides, she might already be involved with someone we don't know about."

Wanda opened her mouth to answer but caught sight of the time and pulled a face instead. "I'd better go and get ready for work."

Sheryl frowned as she looked at the kitchen clock. "But

you've got ages yet, surely?"

"I have to put petrol in the Jaffa on the way. And naturally I can't keep the old dears in the rest home waiting."

With a toot, Wanda zoomed off along the street in her Jaffa-coloured Hillman Avenger. Sheryl waved in response as she made her way home.

There was an envelope sticking out of the new neighbour's letterbox. After a quick check to see if anyone was watching, Sheryl pretended to admire some flowers by the gate, all the while scanning what little she could see of the letter. It was addressed to Miss Marie...but the box flap obscured the surname.

Sheryl looked up in time to see the curtain at the front window fall back into place. She scurried off, smiling to herself. Now she had something else up on Wanda; actually two things—the woman's name and the fact she was single. "So, Miss Marie, what's your story?" she murmured as she hurried along the driveway.

The sun was about to set when a knock on the front door startled Sheryl. Herbert had gone out for his evening walk, Kerfluffle was no doubt doing his evening prowl of the neighbourhood, and she was alone in the house. Only salesmen, or people touting religion came to the front and it was getting rather late for visitors. Should she ignore it? Her curiosity got the better of her.

With trepidation, she opened up, ensuring the screen door was locked. A young, well-dressed man stood on the porch. There was no sign of a briefcase, but he had one hand behind his back.

"Whatever it is you're peddling, I'm not interested," Sheryl said, preparing to close the door.

"Oh no, Madam, it's nothing like that. I'm looking for someone, that's all. A young woman, new to the area, by the name of Rosemarie." He smiled, revealing even white teeth. "I got halfway here and realised I'd left the address behind, silly me." He looked suitably sheepish. "She lives on this street but I can't remember what number she's at."

"Rosemarie? I don't know anyone of that name." She paused to think. "Now there is a young woman who's just moved in next door—but her name's Marie."

"Yes." The man's face lit up, "That would be her. She shortens it to Marie."

"What do you want with her?" She didn't like the way he kept his hand behind him. It seemed suspicious.

"I have something for her." He pulled a bunch of flowers out from behind his back.

Sheryl warmed to him in an instant and she smiled. "Are you her boyfriend?" She didn't wait for an answer. "We were wondering if she had one. She lives just there," she said, indicating with her thumb.

"Thank you so much, Ma'am," he said. "Only, please do me a favour, and don't let on I'm looking for her. I want it to be a surprise." He gave her a conspiratorial smile. Sheryl beamed back. She loved a good secret.

"I'm only pleased I could help you." What a nice young man. And not bad looking either. Wait till she told Wanda she had met the young woman's beau!

Marie settled down on the couch to watch the news. She was used to the house noises now and no longer jumped at every creak. Besides, how was the man going to find her here in this little out-of-the-way place?

Tonight she had a proper meal on the tray; a decent steak with onions and steamed vegetables. Hmm, a glass of red wine would have gone well with the food—but there was none in the house.

The news tonight all seemed to concern the prime minister and his rather startling decisions. She had lived in this country for a couple of years now and still couldn't fathom New Zealand politics.

Halfway through her meal, she realised she had forgotten to lock the front door—but she was too comfortable to move now. This neighbourhood seemed safe anyway—there had been no reports of crime since she had moved in. But she must remember to lock up straight after dinner.

The slight creak behind her barely registered.

"Now I've got you," a voice said. And everything went black.

Herbert had left it rather late for his evening walk. The sun was already below the horizon, and it was nearly dark as he passed Young's dairy and turned the corner into the cul-de-sac. The street lights were still flickering into life but they were about as much help as Christmas decorations, so he turned his torch on to avoid stumbling over the uneven pavement. When was the Council going to do something about it?

Most of the neighbourhood houses had lights glowing through the drawn curtains and blinds. There was only one lamp on at next-door's, but as he watched, it went out. How odd. Why would the young woman be turning the light off so early? The TV was still flickering through the small gap in the curtains. He could hear some strange noises—a thud and a sort of muffled scream, which could be a cry for help. Probably just the TV. But no, it sounded more real than that. Should he investigate or was he just being nosey?

He crept along the shadowy path leading to the house and noted with puzzlement, a discarded bouquet of flowers glowing pale on the dark grass. There was no response to his tap, but the door yielded. A woman on her own, not locking the front door in the evening? Something was very wrong here.

He turned the torch off and stepped into the hallway. It was years since he had been inside this house, but if he remembered correctly, the lounge door was on the right. By the glow of the TV he could see it stood open. Every nerve in his body vibrated as he tensed for action. He tiptoed in, and the scene that greeted him made the hairs on the back of his neck prickle.

In the flickering light, he saw the standard lamp horizontal on the floor and the dark shape of a person leaning over a body lying on the couch. Herbert crept closer, the muttering of the TV masking his footsteps. Raising his torch, he smacked it down on the man's head. The figure collapsed to the floor with a small groan. With shaking hands, Herbert found the light switch and flicked it on. The woman lay unmoving on the couch, head covered with a black cloth bag. Praying she wasn't dead, he searched for the phone in order to ring emergency services.

"What 'as 'appened?" a muffled voice said, "'oo is there?" The woman was trying to sit up.

"I'm Herbert. I live next door. Are you alright?" he asked, as he struggled to remove the bag. "Are you hurt?"

"I am fine, I am not injured but it is 'ard to breathe in 'ere. Get this thing off, vite, vite!" She was starting to sound panic-stricken. With fumbling fingers, Herbert finally succeeded in loosening the bag and pulled it off.

"Thank God!" she said, gulping great breaths of air. "Untie my 'ands, s'il vous plait. Then ring the police. The phone is in the kitchen."

After undoing the bindings with fingers made clumsy with haste, he dashed into the hall where he dialled emergency services and called for help. Then he rang Sheryl, explained the situation in brief sentences, and asked her to come over to take care of the young woman.

For want of a piece of cord, he was tying the bag around the prone man's hands, when Sheryl entered the lounge carrying a hipflask.

"What happened? Who is he?" she asked, as she took in the scene. Then she caught sight of the young woman sitting mutely on the couch. And did a double-take.

"Belle? What are you doing here?" Sheryl stared harder and frowned. "Oh no, of course you can't be Belle, you're far too young."

"You must be Sheryl," the woman said, with a weak smile, still evidently shaken. "Belle was my dear maman."

Herbert suddenly found it necessary to sit down on the nearest chair.

"She told me a lot about you and 'Erbert. I'm sorry I 'ave not been friendlier but I 'ave been trying to keep a low profile because of," she pointed at the unconscious man, "'im. Now I can explain everything."

"Before you do, you'd better have a swig of this brandy, dear—it's supposed to be good for shock." Sheryl poured some into a handy glass and then eyed her husband. "You look as though you could do with one as well, Herbert."

She handed him a capful, which he swallowed in one gulp. And he didn't just need it for the shock of the evening's events. Meanwhile, Sheryl had turned back to the young woman. "Now tell me all about it."

"This man 'as been stalking me for some time, first in Auckland and now 'ere..." The young woman gripped the glass so tightly her knuckles turned white. "It all started with mysterious phone calls. I would answer and there would no one at the other end. It was so frightening. Then there were strange notes addressed to me and left in my letterbox. They said I should leave this country and never return—or suffer the consequences. I became aware someone was following me, but I could never get a good look at 'oo it was. The day someone broke into my flat and scrawled 'Go back to France!' on my wall, in what looked like blood, but turned out to be red paint, was the last straw. So I changed my name and moved up 'ere, to Emory. Where I thought I would be safe—but it was not to be."

Sheryl gulped. "I'm partly to blame for that. He knocked on my door, looking for a Marie—I thought he was your boyfriend...I pointed him in your direction."

"Don't feel bad. You were not to know. I call myself Marie Beauchamp—Beauchamp being my mother's maiden name, but my name is really..."

"Rosemarie," Sheryl murmured, "Rosemarie Henderson. The last time I saw you, you were a tiny baby in your mother's arms. Your parents split up not long after you were born and your mother took you to France. So that explains the accent. Do you remember Rosemarie, Herbert?"

He most certainly did.

"Are you alright? You've gone quite pale." Her concerned voice seemed to come from far away. "Has it all been too much for you?"

A groan distracted her as the stranger came to.

His eyes fluttered open, and with some effort, he sat up. "Where am I? And why does my head hurt?" He focussed on Rosemarie. "What did you do to me, you cow?"

"Don't you talk to my daughter like that!" Herbert blurted

it out before he realised what he was saying. Three pairs of eyes turned to him.

Sheryl gaped at him. "Your daughter?" It was her turn to sit down heavily.

"You're my father?" Rosemarie asked, her mouth also open. "'Ow can that be?"

"So it was you! You're the one who caused all my dad's misery!" the young man said, fury making him flush puce. "His first marriage split up because you couldn't keep your hands to yourself. But he never told me who the man was." He made a feeble and futile attempt to threaten Herbert with his bagged hands.

Sheryl got up from the couch, marched over to Herbert and raised her arm as if to slap him.

"I'm sorry," he whispered. With a shake of her head and a look of disgust, she lowered her hand again and turned on her heel. He jumped as she slammed the front door on her way out. Then he sat, staring at the carpet without a word.

Sirens could be heard approaching and then red and blue flashed through the curtains. There was a hammering on the front door, but before Herbert could make his rubber legs work to go and answer it, two burly officers strode into the room, followed by a policewoman.

After the statements had been taken, and the young man led away in handcuffs, Herbert claimed the hipflask and excused himself, leaving Rosemarie in the care of the policewoman.

"Sorry, but I have to go and do damage control with my wife," he said to Rosemarie, trying hard to keep the wobble out of his voice, "but I'll come back tomorrow morning and explain everything. Will you be alright here on your own tonight?"

"Yes, I'll be fine. Especially now that creep 'as been taken away."

The house was in darkness. Herbert had to use his torch to find Sheryl, who was sitting in the lounge, head in hands. He switched on the lamp rather than the harsh overhead light. His son and daughter seemed to give him accusing stares from their photos on the mantelpiece and he averted his eyes.

"I am so sorry," he whispered.

"Why?" Sheryl asked, peering at him from between her fingers. "Was I not good enough for you? How many others have there been?"

"None!" He didn't want to push his luck by taking her hand, so he sat at a safe distance. "You've been a wonderful wife to me and no, there have been no others, before or after. The fault is entirely mine and I am totally ashamed of myself."

"And so you should be."

He was horrified to see mistrust in Sheryl's eyes.

"I'll try to explain."

"This should be interesting." Sheryl gave him a cold, humourless smile.

"Belle came over one day, very upset. She was looking for you, ironically enough. I can't remember where you were—perhaps at your sister's? She had a bottle of red, meant to be for you and her. Anyway, she claimed she just needed someone to talk to. She parked herself on the couch, opened the bottle and started talking and drinking. I accepted her offer of some wine, which of course in hindsight was a really bad idea, but I only wanted to keep her company, help her out by listening..."

"Ever the nice guy, aren't you, Herbert?" Sheryl said, her

tone dripping with sarcasm.

"So she ended up pouring out all her problems; how her husband didn't seem to understand her, how she had been married for all those years and still had no children. I had no intention of going anywhere near her but she wanted a hug and, well, she looked so sad, so I gave her one, you know, just to comfort her. But by then we'd consumed the whole bottle between us and...one thing led to another and..."

"And you never told me?"

"I thought if I did I would surely lose you and I didn't want that to happen. I still don't! Besides, I wasn't even sure anything had, um, well, you know, occurred—that wine crept up on me and I don't remember much after that. Then the following year, she visited with the baby in her arms and dropped a bombshell on me. She informed me the child was mine. Naturally I was horrified. She said her husband was convinced she must have strayed because he was reasonably certain he was infertile. He had finally only just challenged her about it. But she didn't tell him who the father was. Then he demanded she leave so she was planning to go back to France before the week's end. I offered her some money, my own money that is, to help her with the baby, but she refused."

Sheryl turned red-rimmed eyes to him and stood up. He rose also, unsure whether his shaky legs would hold him.

"I'm going to stay with my sister for a few days, to give me time to think about this. Of course, I don't even know whether to believe you or not. I have no idea when I'll return. Or if I ever will."

Her words chilled him.

"I understand you need time to process it, but please come back." He knew he was begging, but didn't care. He was prepared to go down on his knees if necessary. "Let me drive you there."

She gave him a look of pure disgust and shrank away from him.

"No! Right now I don't want you anywhere near me." She spat the words out. "I'll catch a taxi. But let me leave you with this thought. How are you going to tell your children what you've done?"

How indeed was he going to tell Steve and Leanne they had a half-sister? Herbert sank back down onto the chair in abject misery.

Wanda let the curtain fall back into place. What was with the police cars next door, and who was the young man she had seen escorted out? Then the taxi had gone past. She had only caught a glimpse of the woman in the back seat but she could have sworn it was Sheryl. Had she left Herbert? If so, why?

It reminded her of the day she herself had left in a taxi in an effort to escape that lunatic of a husband she had married when she was so young and naïve. Billy Marsh. He had been Prince Charming right up until their wedding day and then bang, his true colours had shown and he had turned back into the toad he had been all along.

True, Billy had never lifted his hand against her—that would have left physical marks and he wasn't stupid. No, it had all been verbal abuse, telling her she was useless, worthless and stupid, and how lucky she was to have him, because no other man would want her. It had scarred her soul. It wasn't a wife he was after but rather a subordinate, a servant, someone he could have power over.

Then there were the affairs. How many times had the phone rung and there had been no voice on the other end when she answered? And the nights of him supposedly working late. Oh yes, Billy had been clever and sneaky and she had had only suspicions and no proof—until one night she followed him and caught him out. It had been the last straw in her collapsing marriage. So she had returned home, packed her stuff and left.

After drifting around the country for a while, evading and avoiding Billy, she had eventually blown into Emory. When Billy finally managed to track her down, it was only to get her to sign the divorce papers. So, free of him at last, she had stayed, put down some roots and tried to forget her past. That nosey Sheryl hadn't helped though, with all the questions she asked.

Wanda had always been a hard and willing worker—waiting on tables, helping in the kitchen at restaurants and working on orchards down in the South Island. Still was in fact. It had been no trouble to land a job here in Emory, in the rest home. Through saving hard, she had managed to squirrel away enough to put a deposit on this house.

Here she had met a special man, one who had treated her with respect. But, and there was always a 'but', he was already taken. A no-go zone. She sighed. Oh, there had been other men of course, but no one she would consider spending the rest of her life with. So she had amused herself trying to matchmake others, perhaps to make up for the lack of love in her own life, and enviously watching other couples enjoying their marriages. And here she was, a middle-aged woman living on her own in this backwater. Until now. Did she dare hope?

All was quiet on the street again. Still lost in thought, Wanda prepared for bed.

The night seemed interminably long as Herbert fretted over Sheryl's absence. Finally, the morning arrived. After a lonely breakfast, which he could hardly eat, he went across to Rosemarie's house. Over a cup of tea, he explained everything. As he talked, he was aware of Rosemarie staring at him.

"Are you really my father?"

"That's what Belle told me."

"That could explain why the man I thought was my papa didn't want to know me," she murmured.

"Well, I want to know you." He reached out a tentative hand and placed it over hers.

She smiled at him. "I realise we're not really well acquainted yet, but I'm sure I couldn't have asked for a nicer papa. When my so-called father didn't want to know me, I felt as though 'alf my identity had gone. Now I feel as though I 'ave it back. Maman always spoke 'ighly of you. Perhaps I can see why now."

"You do resemble your mother," he said, regarding her thoughtfully. He tried to see something of himself in her but couldn't really. Although there was a hint of his own daughter, Leanne, about her…and perhaps a touch of his mother as well.

"How is Belle these days?"

He was horrified to see Rosemarie well up.

"She's been gone five years now. Dear maman." Rosemarie gazed into the distance. "She saved my life—but lost 'er own. We were crossing the street one day when a car came towards us. I expected to 'ear screeching brakes but instead I swear 'e revved the engine and accelerated towards us…Maman pushed me out of the way just in time but…she was gone in an instant." A tear slid down her cheek. "Nobody got a good look at the driver or took the licence plate number and 'e was never caught. The police thought per'aps 'e 'ad put his foot on the wrong pedal."

Herbert fished a giant hanky out of his pocket and held it out to her.

"Don't worry, it's quite clean." He watched as she dabbed her eyes with it and blew her nose. "Something's been bothering me. What did that young man mean when he said about me causing his father's misery?"

Rosemarie seemed to ponder his question for quite some time.

"I wonder," she said, slowly. "Maman told me, papa—I mean the man I thought was my papa, married again and then adopted a son. I don't think that marriage lasted either. Could the stalker be the devoted adopted son perhaps? Maybe 'e is bitter and blames maman, me, and now you, for 'is father's sadness. If 'e is the stalker, it would explain 'ow 'e found me because my so-called father is one of the few people I gave my new name and address to."

The trill of the phone interrupted her, and she hurried into the kitchen to answer it. Herbert couldn't hear what she was saying, apart from a couple of loud expressions of surprise.

She returned, looking even more thoughtful. "That was the police. Apparently the young man 'as not only confessed to trying to 'arass, and attack me, but also to running down my mother in France. 'E was over there on a business trip, and just 'appened to be in the area." She sounded sarcastic now. "'E tracked us down with no intention of 'arming us but merely to give us a scare and teach us a lesson. But when 'e saw us crossing the road, 'is anger got the better of 'im. The lunatic! Madame Guillotine, she is too good for 'im!" she said, her bitterness almost tangible.

Herbert stayed for as long as he could, partly to comfort her, and partly to put off his return to his own house, which felt so empty without Sheryl. Yes, she got on his nerves several times a day, but he missed her so badly. At last, he got up to leave.

"You don't want me to move away, do you?" Maria asked.

"Of course not! Why would I?"

"I don't want to cause friction between you and Sheryl."

"None of this is your fault in the slightest. It's mine completely." He hung his head. "Besides, she left me last night."

Maria held her hands up to her mouth, clearly dismayed. "I'm so sorry. I do 'ope she will come back, and soon, and that you can work things out between you. Is there anything I can do?" She shrugged in a helpless way. "Come over for your meals if you want."

"Thanks, but I'm afraid I wouldn't be good company at the moment."

On the third evening of Sheryl's absence, Herbert sat gazing vacantly at the TV, absent-mindedly stroking Kerfluffle. There was a knock on the back door and he leapt up, sending the cat flying. Could it be his darling? When he peered through the screen door however, his hopes were dashed.

"Oh hi, Wanda," he said, not bothering to hide his disappointment. "Sheryl's, um, not here at the moment." He hadn't told anyone she had gone, other than Rosemarie.

"I know. I saw her go off in the taxi. She's left you hasn't she?" Her words were like an arrow in his heart and the pain was so great he could do nothing but nod in a dismal fashion.

"Actually, it was you I wanted to see. Can I come in for a minute?"

"If you want." He opened the screen door without enthusiasm. The last thing he felt like right now was a visitor. "I'd better warn you I'm not great company." But even in his misery, he raised his eyebrows in surprise as she tottered in on high-heels, dressed up to the nines. "Is there something wrong with your eyes?" He could almost feel a breeze from her fluttering mascara-clad eyelashes, and the alcohol fumes on her breath were nearly as overpowering as the perfume she was wearing. She plonked a bottle of wine on the kitchen bench.

"Would you like some, Bert?" He winced at being called 'Bert'. "And I'm not necessarily talking about the wine. As I said it was you I wanted to see." With that, she opened up her coat. While he stifled a retch at the sight of her scantily-clad body underneath, she launched herself at him.

"Oh, Bert, Bertie darling, I've wanted you ever since I first laid eyes on you," she murmured, running her fingers through his hair.

At first, he stood frozen, too stunned to move or speak. Then disgust goaded him into action.

"Leave me alone, woman!" He pulled her limpet-like hands off him, although it was about as easy as detaching an amorous octopus.

"Get lost!" He spun her around and pushed her towards the open door, and straight into Sheryl, who stood on the porch.

"Thank you, darling," Wanda said, grinning smugly as she strutted past his wife.

"Sheryl! It's not how it looks," Herbert called to her retreating back. "Please don't go…"

But it was too late. He meandered despondently back into the lounge and flopped down onto the couch, once again disturbing the cat. That was it, he had well and truly burnt his bridges now. Or rather, Wanda had—he had never warmed to that confounded woman! He had been kind and polite to her—just like he was to all the women he knew—but that was all. Now it seemed clear he had been too nice to her and she had so gotten the wrong end of the stick.

All hopes of reconciliation between him and Sheryl died. He must have sat there for a good half hour, staring at nothing and wondering if he should get stuck into Wanda's bottle of wine. A noise startled him and he turned to see Sheryl standing there.

He sprang to his feet. "It wasn't how it looked, I have no interest in that stupid woman, I swear. I don't even like her!" To his surprise, Sheryl held up her hand to stop him and smiled.

"I know, I heard everything. I was just getting out of the taxi when I saw her totter up the steps in those ridiculous high-heels. So I stood on the porch listening, wondering how you'd react. You passed with flying colours."

"I was so scared you weren't coming back." He studied the carpet, feeling as awkward as a schoolboy trying to ask a girl out on a date.

"I followed Wanda back to her house and gave her a right telling off. I told her to keep her thieving hands off my husband."

"Really? So I'm still your husband?" Relief flooded through him.

"I want to come home—but can I trust you?" Sheryl asked.

"Of course!"

"Can you swear to me it was only that one time, long ago?"

He looked her straight in the eyes. "I swear. On our children's lives. It's a distant memory now and I've never so much as glanced at another woman since."

"It's going to take a while to forgive you completely but I'm working on it." She gave him a mischievous grin and rubbed her hands together. "I'm dreaming up ways of making you pay."

"I'll do anything, just don't leave me again!" he said, moving over to her.

"Anyway, who else would put up with you?" She pretended to think. "There's always Wanda I suppose...but I doubt she'll be bothering us anymore..."

"Please, no!" He groaned, and then looked at her with an eyebrow raised. "You haven't done her in, have you?"

Sheryl merely gave him an enigmatic smile as he took her in his arms.

Wanda pulled the covers over her head and sobbed. She was such an idiot. How was she ever going to show her face on the street again? No doubt, big-mouthed Sheryl would have told the whole neighbourhood about her idiotic behaviour by now.

Ooh, how her head hurt now she had sobered up—she had well and truly overdone it on the Dutch courage. Once she had drunk the house dry, she had been unable to bring herself to go out in public to get more supplies. So, with aching head, and desperation giving her the energy, she had searched high and low but couldn't locate so much as a bottle of cough mixture. What she would give for that wine she had left behind at Herbert's right now...

Then she'd had to drag herself to the phone to call in sick at work. She really did feel close to death, but of course, it was self-inflicted.

She should have known Herbert would remain faithful to his wife. But then why had Sheryl left him? Not that it mattered; she was clearly back to stay.

Had it really been worth making a fool of herself over Herbert? True, he had always been sweet to her and she had fancied him something chronic—when she saw Sheryl leave, she had seized her chance. But clearly she had been picking up on the wrong signals and now her feelings for him were dead.

He wasn't even that great a catch. Not compared to the love of her life, her childhood sweetheart. It hurt to think of him and how madly in love they had been, so long ago now. Her darling had proposed to her just before he had enlisted and they had set about planning their wedding—although naturally it had to be a simple affair due to shortages of supplies, being wartime.

But before the big day had arrived, he had been sent off to Europe to fight. And she had never seen or heard from him again. Just before his family had moved away, they had told her he was missing in action, presumed dead. They hadn't kept in touch.

For a full year, every time someone knocked on the door, she had run to open it, expecting it to be her fiancé but had always been disappointed. At last, she had given up, and accepted he was lost to her forever.

Just when she had been feeling so low, filled with grief for her lost love and incapable of making wise decisions, Billy had come along. The charmer had swept her off her feet and into marriage.

What a mess she had made of her life, and now, once again, she had been a complete idiot. Depression engulfed her. The way she saw it, she only had two options, both drastic—sell up and move away—or do herself in.

There was no response to Sheryl's first knock. She pressed firmly on Wanda's doorbell but couldn't hear any chime within—it had probably died of disuse. She rapped on the door again, hard this time. No footsteps, no twitch of the curtains, nothing. Wanda was clearly home—the Jaffa was parked in the carport and she never walked anywhere if she could help it, so the lack of response was concerning. Sheryl tried the handle but the door was locked.

On her way around to the back, she noted the bedroom curtains were shut. To add to her alarm, Kerfluffle, looking grumpier than ever, sat on the back step. As far as Wanda was concerned, there was an open door policy for the cat, so if he couldn't get in, there must be something wrong. After pounding on the back door, she turned the handle and it creaked open. With much trepidation, she entered.

"Hello," she called. No answer. There was a noise behind her and she spun around, but it was only the cat, who had followed her in. With her heart pounding, she walked into Wanda's bedroom. In the gloomy, smelly interior, she could just make out a dark form on the bed. It took her eyes a moment to adjust to the dimness. Then she could see it was Wanda lying on her back, clutching a photo in one hand and a small brown glass bottle in the other. There were little white pills scattered around the pillow.

"Oh no, what have you done!" Sheryl felt for a pulse.

"Aaaahhh!" Wanda screamed, and sat bolt upright.

"Aaaahhh!" Sheryl screamed back.

"What do you think you're doing!" Wanda shouted, and then clutched her head with a groan.

Sheryl held her hand to her pounding heart. "I came to see if you're alright. No one has seen you for two days. How many pills have you taken?" she asked, panic-stricken.

"Pills?" Wanda sounded confused and then noticed the tablets. "Oh, you mean the sleeping pills? I took two and I must have fallen asleep holding the bottle."

Sheryl breathed a sigh of relief.

"Can't a body have a little privacy now and then?" Wanda asked, in a sulky tone. She lay down again with her back to Sheryl. "I suppose you've come to gloat." Still clutching the photo, she pulled the pillow over her head. "Leave me alone. Let me be miserable by myself."

"I brought baking."

"I'm not hungry," Wanda said, her voice muffled, but her stomach growled loudly, betraying her.

"I could do with a cuppa." Sheryl hoped it would get Wanda out of bed.

"You're not going to leave me in peace anytime soon are you?" Wanda wobbled up, but the photo remained under the pillow—Sheryl itched with curiosity to see who it showed—and unsteadily led the way into the kitchen. She removed unwashed dishes from the sink and with shaky hands, filled the jug.

"I suppose you've told everybody what an idiot I've been?" She rinsed out dirty mugs with much clattering.

"I haven't breathed a word to anyone," Sheryl said, as she searched for clean plates in the cupboard.

"Really?" Wanda said, in a snarky tone, "that's not like you. I didn't think I'd ever be able to show my face around here again. Does this mean I don't need to move?"

"I won't tell anyone on one condition—you must promise you will never try that again." Sheryl attempted to catch Wanda's eye to glare at her but her friend avoided her gaze.

"Don't worry, you're quite safe," Wanda said, blushing. "It's obvious he's a one-woman man." She shakily filled the teapot, spilling hot water onto the bench. "It's just that he was so nice to me. Not many men have treated me that well. With such respect."

"That's sad," Sheryl said, and meant it. "I guess I take it for granted." She frowned as Wanda tipped the teapot to pour. "Most people like tea in their, well, tea." She eyed the clear water. "Go and sit at the table. You're in no fit state to be in charge of hot drinks."

Wanda sank down on a chair and put her head in her hands. "Sorry, I'm not thinking straight."

Sheryl organised the drinks and food and joined her. Then Wanda started talking, pausing only to inhale some of Sheryl's delicious scones. Sheryl heard all about Wanda's sweetheart, Bert. So that explained why Wanda had called Herbert 'Bert'. He had told her how much he hated it. Then Wanda talked about the prat she had married. Sheryl listened without interrupting.

"I had no idea," she said, wide-eyed when Wanda had finished. "Now you've told me what you've been through, I can begin to understand why you did—what you did."

There was silence while Sheryl mulled over what she had just heard and Wanda drank her now-cold tea.

"Can I ask why you left Herbert?" Wanda asked, gazing into her cup.

Sheryl pressed her lips together and shook her head. "I'll just say he made an incredibly stupid mistake a long time ago. But it's all in the past, we've put it behind us and moved on." She sent Wanda a piercing stare. "I know I can trust my husband one-hundred percent, and my marriage is secure."

Wanda hung her head, once again unable to meet her friend's eyes.

"Sheryl, I am truly sorry for what I've done. Not just for trying it on with Herbert, but for being a complete cow. I should have been there to support you. Instead, I tried to pinch your husband at the first opportunity. Can you ever forgive me, a silly, lonely and desperate old-ish woman?"

"Yes, already done, you nitwit," Sheryl said, with affection and a chuckle at Wanda's description of herself. "Otherwise, I wouldn't have bothered to come over and check up on you. I would have just let you rot."

"Perhaps you should have," Wanda said, with obvious self-pity.

"I couldn't do that, I'm your friend, remember?"

"And you're such a good one too. I don't know why you

put up with me."

"Me neither," Sheryl said, and grinned.

For the first time since Sheryl had arrived, Wanda's face brightened and she grinned in return.

"Do you want to see a picture of Bert?" she asked, before disappearing into the bedroom. She returned a few seconds later and handed a faded black and white snap to Sheryl. It showed a handsome young man in uniform.

"That's my Bert," Wanda said, sounding wistful.

Sheryl kept her word and Wanda avoided Herbert—not that she could face him anyway. Life on the street returned to its usual mild chaos and the months went by.

Until one day, there was a tap on the front door, so faint Wanda thought she had imagined it. She cracked the door open. A stranger stood on the path with his back to her. His thinning hair was a steely-grey, and he leant on a walking stick. A battered old Vauhxall Viva was parked at the kerb.

"Hello?" Wanda said.

The man didn't move.

"Hello?" she repeated a lot louder. He jumped when she spoke, spun around and limped toward her.

"Sorry, I'm a little hard of hearing. I'm looking for Wanda Summers."

"Yes, you've found her." She squinted at him, wondering if she had seen him somewhere before. There was something familiar about him.

"Wanda?" He looked her up and down and gave a sigh of what sounded like relief.

She frowned at him. "I'm sorry, but who are you?" Could it be...? She didn't dare get her hopes up.

As he drew himself up to his full height and saluted, the years seemed to fall from him. "Robert Thomas Bennett at your service!"

"Bert?"

Wanda had to pinch herself—was this really Bert, her long-lost darling, sitting opposite her, casually sipping tea? Naturally, age and the war had ravaged his looks, and at first, she felt awkward around him—it had been so long. But after a while, she found herself chatting to him like the old friend he had been, and the Bert of her youth came shining through. She was beginning to feel young again herself.

He told her he was now working as an engineer and living in Auckland, but when he discovered her whereabouts, he decided to visit some friends who lived nearby. He had arrived the previous day and was staying for a week.

"So what happened to you all those years ago?" she asked, trying to be gentle, knowing her question might bring back painful memories.

For a moment, Bert looked truly ancient.

"I was shot down over enemy territory and ended up in a POW camp with a mangled leg." He shuddered. "It's not something I like to recall or think about. Anyway, to abbreviate a decidedly long and grim story, it took many months for me to get back to New Zealand. By that time, my family had moved away from your neighbourhood. I did my best to track you down but to my great dismay, I discovered you'd married. I was devastated to find out you hadn't waited for me."

"But I did wait for you! For at least a year. Then after not hearing from you or about you, I gave up and accepted the inevitable—that you must be dead."

"Yes, I finally realised you must have thought I'd been killed in the war. So, thinking I'd lost you for good, I too married. My wife was wonderful and I grew to love her over time." The faraway look in his eyes made Wanda's heart sink. "But she wasn't you." He smiled at Wanda and elation surged through her. He had spoken about his wife in the past tense. Dare she hope?

"So where is she now?" she asked, and held her breath.

"She passed away a couple of years ago," Bert said. Wanda made the appropriate sympathetic comments, but her heart sang. "Naturally I mourned for her," he continued, "and I still miss her." Sorrow flickered across his face. Then he brightened and gazed at Wanda with tenderness. "But I never forgot you. After a decent length of time had passed, I decided to resume my search for you. I just wanted to know what had happened to you, how you were faring, and I confess, in case there was the remotest chance you were on your own again. Thank God you returned to your maiden name, because that was the only one I knew you by—and that's how I found you. Also it showed me," Bert gulped, "that you're single. You are, aren't you?"

Wanda could only nod, being too full to speak.

Bert looked delighted. "So it's just you and the cat?" He glanced at Kerfluffle sprawled out on his usual chair, before returning his gaze to her.

"I couldn't get any more single. Even old Fluff Bum's not mine, he just spends his days here."

"So, no competition at all!"

"Not even from the cat." It was a silly thing to say, but she was incapable of intelligent speech right now.

"And now I've found you, and here I am!" he said, with a flourish. "That's if you want me in your life?" His little-lost-puppy expression melted her heart. She gave an emphatic nod.

But his obvious delight at her response swiftly turned to dismay when he caught sight of the clock.

"Oh no! Where has the time gone? As much as I hate to leave you, I must go. I told my friends I would be home for dinner." He took her hand and held it as she walked him to the door. Then he gently kissed her cheek.

"Would you like to go out for lunch tomorrow?" he asked.

"Very much so," she replied, and prayed she could change her shift at such short notice.

"It feels as though you've only just got here, Bert. I can't believe your time is almost up already. Do you really have to leave tomorrow?" Wanda knew she sounded whiney, but she couldn't bear for him to go. They had spent as much time together over the last few days as his loyalties and her shifts would allow. Now she picked at her dinner with little appetite.

"Yes, I'm afraid so. I have to get back to my clients." Even in the dim light of the restaurant, she could see he looked downcast. Then he plastered on a brave smile. "But it's not as though I'm leaving the country. We can stay in contact via phone and letter. And Auckland isn't that far away—you could drive down for a visit. I certainly plan to return to see you. Anyway, let's not spoil our last evening together. Isn't this meal delicious?"

They attempted to make small talk, but lapsed into silence; Bert seemingly lost in thought and Wanda dreading his departure. Finally, they finished eating. Bert wiped his mouth on his serviette with great deliberation, smiled at her and reached for her hand.

"I've just been thinking—which is a dangerous thing to do!" He inhaled deeply and gulped as though nervous. "What are you doing Saturday, in three weeks' time?" Without waiting for an answer, he rushed on. "I know we've only just got reacquainted, but life is short, and we don't know how much time we have left on this Earth, particularly at our age." He gave her a wry grin. "I would go down on one knee—but I might not be able to get up again." Wanda held her breath and Bert continued. "My proposal from all those years ago still stands. What I'm trying to ask you once again, is will you marry me?"

For a moment, Wanda was lost for words and could only nod so hard, her head was in danger of detaching. She squeezed his hand.

"I still have the ring," she murmured.

"There you go, dear." Sheryl pushed a glass of bubbly into Rosemarie's hand. Ever since Sheryl had forgiven Herbert for his misdemeanour, she had treated Rosemarie as her own daughter and taken her under her wing.

Now Sheryl peered through the canopy of the tree at the clear blue sky. "We couldn't have asked for a nicer day for a wedding. What a brilliant idea to have the reception under the oak tree so the whole street could attend." She grinned. "I'd better go and do my matron-of-honour duties, or Wanda will think I've deserted her. She and Bert are about to cut the cake." She headed back into the crowd again. "Make sure you save some bubbly for when we toast the bride and groom," she said, over her shoulder.

"That's got to be the longest engagement in the history of all time!" Bert said in his short speech, "but definitely worth waiting for." The crowd laughed and raised their glasses to toast the happy couple. Rosemarie stood apart from the joyous throng, sipping her wine and watching the revelry going on. There was rustling and giggling overhead and she looked up to see a child astride a branch.

"Go, horsey, go!" the girl shouted, urging on her imaginary mount. To avoid the risk of falling leaves, twigs and children, Rosemarie moved away from the oak tree and thus was the only one to hear a car pull up in the street, Dave Dobbyn's 'Outlook for Thursday' blaring from the radio. She turned to see a man unfold himself from a shiny Triumph Spitfire convertible, and look over towards the celebration. No one else seemed to notice him.

"Allo, can I 'elp you?" she called, as she moved towards him. "Are you looking for someone?"

His eyes lit up at the sight of her.

"Not anymore!" He smiled, revealing straight teeth that gleamed in his tanned complexion. "What's the celebration for?"

"My neighbour, Wanda, 'as married her child'ood sweet'eart. She thought it appropriate to 'ave the reception under the oak tree for all the neighbour'ood to enjoy."

"Finally the matchmaker has made a match for herself," he murmured. "So you live on this street." His face seemed to brighten even more. "Which part of France are you from?"

"A small town, not far from Paris. Have you been to my 'ome country?" She gave the attractive man her most winning smile and didn't let on she was a born Kiwi. Nobody had flirted with her for a while, and she was enjoying the experience.

"Oui, I lived there for a year. I've only just arrived back in New Zealand."

As they chatted, she found herself wanting to drown in his hot-chocolate eyes. It seemed he couldn't take his gaze off her either.

"Sorry, where are my manners? I haven't even introduced myself. I'm…"

"Steve! What are you doing here?" Herbert strode towards them, all smiles. "It's so good to see you, son!"

Rosemarie felt the blood drain from her face.

"Hi Dad, surprise! I was just chatting to this lovely young woman," Steve said, without taking his eyes off her. Herbert must have noticed her horror and his son's glow, put two and two together and come up with the right amount, for he too, went pale.

"Oh," Herbert said, his voice flat. He put his arm around his son's shoulder and led him away, with Steve glancing back at her every few steps. "There's something I need to tell you, lad…"

5

by Teresa Herleth

Three packed lunches lay on the kitchen table. An apple, sandwiches and home-baked biscuits wrapped in crisp, greaseproof paper.

Wilhelmina was dressed for the day in a vibrant floral dress in shades of purple that accentuated the white of her long hair, coiled delicately on top of her head. Having finished the lunches, she was busy preparing tea, toast and cereal for the rest of the family. She could hear the predictable dialogue of the young teenagers on this 'first day back at school' morning; uniforms, bathroom, socks and pencil cases. Wilhelmina smiled. The smile shrank and disappeared as she recognised the colourful figure of Cecelia Devenish swish by, her wispy blonde hair contemptuously uncombed.

Cecelia was always the first to leave the house, and even today, without so much as a good luck to her children, the front door closed with a loud thud.

Wilhelmina never said anything, but she disapproved of her nephew's wife. It wasn't her place. *At least an absent fool is better than a present one.*

"Morning, Nanty," said Skylar, the youngest, as she entered the kitchen. She sat down and helped herself to a bowl of Weet-Bix.

It took a few moments before Wilhelmina realised what was different about Skylar; her long ash-blonde hair was brushed and plaited down one side. A silent mouse trap sprung in Wilhelmina's heart. The two of them always had the kitchen to themselves and, normally, Wilhelmina would carefully and lovingly do Skylar's hair for her. *Bless. Of course, this was Skylar's first day of high school. Change seems to happen faster than ever these days.* Wilhelmina was sad, and for the next few moments she busied herself wiping the bench tops.

The eldest, Floyd, was the next to enter the kitchen, a tall young man of fifteen, the spitting image of her brother, his grandfather—dead now, just as many years as his grandson was old. Floyd, hair wet and his shirt still loose, frowned at the lunches on the table.

"Nanty..." he began, but Wilhelmina interrupted.

"I know, I know, but I've made it look like you made them yourself. See..." she declared holding up the packed sandwiches that looked haphazardly wrapped.

Floyd shrugged; grunted a begrudging acceptance of Wilhelmina's compromise. He stuffed his lunch into his school bag and sat down to devour four slices of peanut butter toast, a glass of milk and a banana. Within five minutes, Floyd had come and gone, the thud of the front door his farewell.

Just like his mother, thought Wilhelmina with a twinge, *at least that is where the similarities end.*

Skylar's scraping chair pulled Wilhelmina's attention back

to the present.

"See you, Nanty. Thanks for breakfast."

"Have an amazing first day, sweetie," Wilhelmina responded giving her great-niece a big hug—*thankfully something she hasn't grown out of just yet.*

The front door closed softly.

Two down, two to go.

The morning was unfolding as usual. Wilhelmina buttered four pieces of toast, and put Vegemite and cheese on two of them, honey on another and peanut butter and jam on the last one. A glass of milk waited next to the sweet toasts and a rapidly cooling black tea waited with the cheese toasts.

Juno, the middle child, was followed by his father into the kitchen. They both warmly greeted Nanty, sat and silently began their breakfast.

Juno was finished and out of his chair before Michael Devenish had even finished half of his first toast.

"Hey, all the best, young man. Watch out for your sister, aye!" Michael smiled at his son.

Stuffing his lunch into his bag, Juno smiled his goodbyes and ran out of the house to be in time to catch the bus.

Wilhelmina cleared the table around her nephew and started the dishes. She was just finishing as Michael was putting on his coat. Drying her hands, she followed him into the hallway where he stooped to pick up his briefcase before opening the front door. Together, they walked down the path to the letterbox, where Michael stopped and peered at his aunt, who had always been more of a mother to him.

"You know; I'm sure dad's paints are somewhere in the loft. Why don't you take that up again? You could set up the little table in the front room. We never use it anyway."

With a big smile, Wilhelmina tilted her head slightly to look back at this man she loved as her own child. "That is a lovely thought, Michael." They hugged and she watched him as he walked off quickly up the road. Wilhelmina collected the newspaper and post, then moved slowly back toward the house that had been her home for the last thirty-three years.

She had come to help her much older brother with his children when his wife had unexpectedly died. She had known exactly what was to be done, and one thing had led to another; first a surrogate mother to the four children bereaved at a young age—Michael being the youngest at two years—then a nurse to her ailing brother; and then a nana-aunty—hence her name, Nanty—to her brother's grandchildren he had sadly never had the chance to meet.

Now Wilhelmina wasn't sure what she was doing. The children were growing up and she wasn't needed any more.

The front door stood ajar, waiting for her to enter, *but to what? Chores? I guess I have the newspaper.*

She would start with that and then maybe she would find those paints. The front door clicked softly as she pushed it closed.

Outside, Leo was not normally the quiet, invisible young boy he was at home. However, today he had very little to contribute. It was the first week of Leo's second year of school, the teacher had just explained their homework project for the term and everyone was sharing what they knew about their parents' childhoods and their grandparents' lives.

"How about you, Leo? What would you like to share?"

Leo was jerked out of his thoughts and stood slowly, unusually quiet.

"Um..." He was at a loss, uncomfortably aware of how little he knew about his father or his father's parents.

He tried again. "Um."

A few quiet giggles rolled through the class.

"Do you still have grandparents? Where do they live?" the teacher asked encouragingly.

Of course! Leo remembered he did know a little about his mother's parents.

"My mum's parents live in Wellington. Grandma was an air-stewardess in Australia, she grew up there. My grandpa was a businessman. They met on the plane." With a sigh, Leo plonked back into his chair.

"You've forgotten to tell us about your father's parents." The teacher kindly reminded him.

Without standing up, and super-conscious of everyone watching and waiting, Leo softly said, "I don't know, Miss Roberts. I'm sorry."

The class thought this was hilarious. Clever Leo didn't know something; something one didn't need to have brains to know.

Listening to the stifled sniggers and giggles, Leo felt miserable. Normally the children left him alone. They weren't friendly, but they had never been cruel like this; like his dad.

Ashamed that he couldn't answer such a simple question, Leo silently vowed to find out. Whatever it took, somehow he would learn about his father's family. He would take the homework project seriously. Very seriously.

Although born full term, healthy and bright, Leo Franklin Brunnet was a delicate wee thing. Perhaps, had Leo been born ill or with some evident sickness, the father-son relationship may have been different, however this was not the case. He was small in stature, compliant and uncomplicated. Even by normal standards, Leo was an angel during his 'terrible-twos' phase. Frank Brunnet was unable to relate to his son, and yet he was, undoubtedly, his son. Sharp green eyes, dark curly hair, and even, strangely enough, the same birthmark—a small round unimpressive spot—on his upper left thigh. Frank was disturbed by his young son's quiet and calm nature. Having been raised on a farm with the tough get-on-with-it culture, Frank retreated more and more into his work.

And so, for Leo, his father was a busy, distant presence, sharp and sarcastic in tone; prone to sporadic, unpredictable verbal outbursts of anger and frustration, especially when no second child came in the few years after Leo's first birthday. Leo learnt to stay out of sight and not to fuss. For a while during his first year at school, things had been better because his mother was pregnant again, but when Jamie was born things turned sour.

It was normal to avoid his father, and Leo only spoke when spoken to. Occasionally he would ask a question or share something when he thought it was safe, and so it was no wonder really that he knew nothing about his paternal family. But Leo would find out, even without his father's help, he would find out something, anything.

Gareth Wimpress crouched over a well-groomed vegetable patch. However, something wasn't quite right. The vegetables looked spindly, pathetic, a comic contrast to Gareth's large bulk.

For three years, he'd cultivated a tidy array of edibles and for no particular reason this lot were stragglers. The weather had been perfect so far; warm spring days and reasonable nights with just the right amount of rain. It was the beginning of February, and not even the slugs bothered sampling Gareth's puny plants.

In a surge of anger, large thick-fingered hands began to

pull up and toss more than just the weeds. Within half an hour, the sorry sight had become an empty patch of earth. Raked lines meticulously patterned the brown, dusty surface; the wheelbarrow and rubbish sacks full of the green miscreants—a pile of shame.

The heap of green waste didn't impress him; he would have to start again.

Gareth was at a loss. The garden had become his friend. A constant, compassionate, straightforward, simple and uncomplicated friend. Someone who needed him as much as he needed them. His vegie patch never demanded more than a bit of TLC.

Gareth's burst of energy and adrenaline had cleared a path, both literally and figuratively; Gareth's chest clamped over his heart as memories and feelings moved in.

Rejection, dismissal, Bonnie's bright red lips moving, the wallpaper and its Victorian dressed aliens, and brain numbing despair.

Three years ago, he had had to start again. He had uprooted everything, tossed the lot aside, his career, and his life into a deep dark pit. No wonder his current situation had pulled those memories back into the light.

He would have to start here again too. But where? What was the problem with the vegetables? Maybe the plants had been no good. He'd purchased them from the dairy down the road—they'd just begun offering punnets of flowers and vegetables this spring. He guessed he'd have to trek across town to the large garden centre. Surely, they would still have punnets of vegetable plants. Not that he liked to put anyone down, but Gareth had to admit they would probably have a better idea about seedlings than the dairy.

Leaving everything as it was, Gareth went inside—he couldn't stomach the thought of gardening anymore. He'd go to the shops on his next day off.

Leo spent all weekend in his room working on the design and layout of his family tree. Thankfully, the weather had been dull and boring and so Leo's quiet busyness indoors wasn't challenged, the normal insults from his father about not growing into a big strong man were absent. 'If you don't use it you'll lose it, but in your case you need to build them up first', Mr Brunnet would berate his first-born.

The family tree was currently quite lopsided. Leo knew his mother's family by name, having visited his grandparents a few times in Wellington, but had yet to ask his mother for more details about them. He wanted to focus on the visual display of the family tree first.

Leo was happy with the layout. He had branches pencilled in to show the relationships and connections between people and used a big outline of a leaf for the individual names. Surrounding each name were small leaves which would hold the key facts about that person.

So far, he had his and Jamie's name down by the trunk of the tree with small leaves for their dates and place of birth. Above these was his mother's name, with five leaves fanning out, one for her date of birth, another for the place, her high school and the last two leaves side by side connected her name with his father's name. These two leaves would be for his parents' place and date of marriage.

Leo still hadn't asked what his father's full name was. At the moment, the leaf was blank.

He had his granny and grandpa's names written in and the smaller branches and bunches of leaves were for his mother's siblings and their children. He didn't know his cousins or aunts and uncles very well, but his mother had had the brilliant idea about writing to them with a list of questions. He would write to his grandparents too, that would be his job for next week. For now, Leo continued adding decorative detail to his tree.

Later that week, when the family were sitting around the dinner table, Leo quietly asked his parents, but mainly his mother, if he could have an envelope.

"I've written a letter for grandma and grandpa. I'd like to send it to them." Leo shared.

"Harrumph! Don't make a habit of it," Frank Brunnet replied. "Why do you want to write to them anyway? You don't even know them!"

"I remember the plane ride and the steps to their house. And Grandma's cooking, especially that pudding—the one with custard and fruit in a big bowl," Leo said smiling shyly.

"Trifle, you mean." Cynthia said.

"Yeah—," began Leo

"Well I don't know why you should remember her food because if this is anything to go by—," and Frank stabbed his knife at a boiled potato on his plate, "—she either taught your Mum nothing, or you all have no idea what good food tastes like." Frank sneered at his son and wife and then roared with laughter.

"God. Don't look so serious, it was a joke! But I could do with a bit of trifle myself, love. How about you go whip some up for us."

"We don't have any cream or sponge, Frank. I'll make some for tomorrow," Cynthia said, calmly.

It wasn't often Frank was home early enough to eat dinner with her and Leo. Little Jamie was already in bed, thank goodness, which wasn't always the case. Cynthia sat there stiffly, feeling incredibly awkward and yet grateful that Frank's work normally kept him working long hours.

"By golly, woman, you're useless. Don't worry about it." Frank huffed, shaking his head. He wolfed down the last of his butter smothered-potatoes and sausage.

Silent, and mostly hidden behind the table, Leo watched his father leave the kitchen. He hated it when his dad was home early. He hated it because of how his father made his mum look when he was around. Like now, he couldn't look at his mother so he concentrated on finishing his dinner, wondering if he would be allowed to have an envelope or not.

After a while, when the noise of the TV from the lounge had turned to a comfortable buzz in the background, Cynthia spoke.

"I'll get you an envelope, dear. Do you need it tonight?"

Leo was finally able to look at his mother. She was almost her usual self.

"I want to send it on Friday."

She nodded, smiling. "Not a problem. Now, you go get your things ready for school tomorrow, and then get ready for bed. I'll come as soon as I've finished here." She stood holding her still full plate, reached over the table to pick up her husband's, and walked to the sink.

Leo carefully placed his knife and fork together and slipped silently out of the kitchen.

"How long will it take, Mr Young?" Leo asked, chin and hands resting on the counter in the local dairy. He'd had breakfast, but the smell of cream doughnuts and hot pies, made Leo's nose and lungs work a little harder.

"Oh, about a week I'd say. It's good you came before the end of the day, lad. The postie doesn't run very fast on the weekend." Mr Young winked at Leo, who knew he was being teased.

"I suppose I won't get a reply for another two weeks. I mean, by the time grandma has read and answered my questions and then posted a letter back it will be maybe even three weeks." Leo responded matter-of-factly, if a little disheartened, his nose wrinkling in thought.

"I suppose not, young Leo. I suppose not," Mr Young said. "Is it urgent?" he added, watching Leo expertly place the stamp in the right place.

"It's an important homework project," Leo replied, as he handed over the letter.

Limited to what he could carry, Gareth took longer than he wanted in deciding what to buy. Leeks—he could also use them as onions—mixed lettuce, tomatoes were a must. Mixed brassicas, silverbeet and beans. He found a packet of late-variety sweetcorn, and decided to risk trying to raise pumpkins and watermelons from seed. He also bought a fresh packet of carrots and beetroot—again trying a new brand and variety just in case.

He'd have to make do with that. It would be a couple of weeks before he could buy more seedlings. He had a few more day shifts ahead, and then ten days of night duty. Although his job at the abattoir was hard going, it was well-paid and kept him fit.

It had gone noon by the time Gareth jumped back on the bus. He was eager to go home and get stuck into the physical work of replanting. Maybe he would arrange the garden differently, have a repeating pattern in the four beds.

He noticed the trees in the park had been cut. A shame. He wasn't sure about how to organise the garden. Well, he'd see. Maybe he should have walked home.

Sitting on the bus presented Gareth with the problem of not having anything to do. The gentle rocking of the bus sharpened his memory of last week's disaster in the garden.

Dull and rusty memories poked Gareth at the back of his eyes, drawing his attention, if not his blood; Bonnie dressed impeccably as always, beautiful and tall in her high-heels; lips bright red. "You won't understand, I thought it would be enough." It could have been, but Bonnie wouldn't consider adoption, "It's just wrong." She had talked for a long time. He barely understood what was said then, and definitely didn't know now. The message had struck sharp and true though. He had failed as a husband. "It's a woman thing..." And then that look of raw disgust when he'd suggested they both get tested. Gareth jerked ever so slightly in his seat.

Infertile—maybe his garden had run out of steam. Could that be it? Did soil have those kind of problems? But where did you start? It wasn't as if there were soil doctors like there were for humans or animals.

Bother. It would have to wait until after his night shifts.

Distracted with these thoughts, Gareth, on autopilot, rang the bell and carefully stood up with his bags for the next stop.

A young boy in front of Gareth also got up as the bus came to a halt. It was only when Gareth saw the small box suitcase that he recognised his neighbours' son. Gareth wondered where he had been on his own. The boy glanced up at him, and smiled. Gareth smiled back. *Leo! That's right.* Gareth remembered the boy's name as he watched Leo step off the bus in front of him. He was a small boy with a great pompom of curly, brown hair.

Gareth didn't really know his neighbours. He only knew their family name was Brunnet because it was on their letter box and he had had, over the last year or so, the odd conversation with young Leo. The Brunnets had another child, but Gareth had no idea if it was a boy or a girl. He smiled again at the boy walking at his side, who always seemed to be carrying some form of box suitcase—they looked like old hat boxes with handles.

"What have you got there?" Leo asked Gareth.

"Vegetable plants. Punnets of seedlings," Gareth answered. "How about you? Where have you just come from?"

Leo looked pleased by Gareth's question. "The library," he said. "It's amazing. Full of everything. I've been learning more about...about my family tree."

Gareth noticed the boy had large, dark-green eyes. "Choice."

"We have to do it for our homework project."

"Do you think the library could help me with my garden problems?" Gareth asked, humouring the child's obvious enthusiasm with the library.

"Oh, yes!" Leo exclaimed.

Gareth glanced down to make sure Leo wasn't making fun of him. He genuinely hadn't expected such seriousness.

"There's a whole section for gardening," Leo declared, and glanced up at something invisible in the sky. "I...think they...are in the five-hundred books." His dark eyes turned back to look up at Gareth, questioningly.

"Do you know anything about the Dewey Decimal system?" the boy asked.

Before Gareth could say anything, Leo continued talking— Gareth's face obviously had said enough.

"Some guy called Dewey thought of it. All the same kind of books get placed together, animals, plants, maths, science.

It's the most ef-a-shint way to organise different kinds of books and is used world-wide."

Gareth had a lot to think about, however Leo had stopped and was still talking excitedly to him.

"I would never have thought it myself. But there you have it. You can find the phone number for anyone in the whole country…if you know their names…and if you know where they live." Leo's gloomy last sentence was not lost on Gareth, even though he wasn't exactly sure what Leo had been talking about. Gareth did his best to pick up from where he could.

"So you know this person's name?" he asked, tentatively.

"Yeah," came the reply. Leo continued walking. They were about half way home.

"But you don't know where this person lives?" Gareth questioned.

Again, "Yeah."

"Hmm." Gareth unconsciously began to mumble aloud. "It would cost a lot and be awkward calling all the names in the phone book. I guess there must be quite a few of them. What about sending a letter? Although that would also take a long time to write so many letters." Turning to Leo, "How many—".

"No it wouldn't!" shouted Leo suddenly, with a jump. "That's it. Come on, we have to tell Mum."

Leo grabbed Gareth's large hand and hauled him along the footpath. With no time to respond, *today is full of surprises,* Gareth was dragged down the path like a toy on a string.

Before he knew it, Gareth was standing in the Brunnet's doorway being congratulated for the brilliant idea of photocopying Leo's letter.

"And he's going to the library to search about his gardening problems," ended Leo, with a satisfied grin.

Gareth was lost for words. So much was happening all at

once, nothing seemed to work, he didn't know where to begin processing, let alone responding.

"Well, it was very kind of you to walk Leo home." Mrs Brunnet smiled kindly. *Such perfect white teeth.* "Thank you for giving up your time. This school project means a lot to him."

Her hair is so different to her son's. Such a smooth controlled cut, coffee-brown—were the only coherent thoughts Gareth seemed to manage. He couldn't believe he hadn't noticed how stunning his neighbour was.

Blushing deeply, Gareth attempted to respond. "Yes, he… it's…anytime. I mean…" Gareth took a deep breath and smiled sheepishly. "Thank you."

"Well, Mr…?" Mrs Brunnet began.

"Gareth. Just Gareth." He gave an apologetic rustle of his plastic bag-filled hands.

"Well, Gareth, I'm Cynthia. Thank you. Leo, what do you say?"

"Thanks, Gareth." Leo called out, as he walked into the house.

"Enjoy planting your vegies," Cynthia said, stepping back a little into the house.

"Oh, yes. Likewi…good day, Mrs Bru…Cynthia." Gareth turned hastily, retreating, embarrassed with himself.

It was mid-March, Saturday morning, the house was quiet. The family were all out at sports and the sun was still high enough to stream into half of the front room where Wilhelmina sat reading the newspaper from beginning to end. Her long, white hair, curled elegantly up in a bun on top of her head as usual, shimmered in the light.

With increasing curiosity, Wilhelmina had been reading through the job vacancies, toying with the idea of adding something to her ever-simplifying timetable. Her brother's paints lay collecting dust on the table to her right. She just hadn't found the urge to be creative.

However, this morning, her soft blue eyes shone slightly more vibrantly as she reread one particular job request:

Required: flexi times.1-2 days wkly.
HIGHEST DISCRETION.
Visual support for female senior drawing classes.
Travel costs covered. Wage negotiable. Call Ruth, 4821.

Although unmarried, and with no personal experience in the intimacies of relationships, Wilhelmina was not completely innocent or ignorant. She was sure she knew what 'visual support' referred to. Wilhelmina felt strangely drawn to the idea. Surely, she could sit and pose for a group of senior women. Couldn't she? *Oh gosh, don't be ridiculous, Billie, really.* And she energetically turned the page in that no nonsense ruffle-shake manner only newspapers require, when there was a knock at the front door.

She hadn't noticed anyone walking up the path, so engrossed with the prospect of being the 'subject' of a drawing class, the knock had startled her.

Feeling as if she'd been caught in the act of something unmentionable, Wilhelmina tossed the newspaper on to the other sofa, well out of her reach, before going to open the door.

A very large man in his thirties stood back from the door. A shy, splayed-tooth and slightly awkward smile spread across his clean-shaven face. Hovering on the front step, in a rather comical contrast to the man, was a young boy—a dark shrub of curly hair topping a cheery, excited face—who was already chatting away.

They both looked familiar, Wilhelmina wasn't quite sure why, but as she paid closer attention to what the young boy was saying, she worked it out.

"It's very important for the soil and his soil needs lots of compost and so we need more—um..." turning to the man he asked, "what's it called again?"

"Carbon and nitrogen, Ma'am."

"Oh, yes those. And that means food scraps, leaves, lawnmower grass and anything like that. So we're asking everyone on the street if we can take these things out of your hands. We live just across the road, we're neighbours."

Wilhelmina wasn't sure if he referred to them all being neighbours, or if the man was the boy's neighbour and not his father.

"We can come every week to take them off your hands. It won't cost you anything, Ma'am," finished the boy quite seriously.

"I see," Wilhelmina said. "You live across the road and want to take any kitchen or garden waste off our hands for your garden?" She directed the last two words at the man.

"Yes, Ma'am," he replied, and laid a large hand gently on the boy's shoulder. "This is Leo. Thanks to him, I'll be able to save my garden. And I'm Gareth, Ma'am, live right opposite, at number 15."

"Pleased to meet you both. Please call me Wilhelmina." She shook their hands and quite spontaneously asked them in. "While I have a think about how I can help you and your garden, Gareth. And I am curious to hear how you came to the rescue, Leo."

Wilhelmina showed her unexpected guests to the kitchen, one eager, the other reluctant, but obliging. She put on the kettle, and was grateful for the distraction.

By the time the three had drunk their cups of weak, sweet

and milky tea, which they all liked, Wilhelmina had learnt a number of things. A few weeks back Gareth had given Leo the idea of photocopying a letter, which was to be sent to a large number of people with the last name Brunnet. Wilhelmina wondered what all that was about, but the story continued; Leo had then suggested Gareth go to the Library. Wilhelmina learnt that Gareth didn't know anything about the Dewey Decimal system, which little Leo quite innocently shared to Gareth's embarrassment. The large man seemed to shy easily, she noticed. At the library, Gareth had read and learnt a lot about gardening, especially organic gardening, and how to improve the soil's fertility by adding compost. Knowing nothing about compost, his research continued and he learnt how to make it with what was already lying around home.

Gareth's garden was large and being only one person, even if he was a large one, Gareth simply didn't produce enough food scraps, nor could his spartan-like grounds produce enough green waste efficiently . So Gareth, just this morning, had left the house to investigate if he could purchase 'carbon and nitrogen' compost materials.

Meanwhile, having just received his first letter back from the many he had sent out, Leo was eager to open it with Gareth. "I'm not sure why, we barely know each other," Gareth said, with a shy, but pleased grin.

Leo had meet Gareth coming out of his home and insisted they open it there and then. Together, they sat on the front steps and read the letter. It wasn't Leo's long-lost grandparents, but the writer wished Leo all the best with his search and homework project.

Disappointed, but not deflated, Leo had turned to Gareth and asked where he had been off to and if he could come with him. When Gareth had explained what he wanted to buy and for what, Leo stood up and simply, matter-of-factly declared, "Let's ask Mum. You could mow the lawn for her and take the grass away. Hey, let's ask everyone on the street!"

Suddenly, Gareth's problem had become Leo's mission and unable to resist the small boy's excited conviction, Gareth agreed to knock on the doors along their street. So the two of them had gone up the street on the south side and were making their way back down the north side.

They had such great responses, Gareth had to ask for a scrap of paper and pen off the lady a few doors up, to record when and where he would be welcomed to pick up scraps and grass clippings.

Wilhelmina had thoroughly enjoyed the recounting, mostly told in Leo's fast-paced, yet very serious tone. She had told them if they cut the grass at the back of her house, which no one had time nor the inclination to do, then they could have the cut grass. That had Leo right out of his seat, asking where the lawnmower was. Poor Gareth, having warmed and relaxed as the story unfolded was suddenly stiff with awkwardness, despite Wilhelmina's belly laugh. Gareth was able to persuade Leo to continue and finish their door knocking, and then after lunch, they would return, if that was okay with Wilhelmina, to mow and collect the grass.

With the house to herself again, Wilhelmina fussed about in the kitchen for a while, but simply couldn't avoid her thoughts any longer. With long strides, she entered the living room and went straight to the newspaper, found the job vacancy page and easily spotted the one that plagued her. Something about the conversation with the two unexpected visitors had bolstered Wilhelmina's initial *why not* response to the advertisement. But as she read it again, she faltered. What was she thinking? She was a plump old lady, who had led a very conventional life.

Since leaving Wilhelmina's place, Leo and Gareth had

continued down the north side of the street and around the cul-de-sac. Almost everyone was happy to have Gareth come and collect any garden waste, but he was surprised at how many families were happy to mow their own lawn. Only Mrs Rudd, on the turning bay, accepted the exchange of Gareth mowing her lawn in return for having the clippings. She said she would have given them to Gareth anyway, but as it was, a bit of help was always appreciated.

"Why do you think no one answered the door next to Mrs Rudd?" Leo asked Gareth, as they turned onto the path to his house. "We could hear someone was home."

"Maybe they were asleep, or out the back, or weren't wanting to be disturbed. Maybe they thought we were sales people," Gareth replied, and walked up the steps to knock on the front door of the Brunnet's home. They heard the sound of the TV filter through.

Leo harrumphed, not convinced.

"It doesn't matter, does it? I now have an endless supply of green waste, thanks to your clever little idea." Gareth smiled broadly and patted Leo on the back. "Thank you for...well, thanks."

"You're welcome. It was fun." Leo responded brightly.

Gareth turned towards the door again, and was about to knock a second time, when he realised with a pang, what he had thought was the TV blaring, was actually the tones of a very loud and unpleasant argument.

Before really thinking, Gareth thumped loudly on the front door.

"Hello," he called, hopefully, cheerful and confident.

The voices, or rather voice, stopped abruptly. There was a pause, and then Leo and Gareth heard heavy foot falls walking towards the door. Concerned, Gareth glanced at Leo, who had a strange look about him, but there was no time to wonder about that; he gently pushed Leo back down the steps. Gareth stood at the edge of the patio.

Leo was suddenly aware of how tall and large Gareth was, standing under the awning, his head almost touching the wood. *If he had hair like me he would be touching the roof,* Leo thought, with a smile.

As the door swung open, Leo's smile disappeared, and he froze. Normally he would avert his eyes, but somehow it was different because his father's dark, frowning eyes bore into Gareth rather than him.

"What?" Frank asked sharply, still not noticing his son.

Frank looked mean. However, he was considerably smaller than Gareth, who boldly launched into the spiel he and Leo had been saying to all their neighbours.

"I'd be happy to mow your lawns, you know, with no cost to you, in exchange for taking the clippings away for my composting." Gareth finished.

"We're fine..." but before Mr Brunnet could slam the door, Gareth continued, projecting his voice a little more. "Well, if you ever need any help, with anything, I'm just next door. Just a holler away." He turned and held a large hand out to Leo, saying, "and thank you again Leo," then facing Mr Brunnet again, "your son is a great chap. Clever, helpful and very brave."

Leo walked up the steps slowly, casting a quick grateful glance at Gareth. Frank, slightly taken aback by the sudden unveiling of his son, had no choice but to step back into the house and hold the door open.

Gareth was granted a view into the hall, and saw the slight figure of Mrs Brunnet, her shattered heart visible in the look on her face.

"Good day, Cynthia. Thank you for Leo. Remember I'm available anytime. Have a..." but Frank forcibly shut the door, cutting off Gareth's goodbyes.

It took a few moments for Gareth to collect himself and

move off the Brunnet's porch.

Shaken by the experience, and feeling a deep concern for Leo, Cynthia, and her baby, Gareth realised—sometime later—that he had somehow walked home, set out lunch and that the kettle was boiling. This snapped him out of his trance, and he suddenly remembered he had said he would go back to mow Wilhelmina's lawn. As Gareth hurriedly finished his lunch, familiar, if distant, memories of bodybuilding came to him.

As soon as Wilhelmina opened the door for Gareth, she knew something was weighing heavily on him. Her natural impulse was to hug him tight and ask him what was wrong, but she barely knew him and so merely opened the door with a chirpy, "Hello again."

Gareth smiled weakly.

"Sorry to be late, Wilhelmina. I...I...I had some lunch."

"Come on in, Gareth. Let's have a drink before you start on our lawn." Wilhelmina chatted meaninglessly as she prepared two cups of tea. Gareth did his best to participate, but they sat in silence for a time, sipping away at their drinks.

Wilhelmina couldn't help herself. "A problem shared is a problem halved, Gareth."

He looked at her, took a deep breath and spoke softly. "Why are some people such bullies? It makes no sense, she's such a wee thing." He shook his head staring into his cup. "At what point...is it even my place to intervene? People argue. What could I do? I'd probably just make things worse." Gareth looked up at Wilhelmina, appealingly.

"Did you do anything?" she asked.

"Yeah, I pretended I hadn't noticed, but reminded her, them, that I was just next door if they needed me." He laughed feebly and then stopped, a grave shadow passing across his face. "It broke my heart to have to let Leo enter the house with...with that horrid creature." An image of Cynthia's broken look blinded Gareth briefly; he had to shake his head again. When he looked back up at Wilhelmina, she was touched by his look of genuine concern.

"You did all you could, Gareth. It's terribly sad, but the truth is she will have to make the next move, unless of course he steps over the line and, well, does something wrong in the eyes of the law."

"Oh, God!" Gareth exclaimed shocked, sitting up straight and strong in his chair, "I—let's hope it doesn't come to that," his eyes now a steel blue.

Wilhelmina saw and intensity in his steel blue eyes and had to look away. There was a hidden strength in the gentle-giant persona Gareth carried. But when she looked back up, his bulky shape was hunched over the cup of tea, lost between his two large hands. She wondered what his story was, why he couldn't keep his great frame filled with the strength she had just had a glimpse of. Probably the same reason why she battled with the interest evoked in her by the job listing. *Shame.*

She wished she could do more to help Gareth, but she knew this was his journey to make, just as she would have to face the emotions whirling through her.

They finished their tea silently, and then Wilhelmina showed Gareth out the back.

There were only five weeks left of the term. Since that first hurtful week, Leo had been able to impress the class with his family tree design and the information he had received in the helpful letters from his mother's family. Today he was meant to share about his father's family, but because he still had had no news, he reasoned it would be enough to share how he was searching for answers.

"My father is alive, but he doesn't talk about his family. I don't know why. My mum doesn't know why. She remembers meeting his parents at her wedding and they were lovely people. My mum knows my father comes from a big family, at least a few older and younger brothers and sisters. He grew up in the country and somewhere south of Auckland. Mum showed me my dad's birth certificate so I could write in his full name and his parents' names too." Leo pointed to the right hand side of his family tree design, now coloured in a little bit and completed on the left-hand side.

"Because I can't get any answer from my dad, I had to think of some other way to find out about his family. Samantha Dawes gave me the idea of going to the library for help. I explained to the librarian what I needed and she showed me this amazing computer called the microfiche which is a magnifying machine. She helped me write down all the addresses and phone numbers for the family name Brunnet. Oh, yeah, Mum showed me Dad's birth certificate so I knew he was born in Waikato and so me and the librarian decided his family were probably still there. We found nine different Brunnet names in the Waikato area. I thought I could send them each a letter explaining my homework project, but writing nine letters was going to take a long time, but my neighbour, Gareth, gave me the idea of photocopying my letter." Leo held up his written letter and a photocopied letter.

"I'm still waiting to hear back from my grandparents. But I think they must be busy. These things take a while, you know. I did get a letter from one of the people called Brunnet." Leo held up another letter. "He wished me luck and was sure I would hear back from my grandparents." Leo looked over at the teacher with a big smile. "That's all I have, Miss. Any questions?" he asked his silent classmates.

The evenings were shortening, but there were enough hours of light left for Gareth to fit in a bit of gardening after his day shifts. It was still warm, especially when sweeping the leaves off the road under the large oak tree at the end of the cul-de-sac. Gareth would use the leaves for his second compost heap. He wouldn't have the time to make it until next week, but collecting the supplies was essential and had to be done when there was time.

Ever since Gareth had encountered Frank Brunnet's true colours, he had kept one eye and ear on the house next door. Obviously, he had to continue to work and so wasn't always around, but he made sure his presence was seen and heard, when he was home. He had even begun keeping the front porch light on overnight. Gareth hadn't seen Frank since, but had heard him occasionally. He also made sure he crossed paths with Cynthia and her children, boldly reminding them he was just next door if they needed anything. Although he had managed to walk Leo to the bus stop quite a few times now, he had never been able to raise the subject of his father. Gareth had no idea how to start such an awkward conversation.

Leo tended to lead the conversation anyway, Gareth thought with a smile, as he pushed the wheelbarrow full of leaves back towards his place.

He noticed the lights were on in the Brunnet's house, even

though it was still relatively light out, and he couldn't detect the familiar noise of the TV.

Maybe Frank was on a work trip; he was occasionally called away for a few nights, something Leo had shared about his father.

On his way back to the oak tree, Gareth saw shadows moving about in Cynthia's kitchen; nothing out of order. Even when the sound of a breaking plate reached him, it didn't rouse any alarm. Someone must have dropped it, was his immediate thought, and he continued past, down the path towards his compost.

There were loads of leaves, so many Gareth wouldn't have the time to collect them all this evening. He would do more tomorrow. Gareth assumed none of the neighbours minded him taking them. He'd noticed a few faces peering out of the homes closest to where he swept, but as of yet no one had challenged him.

Gareth was almost at the tree when he heard another crash. He paused. Where did it come from? Was the neighbourhood having a bad day dropping plates? But then he heard the high-pitched wail of a distressed infant.

Letting go of the wheelbarrow, Gareth spun around and with long, leaping strides, was quickly at the bottom of the Brunnet's path.

The hushed, but angry voice coming from the kitchen, was now audible. With a jolt, Gareth realised why, the kitchen window had been broken and a pot lay up-side-down on the lawn a few yards from the house.

Gareth's heart thumped heavily in his chest. He was glued to the pavement. The battle of uncertainty, concern and Wilhelmina's words of 'wrong in the eyes of the law' careered through his mind. 'What the hell is *wrong* in the eyes of the law?' he screamed, silently. As far as Gareth was concerned, it was wrong how Frank treated his wife.

Gareth couldn't make sense of what was being said, he should have, but the thoughts and fears in his mind were louder.

He had to do something. He should just walk right in. But what if the door was locked? What about the back door? Was Cynthia closer to the front door? Would she run to open it if he knocked? What if she didn't make it? Should he run home and call the cops?

He heard what sounded like a large object being thrown into the wall and thumping to the floor. There was no time for the police; he had to get in there now.

Before he knew it, Gareth was in front of the door holding his breath. He'd try the door and if it was locked, he'd just knock it down.

To his surprise, the door was unlocked, and Gareth stumbled slightly into the brightly-lit hallway. Gareth spotted Leo in his pyjamas, creeping down the hall towards where the drama was happening. As soon as Leo saw Gareth, he ran to him, and tucked himself behind him holding on to his jeans.

The kitchen was to Gareth's left. The baby was crying, but from farther down the hall. The children were safe, disturbed, but out of harm's way.

Gareth stepped into the kitchen doorway, his large frame casting a strange shadow into the room, the warm presence of Leo still on his leg.

It only took Gareth a few seconds to take in the scene; half the dinner dishes were stacked on the drying rack, a few were still in the sink and on the bench. A shattered plate lay on the floor just in front of the sink. The table was askew, a large dent in one of the cupboards showed where the table had violently been thrust against it and a few of the chairs lay on their sides. Frank stood where the table should have been, face flushed and chest heaving. Cynthia had her back

Emory

pressed up against the refrigerator, just a few feet away from Gareth.

Everyone was frozen in place and time.

Then Frank started yelling at Gareth. But it wasn't until the enraged man started walking towards him that Gareth heard what he was saying.

"This is none of your business, you great oaf. Get out! Get your great pile of pathetic meat out of my house. How dare..."

Neither of the men would have anticipated what happened next.

Cynthia suddenly stood between them, fists clenched and shaking.

"Your house?" she spat. "My parents bought this place for us! For our family. Family! Ha!" She paused. Something about having Gareth there, kind, gentle Gareth who had done more for her little family in these last few months than her husband had in six years, had flicked a switch inside her. All the hurt, shame, frustrations and injustices of the last years burst into flame, a hot burning flame of courage.

Her voice became cold and quiet. "Family is a way of life, not a given. You stopped being part of this family a long time ago, Frank. And now it's enough. No more. You are free to go. In fact...you get out!" and she stepped back. Eyes still on Frank, she guided Gareth and Leo back into the hall making the way to the front door, which still stood wide open, clear.

Cynthia grabbed the car keys off the little side table in the hall, stepped back into the kitchen and tossed them at her husband, who instinctively caught them.

"Get out," she said again, calmly, but firmly, and then stepped back next to Gareth.

Frank recognised the woman he had first met in his wife's sudden strength, and knew in his heart that he really

134

had messed things up. The pain and shame of it was too much, and an ice case wrapped around his chest. A sense of preservation remained intact and so, stone faced and stiff, Frank walked out of the kitchen without a glance at his family, out the front door and down the path to his car. Frank roared off into the dark night.

For a time, everything was suffocatingly silent.

The crying baby brought them all back to life and action. Cynthia raced off down the hall; Leo stepped out from behind Gareth and pushed the front door shut.

Gareth moved back into the kitchen. He straightened the table and put the chairs right. Leo had found the dust pan and brush and handed Gareth the broom. Together, they quickly and silently tidied the smashed plate up. Leo returned the brooms to their cupboard and Gareth put on the kettle. Then they sat down and waited.

An exhausted looking Cynthia stepped into the kitchen shortly after. Before she could say anything, Gareth was up and out of his seat.

"Don't worry. Get to bed. I'll finish up here. I'll stay. On the couch, or something."

Too exhausted to argue, and wholeheartedly grateful, Cynthia nodded with a soft smile. "Thank you, Gareth. Come, Leo," and the two left the kitchen holding hands.

Instead of making a drink, Gareth used the water from the kettle to finish the dishes. He was about to search for the laundry to find something he could use to board up the broken window, when Cynthia appeared.

She lay a blanket and pillow on the clean table and a roll of gaffer tape.

"Plastic bags are under the sink. Thank you, I..."

"Of course," Gareth replied, warmly. He knew what she wanted to say and understood things would be a bit muddled for her just now. "You need to sleep."

She nodded. "Good night then."

"Good night, Cynthia."

With Cynthia and the kids tucked up in bed, Gareth sealed the broken window as best he could; locked all the doors and secured the windows and then pulled one of the arm chairs into the hall. He wouldn't get much sleep sitting in the chair, but he probably wouldn't be able to sleep lying down either. At least this way he would know the family was safe and he'd be right here if Frank thought he could come back in the middle of the night. He would call in sick tomorrow, and get a locksmith to come and change the locks. The glass could wait.

Gareth carefully pushed his hand into the middle of his compost heap. He was surprised by how warm it still was months later. Obviously, the beneficial bacteria were still decomposing the raw materials he had collected from the neighbours: grass clippings, food scraps, weeds, leaves, hedge clippings; he had just tidied up the hedge between his property and Cynthia's. In fact, at her suggestion, he had cut a gateway through the hedge into her back yard the day before yesterday.

He felt good knowing he could get to them more easily, should they need anything. It was only a little over a week since Cynthia had sent Frank packing—thank God he had been there; who knows what that man would have tried otherwise. However, so far there had been no trouble.

Frank had called a few days after the whole incident, to request his things. Cynthia had asked Gareth if he would be there to let him in and supervise; she would take herself and the kids to the park.

Saturday morning, he had walked over. She gave him the key and hurried away, the kids bundled up.

Inside, Gareth saw that Cynthia had respectfully gathered and neatly boxed up her husband's things and anything else she thought he might want to take with him, such as the TV and the cassette player. She was a good person.

Gareth waited in the kitchen with an untouched cup of tea for an hour before Frank's car pulled up. Frank hadn't seemed surprised to see him. No words were exchanged.

Gareth had hesitated, but then decided it did no harm to help the man load the car with his things. Within half an hour, Frank was gone, and Gareth locked the front door with the new key and returned home with a lighter heart.

Gareth patted his compost. He was happy for Cynthia and the kids, and guiltily pleased they appreciated his support. It was nice to be needed again, and by humans, not just his garden.

Gareth smiled at this; although the joy he got from gardening, and making compost, continued to surprise him. He was curious to see how the next pile would go, especially now he had a new ingredient.

Gareth had had the great idea of collecting sheep droppings from the farm land at the back of his property.

Arriving home from night shift just as the sun was rising, Gareth, armed with yellow kitchen gloves and a few hessian sacks, had quietly clambered over the fence. It had taken him a good few hours to fill two sacks with the small round pebbles—black gold to the composter—and people were beginning to stir in their homes by the time Gareth returned home to shower and slip into bed.

Now it was sometime after 2.00p.m., and Gareth had finished getting ready for his next pile of compost, which would include his early morning harvest.

He had already prepared a thick layer of twigs on the

ground, which would allow for better airflow. Next had come a not-too-thick layer of grass clippings, a layer of dead leaves and lastly a few litres of water sprinkled over it all.

He would add a layer of food scraps later, when he returned from trimming Wilhelmina's front hedge. Her clippings would also be added to the large piles of various materials waiting to be compiled into a compost heap. There was a large pile of fresh lawn clippings from Mrs Rudd at number 27, the two sacks of sheep pellets, another large pile of various dead brown leaves and plants, a large bin of food scraps collected from the neighbours and another pile of old dried grass clippings.

Proud of his progress, Gareth slung a few large sheep wool-sacks into his wheelbarrow, where his clipper machine already waited and made his way across the road.

It was the end of the week, quiet, only a gentle breeze stirring the surprisingly comfortable warmth of early May.

Wilhelmina was already sitting on the front porch drinking lemon water, half in the sun, half in the shade.

Gareth enjoyed the silent and simple ritual of having a drink before getting stuck in. Something Wilhelmina had established ever since he and Leo had first knocked on her door.

Wilhelmina briefly explained to Gareth what she wanted him to do with the hedge, and then they worked in comfortable silence, except for the buzzing chatter of the hedge clipper.

While Gareth trimmed, Wilhelmina weeded the front flower beds and sliced the grass along the concrete paths with a lawn edger, a great little tool Gareth had been meaning to ask if he could borrow.

Half way through the job, Gareth paused to refill the petrol tank and decided to have a rest. It was heavy going. Lifting and swinging the beast of a machine engaged different muscles to those Gareth normally used at work.

He filled his glass with lemon water and sat watching Wilhelmina. He wasn't sure how old she was. Despite her pure-white hair, he didn't think she was that old, and he was quietly impressed by how flexible and nimble she was, considering she was by no means a small woman.

Gareth was embarrassing himself with the images popping into his mind. Wilhelmina's size reminded him of the large pale-green pears he had eaten as a child, plucked off the tree in his grandparents' back yard. Sometimes, they had been bigger than both of his child-sized hands, plump and perfectly symmetrical.

Just then, the three Devenish children bounded into view.

Gareth was grateful for the change of focus and the chance to move away from his last train of thoughts.

Wilhelmina momentarily looked up from what she was doing. "Hey. How was school?"

The standard replies of "fine", "good", "okay", made her laugh out loud. She rolled her eyes in good humour at Gareth, before turning back to her weeding.

Standing up, and stepping out of the way, Gareth nodded gently at the children as they came towards him.

"Hey, Gareth," Floyd said, and paused at the bottom of the steps looking up at the tall man hidden in the shadow of the veranda.

Gareth noticed the old SLR camera casually and comfortably held in the boy's hand.

Wilhelmina had shared a lot about her great-nieces and nephews, but Gareth couldn't remember her saying anything about Floyd taking photography. Gareth suddenly felt as if the teenager was seeing him fully for the first time.

"Afternoon," Gareth replied, with another nod.

Floyd followed his siblings inside.

Feeling awkward, Gareth drank his water, swapped the

glass for the hedge clipper and walked back to the hedge.

After a few careful and powerful sweeps, Gareth was lost in the rhythm of trimming and the vibrating hum of the motor.

When Gareth was almost finished, he noticed out of the corner of his eye, someone crouching next to Wilhelmina. He took a quick look and saw Floyd with his camera; Wilhelmina was listening attentively to something he was saying to her.

The next time Gareth looked their way, Wilhelmina, sitting back on her heels, was unsuccessfully attempting to brush the silvery wisps of loose hair out of her face with the back of her gloved hand, while Floyd half-knelt, half-crouched behind the camera, focusing on his great-aunt.

Gareth could see and identify with Wilhelmina's discomfort. Not wanting to intrude, Gareth efficiently finished the small section of hedge and then walked back along it, away from the clicking camera, making minor touch-ups as he went.

Job well and truly done, Gareth walked back to the veranda and his wheelbarrow, motor still running. Whistling a meaningless tune, Gareth turned the hedge clipper off and banged about noisily. He grabbed the rake and a sack and began scraping the clippings together.

At the sounds of soft giggles and laughter, Gareth sneaked a peek and gave a deep sigh. Wilhelmina looked to be enjoying the attention.

Gareth relaxed into the cleaning up, and was finally able to get excited about completing his second compost pile. He wanted to make the most of the unusually warm weather to start off the decomposition process, because it would slow down as soon as the weather turned. He hoped to have enough completed compost available for when spring came again.

The condensation-speckled mirror crinkled Wilhelmina's reflection. *What was there to lose really?* Art was, after all, not just about human beauty, but about form, light and composition, something she had been forced to remember that evening. Floyd had shown her the black and white images he had taken and developed at school.

Wilhelmina had had to sit down as she saw the photos of her in the garden.

Floyd had beamed with pride and she couldn't help but admit that the shots were good. Very good, even if the subject matter was her.

The images were close-ups of her face and hair; ones of her laughing; ones of her gloved hands blurred in their motion of ripping out weeds; ones of her silhouette, crouching, with the house out of focus in the background. They were magical.

So what if she was voluptuous, plain looking and in her late fifties, with unusually white hair? The human form, no matter how socially ugly, could become a beautiful, amazing piece of art with the right attention.

Wilhelmina smiled as her heart swelled with pride for her dear, growing-up Floyd. He had an eye for composition, detail, angle and light. He would surpass his grandfather's artistic ability at this rate.

She wrapped a faded blue towel around her large hips and another around her bosom. Another towel, pink and flowery, she used to wrap around her thick, waist-length hair.

Wilhelmina decided, in the steamy, soap-smelling bathroom that she would call Ruth. She would offer herself as a visual support, in the name of art and artists refining their skills.

Mind made up, shoulders back, Wilhelmina smiled at herself in the mirror before turning to unlock and open the bathroom door.

The following morning was a Saturday. The children were whisked off to their respective sports events and Wilhelmina had the house to herself by 8:00a.m.

With a hot milky coffee, she sat on the stool next to the phone in the hallway, the newspaper folded open on the listings page, the wanted ad circled in pen.

Wilhelmina was inwardly jittery, even a tad sick in the stomach with nerves. She hoped Ruth was home, she hoped she wasn't too late; it had been over two months since she first read the advertisement. She hadn't had the courage to read through the listings since then, so she had no idea if the senior drawing class still needed someone.

Taking a deep breath, pushing all thoughts aside, Wilhelmina picked up the phone, dialled and waited; heart thumping, stomach wringing its wobbly hands; her breath shallow. She wouldn't leave a message if it...

"Good morning, Ruth speaking."

Here we go.

"Good morning, Ruth. My name is Wilhelmina and I'm calling about your advertisement from a while back now. Um, are you, by any chance, still needing a, ah discreet model for your senior women's drawing class?"

There. I've done it.

And Wilhelmina quivered ever so slightly as she relaxed her breath.

The rest of the telephone conversation bubbled and flowed like water in a pebbled stream. A thin cream-coloured skin formed on Wilhelmina's coffee, and before she knew it she was locking the front door behind her. Unable to restrain the smile on her face, Wilhelmina stepped into the bright and crisp morning air, a delightful sense of purpose wiggling through her veins.

As Wilhelmina crossed the road, Leo, his mother carrying Jamie, and Gareth, laden with suitcases, stepped onto the path just a little way ahead of her.

Leo was already running towards her with a huge grin, so Wilhelmina had no choice but to stop on the pavement and wait for the boy, who was excitedly swinging one of his famous box suitcases.

"Morning, Leo. Do tell." Wilhelmina's smile broadened because Leo had already been excitedly explaining.

"—and so we're taking the bus to Hamilton. And they'll pick us up and I'm gonna spend a long weekend at Kuia and Kura's farm. That's grandma and grandpa in Maori. I'm part Maori. Choice, huh!"

"Leo, that is very exciting. Good morning, Mrs Brunnet, Gareth. Shall we walk to the bus stop together?"

"Where are you going?" Leo asked taking the lead down the path.

"I'm starting a job with a drawing class. I'll be their visual aid support person." Wilhelmina's eyes sparkled with glee at her clever use of words, protecting her little secret.

For most of the bus ride, Wilhelmina listened to Leo's vibrant comments. Briefly, it was nice to be a part of his up and coming adventure. *We are both on a new journey. Both life changing, if in different ways.* And yet it was lovely to sit with her own thoughts again after Gareth had led them all off at the main bus station.

Wilhelmina was charmed by the gentle tenderness growing between Gareth and Cynthia. She was glad Leo and little Jamie would have a male role model, and this time a positive and supportive one, in their lives. She wondered how long it would be before the two adults recognised they were meant to be together, and re-establish a family unit.

Wilhelmina appreciated the years she had had raising young children, but it was now the right time to stretch out and change direction. Do something for and with her own self.

It was scary heading into the unknown; however, it felt right, very right.

When Wilhelmina arrived at Ruth's door, she knocked without hesitation.

Moments later, the door swung open and a welcoming smell embraced Wilhelmina as she stepped through.

6

by Rob Burt

Plus les choses changent plus elles restent les mêmes, so they say. The French that is. The more things change the more they stay the same.

What do you reckon?

It's twenty-two years down the track now, since I first stepped on to this piece of land down here in the South Pacific. A thirteen-year-old boy mesmerised by the freshness, the cleanliness, the smooth green carpets of grass lining the pavements and street, the white picket fences and leafy hedges all in a row.

And now? Well, what can I say? A Fokker Friendship flies low over the great oak tree from which I took my never-to-be-forgotten tumble. It stands proud, the sole visible beacon from that past. Otherwise there is not much else that is recognisable.

If I stand under the oak, as I'm doing now, I can gauge roughly where our house was. I can see Jake's place, or at least where Jake's place was when I was last here.

It was such a shock taking that first step over two decades back. The madness of India had become a distant world, yet I felt myself to be a stranger in this strange land.

So maybe the French were right. Yes, some things may have shifted, but at heart, they are still the same. A house is a house is a house, aye? Once white, then green, but still a house. Trees might be taller and they might be able to bear my weight as I scramble around on their upper limbs, if I still did that sort of thing, but they are still only trees.

And what about that thirteen-year-old? Do we see him around? What has become of him? Back then I knew him intimately, well at least as intimately as any thirteen-year-old can know himself. Now he is only a memory, shaped and given form by the intervening years, and memory as we know, is an unreliable beast that must be treated with caution. Selective, self-interested and biased, memory is not to be trusted. So let us allow our imaginations to come into play, if you will, and pause outside an imagined number fourteen Oak Tree Lane? And there, let us imagine that thirteen-year-old's bedroom opening out at the front of the house. It would have been slightly to the right.

Let us imagine him, if you will, gazing out, traces of sadness around his eyes. See the poster of his beloved Bishan fixed to the wall behind him, a daily reminder of a life he has left behind and an anchor for him to cling to, as he navigates the turbulent waters of his new life in this strange land.

Namaste! My name is Abhimanyu Chincholikar, which I guess must be quite a mouthful for you to get your tongue around. You can call me Abhi if you like, but do not, under any account, do so in front of my mother.

She has been taking a very oppositional stance to many of your western conventions, has my mother, including your practice of abbreviating names.

"But, Ma," I protest, "they have much trouble pronouncing our words."

She will stamp her little foot. "So what? We have to get our tongues around their impossible language, so why shouldn't they do the same for us?"

So there, be warned! You argue with my mother at your own peril. Compromise is not on her map of the world.

As I tell you this, I'm sitting cross-legged on my well-made bed, another *Ma law*, while behind me the figure of Bishan watches over me. I am gazing out through my window, which is veiled by lacy, white curtains. They are perforated so I am able to furtively see others, while they have no sight of me. *That* appeals to the secretive side of myself that I keep well hidden.

I am looking out at Oak Tree Lane, which is our street, my street. The house I am peering out of is our home. As I speak, the street is bereft of life, human or animal, although of course there are trees and other plants. There is not a soul to be seen, not a sound to be heard.

It is so different in this country. I have been here six months, and I am still struggling to come to terms with it.

Back home in Madurai there would be a constant river of people flowing past. I miss that. However, Papa says, "There is no back home. This is home now."

But I am running ahead of myself, polite Indian boy that I am, I must introduce you to my family, before I proceed further. Ma is Rasheeda, and she is the energy that drives our family. She has a sharp mind and an equally sharp tongue, and while it is my papa who, according to Indian custom, is the head of the family, it is my ma who calls the shots. As I said earlier, you do not mess with my mother.

Papa is a mathematician and it is because of his work that we came here. "Why move at all?" Salika and I protested, when we learned of our move to New Zealand.

"For a better life for us all," Papa replied, cryptically.

So that was that. He too has a sharp mind as befits a mathematician, but his tongue is soft and smooth and he is no match for ma in the arguing department.

Salika, my behan, my sister, is seventeen and in her last year at school. Brothers rarely see beauty in their sisters, and I am no exception. The reality, however, is that for a young Indian woman, she is unusually tall, and from the glances she gets from young men, I can only assume they find something appealing in her appearance.

I must also confess that her attractiveness has been of benefit to me as I search for friends in this new land, but more of that later.

Salika, however, is not just a pretty face. She can match ma in being uncompromising, especially when it comes to defending her independence. Only two nights back, there was a heated exchange at the dinner table, around the possibility of importing a young man from Tamil Nadu, whose family had expressed interest in him marrying Salika.

"I do not buy any of that arranged marriage crap," she yelled at Papa. "I am going to be an engineer and build bridges, so do not go making marriage plans for me. I will not have it."

Ma gently encourages my sister to show some respect to Papa, but it comes across as soft, and even my mother knows not to push it.

"Where does she get these ideas from?" says my father, rolling his eyes and glancing in ma's direction.

The last member of my family is my nani, my father's eighty-five-year-old mother. There is not a lot to say about, or to Nani, as she speaks neither Hindi nor English, and can only understand Tamil, which is the native tongue of the Tamil Nadu.

The rest of us speak only Hindi or English. Dada, my father's papa, died three years ago and since then Nani, a staunch Hindu has embarked on a spiritual journey that she says will unerringly guide her towards her death and final reunion with Dada.

Her journey involves the writing and rewriting of the Bhagavad Gita and since Dada's death; she has completed it once, and is now on to her second lap as it were. It is just writing; no chanting, no prostrations, no music, no incense or candles. Just writing six hours a day every day, her small, wizened features poised a few inches above the page, her pencil gripped firmly by her bent, arthritic fingers. Whew!

I respect Nani's perseverance, but my young, rational mind struggles to see the point of it.

Then, of course, there is me, Abhimanyu, or Abhi if you say it softly, and I will have lots to say about myself.

I crash through the kitchen door, kicking off my sandals, and adding them to the rubble of shoes that have now colonised much of our small back porch. I grunt wordlessly in response to my mother's affable greeting, grab a still-warm samosa and stuff it into my mouth. My bedroom door slams behind me.

It has been a day from hell! Actually, more like a month from hell. Samosa crumbs cascade down, littering my white bedsheet as I gaze at the ceiling.

My mouth would open and wail, if it wasn't so full, but my eyes, under no such restraint, surrender to the deluge of hot tears that have dammed up behind them.

Nothing particularly awful happened today, well, no worse than any other day. In fact, it was just a continuation of the unrelenting awfulness that has been my lot since we arrived six months ago.

At school, as always, I feel I'm invisible. No one notices me or says hello, and they seem to look right through me. Am I really here? Perhaps I'm a ghost? Teachers still cannot pronounce my name, in fact one calls me Abba, as though I'm a Swedish rock group and, as you can imagine, this leads to cruel mocking from my classmates.

"Fucking curry-muncher," one thuggish boy muttered, as he shouldered past me during the break today.

Through a curtain of moisture, I see my poster of Bishan filling the wall at the end of my bed. Back home this was the most prized possession, of all my prized possessions, but since I have been in this god-forsaken country, I have felt so swamped with dark feelings; I have not taken the time to look at, or talk to my hero.

Poor me! Poor Bishan!

But of course, Bishan is not poor and most certainly does not need me. I, however, am poor and now at this time, most certainly need him. There was a time, not so long ago really, when not a day would pass without me chatting to Bishan in awe and adulation.

Recalling that now, allows me to go back to those times and I can feel an edge of the darkness in me softening, as a little gladness makes its way into my heart.

Bishan Singh Bedi. Shall I tell you about him? Well I am going to anyway, and if you have never heard of Bishan, then you are in for a treat.

Bishan Singh Bedi is, unsurprisingly, with a name like that, an Indian. However, he is not just any old Indian. He is in fact one of crickets' greatest spin bowlers of all time, not only in India, but in the cricketing world.

Looking at him as I speak, I see a Sikh man of slim build, hands on hips, his turbaned head tilted slightly to his left, the promise of a smile playing around his mouth and eyes.

It is as though he has just seen something amusing, but his gaze remains steady as he eyes the camera.

At his best, and this biased dreamer holds that Bishan is always at, or near his best, he is virtually unplayable. Australians, Englishmen, West Indians and New Zealanders alike do not know what to do with him.

My pa loves him almost as much as I do, and on that one never-to-be-forgotten occasion, after an overnight train to Madras, we watched Bishan deal to the English. It was the third and final test, and with match figures of eight for forty-two, he tied them in knots. They were destroyed. We won the series two–one.

The Indian National Papers sang his praises for days on end; we could not get enough of him. Superlatives such as magician and conjurer filled their reports, and a visiting English commentator described him as 'graceful, even beautiful, and full of guile'.

The image of that small Sikh man, dwarfed by a stadium of sixty thousand screaming Indians demented with joy, is imprinted in my memory for all time.

It was the beginning of my own journey, where I vowed, as best I could, to emulate him and develop my spin bowling skills as he has.

With my father's support and enthusiasm, I set out to achieve that. On the streets, and at school, I practised until the skin on my fingers was frayed and raw, and while I would not say I exactly prayed to Bishan, I did chatter away to him each evening, telling him of my progress, until sleep laid claim to me.

There was a time when, burning with enthusiasm, I would light a candle at the foot of his poster. There were a few occasions when some sandalwood incense was burned, but at my mother's insistence, this practise ceased.

"Ganesh yes, Krishna yes, Bedi no!" she snapped. "He is a

man, not a god!"

The cricket coach at school took notice of my bowling, and though I was only twelve at the time, he included me occasionally in the Third Eleven. At the end of the season, I was a regular, and two months before we came here, I was the leading wicket taker for the whole grade. My father took photos of me in my whites, and together we crafted a letter to Bishan, expressing our admiration of him and including my season's statistics.

I have yet to hear back from him, but that is alright, as he has been putting the Australians to the sword on their own wickets, and very few players have ever achieved that.

About that time, my coach talked about putting me forward for inclusion in the Tamil Nadu Development School, but we came here instead.

"May I come in, little bhrata?" asks Salika, who, in two strides is across the floor and onto my bed before the words are out of her mouth.

"Aaiye, nice of you to ask," I grumble, in feeble protest.

Mischief lurks behind her smile. "You have been looking a little unhappy these days, Abhimanyu. Perhaps it is time for one of our brother-sister chats, eh? We haven't had one since we arrived here, and I think we are long overdue."

I shrug indifferently. "If you like."

"If *I* like! Little bhrata, I did say you looked a little unhappy, but frankly, you have been a bag of misery for weeks now. That worries me. We need to talk!"

Salika and I generally get on pretty well. Initially we did nothing but scrap, but then we progressed to a more good natured sort of bond. However, from the time our move to New Zealand was first mentioned by my father, we had begun to have occasional heart-to-hearts. We shared, not only our sadness at whom and what we would be leaving behind, but also our fears about what might lie in wait for us on those distant South Pacific Islands.

These were not easy things to talk about with our parents. They seemed to interpret them, correctly I might add, as signs that we did not want to go. If we started to protest about the move they would become defensive, we would close down and the issue would not be raised again.

So over the last six months, with Salika and I not talking, my sadness and fear had snowballed and were now rampaging through my body, unexpressed and out of control. Yet, for reasons I do not understand, I could not bring myself to talk to my sister about any of this.

"As always, behan, you are spot on. I feel like shit and don't know what's happening to me. I've never felt like this before." The words spill out of my mouth and tumble over each other.

"New Zealand is so strange, so different. Not only am I longing for all the things I knew I'd miss, but I'm also missing those things I imagined I would gratefully wave goodbye to."

"Like what?"

"Well, for a start, it was no surprise I would miss Falgun and Razez. They were like my brothers. So much of my day now seems to be spent in la-la land, day-dreaming about them, seeing their ugly faces, hearing their never-ending laughter. I see Falgun's missing eye and watch Razez hobble along on his crooked foot."

My eyes moisten as I speak.

"But what has shocked me is that I'm missing those things I thought I would be glad to see the back of; hordes of mad Indians blocking city streets, the never-ending babble of their voices, and the shrieks of wallahs at their stalls. Even the mountains of rubbish littering sidewalks, the stench of urine and shit, and the cows trying to disembowel me on the corner of every marg."

"Yes, I know what you mean." Salika nods.

"Then there is this dream, Salika, that comes again and again. In it, the Meenakshi Amman is a giant pile of ancient rubble covered in moss. Crowds pour through the central square as always, but I am the only one who sees the great temple is no more. Tears stream down my face, my heart feels as if it is breaking and my wail is a solitary cry.

"One night, I awoke in the dream. Pa was holding me and stroking my head. 'Acha, little one,' he was saying, 'we are all here with you.'

"But above all," I continue, "I miss that oppressive South Indian heat. I miss the shade and scent of the tamarind tree as it shelters me from the forty-five-degree inferno that is summer in Tamil Nadu."

I pause. "I never thought I would hear these words come out of my mouth, Salika. I so much wanted to experience this country's cool greenness, something I had only seen in movies or on TV. Yet now that I have it, I don't want it. I want to go back home!" I sob.

Salika gazes softly over at her young brother. Shoulders slumped, head hanging; his chin is now almost resting on his chest. His shirt is showing a rapidly widening stain of dampness and an icicle of snot hangs from his nose. Yes, he is thirteen years old, but he is thirteen going on ten. Physically he is still just a boy and a small boy at that. So conscious of his lack of height and how he is dwarfed by nearly all his peers, he flails at the world, trying to punch above his weight.

He has always used his sharp mind, his way with words, and his prowess on the cricket field to prove his worth and win himself friends. But that was back home, and none of that, for the moment at least, is carrying much weight in this foreign land. Her little bhrata, she sees, is lost and lonely.

Something shifted this week. Don't ask me why, as I haven't a clue.

It felt as if someone or something, reached into the black cloud that has enveloped me since I came to this country, and drew me out into the light. I keep looking about suspiciously, waiting for the darkness to descend again, but it all seems to have melted away. I'm left wondering, how something so dense and remorseless could have suddenly disappeared? Surely there would be traces of it in the air or drifting mist-like across the land, but no, there is nothing to be seen. Not that I'm complaining, mind you.

One thing happened that may have caused the darkness to go, or on the other hand it may be that the lifting of the cloud has allowed this thing to happen? Who knows?

I have found a friend, or is it perhaps that the friend found me? However, I must move with caution as this Indian boy has a bad habit of running ahead of himself.

So here are the bare facts; a conversation was had, names were exchanged, hands were shaken. Nothing more than that. But it's a start, wouldn't you agree?

His name is Jake, and I think we have some promising things in common. We are close in age; we go to the same school and—listen to this—we both live in Oak Tree Lane!

In fact, at a stretch, you could say we are neighbours.

In other things, however, we are quite different. He is white and, I'm, well, black. Tamil black, which is about as black as it gets. Jake is taller than me, but then everyone is taller than me, and he is an only child. As you will know by now I'm one of two children.

Shall I tell you how it happened? Well, I'm going to anyway. Whose story is this?

It was before school at the end of last week. As always, I'm running late and know late for the bus means late to school, which means two lates in one week, and that means lunchtime detention and writing a five-hundred-word essay about being late. So there I am, running along Oak Tree Lane, when this tall, lanky figure, all arms and legs, pulls alongside me.

"Hey, slow-coach, you'll have to do better than that," he grins, "we've got two minutes at most."

With that, he stretches out, but not so far as to leave me flailing in his wake. In fact, he stays just ahead of me, wordlessly inviting me to keep pace with him, encouraging me on with occasional glances in my direction.

"Two seats at the back," he gasps, as we clamber on board and sit wordlessly, allowing our panting to subside.

"I saw you a week back, running for the bus then as well. Are you always late?" he says, breaking the silence.

"I have to run for everything, late is my middle name."

I notice our arms resting side by side, his paleness in contrast to my darkness, white against black.

"I do this trip five days a week without fail, so how come I've never seen you before?" I ask.

"Hmm, well, there is a bit of a story there which I might tell you about sometime, but for the moment, let's say I've had a year away from Mum and Dad."

"So, a holiday from school too?"

"Na, I've been at boarding school and then with my aunt and uncle for the holidays. Now, no more questions Mr Detective. Tell me about you. What's your name? Where have you come from?"

"I'm Abhi, and I'm from India. My father got a job here six months ago, and now we live here."

I paused, not quite believing the words coming out of my mouth. *Now we live here! I had been saying to people 'oh but we're only here for a little while,' or 'we will be going back to India when,' or 'once my dad's work's finished'. It was as though, if I repeated it often enough, it would happen that way. Yet here I am, now unexpectedly accepting the inevitable as it were. How come?*

"Jake," he said, suddenly thrusting out his hand. We shook with due solemnity, got off the bus, and headed across the school grounds, going our separate ways.

So that was it. I would not see Jake again for a week. No trace of him in our street, nor on the bus.

In my mind, I would begin fashioning the shape of our friendship, long heart-to-hearts, swimming, biking and taking him home to meet the family and sample Mama's freshly fried samosas.

There, see! As always, I was running ahead of myself; an easy recipe for disappointment.

Actually, Jake and I would become very good friends as it turned out, but not in any way that I might have predicted.

I fish around in my pockets for the letter that arrived a few weeks back. It was from Jake and it was hearing from him after all this time that prompted me to make this journey up here, back into the ghosts of my past.

He is, he tells me, living out the back-of-beyond in Northern Saskatchewan, married with a family, and now an industrial electrician working in the bowels of some uranium mine.

I spread out the crumpled letter on the bonnet of my car, and with it the article he had cut out from one of the Canadian daily papers. It records the changes provincial areas of New Zealand are wrestling with as they face significant infrastructural developments. He included two aerial photos. They are side-by-side, one of Auckland and its extensive growth into the outer farmland. The second is of Oak Tree Lane, as we knew it, and Jake has marked our homes with our initials.

I hope this letter finds you Abhi, he writes. When I saw this article all my memories of our friendship and the sanctuary that your home and family provided for me came back as clear as though it all happened yesterday. I feel full of emotion and gratitude as I write this, he says.

My own memories and feelings of that time also surge up in me as I reread Jake's words and then once again, turn and gaze around at this land which was once our street.

I don't know which came first, seeing Abhi outside that morning or hearing my mother. My friend was at the window, my mother down the far end of the house. I glimpsed his face, wide-eyed, fearful, as my mother's shrieks reverberated off the walls and rolled down the hallway.

I'd been on at him for a while now, to come to my place, to see my collection of kites and flags, my photo display of brightly coloured and tiny, yet lethal, Amazon frogs.

"Come on over, why don't ya?"

"Hmm, perhaps, I'll think about it."

"What's there to think about, Abhi? It's simple. Two minutes from here to there. We're not going to eat you."

Well now Abhi was here, but his timing was not great. Sure, we were not going to eat him, but we were instead putting on a show, one where my dad was smacking my mum around.

Welcome to my life, I thought.

From the frozen look on Abhi's face, there was no mistaking the fact that he had heard my mum's cries, now slowly subsiding into short yet persistent bursts of wailing.

I was used to it, but even so, to have my new friend, my only friend if I'm to be honest, witnessing the violence was humiliating. Yet to say I'm used to it, I conceal how deeply shaken I always am by the sound of my Mum's crying.

Not that this morning's episode comes as a complete surprise. The rapidly growing stack of empty bottles by the garage, loud voices during the night, my dad's increasingly red face, were all evidence I had pretended not to see. My family life was once again in a state of free-fall.

Those last twelve months at Uncle Din's, had luckily taken me away from all this, even though concerns for my mum were never far from my mind.

"It's not your responsibility, Jake," Aunty Sara used to say. "You're only sixteen. Your mum has to decide that your safety and hers are more important than her loyalty to your dad. For the moment, at least, she's unable to do that."

So, twelve months of no screaming, then back here, riding on the wings of a promise. A fresh start, a new beginning. Dad at AA, back at work, them both on the couch watching TV in the evenings, holding hands. Mum all smiles at last.

I open the door. Abhi, stunned and immobile, stands like a small brown statue of some unknown Indian deity. Mum's now-gentle sobs are wafting around us.

"Not a good time to be here," I whisper. "Can we go to your place?"

"Sure," he replies, in equally hushed tones as though we are in the process of trading dark secrets.

"When my dad's like this, it's best not to be around."

We walk in silence, the sounds of crying receding into the distance; the familiar pain in my guts now resurfacing. I wonder whether Indian men get drunk, whether they beat the crap out of their wives. I wonder what Abhi is thinking, I wonder what he will say to his parents. I wonder...I wonder. Barely a two-minute journey and yet so much wondering.

I'm scared!

"Ma, this is Jake," announces Abhi, as we come through the back door, my ears still straining for any traces of my mother's cries.

"Namaste, Jake. Welcome to our home." She smiles. Abhi's mum is beautiful and I feel the pain in my tummy begin to migrate to that space behind my eyes, where it threatens to come riding out on a river of tears.

A plate of delicious smelling, little cakey-looking things is plonked down in front of us, and it is all

I can do to stop myself from scoffing the lot in one go.

My friend's frozen features have begun to melt a little and he smiles at me. There are no questions, just chitter-chatter about this and that, and gradually the tightness I have lived with over recent weeks, begins to unwind. I feel as if I've been here forever.

"You're always welcome here, Jake," Abhi's ma says, as I'm about to leave later in the day. "Don't wait to be invited. Don't be a stranger."

And so I wasn't.

Of course, I was to find out in the ensuing weeks that the moment we walked through their door that morning, Abhi's Ma knew something was up. The look on her son's face spoke volumes and without pushing or prying, she gently reassured me to the point where I felt their place was almost a second home. I never told her what had been happening and she never asked. She just kept opening the door and her arms, so it became the most natural thing in the world to go there, whenever I needed or wanted to.

Abhi seemed to accept all this as normal and, over time, I began to confide in him about what had been happening in my life. The rest of his family also seemed at ease with my presence, his papa, his sister, and his strange nani, who always seemed to be writing something. She never spoke to me, but then as far as I could tell, she never spoke to anyone.

Abhi talked about his life in India, the friends he had left behind, and that Indian cricket player whose picture was on his bedroom wall. He proudly recounted the man's feats he knew off by heart, and he clearly conveyed his love for the game.

I'm not a cricket-playing-person; in fact, I'm not an

anything-playing-person. But I could see, for reasons I didn't then understand, this man on the wall was someone very important in Abhi's life.

I knew Abhi had been invited to start going to cricket practice after school and there had been some talk of him being asked to practice with the senior boys. One day after several weeks of making myself at home with this family, his pa walked with me to the gate as I was leaving the house.

"We are very glad you come here, Jake," he said. "Abhi is a much happier boy since you are his friend. When Abhi is happy, we also are happy.

"This Saturday, he has been selected to be in the College First Eleven squad, and of course, we are all proud and happy for our son," Pa confided. "It is the custom in our country to celebrate a son's success with a special meal before the game and then to dress in our Indian clothes and go with him to the game. We will all support him and applaud his joy and his success. We want you to join us, Jake, to be with us as we celebrate with Abhi. Please say that you will come."

Mr Jason Mathews, Dean of Form 3A was something of a mystery. On the one hand, there was his mathematical-self; an embodiment of uncompromising precision, a pillar of exactitude, a lover of grace and symmetry. On the other hand? Well...on the other hand, not to put too fine a point on it, there was his chaotic-self. His office, where he stood, was a manifestation of this chaos; papers and books, pencils and pens, and even the odd article of discarded clothing were strewn about, as though a small hurricane had just passed through.

Jason scavenged, unsuccessfully, through the rubble on his desk for those notes from last week's meeting with Mr Chincholikar. While he awaited the arrival of Ross Jamieson, the school's Phys. Ed. master, he recalled that meeting, and with it, Mr Chincholikar's barely concealed distress for his son Abhi.

Prior to arriving in NZ earlier in the year, Abhi had, according to his father, always been a happy child, confident, outgoing and full of life. But since their arrival it had all been downhill, and now Abhi seemed isolated and miserable. The family were beside themselves. What could the school do to help? Did we have any suggestions?

Jason had noticed the boy when he first arrived, not only because he seemed very small, but also because he was so adept at maths. Abhi was always on his own and seemed pretty fragile. Jason had a clear memory of a time when Abhi's classmates had teased him about the unusual smells emanating from his lunch box. The lad had wept inconsolably.

The father had also mentioned, somewhat in passing, that back in India his son had loved cricket and had been a more than useful spin bowler and it was this that had prompted Jason to arrange a meeting with Ross Jamieson. Wasn't it only at the beginning of term he had heard Ross complain about the First Eleven's abysmal track record, and the current absence of halfway decent bowlers?

Jason's mind had also gone back to last year's Student Development Seminar for the school's Deans. What was it they had said? Something about identifying strengths? Go to where the students are doing well already? Build self-esteem? Something like that anyway. A movement at the door caught his eye.

"Hey there, Ross" greeted Jason. "How's it been going out

there in the world of Phys. Ed? What sort of form have the boys been showing this winter?"

"Hmm, bit of a mixed bag really," Jason replied. "The seniors, as always, have never been in the race, but the juniors are showing some promise in most sports and, in fact, in hockey, they've been seriously competitive."

"So there might be light at the end of the long, dark tunnel," Jason mused.

"Mmm, yes, I thought I glimpsed something once." Ross smiled.

Jason noticed the scrawled notes on his cluttered desk and recalled the reason for this informal meeting. He picked them up and held them triumphantly aloft.

"Abhi Chincholikar," he proclaimed.

Ross looked puzzled.

"Abhi's that Indian boy in 3A," Jason said. "You don't know him?"

Ross shook his head.

"His father came to see me a while back, as he's been concerned for him since they arrived in New Zealand six months ago. The boy's been unhappy at home and the father reckoned he was seriously homesick. He has become mates, quite recently, with young Jake Hudson in 4B, but apart from that, Abhi has struggled to make friends."

"Hmm." The Phys. Ed. teacher examined the ceiling. "I did see this Indian kid at the Midwinter Sports Day back in July but he looked so young I thought he must've been someone's little brother."

"That would have been him," Jason replied, "looks like he's ten years old."

"So," Ross muttered as he tilted his head to the side with a quizzical half-smile, "where do I fit in with all this, Jason?"

"Well, I've thought of a few things we could do here to help the situation," the Dean replied.

"Such as?" Ross asked, suspiciously.

"Well, at my end," Jason said, "I've had Abhi for maths and as he's a bright kid, I've moved him into the High Performance Group. I had wondered whether it was a bit premature, but so far so good. He's only been there a week or so and he's clearly up with the best of them. I can see it's given him a bit of a lift. In fact, Mr Chincholikar rang yesterday and expressed his appreciation. He said the boy already seemed a little happier."

Ross nodded. "But I still don't see...?"

"At our first meeting, Abhi's father mentioned that in India, Abhi had been a better than average spin bowler. In his last season there, he had topped his grade for wickets taken and had been considered for the State Development Squad. But then they came out here."

"Okay, so...?" Ross seemed to be playing dense.

"Well, mate," Jason growled, "you've been grizzling forever about how the school lacked quality bowlers. In fact, as I recall, you thought that problem was at the heart of the First Eleven's appalling record in recent years."

"You're right. I have said so repeatedly and I'm almost sure that is the issue."

"Here's your chance to turn it around," Jason said. "Why not take a look at Abhi? It can't do any harm, can it? It might boost the school's cricketing fortunes and at the same time help this kid settle in a bit and feel like he's part of the place."

"Fair enough," Ross replied. "Practice starts the week after next, so I'll tap him on the shoulder, and if he's interested, we'll give the boy a run."

It was several weeks before Jason again ran into Ross in the Staff Room, and he had forgotten about Abhi and the cricket team. The boy had been doing very well in the HPG, his classmates clearly respected him and so the cricket had slipped his mind.

Ross was enthusiastic. "You were right about that Indian boy. With a cricket ball in hand, Abhi's been a revelation. No one in his age group has even the faintest idea about what do with him, so I've moved him up into the senior squad. He's tied them all up in knots too. Even the best batsman in the school is struggling to deal with his bowling."

So, young as Abhi was, Ross had taken the plunge and selected him for the First Eleven in the coming Saturday's annual fixture against St Peter's Collegiate.

"I'd like you to come along if you can," Ross said. "Afterwards we can drop into the Green Thistle for a pint, eh? I think I owe you, Jason."

"You're on, Abhi," says Mr Jamieson, squatting in front of me. "Just hold your end up. That's all you have to do. Featherstone is still there scoring runs and our total is not too bad at all. So do your best. Don't go for any slogs. Just defend your wicket. We're one hundred and forty for nine against St Peter's. A much better total than anyone dreamed we were capable of, including ourselves."

Cries of "Go for it, Feather!" echoes around the team, and there's a buzz of excitement and chatter. Who would have believed it? Feather, against all odds, continues to defy their main strike bowler, a giant we have nicknamed Goliath, and for good reason. He is the size of a large truck and pretty quick to boot.

What makes him less fearsome to me, however, is that he is clearly tiring and losing control; spraying the ball all over the shop.

"You just have to stay there, Abhi. Let Feather score a few

more runs." Mr Jamieson puts his hand on my shoulder.
"Now go get 'em."

I start my journey out to the centre of St Peter's Collegiate
Oval. The grass, as always in this country, is green and lush,
and the playing field is lined with tall, slim trees that look
as though they are reaching their arms to the heavens in
prayer.

I glance across at my family, seated around their blanket on
which is littered the remains of our lunch. They are smiling
and waving, calling out words I can no longer hear.

Jake's blond hair and pale skin stand out against the
darkness of my family.

My team mates shout words of encouragement, as I keep
my head down walking out to the wicket. I don't want to
meet the eyes of the opposing team, especially Goliath, who
appears to have had a renewed burst of energy, having taken
the last two wickets in quick succession.

My pads are too big for me, but they were the smallest
ones in the kitbag so the tops have been folded over and
strapped down. It gives my legs a bulky look that contrasts
with my small size and skinny upper body. I fear I look
ridiculous.

Walking in them too, is a challenge. It feels more like
waddling than walking. Goodness knows how I will run.

I'm now very nervous, so I do what I always do in this
game when I am scared. I imagine Bishan watching me, his
half-smile now something much fuller. He is nodding his
approval.

I'm close to the opposition now, and out the corner of my
eye, I see them all watching me shuffle along like an old
man.

"Hey look at this little fella."

"Does your mum know you're out here on your own?"

"Are you standing in for your big brother?"

The calls are good-natured and there is a round of gentle applause from them as I reach the wicket.

"Don't worry about them, Abhi," Feather says reassuringly, as he comes over to meet me.

"Keep your head down and defend. I'll try to get a few more runs, aye? We're doing pretty good I reckon."

I centre my bat in the crease and finally standing up straight for the first time, I look around the field. In the distance, I can just see the very small figures of my family and Jake watching me while the opposing players have now gone into their crouch positions.

At the other end I see Goliath tossing the ball nonchalantly from one hand to the other, while his white trousers show evidence of the red smear where he has tried to revive some of its shine.

My heart is pounding in my chest, but that's not new for me as, regardless of whether I bat or bowl, my heart always chugs away in there like a small engine.

I take up my position, crouching slightly, correcting my grip on the handle and adjusting the spacing of my feet. I turn side-on and look towards Goliath, who has begun his run toward me. He looks for all the world like a charging grizzly bear.

I breathe out and settle down, awaiting the arrival of that first ball.

I'm off in a reverie now, reliving that day. Not many runs off my bat, but I managed to hang in there for those final overs. However, in doing that, I cannot lay claim to any great skill. My small stature, combined with the Goliath's wayward bowling, meant all I had to do was duck and weave.

Bishan would have approved.

In those five overs, Feather made a further fifteen runs and then he was out and St Peter's came in to face the music.

Their innings was to become my moment, or moments, of glory. They were all gone for seventy-five, and I took six for thirty-four, allowing us to win by almost one hundred runs.

I was carried off on the shoulders of my team mates. It was the first time in two years, our First Eleven had won a game and we had never beaten St Peter's before.

Monday assembly at school was something of a riot. We were applauded and cheered for what seemed an eternity. My back was slapped so often and so hard, that I feared my spine might dislocate.

We were heroes.

The local paper joined in the celebrations and devoted a paragraph in the Weekend Round-Up, where mention was made of 'the wily young Indian spinner, Abhimanyu Chincholikar, who destroyed St Peter's with a display of spin bowling that would not have disgraced a Senior Representative side'.

So while I seemed to suddenly have gone from boy invisible to everybody's hero, the shift was, in fact, much more gradual, painful and internal. Jake's friendship was the start and the promotion into the elite maths class followed that. My self-confidence, never an issue in India, began to slowly regather itself and the invitation to join the First Eleven Squad was the icing on the cake.

After that, I was up and away. I achieved well in my five years at College, especially in Maths and French. Needless to say, I was to be an automatic selection for the First Eleven and in my final year was made captain.

Throughout those years, I made a good many friends, some of whom have endured to this day.

Jake's life at home turned the corner early the following year, when a neighbouring woman, so troubled by the persistent sounds of violence, laid a complaint with the police.

Two officers visited the home and, in no uncertain terms, laid the law down to Jake's dad. The drinking was to persist somewhat, but the violence ceased. About a year after their visit, Jake's dad moved out of their home.

Jake and I remained firm friends until we went our separate ways, Jake off to Auckland, to embark on an apprenticeship, and me two years later to Wellington to attend Uni. While we stayed in touch with each other from time to time, we gradually drifted apart and I had no contact with him until I got his letter.

As for my family, my nani breathed her last in my final year at college, and while I'd actually lost track of her progress, ma believed she was into her fifth rewriting of the Gita, albeit in a totally illegible script. My ma and papa returned to India, when papa retired, saying they wanted to die in the country they were born in.

Salika surprised everyone. In spite of her feisty opposition to arranged marriages, she was quietly led away by a previously unsighted man from Chennai. She now lives there in marital bliss, I am told, with three children, and makes a mean masala dosa. Who in the world could have predicted that?

As for me, well I did a mathematics degree, like my papa, but there the similarities end. I also majored in French, a language and culture I have always felt inexplicably drawn to, and then went on to train and work as an Air Traffic Controller.

It's somewhat ironic, considering the total transformation I see around me here.

I remain happily single, with no desire to leave New

Zealand. I visit my parents and sister every other year, but have never once felt tempted to join them over there. All those aspects of India that I so achingly missed twenty-two years ago now seem an anathema to me. I like my comforts. Ya!

I visited France on several occasions and spent a year there, teaching English and Maths at L'Ecole Polytechnique in Marseille.

While I savoured the food and culture of this Mediterranean region, I missed New Zealand very much and learned where it is my heart actually lives.

As for cricket, well I played for the first few years at Uni, but gradually my enthusiasm waned and I eventually walked away from it. Too many other novel and interesting things snared my attention I guess.

And Bishan? He is still in my life, although now in a much subtler way. His picture finally migrated from my bedroom wall to my bedroom cupboard, where, rolled up, it remains to this day.

My papa sent me an excellent biography of Bishan Bedi ten years ago, and while reading it, I put the poster up on the wall for old times' sake. What I didn't anticipate was what an intensely emotional experience it would prove to be. Many of those feelings that had coursed through me during those early months in this country resurfaced, as I read Bishan's story and gazed at his photos.

I understood, perhaps for the first time, what a painful journey of self-discovery that time had been for that thirteen-year-old Indian boy. And I was reminded how the lessons he learned twenty-two years earlier, had served to inform and sustain him over the ensuing years.

The familiar sound of a low flying plane fills my ears with plaintive roars. The road is busy with traffic and I wonder if the corner dairy, still there after all this time, is reaping the benefits of this. This business of life here brings me back to the present and looking around me, I speculate as to how what was once such a quiet little cul-de-sac, has been transformed into something like Grand Central Station.

Yes, everything has changed and yet, in matters of the heart nothing is that different. A place is a place is a place, aye?

I turn away and start to make my way towards my car.

7

by Kamala Jackson

When Howard turned the key to the house and opened the door, he grinned at her.

"I'd like to carry you over the threshold, but under the circumstances..."

She smiled back at him, her hand going to her stomach. Twins, they were expecting twins, and they already had Brad.

She walked into the house, which had the raw smell of new concrete, the ranchsliders and windows were dusty and smeared. The house, a shell really, felt cold, but she immediately began to think of curtains and wallpaper. A brand new, three-bedroomed-house, bought impulsively, by Howard, without any prior discussion. What had he said?

"I thought I'd just drive out to the new development and have a look see, and there was this one practically finished. They were just putting the iron on the roof. Well, it was an opportunity not to be missed and we had enough for a deposit. So here it is, our dream home."

"It's amazing," said Janice, wondering if a clinker brick with aluminium joinery on a new section with no trees, the top soil removed and clay and rubble everywhere, was really her idea of a dream home. She reached out and let her fingers run over the orangey-bubbled glass pane beside the front door.

"Come on," said Howard. "Lots to see." There were three bedrooms, the master with an en-suite, which, like the family bathroom had marble-like Aakronite benches and gold-coloured taps. Janice could imagine Brad in the avocado bath with his rubber duck and the red whale that spouted water.

"The kitchen, Janice." Howard was always forging ahead. "Come on."

The kitchen was empty, except for the insulated ends of electric wires sticking out of the wall.

"Stove here," said Howard, conjuring it up. "Dishwasher, fridge."

"It's great. I'd like a bench here under the window, and here against this wall with wooden cabinetry above. What do you think?"

He had already moved on.

"The dining room, the...What's holding you up?"

Janice waddled through the door.

"Twins."

As she said the word, there was a sharp tearing in her belly.

"Yeah, right." She knew his point of view. Peasant women gave birth next to the paddy field, then got up and went back to work with the infant swaddled on their back. A lesson for all Western women who made too much of a performance about something entirely natural.

"And now for the pièce de résistance."

Howard threw open a door, but whatever was there had to wait, because the twins had decided to make their entrance.

"Howard, dear. The twins. We need to go to the hospital."

He frowned, his dramatic moment spoilt, or if not spoilt, postponed.

"Are you sure?"

"Now!" yelled Janice, and Howard was beside her, holding her.

"I'm here, honeybun. Everything's going to be all right. Just take it easy."

Janice leant on him and swore loudly, the pain so bad it felt her guts were being torn out.

The birth was difficult and she needed to rest and get into a proper routine with the two babies, so it was three weeks before she returned to their new house and saw what was beyond the door Howard had flung open. The pièce de résistance. A sunken lounge with a raised brick fireplace and a ranch slider opening on to the deck. She liked it. She went out and walked to the end of the deck.

"Oh, look."

Next door was a lovely weatherboard cottage with a tiled roof.

Howard was not charmed.

"Hold outs," he said. "Wouldn't sell."

"If it was mine, I wouldn't either. I couldn't leave those established flower beds and fruit trees." *No way!*

"They're old. Soon pop their clogs, and then the land will be available for a decent modern house like ours."

While Janice had been laid up, Howard had gone ahead and ordered wallpaper, carpet, lino and drapes. She would have liked to have shopped around with him, been involved in the decisions, but as he said they needed to move an active little boy and two demanding babies out of her mother's small place as soon as possible. Even the most devoted nana needed her own space, and some peace. But, still. It was a shame, the rush, the bad timing.

She saw the whiteware Howard had installed was expensive, European stuff.

"You didn't get Fisher and Paykel," she could not help saying.

"Fisher and Paykel!" Howard laughed.

"Mum swears by it."

"Honeybun. Don't be so small time. Top of the line, European. Nothing but the best for my wife."

"Can we afford it?" she asked in a small, tight voice.

"Of course, we can. With a credit card. Man's greatest invention since…"

A loud furious baby yell from the next room interrupted him. The other twin woke and joined in.

"You're needed, darling," said Howard, kissing Janice on the cheek. "I'm off. See you later."

"Where are you going?"

The answer was a slammed door, and the twins redoubled their efforts.

After she fed the baby girls, twins, but not identical, she marvelled at how beautiful they were and yet how different. They even suckled differently, one greedy and kneading her breast, almost hurting, with her little fist, the other equally focussed, but quiet and neat, and when she had finished, gave Janice a beautiful smile.

Janice put them down to sleep and then started the unpacking. Howard had got as far as unloading stuff and bringing it through the front door, but now had left everything to her. She opened the first packet to hand. It was king-size sheets for the king-sized bed he had installed in the master bedroom. They didn't need a bed that big and it meant they'd had to buy larger sheets. Her mind started going down the usual track of worrying that Howard was spending too much too fast. She told herself to stop thinking about it and just concentrate on the unpacking.

Half an hour later, there was a knock on the door.

Janice opened the door to an elderly woman with bright eyes and a greying brush of ginger hair.

"I'm Pat," she announced. "Your next door neighbour."

"Hello, I'm Janice. I'd like to invite you in but the house isn't set up yet."

"I know. We saw the moving van arrive and your stuff carried in. Then your husband left shortly after. I told Max, that's my husband, that lady with the two babies is going to need help. I'm going over. And if you think I'm pushy, well I am, but I genuinely want to help. Now how far have you got?"

"I'm in the kitchen with the pots and pans, and the dishes and the cutlery and the table cloths and cleaning products, and working out where they should go," said Janice surprising herself. She was usually more reserved with strangers.

"I'm good with kitchens," said Pat. "Now I'm going to move that chair into the kitchen and you can sit on it and tell me where you'd like things to go."

Pat started grappling with an easy chair.

"Please be careful. I'd hate you to hurt yourself."

"Don't worry about me, I'm a tough old nut. You just stand clear."

"So you live in the cottage with the lovely garden," said Janice.

"That's right, Max and me. We've been here for forty-five years."

"You must have hated it when the developers started bulldozing the place."

"You've got that right!" Pat pulled a face and then laughed. "It's not all bad. Max and me have probably reached the age when it's good to have neighbours. One of us might fall down and break a leg. Or, one of you might have a problem, and Max could help. He's good in a crisis."

Janice thought if Max was anything like Pat, he probably was. Pat was not only good at kitchens, she was efficient and decisive about unpacking and putting away clothes, shoes, toiletries, ornaments and rugs. Working together, they had more or less finished the job, except for Howard's computer, fax and general office stuff. Pat had come up with some good ideas about where to put things. When Janice didn't agree she said so, and Pat let it go, except once when their difference of opinion developed into a friendly argument and they had laughed their way to a compromise.

Pat was very easy to get on with, but she was strange about the twins. When Janice nursed them, Pat said they were beautiful and Janice very lucky, and then walked away into the kitchen. Usually people went gooey over the babies and wanted to talk about them.

"Where do you want the spices put?" yelled Pat. At that moment Janice didn't care, she wanted to concentrate on her babies.

"Somewhere near the stove."

"Okay, boss."

Later there was another yell from Pat.

"There's a laundry basket full of clothes. Do you want me to put on a wash?"

After that she got out the Windolene and set about cleaning the windows.

Janice was left to get on with nursing the babies, burping and changing them, kissing them as they smiled and gurgled and grabbed her fingers. When Janice had put the babies down, Pat appeared.

"I'm that thirsty I could drain the pond in the park. I see you have no instant."

"Sorry, that's something I forgot to get. We're mainly tea drinkers ourselves."

"Good thirst quencher," said Pat. "You go and sit yourself on the deck and I'll bring it out."

"Yes, boss," said Janice.

The late afternoon sun was pleasantly warm and Janice listened to Pat talk about the families who had lived in Oak Tree Lane for years and those who had recently moved in. Then she said she had better get home. She had planned sausages and mash, real comfort food, for Max. She preferred to give him what he liked, but, though he wasn't big on salads, she might sneak in a couple of lettuce leaves. They were laughing when Janice heard Howard's key in the lock. He stopped short in the doorway.

"What's going on?"

"Pat's just going. She was helping me unpack and we got heaps done. Thanks Pat, you don't know how grateful I am."

"You're welcome. Anytime you need a hand, just give me a shout. Bye, Howard."

When the door had shut, Howard repeated, "Anytime you need a hand, just give me a shout? Janice, I don't want that woman in my house again."

"Your house?"

"Okay, our house."

"Howard, I'm on my own a lot. I need to find friends in this cul-de-sac."

"Friends? What do you and that old bitch have in common?"

"Well, we're women and we have experiences in common.

Look, I don't have to justify who I choose to have as friends, and I like her tough, no nonsense attitude to life."

"So when I have mates round for a barbecue, your new friend would fit right in?"

"No, and she wouldn't want to be there. I don't like all your friends either. Shall we just leave it at that?"

Howard looked around.

"Where's Brad? My little man."

"Braad," wailed Janice. "You were to pick him up from mum's, remember?"

"Oh shit." Howard grabbed the new, green telephone.

"It's not—"

"Connected," finished Howard. "Those useless bastards. It's about time there was competition in the phone business." But he put the receiver back gently enough in its cradle. "Well, honeybun, what have you planned for dinner for the two men of the family?"

Janice hadn't planned anything.

"There are baked beans in the cupboard, eggs, and the bread's okay for toast." Like Pat, she might sneak in some lettuce leaves.

"Not the sort of meal a guy wants when he gets home from a hard day's work."

"Exactly the sort of meal a wife wants to get when she has had a hard day's unpacking, arranging and putting away."

"Humph. You've done a lot," conceded Howard, looking around. "How about Brad and I pick up some takeaways on the way home?"

"Great," said Janice. She moved towards him and their mouths came together. There was something, call it love, attraction, need, a combination, whatever, it was still there.

Howard decided they had to have a fence. A high fence between Max and Pat's place and theirs, but not one at the back where the single mother and her backward daughter lived. The mother was too stuck up to bother them, but easy on the eye.

"For privacy," he explained "Those two are retired, home all the time, nothing to do but be nosy."

"I won't be able to see their garden. I'll be making my own, of course, but it'll take a while."

"What do you want a garden for? It's just more housework, which I thought you didn't like."

"Housework?"

"Outdoor housework. Mowing, pruning, weeding, watering. What a drag."

"Colour, fragrance, seasonal change, birds, nature, life."

"You're such a romantic, honeybun. No, seriously, I need to concrete the back for the Land Rover, the boat and trailer, the barbecue, etc."

Janice did not like the sound of 'etc'.

"We don't want Brad and the twins playing outside on concrete!"

"You could always take them to the park. More room there."

"I don't have a car."

"That's the next thing on the list, honeybun. You like Toyotas, don't you? That's another thing to be parked out the back."

Janice refused to leave it like that, and after a lot of haggling Howard said she could have a third of the space. Mentally she downsized the garden to a small lawn for the kids to play on that she would mow, a washing line, a shade tree, a thornless climbing rose, a lemon tree, a narrow border for herbs and annuals, and somewhere she would squeeze in a flowering, scented shrub. A luculia, perhaps.

Compromise was part of life, an unavoidable feature of living as a couple, as a family, though Janice preferred the phrase 'give and take'. It sounded more even-handed, more generous. The 'compromises' that she and Howard had come up with over the years were more like skirmishes won or lost. In fact, she was quite battle fatigued, and the good aspects of coupledom had become routine. She thought he must feel the same, and when she suggested they go to couple counselling, he rubbished the idea. No chance of a compromise there.

She had seen very little of Pat apart from a, "Hello, how are you?"

It was the children who kept her in touch with the passing of time. Fi and Lou were now four, and Brad almost nine. They had celebrated four Christmases here, and eight birthdays. Had put on too many barbecues for Howard's bragging buddies and their girlfriends, that Howard did not hesitate to flirt with.

They were having another barbecue that evening and she had a list of food and drink to get from the butchers' and the liquor outlet. She would make coleslaw and a tomato salad for those who were not exclusively carnivore.

Brad was at school, the twins at kindy, and she was getting ready to go out when there was a rush up the steps and a banging on the front door.

Pat, looking a lot older now, was distraught and gabbling.

"Thank God, you're home. It's Max," she said. "I've called the fire brigade and our doctor. Janice, I need to have someone, you, with me."

"Of course." Janice closed the front door behind her.

"Has Max had an accident?"

"No, dear. My Max is dead."

"Oh, no. I'm so sorry."

Why the fire brigade? But Janice didn't ask. Pat was rushing, and Janice hurried to keep up with her.

"He's had a heart problem, was supposed to take things easy, but he said he was okay to do a bit of pruning. I said he knew his body, and if anything didn't feel right he was to come in."

By then, they were through Pat's house, down the back steps and in the garden, and Janice saw Max straddling a branch of the old apple tree. He was leaning towards the trunk, his forehead resting against it. His body seemed perfectly balanced, in no danger of falling. A pruning saw had slipped from his grasp, and lay on the grass. So did a ladder.

"Are you sure...?" began Janice.

"Dead as a doornail. Max, you bastard, you didn't say good-bye. You didn't give me a chance to say sorry, to say I loved you, nothing. You're a bastard for leaving me like this."

Janice was alarmed at Pat's vehemence. She put an arm around her.

"Come, we'll go inside and have some tea." She added, "He looks so peaceful. Beautiful."

"Looks peaceful about leaving me in the lurch," Pat said fiercely, but she let Janice steer her up the back steps and onto a kitchen chair.

Janice walked towards the bench, to the electric jug.

"Not another bloody cup of tea," said Pat. "Brandy."

"Where do you keep it?"

"That cupboard there."

Janice opened the painted blue door. Inside there was a collection of bottles. As well as the brandy were two whiskies, a bourbon and a sherry.

"Have some yourself," said Pat. "They're not there for medicinal purposes."

"Thanks, but I won't. If you don't mind, I'm going to have a bloody cup of tea."

She smiled as she handed Pat a glass of brandy.

"You're a good one," she said, gulping a mouthful and closing her eyes.

Janice asked Pat if she had any relatives in Emory.

"No, only Max's sister in Australia."

"Would you like me to contact her?"

"Not tonight, love, Not tonight."

Three firemen arrived without their usual fanfare. Janice and Pat stood outside to watch Max taken down from the tree. The men did it sensitively, supporting the body at all stages so there was a minimum of uncontrolled flopping, which made Pat cringe. The largest fireman carried Max over his shoulder and he was laid down on the bed in the spare room.

When an elderly doctor arrived, Janice left Pat with him and stayed in the kitchen to use the phone.

"Howie?"

"Hello, honeybun. Everything okay for tonight?"

"Not really. Max has died and I'm with Pat."

"Max who?"

"Our neighbour."

"Oh. Well, that's a shame. Nice enough bloke, but not our sort. So what's it got to do with us?"

"Pat's only relative is in Australia. She needs someone with her."

"Okay, why you?"

"She asked me."

The doctor had come into the kitchen and was waiting presumably to speak to her. He went to the open back door and stood on the steps looking out. He was giving her some privacy to finish her call, but she felt embarrassed that someone would hear one of her tortuous conversations with Howard.

"Well, I take it you have everything under control for tonight's barbecue?"

"That's just it. I've not had the time to go to the shops, and the kids need to be picked up."

"What exactly are you saying, Janice?"

"That if you want a barbecue tonight, you'll have to do everything, or cancel. I've got to go now, Howie. The doctor's waiting to speak to me. I'm sorry."

As she put down the phone, his voice was still audible, an angry squawk. She was flushed, and resentful that Howard didn't make things easier for her. He would see this as her failure, her failure to manage their life without inconvenience to him.

"Are you all right, Mrs...?" The doctor was looking at her in a professional manner.

"Fraser. Yes, thank you."

"I suggest we sit at the table."

Her shoulders relaxed. Sitting, resting was exactly what she needed. She smiled at the doctor.

"This is very good of you, Mrs Fraser. I can spot an overworked wife and mother when I see one." He told her that he had given Pat a light sedative and she was sleeping. "When she wakes, give her something light to eat. Soup, or a poached egg. At the very least a hot drink. I'm leaving this small bottle here, in your care. Don't leave it where Pat can find it. She can be rash. When she wants to sleep give her two teaspoons. Are you willing to take on that responsibility, Mrs Fraser?"

"No, yes. Yes," she said.

"Good woman. When I first came to Emory and opened my clinic as a young, newly qualified doctor, Max and Pat were the first to sign up as patients. I came to know them well. A very devoted couple. Pat will take this loss hard."

He stood.

"I'll put a call through to the funeral director and ask them to come round this evening."

When he had completed his call, Janice walked with him to the door.

"I think I can guarantee that after I have left, neighbours will come knocking. You should be able to leave someone with Pat if you need to check on things at home."

The doctor—she had forgotten to ask his name—was right. After ten minutes the first knock came. As the news passed around the houses, visitors arrived with food: pikelets, curry, leek and potato soup, a whole cooked chicken, and peanut brownies.

The funeral people came about 4.30p.m. Pat was still asleep.

Janice went home at 8.00p.m. to check on the children. The carousing from the backyard seemed indecent. Theirs must be the only house where the death in the street was not being respectfully acknowledged.

The children were in bed, but not asleep.

"Have you had something to eat?"

"A sausage," said Brad. "It was squishy in the middle. It was yuck."

"Yuckee," agreed Fi and Lou, screwing up their sausage-smeared faces. Janice washed their faces and hands with a soapy facecloth. Dried them.

"Well, tomorrow morning, come round to Pat's. I'll make

pancakes for breakfast. How about that?" asked Janice.

"Choice," said the kids, automatically. The twins whispered together, then looked at her, waiting.

"Why aren't you home, Mum?" asked Brad.

"Because I'm looking after Mrs Settle. Her husband, Max, died today. He was old and Mrs Settle is very sad. Now, you kids, snuggle down into bed, heads on pillows, blankets up to your chins, shut your eyes." She kissed each of them. The soft, wet mouths. "Night, night. Sleep tight."

Their eyes fluttered open.

"It's too noisy," said Brad.

"It is a bit." She looked out the window, but couldn't make out much from the light of the barbecue and three shuddering candles. The raucousness repelled her. She smelt burning meat, got a sense of movement, the clink of bottles. A couple seemed to have reached an amorous stage of drunkenness, twining arms and glued faces. As they paused to take breath, Janice saw the man was Howard. The woman looked familiar, but she couldn't place her.

"What's happening, Mum?" Brad was out of bed.

She fastened the window shut and pulled the curtain across.

"Just adults behaving badly. Now, I'm going to read you a story."

"Yaaay."

After they had fallen asleep, Janice slipped out of the house, giving the barbecue a miss. Someone was going through the fridge in the kitchen.

"Bugger, they're out of tonic."

Outside, Janice passed Peter Mansell in the street.

"What a terrible racket coming from that house," he said.

"Terrible. No consideration for others."

"I'm thinking of ringing the police."

"Good idea. I think you should."

"Hang on," he called after her. "Isn't that your house?"

She ran up Pat's path. It was, but not her responsibility. It was all up to Howard and, as for herself, she had better things to do.

"Grief," Pat Settle told her cat, Minx, "is not just one thing. I'm grieving for twenty things. Twenty! I made a list."

The handwritten list, Blu-Tacked to the fridge door, flapped in the breeze from the window. Morning sun fell on the rag rug, brightening the faded colours. Minx flopped down in the warm light. Pat was scrubbing the porridge pot. Grief, it was such hard work.

"Number one. Max's snoring. You don't believe me, do you, Minx? It drove me mad. I'd poke him. Hard. Tell him to turn over. Sometimes I staged a protest. Took myself to the spare bed."

Pat Settle wiped dry her bowl and spoon, put the small pot in the nest of saucepans in the cupboard.

"To be honest, I think I liked making a fuss. Now, no more snoring and the nights are quiet. Quiet as...too quiet." She sniffed.

Pat put on the jug, spooned instant coffee into the old china cup with the bluebells on it. There was a small chip on the rim near the handle and a short crack, but she couldn't bring herself to throw it away. Her mother's cup. If it broke that would be something else to add to her list.

She poured some milk on to the coffee powder and stirred. They liked it that way, she and Max, to add the milk before the boiling water. It tasted better.

"To be honest, Minx, most of the time the snoring wasn't too bad. It was sort of comforting. Like rain drumming on a tin roof. Car tyres hissing on a wet road."

Pat turned from the bench and frowned at her cat, lying on its back, stretching voluptuously in the sun, the fur rippling over its fat belly.

"Minx, you're a hard-hearted cat, incapable of grief. A dog would be sympathetic. I'm drinking my coffee in the garden. Coming?"

"Number two. Things Max said. 'You're still the best cuddle in town.' 'Tried them all have you?' 'And the cheekiest smile.'"

Pat swept the wooden boards of the porch. Minx sprawled on the top step.

"Move, Minx." Pat prodded her. Minx obliged slowly, stretching first her front legs, then the back ones, before moving down a step.

"Don't bother hurrying yourself, Minx. I've got all day." After this sarcasm, Pat's spirits dropped. She heard herself sigh.

"Did you hear that, Minx? I don't always know it, when I sigh. Max would hear it. 'Feeling tired love? Come on, put your broom away and sit down. I'll make us a cup of coffee.' He paid attention to me. He made me feel good and he cared for me. I was important to him. His number one person, and he was mine. Now I am important to no one. Not important to you, am I, Minx? If I died tomorrow, you'd just smooch your way into another house. But take my advice and give next door a miss, even if you could scale that ridiculous fence. Max laughed when he saw it going up. 'They don't want us as neighbours, Pat. We're not good enough for them.' I told him Janice wasn't like that. It was that Howard. If he didn't like our house, it wasn't as though we had been delirious about seeing green paddocks replaced with building sites and those ugly brick houses."

"One day, Minx," Pat said, "Howard came charging down our cul-de-sac, did a U-turn and parked with a jerk in front of his house. He blasted the horn and leapt out. 'Janice, come and see this.' *This* was a brand new Land Rover.

"Janice didn't look too thrilled. Perhaps she was thinking of the new clothes her growing kids needed. 'What was wrong with the Toyota?' she asked. 'You've got to think big, Janice. We have to think it to make it. Now go and put out some glasses, we're going to celebrate,' and he reached in and pulled out a bottle of bubbly.

"'Was it the French stuff?' asked Max, laughing when I told him about it. 'He's chasing the dream, Pat. He's chasing the dream.'

"Three months later, Minx, Howard towed home a large boat with an outboard motor. 'Whaddaya reckon, Pat? Will he invite me to go fishing with him?' Well, that Howard was too stuck up to invite Max, and so he missed out. Max was great at fishing, knew the best spots. Could have taught that Howard a thing or two."

"Number three. Sharing. Sharing holidays, jokes, memories. I miss all that. Sharing our tragedy. I would have gone off my rocker, if Max hadn't stuck with me.

"We couldn't have a baby. There were false alarms, and we tried again, and again, until the Doc said no more. The stress and the miscarriages had knocked my health. We decided to go for adoption, but were turned down. 'Too old,' they said.

"When we got home, we went and lay on the bed, hardly saying a word, holding each other close. We were both shell-shocked with grief. We'd been given a life sentence, a life sentence of childlessness."

"I've never told anyone this before, Minx. Except Max, of course. But...but after our big tragedy, I went a bit crazy. Max didn't know. Not at first. He thought I'd let it go, moved on. I let him think that, but secretly, I...I can tell you Minx, can't I? It's not as if you're going to tell anyone.

"I started stealing. It began by accident. I was walking in the street. A woman was ahead, pushing a pram. How I hated new mothers, why did she deserve a baby when I couldn't have one? Her little boy was kicking his legs. He had on blue booties and as he kicked, one of them came off and fell over the side. She didn't notice, which just shows that she didn't deserve...

"Anyway, I picked up the bootie and I was going to call out and give it to her, but it felt so soft in my hand, it was such a pretty blue, I stuffed it in my pocket. That's how it started. My collection.

"I got a couple of toys that way, even a blanket. But it wasn't enough. To hurry things along, I started to shoplift. My heart beat so fast, I thought it would gallop away. I must have looked so guilty. I couldn't believe it when no one chased me down the street. I hurried home so I could take it out and have a good look at it. A red and yellow striped cardy with Mickey Mouse buttons. I loved it. I made sure that things I took would balance, something for a girl, something for a boy, because we could have had either, or both. I got quite a stash and of course I had to hide them from Max, but I wanted them where I could take them out fairly easily and look at them when he was at work. I was sick, Minx, a bit mental. Now don't look at me like that. I can use that word when I am talking about myself."

"I was found out, Minx. I caught the 'flu. Max's sister Jude, sorry, Judith, she's proper stuck-up, was coming to stay. Her annual visit from Oz. Max said not to worry, he would get the house in order. I just slept, zonked out with a high fever and Aspro. I wasn't thinking. Saturday morning, I heard Max's voice. 'What the...?' It came from the spare bedroom. That woke me up. I knew what he'd found. He didn't come straight away. He made coffee for both of us and brought in a tray with my favourite chocolate mint biscuits. 'I found something, Pat. In the guest bedroom. Baby clothes, a suitcase full of them. What's that about?'

"Well, I didn't want to deal with it. Not then. Not ever. I started to cry. Max apologised. 'Sorry, Pat, I know you're not well. We'll have a chat about it later when you're feeling better.'

"At first that felt like a reprieve, but then I realized I wouldn't want to get better, if that was going to be hanging over me. I told him I bought them from an op shop, how I couldn't help myself. But that didn't wash, most of the items were brand new, their price tags still on them.

"OKAY, Minx—I know it's almost your meal time. If you'll just shut up a minute and let me finish, I've got a treat for you. Worth waiting for. You miserable dumb animal, you don't understand a thing, do you?

"So I told Max the truth. I told him everything and he held me and said he was disappointed, but he understood. He would deal with the clothes he said, but I must promise to stop, so I said I would, not really thinking I could. But then he said the possibility of me being caught, being charged, standing up in court, scared him. 'I couldn't bear it, Pat, if that happened to you.' There was something in his voice, in the quiet way he looked at me, that I knew I couldn't just laugh it off. I was his number one person, and I didn't want to lose that. He was the one person in the world who cared for me, and because of that I was a better person than I might have been. The thought of losing him gave me the shivers. I knew then I could give up the baby clothes, for him."

Pat felt that old emotion, a terrifying fear of loss. And now she had lost Max, but not because he had given up on her.

A mew brought her back to the present. She went to the fridge, brought out a packet, and unwrapped a fish-head. Minx jumped up on to the bench.

"Don't think you can eat this smelly thing here, Minx."

Pat went out the back door, across the lawn, past the rotary clothesline all the way to the back fence with the vacant plot behind it. Minx followed, mewing incessantly.

"Go get it, Minx," said Pat as she heaved the fish head high over the fence. It landed on a small bush, slid through the leaves and fell onto the ground. Minx squeezed under the paling. She moved fast for such a fluffy animal, crouched over the fish, securing possession of it, her eyes searching around for possible challengers.

"Once I stopped pinching baby items," said Pat to no one

in particular, "my children, the daughter and son who were never born, had a life in my imagination. Elspeth with her father's olive skin, dark hair and gorgeous smile. Geoff, a ginger like me. Tall, athletic, good white teeth. As they were not tied to time, I could imagine them at any age and out of sequence. At their weddings, as schoolkids, graduates, babies. And I swapped their looks around. The girl having auburn hair, delicate skin with no freckles, and the boy with his father's looks, but taller.

"I grieve for them. Numbers four and five. The daughter and son we never brought into life. The jewels we could never treasure. Geoff and Elspeth.

"I never pinched another item of baby gear. I did something worse."

"The first could not have been easier. Jude, sorry, Judith went back to Oz leaving her ring behind. A huge oval opal, a present from hubbie, a real beauty. She wrote saying she had lost it and was it around the house somewhere? I wanted to get the idea it was in our house out of her head, so I wrote back asking if she had left it in the toilet of the cinema, because she always took her rings off when she washes her hands. She wrote back asking me to go to the cinema and enquire. She sent a list of other places she'd been to the toilet, and sent a photo of the ring with an insurance evaluation. Four thousand dollars, I couldn't believe it.

"Max said I should work my way through the list. I asked him to phone them up. He said they would take more notice if I showed up with the photo and the evaluation. It took me a week. Jude must've had a bladder problem; she'd gone to the toilet so often. And all the time I knew that the sky blue opal was in my button box in the sewing machine cabinet. Keeping the ring was my revenge for all the times I had to sit through her photos of children and grandchildren. It was the baby photos that hurt the most.

"Then Jude wrote to say they'd made an insurance claim on the ring, and Stu was going to buy her a bigger one. Well, why didn't they do that in the first place, instead of making me traipse around like a wally with her list?

"Did I feel guilty? No, I was afraid. Afraid Max would find out. The stress seemed worth it every time I held the ring, moved it in the light and saw the flashes of colour.

"The next one was an old-fashioned brooch, a butterfly with ruby and diamond wings sitting on a gold bar. The catch was loose. It also had a chain that ended in a gold safety pin, for extra security, but the head of the pin had become wide, so the brooch was not secure at all and had fallen forward from the pin, and the pin was working itself out of the lapel of this old lady's costume.

"The brooch reminded me of one my granny's best friend used to wear. I had always liked it.

"Well, Minx, are you disgusted? Stealing from a doddery old dear?

"It was in the new shopping mall. I was sitting on a bench, not minding my own business. This old lady stopped in front of me, so I had a good old look at her near-falling brooch. She stopped there to talk to a friend, and I kept thinking the friend would notice the brooch and fix it, but no, they were skiting about their grandchildren. This one had got an apprenticeship, that one was doing well at university etc. etc. They didn't know how well off they were, while I had nothing, so I decided the old lady could spare her brooch. When her friend finally wandered off, I got up from the seat and accidentally on purpose banged into the old lady, who lost her balance. I caught hold to steady her and in the process took her brooch, which just about dropped into my hand.

"'Oh, dear,' she said. 'I feel quite dizzy.'

"I thought I better take her somewhere to sit down and buy her a cup of tea. I had one too, and chatted with her until she felt better. To stop her talking about her grandchildren, I told her that Max had recently been diagnosed with a heart problem and what changes this made to our lives. How he couldn't garden or mow the lawn, without stopping for frequent rests. The old lady was quite sympathetic, and after a while said she felt quite steady again, and thanked me for helping her.

"I went straight to the Ladies, to the privacy of a booth, so I could take the brooch out of my pocket and have a good look. It was a real beauty, a delicate, Victorian brooch."

Emma is four years old and lives in the present tense. She sees a flower, admires its sunshine colour and the drop of moisture sparkling on the petal. Emma likes shiny, glinting things.

A fantail dances around her.

"Birdie." She tries to catch it, following it to the boundary fence. The fantail flips away. Emma puts her eye to a gap between the palings. The old lady's cat is crouched under a bush, eating. Emma knows it's a girl cat.

"Puss. Puss," she calls.

Puss gobbles. She's very hungry. There's a fishy smell and Emma wrinkles her nose. Then Tyro is there beside Emma. A boy dog. He barks, he squeezes under the fence, runs and stops in front of puss. His tail is stiff and tall, making quick little shakes. Puss grabs something in her mouth and looks at

Tyro. She's angry. He barks, she hisses with her mouthful.

"Bad Tyro. Bad Puss."

Tyro jumps and puss scratches. There's a big fight. They make angry and hurt noises. They roll over and over fast. Emma cannot see which is Tyro, which is Puss. They are both white and black.

"Emmaaaa. Come and say goodbye, sweetheart. Visitors are going."

Mummy is calling.

Mummy lifts Emma, holding her tight. Emma wriggles. Mummy holds her tighter.

"I'm worried about Ems. Hardly talks, she's so quiet. Aren't you, my precious, my treasure?"

"Tresha," says Emma.

"Take her to playcentre. She'll make friends there, learn to interact."

"I know. I should. I'd love to. But you have to help out, take your turn, and I'm sooo busy."

"Sooo busy," says Emma.

"How about kindy?"

"I know; I've thought of that. But kindy's miles away on the other side of town. When they built these houses, they didn't give much thought to the infrastructure, did they? And study takes up so much time. My assignment is due in two days, and I've hardly started."

"Just as well we're going then." Mummy's friend laughs. "Thanks for lunch. That salad was delicious. Really. Next time you must come to my place."

"I didn't mean it like that. If I didn't take time off to socialise, I'd go mad. Just wonder sometimes if I've taken on too much. Now say good-bye, sweetheart."

"Bye." Emma looks at Mummy's friend. She's nice. Emma wishes she was staying. Staying and laughing. Mummy doesn't laugh much. She sighs. Mummy is sooo busy. She wants to be a gee...gee...o...dig the earth.

"So my precious, my treasure, do you want a little nap?"

Emma shakes her head.

"Do you want some juice?"

Another shake.

"Well, what do you want?"

"Garden."

"Garden? You want to go outside again?"

Emma nods. That's what garden means.

"Okay then, for a little while. What's the attraction, it's mainly lawn? When you're older I'll get you a trampoline." She looks at Emma. "You're a deep little girl, aren't you? You already have secrets."

"Secrets," says Emma.

"Mummy's going to sit down now and do some study. Later we'll go for a walk, then Mummy's got to make tea." She sighs.

Emma hears a bark.

"Tyro," she shouts and runs outside.

Puss isn't there. Puss has gone home. But Tyro is there at that fishy, smelly place near the bush. Tyro is busy, digging and digging. Earth flies everywhere. It goes high in the air and then falls on the bush, on the grass, on Tyro. Tyro is dirty but happy. Perhaps Tyro wants to be a gee...gee...o... like Mummy. He likes the smelly earth; he rolls over it. He will smell bad. Emma hopes Mummy doesn't smell when she's a gee...gee...o...iss.

Tyro is back to digging. Emma sees something sparkle and gleam in the falling dirt. Faraway, at the end of the fence, there is a broken bit. Mummy doesn't know about it. Emma goes there now. She starts to crawl through the fence. A nail snags her top.

"Naughty," says Emma.

A ball comes over the fence. It goes big bounce, smaller bounce, little bounce before it becomes still. It's the yellow ball that belongs to the boy in the front house. Emma goes to the fence. The boy is there looking at the fence. He sees Emma.

"Hey you," he yells.

"Hello," says Emma. "What's your name?"

"What? Brad. Hey, could you get my ball? Chuck it over?"

"My name's Emma."

"I know. My ball. It's behind you."

"Will you be my friend?"

"No way. You're a girl. And you're too young."

"No," says Emma. "I'm four."

"See. Not even old enough to go to school."

"I'm too busy to go to school. I'm sooo busy."

"You're nuts," says Brad.

Emma looks at him. She shows him her hand, a dimpled fist enclosing something.

"If you'll be my friend, I'll show you a secret. Tresha."

"Look, Emma. I'm not interested in your secret. I just want my ball."

Emma looks at Brad. He doesn't look at all friendly.

She thinks she's going to cry.

"Okay, listen. If I look at your secret, will you give me my ball?"

Emma nods. She stretches out her arm again.

"You can look, but not touch," she says as her fingers uncurl.

"I've seen it now. It's a ring. So what?"

"Pretty," says Emma. "Precious."

Her fingers enclose the ring, her hand withdraws.

"My ball," says Brad.

"Okay." She turns and runs to the ball. Tyro is barking. He's in the house, at the window. He has seen the ball.

"No, Tyro. This is Brad's ball." And Brad is her friend. She picks it up and runs back to the fence.

"Listen, Emma. You're small."

"I'm four."

"Exactly. And the fence is high. So you'll have to throw very high and very far. Can you do that?"

Emma nods.

"Good girl. Are you ready?"

Emma lifts her arm above her head.

"One, two, throw," yells Brad.

Emma tries very hard. The ball doesn't go very high. It doesn't go far before it lands with a plop.

"Useless," says Brad. "Typical girl."

Emma is watching the yellow ball roll over the lawn. It goes slower, and slower and stops as it sneaks under the fence and hits the concrete. Emma looks at Brad, Brad looks at the ball.

"Thanks, Emma."

She knows he is happy as he picks it up and runs back to his house. And Emma is happy. She has more secrets, precious tresha she can show Brad, her friend.

"I have no intention, Minx, of revealing all my secrets. All my cunning, sneaky ways of collecting my jewels. If I had never met Max, I do believe I could have become a hardened crim. Of course, he found my stash, but not for a while. Time enough for me to amass these beauties, that I still grieve for. Number six, Jude's opal ring, seven, the Victorian brooch, and eight, a pounamu pendant, a genuine antique, not made for tourists. Nine was a half-carat diamond earring, ten, a gold signet ring inset with lapis lazuli. Eleven, something Judith would go mad for, a pearl necklace with a sapphire pendant. Twelve, a platinum eternity ring, a circle of diamonds and rubies. Number thirteen, now that was a necklace of black seed pearls, as rare as hen's teeth. Number fourteen, a gold chain with a pendant engraved with the lovers' initial. Sweet. Did I feel guilty? No, she was careless and spoilt, and he drove a Porsche. Fifteen, a novelty ring, a silver dragon encircling a tiger's eye. The least valuable, but a favourite and I grieve that no one will again see and appreciate all this beauty now buried and lost in the earth.

"Max found the hoard when he went to the button box to find something to replace the missing button on his cuff. He was going to sew it on to save me the bother. He did not deserve the shock he got. I heard him call out. He was pale and dizzy, with pains in his chest. Doctor Preston came and phoned for an ambulance. I was terrified. 'Don't let him die, Doctor. Don't let him die.'

"For days I sat by him in hospital holding his hand, and crying, begging him to forgive me. He wasn't talking. A nurse told me all my crying and carry on would not help him get better. I should talk about cheerful things, she said.

"Cheerful things! I told him the apple tree was coming into blossom and looked ever so pretty. When he came out of hospital I would make apple shortcake with the last of the stored apples. The neighbour across the road came and mowed the lawns without me having to ask. Jude—sorry—Judith, had written him a letter, but it wasn't actually cheery, so I didn't read it to him. I started to worry that if I sounded as though everything was going well, he'd think I didn't need him. So I told him how much I missed him. He was the best husband ever. I didn't deserve him, but I needed him.

"When Max became aware of where he was, I thought he looked at me in a different way. I was gutted. He remembered what led up to his heart attack.

"'You know, Pat, if it had been anyone else I would have called the police.'

"I didn't point out that he had been in no condition to call anyone, that I had called the doctor. I said, 'Go ahead, Max, if that's what you want to do. I deserve it.'

"'I can't do that, Pat. You make bad choices at times, but at heart you're kind and decent. I love you.' He said when he got out of hospital he would bury the jewels, he wouldn't say where. He said I would have to stop stealing. No more jewels, no more pretty things to make up for our tragedy. I spent the whole day eating humble pie, which is not easy for Pat Settle. But I had no choice, if the price of stealing was another heart attack for Max, it wasn't worth it. Simple as that."

"My sainted aunts! Janice you look terrible!" Then Pat noticed that Janice was holding Brad by the hand. "Just joking, Brad. Your mother's as gorgeous as ever."

"Can we come in? I told Brad you wouldn't mind him playing in the back garden."

"'Course." Pat went to the biscuit barrel on her bench. "Come here, young man. Now how many biscuits will we allow him to take?"

"Two," Janice said.

"Take three," said Pat. "Go on." She grinned at Brad's eagerness.

"Minx is out in the back garden. Remember that she's almost an old lady. If you do anything she doesn't like, she'll let you know, and serve you right."

"Yes, Mrs Settle. Thanks." He ran down the back steps.

"Now what is it," asked Pat, sitting across the table from Janice, "that you didn't want to tell me in front of Brad?"

"I got a fax this morning." Janice brought out a folded piece of paper from her pocket, and handed it to Pat. It read: Janice, this should come as no surprise. I'm leaving Godzone (ha,ha!) with Sheryl to start a new life. You and the kids can have the house, cars, boat and trailer. You can't say I'm not generous. Just don't be in the house between eleven and one when I come to pack up. Howard

"What a shocker," said Pat. "Was it a surprise?"

"Totally. I guessed he was having an affair, but I didn't think he'd leave the kids, especially Brad, his little man. Then I thought it would be just like him to say he was leaving the kids, and go and snatch them. I felt so stressed. A little crazy. I went to their schools straightaway and picked them up."

"Good on you. I know what you need right now." Pat got up and brought a bottle of brandy and two glasses to the table. "You could do with a snifter or two. So could I, just hearing about this."

They sipped at their brandy and Pat reached across and

held Janice's hand.

"You'll get over this. A strong, young woman like you." Then Pat laughed and let go. "Listen to me talk. How would I know? I've never had to put up with a straying man."

"You were lucky."

"Don't I know it? You'll have the kids to keep you busy."

"Mum, I'm thirsty."

Pat gave Brad a good-sized glass of Raro.

"You know, Janice, you and the kids are welcome to stay here."

"Why aren't we going home, Mum?"

"We're having a little surprise break, darling. Thanks, Pat. You know, you're my best friend in the world. I'll be in touch."

Janice and Brad went off to pick up the twins from her mother's. They would spend the night at some anonymous motel, where she would break the news to the poor kids.

Poor Janice. So pale, except for the bruised look round her eyes. The weight was falling off her. As the days passed, she had more and more bad news. The bank told her that the mortgage payments were way behind, and now that the family did not have an income, the bank would be forced into holding a mortgagee sale. The Land Rover, the boat and trailer were re-possessed. She managed to borrow enough money from her mother to pay off her own car. She summoned the courage to ring Howard's employer and ask if there was any back pay and holiday pay owing. He told her gently that when another member of staff had taken over Howard's accounts, he found Howard had been embezzling money from their clients. There was a warrant out now for his arrest, also for the arrest of Sheryl, his secretary. He warned Janice that the police would probably want to interview her about Howard's whereabouts.

Janice went to Pat's. She broke down. "I knew he was impatient. He wanted everything NOW, but I never thought he would do anything illegal. My children's father a criminal. It's so shaming."

Her 'best friend in the world' was a crim too, but Pat reckoned that was something Janice didn't need to know, she was carrying such an emotional burden.

"I hate that house, and everything bought by Howard."

She and the kids moved into the cottage with Pat and Minx. A bit of a squeeze, but they managed. Janice decided the kids didn't need to know the truth about their father till they were much older. She had the hard job of convincing them, that though he didn't love their mum as much as he used to—he had a girlfriend now—he still loved his children. The puzzled distress on their faces broke Pat's heart. How could their father not love their mother, and if he loved them, why had he left?

Pat kept the girls busy making biscuits, which they all ate too many of. A neighbour's son was invited over to play cricket with Brad, but that ended in tears when the boy repeated some gossip about Howard.

"Is not! Is not!" shouted Brad. "I hate you!"

Janice told the boy it wasn't kind to repeat things he'd heard. He couldn't be sure they were true.

"Tis true. Dad said."

"You skedaddle before I wash your mouth out with soap."

Poor mite, thought Pat. Brad was set up for a fall later in life, but that didn't make her soft with him.

Janice decided to hold a garage sale. Apart from clothes and the most loved toys, everything was for sale. Pat and Janice spent a week researching and pricing the stuff: Howard's European whiteware, the kingsize bed, unopened wine, beer and spirits, lamps, paintings. They put a sign at the opening of the cul-de-sac, and a notice in the evening paper. The start time was 8.00a.m., but they knew the dealers and early birds would come at 5.00a.m. Later, the neighbours would arrive to pick up a bargain, but mostly out of curiosity to see the evidence of the scandalous Howard's lifestyle. The plan was for Janice and the kids to eat takeaways and camp overnight in their sleeping bags.

In the evening before the sale, Janice and Pat sat on the deck and sipped a small Cointreau each, enjoying the alcoholic, citrus sweetness. Brad came up, followed by Emma. He didn't seem to mind her tagging along, which she did whenever she could.

"Mum?" Brad held up his cricket bat. "How much do you think this is worth?"

"Oh, what do you think, Pat? About two dollars?"

Brad looked upset. Then he said bravely, "Well, Mum, you said we needed every cent we could get, so I guess two dollars is okay."

He was offering his favourite possession for the garage sale.

"Come here," said Janice. She hugged Brad. "I don't want to sell your cricket bat. It's your favourite thing."

"But, Mum, I want to help. I'm not too little."

Pat had never seen a small boy's face look so serious.

"I reckon," Pat said butting in, "you might get ten dollars for that."

"Choice," he said. "Please, Mum. Pleeease."

"Mummy's very grateful. Whatever we get for it will be a plus. Thank you, darling."

"Choice." He jumped up and down. "Emma wants to help, too."

Emma came forward shyly. "Tresha," she said. "Pretty." Her uncurling fingers revealed Judith's opal ring.

Pat and Janice both gasped, probably not for the same reason. They spoke at the same time.

"Where did you find it?"

"Is it your mother's?"

Emma shook her head and said, "Mine."

"Where did you find it?" Pat repeated, trying to be patient and gentle. Not easy for Pat Settle, especially when her lust for jewellery was making a forceful return.

"In the earth." Of course, where else? But Pat had an idea about which bit of earth it could be. The back section where cats and dogs and neighbourhood children played. She had seen Emma there, several times, on her little haunches, poking at the ground.

"It must be worth a lot. I suppose we should contact the police," said Janice.

Brad and Pat both yelled, "No!" Brad because he was protecting Emma, Pat because she was protecting—what exactly? The opal?

"About four thousand dollars," Pat said. "I know that ring. It belonged to my sister-in-law, Judith. She lost it when she was visiting one time."

"Why do you say belonged, past tense?"

"Because I know she wouldn't want it back. I spent a week trotting round places she'd been, carrying her insurance evaluation, but no joy. So Judith and her husband claimed on the insurance and he bought another, bigger, opal ring. If she got this back now, it would be an embarrassment to them, and the insurance company. A lot of backtracking and fiddling around. Just a nuisance." Was Janice convinced?

"Thank you, sweetie. It's a very generous gift," Pat said to

Emma.

"Tresha," said Emma.

"But is Emma old enough to know what she's doing?"

"Yes!" yelled Brad, in support of littlies.

"I think I'd better ring Emma's mother and ask her to come over."

Pat managed to stop herself from saying, *That cow.*

"Could I have a look at the ring while you're doing that?"

"Sure." Janice passed it over.

Pat tipped it backwards and forwards to catch the bright red and green lights glinting from the sky blue depths. The other jewels must be where Emma found the opal, or had she found them all?

When Emma's mother came, she tried the ring on a finger, saying how perfectly it fitted, what beautiful colours, etc. She had large capable hands and long fingers. The opal did look good on her hand.

"We know," Pat said loudly, "that the ring originally belonged to my sister-in-law, who lost it and has since replaced it with the insurance money..."

"How much?"

"Four thousand," Pat looked for signs of greed disfiguring the other woman's face, but she was difficult to read. "For reasons, I've explained to Janice, my sister-in-law doesn't want the ring back..."

"The reasons are...?"

Was this a cross examination? She wasn't a lawyer; she was a geologist. Instead of just listening like Janice, she fired questions at Pat like she was some kind of verbal machinegun.

"Emma found the ring. She wants to give it to Janice to sell, because she wants to help Brad's family."

"Do you?" fired the machine gun at her daughter.

Emma nodded.

"Did you put her up to it?" This question was aimed at Brad, and Pat could see Janice getting ready to protect her boy.

"No," said Brad. "Emma knows what she wants."

"Yes," said her mother. "I believe in treating children with respect from the moment they are born, and allow them to develop their own tastes and values and make their own decisions."

Well, that's handy, Pat thought.

"So, if Emma wants to give you the ring, you should respect her by taking it." She slipped the opal off her finger and handed it to Janice.

"And ask a reputable jeweller's shop to sell it on behalf to get a reasonable return."

"Of course. Thank you, Emma, you're a sweetheart." Janice looked exhausted.

Pat also felt wrung out. Her blood pressure had returned to a reasonable level, when Emma, bless her, produced another surprise—the Victorian butterfly brooch.

"Does this belong to your sister-in-law as well?" asked Emma's mother snidely.

"Mine," said Emma.

"No, it does not. I think they're fairly common. Most Victorian grandmothers would have had something like this."

"Yes, I think I have a similar brooch. Did you get this from my jewellery box, Emma?"

"No."

"Tyro dug it up," said Brad, "and Emma found it."

"Tyro dug it," explained Emma, "But he didn't want it. Tyro likes smelly bones. I like pretty things. Precious tresha."

Pat was afraid the whole business of whether or not to call the police would come up again.

But they were all tired. Finders, keepers they agreed. Then

they asked Emma if there was more treasure.

"Secret," said Emma.

Fair enough, thought Pat.

"Here we are, Minx, sitting outside in the garden in the dark. You're not very happy with that, are you? You'd rather be cosy inside. Well, tough, you big ball of fluff, this is my night and I am enjoying it, sitting wrapped up with a blanket in the old deckchair, a hottie on my lap, and a thermos with a hot toddy.

"Remember my list of griefs? I had to remove it pronto from the fridge when Janice came. I stuffed it into my mouth, so you could say the list is internalised. Thanks to a dog and a four-year old girl, the jewels have materialized again, not hidden for ever in the earth, with no one to appreciate them. Bless you, Max. Did you put them in a paper bag? Was your heart hurting when you were digging? I feel sick at the thought. So I replace that grief with this. Sixteen, Max and I never had that holiday we'd planned, visiting the old gold mining regions of New Zealand—the West Coast, Otago and the Coromandel. Both our great grandfathers had come to New Zealand in the gold rush. Perhaps that's where my interest in glitter comes from. Seventeen, this might seem strange, but looking back, I wish I'd been a bit more friendly to stuck-up Judith. I'm not sorry of depriving her of her opal. If you can replace things so easily, you probably don't feel their loss so much. That's my theory. But I wish I had been a bit more civil to her. Max would have liked that, and maybe Judith too.

"Minx, this toddy is quite addictive, ha, ha, but it wouldn't do you any good.

"Eighteen, the closeness, the sex, with Max. We became good at it, and don't tell me that desire fades with age. Nineteen, that Max and I will not grow old together. Twenty, my time for appreciating the feel, the smells, the sounds and sights of this dear earth is running out. Fast.

"I refuse to become old on my own. I have made my plans. Consulted a lawyer. Duped Dr. P into giving me the little oval pills that lace my hot toddy. In my will I have left ten thousand pounds to Judith, though she doesn't need it. When Janice and her mother and her kids come back from their holiday in the Bay of Islands, they will learn that I have gone. My lawyer will tell Janice that she has inherited this cottage. They may not end up living here, but she will have a financial asset and be able to get a home of her choice.

"I have become dangerously fond of Janice, Brad, and the secretive twins, Fi and Lou. I wanted to be an honorary granny, but they have a nana of their own. I know what I'm like. I would've competed hard for their time and attention, and that wouldn't have been right.

"I like that little Emma. I've left her some money and she has the jewels. She has an appreciation of beauty, and glitter and colour. I liked the way Brad was protective of her. Even the most, stroppy, self-sufficient woman needs to know that someone cares for her. Janice will see that Brad doesn't turn into a Howard. Brad said one day, 'Emma hasn't got a dad, and she's all right. So we'll be okay with Mum, and she'll be all right with us.'

"Get a hold of yourself, Pat. Don't start crying now.

"Another sip. Another. Are you leaving me, Minx, now the hottie's getting cold? Good-bye, you self-centred ball of fluff. The back door is open.

"Drowsy now. Can't think. Stars are blurred, can smell blossom…lemon…grapefruit. Hear the murmuring of… sparrows…falling asleep."

Emory

8

by Derin Attwood

Kevin Smith drove his car into the garage, sat for five minutes savouring the silence. With a deep sigh, he climbed out, grabbed his briefcase off the passenger seat, and closed the garage door.

The noisy chaos hit him the moment he entered the house.

"Kev's home, Barb." Darlene paused, as her mother appeared.

"Kev's home, Mum," Jolene mimicked.

Barbara Smith smiled indulgently at her daughters.

Kevin scowled at them. "Dad, to you, missy."

Barbara tittered. "Oh, they're just trying their wings, dear. You're too hard on them."

"I'm not hard enough," Kevin snapped.

"Bye, Mum." Jolene and Darlene raced past them, aiming for the back door.

"Cheese, Darlene!" roared Kevin. "You're not going out

like that! I can see your bum-cheeks."

"Muuuum!"

"Don't be crude, Kevin, talking to my girls like that. Honestly! See, you've made poor Jolene blush. Anyway, I told them they can go out, dear, and this is what young girls are wearing, these days."

Kevin eyed Darlene's Daisy Dukes. Jolene wore a skirt. It was short, and tighter than he liked, but he was aware of the fashions girls wore, and at least she was covered. "No it isn't. That's a costume from a TV show. So if she's headed for a film set, fine. Otherwise, go and get changed."

"We're just going to meet the kids in the park," said Darlene. "All o' them in the street are already there."

Kevin snorted. "No, they're not. I just saw that Indian boy going back to his house with young Jake. And the two down the end aren't there. I saw them earlier with their mum."

"Well we wouldn't let *them* come with us, anyway. Stuck-up geeks," Darlene said, with a sneer.

"Just because they work hard at school, and plan to make something of their lives."

"Muuuum. We're late. They'll go without us."

"The park isn't going anywhere, Darlene," snapped Kevin. "So where are you going and who with?"

"Oh, Kev, don't fuss! Off you go, girls." Barbara shooed them out the door. "You make me angry, Kevin. You're far too hard on them. I'm going to have a cigarette. Go and have a bath, or something. Leave the girls to me." She scowled at him, and pulled her cigarettes out of the phone drawer.

"Barb, Pete McKinley saw Darlene in Danny White's Holden Commodore a few days back. Ya know he's trouble. He hoons around like a maniac, speeds all over the place. We'll be organising her funeral next, because there'll be an accident. Either that or she'll get pregnant."

"Oh, you're just being an old fuddy-duddy. They're happy,

lively girls. Not at all like poor Lara. I do worry about that girl. Her mother makes her study far too hard. Mind you, Bella's nothing to write home about. Single, three children. She calls herself a widow, but there was that man who stayed there last year. And there've been others. I'm not saying anything, but, when the doors are closed, wee-eel—who knows what…"

"Cheese, Barb. She is a widow." Kevin stared at his wife with dislike. "I went to her husband's funeral. It was tragic. The man staying at her place last year was her boarder, and he was about eighty." He walked into the bathroom, and turned on the taps.

Whatever had he seen in her? He was a naive twenty-year-old when they met. She seemed to be sweet, reserved, and modest. She was the daughter of a woman in his mother's knitting group, and his mother introduced them. On their first date, Barb had worn a powder blue trouser suit. Sleeveless, she wore a polo-necked jumper under it, he remembered. He'd admired it. She wore the top of it alone as a mini-dress on their third date. It was very short, but it was the height of fashion, she said. It was also his downfall. The night had been cold, even for May. He'd lent her his jacket, very gentlemanly, he'd been.

That friend of hers, Mick, had passed around his hip flask, 'just to keep us all warm,' Barbara had said. The whiskey went straight to Kevin's head. Not good. Kev couldn't remember doing anything, but Barb assured him he was wonderful. A few weeks passed and she told him she was pregnant. The twins were born seven months later. Twins were always born early, he was told.

He sighed deeply. "Wish I'd let her freeze to death," he mumbled to himself, as he put his foot into cold water.

"What did you say, dear?" called Barbara, as she walked down the passage.

"I said the water's freezing. Why is it I can never get a hot bath?"

"I told you to get a bigger cylinder. That one is just too small. We have a growing family."

"A selfish one," he mumbled, as he wrapped a towel around his waist and walked into the kitchen to boil the jug.

Kevin lay back in the lukewarm water and wondered where it had all gone wrong. He—they had been happy at the start, even though the twins came so quickly. Barb had liked that he was doing well at Woolworths. His steady advance up the ladder to undermanager had pleased her. Now she was unhappy that he wouldn't push himself further.

He would become manager eventually, but not until Mr Morgan retired. That would happen in two years, not long to wait, really. But Barb felt it wasn't soon enough. To become manager sooner, the whole family would need to be interviewed by Mr Samuel, the big boss in Auckland.

While Barb might possibly pass muster, Kevin had no doubt the impression given by his daughters would be disastrous. It might even stymie his chance of becoming manager here, and he wasn't prepared to chance it. Anyway, he didn't want to move. In Emory, he had friends, and could avoid the social circle his wife wanted them to move in.

Barbara had plans. Big plans. The worst parts were a posh house in Morning Point, and membership at the golf club. She even talked about them getting a small boat, so they could join the yacht club. It didn't matter that they both hated boating. 'It would be prestigious,' she said.

Of course, she would prefer to move to Auckland. The only thing that convinced her to drop the idea, was telling her they would have to live in South Auckland, and she refused to go there. She was beginning to question why they couldn't live in posh Remuera, and suggested he commute. He didn't fancy sitting in his car for a couple of hours, twice a day.

He might have considered a move had the girls been better behaved. But until they left home, he would go nowhere. Even then, Morning Point was out of the question. He didn't really like the sort of people Barb would find attractive. He had contemplated leaving her in the past, but as wonderful as it seemed in his dreams, he knew the reality would be horrid. He had learned over the years that his daughters got their snide viciousness from their mother. He could accept that he would still have to maintain the family, but Barb would claim the house and make sure he had nothing to live on. He would have no home and no way to afford one. He would also lose what little influence he had on his daughters.

With a deep sigh, he hauled himself out of his bath, dressed and went to watch the six o'clock news.

Barb talked all the way through the news, mainly neighbourhood gossip, until he had had enough. He turned the TV off and stood. "I'm going for a walk," he said. "I'll get the girls, and we can have dinner as a family for a change." He walked out, hearing Barb bleating in the background about embarrassing the girls in front of their friends and leaving them for a while longer.

As he walked down the drive, he heard the familiar sounds of Peyton Place. Barb had put in a video of her favourite program.

Tommy Dawes jumped out of the oak tree as he stepped onto the grass verge around it. That boy was a tree-climbing fool. Up any tree he could find a foothold in, and this one in particular.

"Not at the park with the others, Tommy?"

"No one's there, Mr Smith."

"Oh, I thought Darlene and Jolene were meeting you all there."

Tommy shook his head. "They got into a car down near our place just after five."

"Whose? Danny White's?"

"Nah! It was a fairly new Audi. Danny's got an old dunger."

"Thanks, lad."

"Barb, did you know they were going off in some boy's car?" he demanded, when he got home.

"Darlene did mention they might meet her young man. He comes from a very good family. You should be pleased. He's serious, mature, and he's a very good catch. She could do worse. And his younger brother quite fancies Jolene."

"If he has a licence, he's too old for her, Barb. And some kid borrowing his dad's car does not make him class."

"Oh no, he owns the car. Evidently, he has two. He lives over at Morning Point."

"What sort of fool do you take me for? No teenager in this town has two flash cars."

Barb blushed. "Well, I—um—Darlene mentioned he was no longer a teenager."

"Twenty! What twenty-year-old is interested in a child?" Kevin took a deep breath. "This is wrong, Barb. They're thirteen. It's illegal. I'm gonna call the police."

"You will not! You'll embarrass them. I will not have a police car outside my house. It was bad enough when they arrested that Keith guy from number five."

"A man of twenty!" He stared at Barb, suddenly suspicious. She was fussing, and she only did that when she was trying to hide something. "What?" He paused. "Barbara, what haven't you told me?"

"I don't know what you're talking about."

"Oh yes you do. Tell me, or you can tell the police."

Barb took a deep breath. "There's nothing wrong, Kevin. He has a good job and his own house, and he's quite smitten with our Darlene."

"And?"

"He's twenty-five," she said, in a small voice.

"Cheese, Barb! Darlene is out there necking with a middle-aged man? Men that age only want one thing from a young girl. They should be home anyway. I'm ringing—"

"No, you're not! Jolene is chaperoning them, and I told them they could stay out until ten. We'll have dinner then."

"They're thirteen. And it's a school night!"

"Oh pish. They'll be fourteen in a few days, and they won't need that much education if they marry wealthy men."

"They're not fourteen until November, Barbara. That's seven months away."

The argument lasted until ten-fifteen when, despite Barbara's ever-louder protests, Kevin finally picked up the phone to dial the police.

Barb slapped her hand onto the disconnect bar as he began to dial the second number. "There's a car in the drive." She peered through a crack in the venetian blinds, and nodded with satisfaction. "Yes, it's them. See, you worried about nothing."

Twenty minutes later, the girls walked in the door. They took one look at their father, and raced down to their bedroom.

"Don't you dare go down and yell at them," Barbara said, and pushed him back into the lounge. "You'll only inflame things. I'll talk to them."

Minutes later, he heard her in the kitchen.

Kevin looked in. "You're cooking for them?" He was horrified. "You didn't tell them off, did you? Cheese, Barb. Those two are going to end up in so much trouble. Who'll sort that out?"

He knew she was angry when she looked up, but moments later, realised her anger wasn't aimed at the girls.

"This is the best chance our Darlene has. You're stuck in that dead-end job, no chance of improvement. Even if you do become manager, Emory is just a hick-town. The end of the road. They would have far more chance to meet well-connected young men if you'd apply yourself and become a manager in Auckland, Wellington, or Christchurch. Anywhere would be better than this ghastly little backwater town, in boorish Oak Tree Lane with trailer-trash neighbours. Darlene and Jolene are city girls, and this is their opportunity. They're stifled here. You're holding us all back!"

She grabbed a large bottle of Coca-Cola from the fridge, picked up the tray and pushed past him.

Kevin sat wearily at the table and sighed. Nothing he said would make any difference, although he was tempted to storm down to the bedroom to tell them all exactly why he wouldn't get a manager's job, but deep down he knew it would be useless.

He was shocked into speechlessness at the sight of the Cola. They had agreed, as parents, the girls shouldn't have fizzy drinks, nor eat junk food at all, except for a few very special times during the year.

For the first time in many years, he pulled open some of the cupboards. Three of them were stacked with junk food. Bottles of fizzy, chips, bought biscuits, bought jam, canned food and a few things he didn't recognise. Interestingly, the two canned foods they had agreed to use occasionally, sardines and baked beans, were not there.

Equally horrifying though, were the half-empty bottles of gin and vodka, all in amounts far in excess of reason. While he'd never seen Barbara drink much, he began to wonder. Why else had she bought it?

Barbara had always discouraged Kevin from entering the kitchen. Her domain, she called it, where she could listen to the girl's secrets and advise them on the problems they were facing as they grew. His proposal that he too listen and offer suggestions were rejected.

"Girls don't talk about their girl-problems in front of men," she declared.

Now he wondered if that really was the reason.

Give Barbara her due; she'd always cooked him a meal, sometimes fairly basic, except on those evenings when she had taken the girls to see her sister, or to the pictures. On those nights, she would leave him something cold on the dining room table.

Realising she wouldn't cook for him tonight, he began to look for the makings of a meal. As he opened cupboard after cupboard, he began to wonder if he had ever really known her. Yes, she would go shopping tomorrow, but there was little that was wholesome in the kitchen.

From the chiller in the refrigerator, he found an old carrot, two wizened potatoes, half a limp lettuce, and a small square of old cheese.

The bread-bin gave up layers of plastic bread bags—sliced white bread, according to the advertising—a food he and Barb had discussed and rejected a few years back. The top one held two heel-end partial slices, days old, dried and unpalatable.

Kev didn't enjoy white bread anyway, and all he could see to put on it was jam. In desperation, and with nothing else there, he toasted the crusts under the grill, sliced the cheese sparingly to cover one piece, and grilled that as well. At the back of one cupboard, he found an almost empty jar of marmite, and scraped that to cover the other crust. A sparse meal, but it had to do.

Having eaten, he walked down to the bedroom. Wearily, he got into his pyjamas, and climbed into bed. As tired as he was, sleep didn't come easily. He could hear Barb and the girls chatting and laughing. Finally, sometime after 2:00a.m. he drifted off.

Kevin woke when the doorbell rang. It was 8.25a.m. and he was late for work. On the three occasions he'd been late before, Mr Morgan had been very understanding. Being late only three times in over twenty years was still a record at the shop.

He swung his feet onto the floor, and realised Barb hadn't come to bed. He wondered if she had slept on the couch, in the spare room, or in with the girls. He realised with shock that he didn't really care. He dressed and walked into the kitchen. It was empty.

A piece of paper on the table bore the legend:

gone to mums—back when I'm ready.
I took the housekeeping from your
wallet. Have to feed ourselves somehow!

His wallet sat on the table, empty. Most of his wages had been in there. He'd withdrawn extra to cover the petrol, power and car insurance. They had plenty in savings, but it would be a tight month. The whole idea of savings was that they didn't spend it.

Whoever had been at the door had gone. The cupboards were as empty as Mother Hubbard's, even the disgusting junk food was gone, and most of the alcohol.

Five peaceful days passed before Barbara and the girls returned.

They chatted and giggled together, and walked out of the room when Kevin entered. Barb still slept in one of the other rooms.

Kevin was generally ignored. It was an uneasy truce.

Barbara and the girls sat at the kitchen table, eating toast and jam. A box of groceries on the bench told him that Barb had ordered from Young's, an expensive alternative, despite there now being a choice of supermarkets in Emory.

It was the first time all four had been in the same room since they had returned from visiting Barbara's mother.

"Glad you're all here, because I think we all need to talk about some changes," Kevin said.

"Are we moving?"

"No, Darlene. We can't afford to."

Barbara rolled her eyes. "You could get a mortgage."

"I've only just paid one off. I don't want another. Anyway,

we need to get some savings behind us."

"Oh, you're so mean!" Darlene screamed. "I can't wait to leave this disgusting hovel."

Kevin bit his tongue. Nothing he said would help things.

"The mortgage was paid off two years ago, Kev. You are the only person I have ever heard of who chose a fifteen-year mortgage and paid it off in ten. But that gives us plenty of time to pay off another. There's a lovely house in Morning Point, five bedrooms, two dining rooms, two lounges, three bathrooms. So lovely." Barbara sighed wistfully.

"Why would we need five bedrooms, and two lounges. The girls will leave home in a few years. Unless you plan to have boarders to help pay off the mortgage?"

"Boarders?" She looked horrified. "Open my house to strangers? Never. Only common trash stoop to taking boarders."

"Not only is that not true, Barb, it's not fair."

"Oh, you would take that Bella's side. Looks as if sugar wouldn't melt in her mouth, that one, but she has that young man there now, and who knows what goes on when the front door is closed. And those poor little children in there too. What're they seeing? Bella could even be offering Lara—"

"Stop it, Barbara! You have an evil mind, but at least keep it to yourself." Kevin was disgusted.

"We'll need five bedrooms so the girls can visit, bring their husbands and children. We'll want them to stay for their holidays and..."

Kevin leaned down and picked up a small roll of paper someone had dropped on the floor.

As Barbara wittered on about the house in Morning Point and long visits, he unrolled it and glanced down.

"This is a school leaving certificate. Darlene? What's..."

She went very still, then patted her permed curls, and

sidled nearer her mother. "I've got a job."

"You're thirteen. You can't get a job until you're sixteen."

"Well, I got one, and the school said I could leave if I had the certificate."

Kevin glanced again at the certificate. "What sane business would hire you? They'd know you're only thirteen just by looking at you."

"They interviewed me over the phone. Millie said I was perfect. I'm starting on Monday."

"What did she want to know?"

"What hours I wanted to work and all sorts of other things."

"Such as?"

"Whether I'd be happy dressing up and could I talk to people and things. Millie said I spoke beautifully."

"What's the name of the business?" Kevin asked.

"It's a private club," Darlene said quickly. "I serve drinks and snacks. I talk to the customers, and dance if they want me to, and they'll take me out for meals and drinks and things."

"It sounds very nice," said Barbara.

"What's the business called, Barb?"

Barbara looked blank, and Kevin turned to Darlene.

"The Turkish Rooms. See it is a real—"

"Cheese, Darl, it's a whore-house!"

"Do not use words like that in front of my girls. And her name is Darlene."

"She'll hear a damn sight worse if she goes to work in a brothel. She'll get a fair visual education, too. You can't work there until you're twenty-one, Darlene. Then you'll be on your back, not eating out in posh restaurants."

"Language, Kevin. Don't be so vulgar. Go to school, girls. Now, I'll…"

"We can't," Jolene said. "We've missed the bus."

Kevin glanced at the clock. 8:48 a.m. He decided there was no point in furthering the argument. "You girls get in the car. I'll take you. Oh, Darlene, open your bag."

"Muuum!"

"Really, Kevin. Some things are private and personal."

"She connived to leave school illegally, and was planning to work in a brothel. I think privacy is a privilege she no longer deserves." He grabbed the bag, opened it and pulled out the six-inch strip of stretch material Darlene wore as a skirt, her old bikini bra, trimmed until it was little more than nipple covers, and a packet of cigarettes. He threw them on the table.

"Did you know she was smoking, Barb?"

Barb shrugged. "I knew she had tried them. They all try it at that age."

"Jolene?"

Jolene handed her bag over. "Just because she—"

"Button it, Missy. I will be checking your bags every day from now on. Now get in the car."

"None of this would be happening if we lived in Auckland."

"Oh, yes it would. It'd be worse, Barb. I'm not prepared to move at this stage. I won't move the girls from school. When they're sixteen, they can leave and do what they want. They'll leave home and not be my problem. At that stage, we can make plans for the next five years, but I'd want to downsize then. We could buy a section, and build a nice new house."

"I will not live in a tiny dump just because you want to. I'd prefer to leave you."

"Any time you like, Barbara."

With the girls in tow, Kevin walked into the school office. "I'd like to see the Third Form Dean."

"The secretary glanced down at a large diary in front of her. "She has an opening next Thursday."

"Now! I'll wait." He gestured to the seats. "Sit down, girls."

The secretary looked flustered. "Perhaps the girls can take a note to her on their way to class, Mr Smythe."

"No they can't. I'm not letting them out of my sight until I sort out the irresponsible attitude this school has to the day-time care of them. And my name is *Smith!*"

She blushed further and picked up the phone. Moments later, a fifth form boy ran in, glanced enquiringly at the girls, collected a note from the secretary and ran out.

"Now it'll be all over the school," Darlene hissed. "I hate you!"

Ten long minutes later, a middle-aged woman walked into the waiting room, glanced at Jolene and Darlene, and held out her hand to Kevin.

"Joan, Joan Allen. It's nice to finally meet you, Mr Smith." She ushered them all into a small office, pointed to two stools for the girls to sit on and angled a chair for Kevin as she slipped behind the desk. "I think it's a good idea to separate the girls, Mr Smith. Have you decided on Darlene's school yet? We'll need to send on her records."

Kevin handed over the leaving certificate. "She's not leaving. This was done without my knowledge or approval. She evidently planned to go and work at The Turkish Rooms. It's a—"

"I know what it is," Joan said, quickly. "She told me you were sending her to a school in Auckland."

"Well, I'm not, and if ever I have plans to leave Emory, I will inform you personally. How could she do this without a parent's signature?"

"Honestly, I don't think it's ever happened before." Joan took a deep breath. "Mr Smith, it's Kevin, isn't it?"

He nodded.

"Kevin, most girls don't leave here until they're between sixteen and eighteen. Then there's no need for a parent's signature. Of the rest, well, we trust the girls, and my goodness, this is a huge shock. Believe me, it won't happen again. I'll make sure of that. The certificates and the rules will be changed immediately."

"You talked of separating the girls. Why?"

"They're very disruptive together. I felt it would be better for everyone if there was a change. We've been hoping you'd come in for a parent-teacher interview. I have written to you. Darlene told me you were often out of town, and her mother wasn't well."

"Darlene is proving to be a very adept little liar."

"Mr Smith. We don't label our girls."

"Then how would you describe her behaviour? I have asked about interviews. She told me you don't do them any longer because the teachers have too much work. So, the word liar is quite tame."

Kevin left the school with a lot to think about; Jolene had been put into Three B, where she would have to work a lot harder and finish her homework. She would be assessed in two months; Kevin had already arranged the meeting. Darlene went into Three G, a general class with a wider range of practical subjects and an older female teacher, known to be extremely strict. Neither girl was particularly pleased.

There had also been issues with their school uniforms.

Darlene's was excessively short and both were far too tight. A look through the 'uniform for sale' cupboard gave an almost new skirt for Darlene, while everything in Jolene's size proved to be too wide.

"So I'll need to buy her a new one," said Kevin. "It's ridiculous. Just four months since I bought those."

Joan glanced at the skirt and then at the twins, sitting sullenly on their stools. "I have a solution. I'm sure Mrs Harris, our sewing teacher would be happy to alter a skirt for Jolene. Jolene can take it to her now, along with a note, wait for it to be done, change and bring her old skirt back here."

"Mum won't let us wear other people's cast-offs, Kev," Darlene said.

"That's enough from you, missy. You will wear that skirt, and you'll do nothing to alter it. Do you hear me? The skirt you were wearing was new, and it looked nothing like that when I paid for it."

Jolene shrugged and nodded. Darlene glowered at her feet.

Kevin's next stop was The Turkish Rooms, where he had an equally forthright discussion with a *Miss Millie*. A threat to go to the police brought the promise of a change in their hiring policy, and he left still annoyed, but satisfied. He arrived at work at 11.15a.m.

Kevin decided to be up-front with Mr Morgan. He liked and respected the man, who also had daughters.

Mr Morgan roared with laughter, commiserated, and thanked him for being honest. "You were seen going into The Turkish Rooms this morning. Don't worry, I put a stop to the gossip, and I will further step on it, but it's nice to know you weren't there for the usual reason. This will go no further, believe me."

He walked into his office, chuckling quietly.

An uneasy peace settled over number twenty-three. Barbara still slept in the spare room, although she had politely suggested they switch and she have the larger master bedroom.

Kevin, just as politely, declined, and she backed off. Other than that, she ignored him most of the time.

Darlene still appeared to hate him, and refused to acknowledge him at all. For the next few evenings, she slumped dejectedly in front of television, and then wandered off to the park, although she made sure she was home by teatime.

However, Jolene settled down to homework in the evenings, and seemed to be enjoying the work.

Kevin made a small desk for each of them, to sit beside their beds. Darlene dumped hers in the back yard, but Jolene used hers when Barbara wanted the dining room table.

Kevin hoped the problems were now over.

In August, 1984, Barbara began talking again about moving to Morning Point, although she had found a different house. She had a flash coloured brochure, which she showed Kevin along with a half page article from The Emory Times, displaying it at its hideous best.

Kevin hated the house. It was everything a comfortable house was not. All sharp corners, sleek lines, little furniture and what was there looked dreadfully uncomfortable. He knew Barbara would copy the furniture style if she ever got the chance to move there, but he was relieved to see the price. It was so far out of their league, even Barbara had to accept it was beyond belief.

"Even if we got top dollar for this house, the bank wouldn't lend us the difference, Barb."

"But if we only needed ten thousand dollars they would, wouldn't they?"

"If we got a second mortgage, we'd have to declare it. It comes down to my ability to repay it, and I couldn't."

He was talking to her back; she'd gone into the kitchen.

"But if we were only about ten thousand short?" she said, as she returned with a tray holding four glasses and something in a bottle with a tea towel wrapped around it like a napkin. "Champagne! We're celebrating." She poured four glasses of something pale and bubbly, and handed one to each of them. "To a new home."

Kevin watched in horror as Darlene downed her glass and held it out for a refill.

"That's enough, Darlene. No, Barb. She shouldn't—"

He stopped speaking when Barbara defiantly refilled the glass, and did the same to her own.

"Oh don't be a spoilsport. We never celebrate anything."

Darlene again emptied her glass before Kevin could take it off her. He took Jolene's glass, noting with relief it was still full. He emptied it and his into a plant pot that was now devoid of the dead plant it had once held.

"I've sold the house," Barbara crowed, waving a strip of paper above her head.

Kevin went pale. "You what!? You can't! It's not in your name."

Barbara laughed. "You'll not complain when you see how much this is made out for."

Kev grabbed the strip of paper, a cheque, but it took a while for him to comprehend the amount it was written for. The numbers seemed wrong. There were too many zeros, but he realised they corresponded to the words.

He sat down heavily. "Someone's playing games with you, Barb."

"I'll cash it and you'll see. He was verrry wealthy, sooo attractive, reeeally posh car, only five hundred miles on the speedometer, and he took me out for a lovely expensive lunch. And he bought a bottle of champagne. It was divine."

"And the name of this man?"

Barbara opened her mouth, took a breath and paused. "I can't tell you. It's secret. I've agreed. If I tell you, well, he might need to pull out. Then we'd get nothing. Would you prefer to live near a sewage plant? Because evidently that's what the Council is going to put on the land behind us. This man is trying to stop it, but you can't tell anyone that. And we don't have to leave immediately. We can take our time finding the right house and redecorate it. Then we can buy new furniture, get it all in as we like. We won't even need to pay rent here. Tony was so sweet about it. Even if we take a year or eighteen months to do it, he's fine with that. Not that we'd want to of course."

It was overwhelming. "It sounds too good to be true. I'll think about it, and talk to Ted Busby at the bank. He knows about these things."

"Don't give him any information. Just cash the cheque, because if you don't, I will. Now we can move into the house of my dreams. Everything will be so much better. I'll mix with the right people; the girls will marry their wealthy fiancés, although Darlene is almost engaged now anyway.

Everything will be just perfect."

Kevin folded the cheque into his wallet, and resolved to take good care of it until he had had a few words in some knowledgeable ears.

"Dad."

Kev glanced up. "Yes, Jo?"

"Her name's Jolene," interrupted Barb. "Don't bother him with all that nonsense, girl. I've told you what to do. Now come into the kitchen and help me with dinner. We'll have prawn cocktails for starters, and I'll add some melon balls. I bought a melon when Tony took me to Auckland for lunch. The supermarkets are so much nicer there. Better quality goods. We'll have a fruit bowl, too, with some petal-fours. Just like we made for dear Prince Charles when he came to visit last year. You can make those, Darlene dear. Come along now. Jolene, get out the napkins and set the table."

Kevin inwardly cringed at Barbara's mispronunciation, and then realised she was speaking to him.

"Did you hear me, Kevin? Go and put your jacket on. We'll dress for dinner."

"Jo," Kev called quietly, as she trailed behind the others. "What is it, love?"

"Nothing really." She looked very unhappy.

"Ask me anyway. I may be able to help."

"Dad, do I have to do what older people tell me?"

"That would depend on the older person. Me—yes, because I always have your best interests at heart. Your teachers generally, the police, and the doctor."

"Mum and Darlene?"

Kev took a quiet breath. That was dicey. "Jo, if you feel it's wrong, it generally is. If you're unsure, come and ask me. You don't have to do what your sister tells you. She's only twenty minutes older than you."

"Mum said I had to. All older people."

"Maybe Mum misunderstood the question." He smiled as she hugged him. It was the first time in a long time she'd allowed him to be that close. "How's school?"

She nodded, and almost smiled. "Hard work, but not as bad as I thought it'd be. I'm even enjoying the homework. Lara showed me how to make a schedule for it, and we study together in the library twice a week. I've worked hard enough to go into Four A next year. It's been fun. I know things I didn't know I knew."

"Good. I'm very proud of you."

"Jolene!" Barb screeched, from the kitchen. "Are you setting the table?"

Dinner was a strange affair; served later than usual, 'society hours', Barb said. She wore her posh dress, and talked of dressing for dinner every night from now on, and getting a fancy new wardrobe, "because I can't possibly wear the same dress every night, can I?"

She'd bought a new bright yellow tablecloth, with hideous orange napkins.

The prawns were palatable, but needed shelling. The melon oblongs, no melon baller, Kev suspected, still had seeds in them. The lettuce under them was more wilted than he liked, and Barb's *petal-fours* were Snax biscuits with a buttery mayonnaise on them.

"Just lovely," Barb said, as she carefully folded her napkin after dabbing the corners of her mouth. "We'll have more meals like this from now on. I bought a lovely new cookery book from Auckland, so I'll begin experimenting." She picked up the wine bottle and filled her glass.

"No more for the girls, Barbara. They have school in the

morning. In fact, if that's dinner, I think they need to get their homework done. I'll clear the table. You'll want to watch Peyton Place."

"I don't have homework," said Darlene. "Mum, can I go to the park?"

"Yes, Jolene can go too. Keep you company. But be home by ten, otherwise your father will fuss."

"No, Barbara. It's almost dark. Jolene has homework."

"Oh, pish, she's still young, Kev. You make that girl work too hard. And tonight is a celebration."

"Go to your room, Jolene," Kev said.

Jolene raced away. Darlene melted out of the room, and the front door banged. Kevin turned back to the table, and realised again, that Barbara was fuming.

"Don't tell my girls what to do," she snapped.

"They're my girls too, Barbara, unless there's something you want to tell me."

"What are you implying?"

He stood, turned on television, and began to stack the plates.

Barb opened her mouth, heard the music for Peyton Place and, glowering at him, sat down to watch.

Must remember that ploy.

He took the plates into the kitchen, stacked them and ran hot water over them. While waiting for the sink to fill, he cut four slices of bread, buttered them and, for want of anything else healthy from the cupboard, grated apple and cheese over it. He turned off the taps, took the plate to Jolene's room, sat and shared the sandwiches with her.

"It's an interesting combination," said Jolene. "I like it. I wouldn't have thought of it."

"My nan's favourite. You'd have liked her. I wish she was still alive. She always gave really good advice."

He said goodnight, took the plate back to the kitchen,

rinsed, dried, and put it away, washed the dishes and left them to drip-dry.

Kevin talked to the bank manager, Ted Busby, at lunchtime the following day.

"I'm glad you came in, Kevin. If you hadn't, I'd have rung and asked you to."

Kevin handed over the cheque. "Is this genuine?"

Mr Busby glanced at it and sat it on the desk in front of him. "You realise there is little I can tell you about another client's account." Kev nodded. "However, this company has been very active in Emory recently. All other cheques written on this account have cleared. By all means, bank it."

"Why would they want to buy my house?"

"They're a big player in Emory, it seems. I can't tell you anything more, because I really don't know. I heard a whisper in the golf club that they do experimental farming on a grand scale, and plan one here. But as I said, it was only a whisper, and it wasn't from a reliable source."

"What would you suggest I do?"

"Cash it. If I was offered that much for my house, I'd be out of there as quickly as I could. Buy something a bit nicer, and put the rest aside for your retirement."

Kev nodded. "Now, why did you want to see me?"

"Oh, yes. There's been some unusual movement in your savings account lately. Unusual for you, that is." He fussed around with some paperwork, and pushed a page over the desk

Kevin stared in disbelief. His last five-year's savings had been reduced by almost a half.

"How? Who?"

"I've sent for more information, but it seems three cheques were cashed on different occasions in Auckland. Have you lost your cheque book?"

Kev slowly shook his head, reached into his jacket pocket, and pulled out the chequebook.

"Could some cheques have been stolen from it? If so, decide if you want us to involve the police. If theft is involved, we would strongly encourage you to."

Kevin opened the book to the relevant section and looked at the scribbles on the stubs. After a few moments of embarrassed silence, he took a deep breath. "Barbara."

"Barbara Smith has signing rights also," Mr Busby said, checking the details.

"Can I somehow ensure that from now on, only cheques signed by me, are cashed?"

"Not without her approval."

"It isn't a joint account; she just has signature rights to it. Can I remove her name?"

"Again, not without her knowledge."

"Oh!" Kevin thought quietly for a few minutes. "I'd like to withdraw all money from my accounts in this bank. Leave forty dollars in this account to keep it open. I imagine I couldn't close it at this stage anyway."

Mr Busby nodded, as he reached into a drawer for the necessary withdrawal forms. "We would be sorry to lose your custom."

Kevin signed at the bottom of a few pages, and handed them back to have the final amounts filled in.

As Mr Busby worked out the interest on his calculator, Kevin stared at the cheque, and tried to think clearly about his situation.

"Now tell me," Kevin said, as the transaction was finalised, "if I opened a new account in my name and deposited my money into it, would Barbara be able to withdraw from it?"

Ted Busby smiled. "We cannot tell her anything about any account here, other than her own, or one she has signatory rights on, and that would be the same in any bank you use. No, she couldn't withdraw from it."

"I'll do that then. I've been very happy with your bank." Kevin handed the cheque over. He filled out more forms, and ordered a chequebook to be sent to his office.

"The cheque will take ten working days to clear, and you should have your new chequebook soon after." Mr Busby shook Kevin's hand.

Six days of relative peace and quiet. Work was easy, Mr Morgan took three days off, and Kevin took over his duties. He'd done it before when Mr Morgan went on holiday, and this wasn't too different, except this time he was told to work out of Mr Morgan's big office.

Evenings were quieter. The television was on of course, and during the news and advertisements, Barbara wittered on about house redecoration and all the things she wanted to change when they bought the new house. Miniature obelisks, Laura Ashley wallpaper, vinyl floors, glass dining tables, venetian blinds and mirrors on all the doors. It all sounded hideous.

Raised voices from the dining room distracted Kevin from his newspaper. Barbara was engrossed with her television program, so he went to investigate.

"And stay away from me!" screamed Darlene. A number of books hit the hall wall in front of his face, and he saw the light go on in the girl's bedroom. He picked the books up and went down to see what had happened.

Jolene had an exercise book open on her bed. She was smoothing out one of three pages. A roll of Sellotape sat on her desk.

"What happened?"

"Nothing really. Darlene wanted to use the table. Evidently, Mum said she could. I didn't know."

"Darlene did that?"

Jolene nodded. "It's okay, Dad, I can sellotape the pages back in. The teacher will be okay; it's still readable. She'll know I've done the work. Anyway, I have more homework to do. I'm fine."

Kev walked into the dining room in time to see Darlene smoothing her uniform skirt out on the table. She reached for a pair of scissors, but Kevin grabbed them first. "You will not do that, Darlene. I told you, this uniform will stay intact."

Darlene glared at him, made a lunge for the scissors, and cursed when she missed. "It's a horrid skirt; it's like wearing a tent."

"Nevertheless, that's the uniform, and it will stay as it is."

"I don't know why Barb puts up with you," she yelled. "I can't wait for her to chuck you out. You are so sad. I hate you!"

"What's going on?" Barbara stood at the door.

"She was about to cut the bottom off her school uniform skirt."

"I said she could."

Kevin stared at Barb in horror. "They've said if she does, we'll have to buy her a new skirt. This is the second one this year, Barb. We can't afford to keep replacing it. Especially as she's been told."

"Oh, that's ridiculous. The skirts are gormless. She's just a young girl. She needs freedom, fashion. Not long constricting skirts like that."

"Those are the rules, and if you have a complaint, take it up with Mrs Allen, the Third Form Dean. However, Darlene's uniform stays as it is. No argument."

"Muu-uum!" Darlene wailed. She threw the skirt across the room, picked up a couple of spoons that were sitting on the table and threw them too.

"Darlene!" Kevin thundered. "Stop it! Now!"

She began to scream.

Barbara stared at Kevin, angrily. "Go to your room for now, Darlene. I'll bring you a glass of something nice."

"No," said Kevin. "Jolene is studying. She shouldn't be disturbed. I'll get Darlene a glass of water."

He took the scissors with him and put them in the everything drawer, grabbed a glass, filled it, and returned to the dining room. Darlene began throwing more things as soon as he appeared. Table napkins, the tablecloth, other spoons and forks. Soon all that would be left would be the good glasses that sat in the dresser.

"Calm down and drink this." Kevin held out the glass, wondering if that too would hit the wall.

"Have this too, dear." Barbara handed her a small pale blue pill.

"What's that?" Kevin asked.

"Just a wee happy pill. It'll help calm her down."

"Valium?"

"It's just one. She's become very nervy with you picking

on her all the time. This will help her settle."

"A glass of water and a few deep breaths will calm her down."

Darlene grabbed the glass off Kevin, swallowed the tablet, and stared at him defiantly.

"You see, Kev. It worked."

"At that speed, it didn't have time to touch her tonsils, let alone work. And you can stop that now, missy," he said, as Darlene took another deep breath.

"Oh, go bite ya bum," she muttered.

Barbara stepped in between Darlene and Kevin. "Go into my room, Darlene, dear. Lie down for a while. You can sleep in there with me, tonight."

Darlene left still mumbling under her breath.

Barbara opened her mouth, but clearly had second thoughts and followed her.

Kevin was adding up the previous week's takings when Barbara walked in.

"I just went to the bank to cash a cheque," she said. "They couldn't, they said there wasn't enough money there. I was so embarrassed. It's ridiculous that you earn so little. You can't even afford to feed your family." Her voice rose, as she spoke.

Mr Morgan stepped out of his office. "Please keep your voice down, Mrs Smith." He turned to Kevin. "Perhaps you'd like to talk in here, Kevin. A little more private. I'll take an early morning tea."

He walked out without acknowledging Barbara, who followed Kevin into the office. He closed the door firmly.

"Please keep your voice down, or our business will be

heard in the shop. Now what's the problem? I know your housekeeping was in there. I talked to Mr Busby this morning."

"Why have you changed the account?"

"Bank security picked up some unusual withdrawals a few weeks ago. They're getting more information, but the withdrawals happened out of town, so it'll take a while to sort out." He sat down behind the desk, watched Barbara and wondered if she would own up to the withdrawals.

"It's most inconvenient. You should have warned me."

"Well, if your housekeeping money isn't in there, I will ring Mr Busby again and get him to call the police."

"Oh, no, I thought I'd get new shoes for Darlene. She has had such a stressful year. I'll leave it until everything's back to normal." She looked around. "What an absolutely ghastly little office. You really should consider transferring to Auckland, although anywhere would be better than here." She swept out of the room, slammed the door, and the outer office door behind her.

Kevin returned to desk, pulled out the bank statement he had received yesterday, sat and studied it for a few minutes. Although Barbara hadn't lied, she also hadn't owned up to cashing the cheques. *Does she think the bank won't find out?* Well, it was time for a few decisions, and Kevin knew not only what he wanted to do, but how to do it.

"Everything sorted?" Mr Morgan put his head around the door.

Kevin nodded. "I've made a few decisions."

"Good. Now act on them. The longer you leave it, the harder it will be. If you need some help or advice, my door is always open."

Four days later, Kevin opened his new chequebook, double-checked his addition, filled out some details on the top cheque, crossed and signed it. Then he folded it and put it in his jacket pocket. He then put the chequebook into an envelope, sealed it and placed it in the office safe. He stood, took a deep breath, squared his shoulders and left the office.

Kevin drove the car into the drive. He sat for a few moments, savouring the quiet.

He left his briefcase in the car, rechecked he had everything he needed in his pocket, locked the car and walked inside.

Barbara sat in the lounge watching a soap opera. The sofa was covered with open magazines and advertising gumpf from shops based in Auckland.

He pushed them aside, ignoring Barbara's screech of protest, leaned over and turned the television off, eliciting another complaint, also ignored.

"Barbara, the cheque cleared, so the money for the house is in the account."

Suddenly, he had her undivided attention, but as he took a breath to continue…

"Darlene! Jolene! Come here. We're celebrating."

Kevin groaned inwardly. This wasn't how he wanted it, although he realised with Barbara, nothing would happen unless she had an audience.

"Oh well, I guess this affects them too," he said.

Barbara ignored him until she had her bottle of bubbly open and poured into four glasses.

"I've sold the house, girls," she said, sipping her wine. "We'll be living at Morning Point within a few weeks!"

"No, Barbara!" Kevin said. "Listen for once. I've made a decision. I'm leaving you."

As what he said registered, she was speechless for a few moments. Then, "But—but—what…"

Jolene raced out of the room. Darlene sat on what Kevin realised was once his chair, and placed her feet on the footstool.

"This is for you."

He pulled a cheque from his jacket inner pocket, and handed it to her.

"Barbara, listen to me. That cheque is made out for half of our money, less the amount you took from our joint account while you were in Auckland a few weeks back."

She stared up at him. "I can't buy a house in Morning Point with this."

Kevin ignored her. "It's made out specifically to you, and it's crossed, so you have to put it into your bank account. You cannot cash it and then pretend you've received nothing. That amount will buy you a very nice modest house and car, with a little left over. You will survive very well, as long as you get an income and watch what you spend. You can keep the furniture, that's offset by the car, which I will keep. I have photos of the furniture, so you can't claim you don't have it."

Darlene leaned over and picked up a glass of bubbly and drank half in one gulp.

Kevin took the glass off her, took that and the bottle into the kitchen and sat them in the sink. Then he went to the bedroom and put the final few items he owned, into a bag. His other possessions had been taken out in his brief-case over the last ten days, and stored in the flat he had rented. He collected his shaver and toothbrush from the bathroom, packed them, picked up the bag and returned to the lounge.

Darlene still sat in his chair, sipping from another glass of bubbly. He ignored her.

Barbara sat on the couch staring at the cheque. "You can't leave me! What about the—well everything? How can I live?"

Kevin sat opposite her, and pulled out the old chequebook. "Barbara, I'm giving you this. It has four cheques in it. That will give you housekeeping money until you organise yourself. Do not write them for more than forty dollars each, or they will bounce. I've taken my name off the account, so you can continue to use it if you like. Mr Busby will order you another cheque book if you ask him to. After that, there will be no more housekeeping. So you'll need to move fast to sort out what you want to do. Now I'm going. I'll let you know where I'm living."

Jolene walked back into the room carrying a suitcase and her schoolbag. "I'm coming with you, Dad."

Barbara stood and glowered at Kevin. "No! Jolene, you're staying here with me. If you leave me, Kevin, I'll make sure you never see the girls again."

Kevin picked up Jolene's bag. "She will come with me. Works out, a child each, although I will pay some maintenance toward Darlene until she leaves school. Jolene will visit you, and Darlene can visit us."

"You can't have Jolene. You're not her father."

Kevin pulled Jolene close. "How dare you say that in front of them? They have been my daughters since they day they were born. If you intend to argue about this, your neighbours can read about it in the court pages of the newspaper, because I will take you to court, and I will drag every sordid detail out of you. It might even make The Truth. But Jolene will be living with me. If you argue about it, you may also be explaining to the police about forging my name on the house sale papers. Last time I checked, that was a crime."

Barbara stared at him, and fumbled for her cigarettes. "How will I manage? Darlene's pregnant!"

"What?" Kevin grabbed the glass off Darlene, again took it and the other two glasses of bubbly into the kitchen, poured them down the sink, and returned to the lounge.

"How far along?"

"Four months."

"I'd suggest the two of you approach Darlene's wealthy young man, and organise some help with baby stuff. What he did was illegal, so I doubt you'll have too many arguments. He won't argue with the police, anyway."

Barbara was stunned. "You can't go to the police. They'll say it was her fault."

"Not when I tell them her age and his."

"Yes they will," Barbara said. "He caught her with his brother."

"That's not ideal, but the police will still—"

"And his best friend."

Kevin was shocked. "Well…"

"And then…"

Kevin pressed his lips together tightly.

"Cheese, Darlene. How many?"

Darlene shrugged. "Dunno!"

"Basically she doesn't know who the father is. Still, she's underage, and—"

"You're not going to the police. I told them all of them I was nineteen. I'll tell the police that as well. They'll laugh you out of the station. Anyway, it doesn't matter." Darlene grabbed Barbara's cigarettes. "I'll be fifteen when I have the baby. I'll go on the Single Mother's Benefit. Mum can too, actually. At least until I leave school."

"You have to stay, Kevin." Barbara, almost on her knees, had tears streaming down her face.

"No. I can't live like this. I've made up my mind, and

despite your promises, Barb, nothing will change it. You'll manage. I still think you should go to the police. I will come too."

"No! That would be so embarrassing. The whole street will gossip." Barb took a deep breath. "What will I do?" she wailed.

"Take Darlene to a doctor, and stop her from smoking and drinking. Be prepared for the police to be involved anyway, Barbara. I intend to tell them. Darlene is still underage, and the school will tell them, if we don't." Kevin picked up the bags and followed Jolene out to the car.

Barbara grabbed his arm when he got to the door. "Kevin, don't go. Things will change, I promise."

He shook her off. "I've heard it all before, Barbara."

"What am I going to do?" she wailed.

"Maybe you should get a job."

Kevin backed the car out, but turned west, and drove slowly around the oak tree.

Jolene waved at Lara as she passed.

"You seem to be good friends with her now, Jo."

Jolene smiled. "She's choice. Mum always said she and her mum were stuck-up bitches, but they're nice. Lara studies hard, and she really helped me at the start. We'll be in the same class next year. She's asked me to be her study-mate. She wants to go to a university in England. She said I was bright enough to go too. I'd like to try for the exams, but it's expensive."

"It's a good goal, and I'm sure we'll manage it. You'll still be at the same school as Lara, and maybe she can come and visit us."

At the intersection to the main road, they both glanced back.

"I'll miss Oak Tree Lane. Some nice people live here. But you've not been very happy here, have you, Dad?"

"Oh, it's a great street. Barbara and I, well we weren't so good together, although, without her, I wouldn't have you."

"Maybe you should have married the street, not Mum."

He laughed. "Come on, honey. Let's go. I'll show you our new home. Oak Tree Lane won't go away."

9

by Derin Attwood

Charlotte spat the tablets into her hand. They left a bitter taste in her mouth. She turned over and reached for the glass that sat beside her bed. Empty, and so was the jug. Maude had forgotten to fill it again. Charlotte wished her grand-niece, her sweet Becky was back with her. Becky would never have forgotten to fill the jug; would never have left her for hours and hours by herself. But Becky was now in England, her big OE, and her cousin Maude had taken over.

She day-dreamed for most of the morning, remembering back to when the house was being built, room by room, as Papa had the time, materials and help. For that reason, the house meandered, some rooms set to catch the sun, others to get breezes on hot days, and others with easy access to the garden walks or the lawn. The bedrooms were built to get the winter sun in the morning, with French doors opening onto the wide veranda, to keep them cool in summer and maybe gather a breeze. The passages were wide, so two people carrying trays, could easily pass, and the kitchen dining room was big enough for the family to share breakfast together. She remembered when it was full of people and noise, ten older brothers, and eventually their fiancées, wives and children. She remembered back to when the house echoed with the sounds of shouts, laughter, and the thud of stockinged or bare feet.

Papa had added a sunny tea room to the north-western corner of the kitchen for her, so she could sit and read her books while enjoying a pot of tea or a glass of wine in the afternoon. It was set for afternoon sun, but sheltered in summer by the large pear tree, conveniently off the kitchen so the heat from the stove would warm it in winter. A French door opened out onto the flower garden, to get the fragrances and breezes of spring and summer. When she was older, her closest friends would join her there, sewing, and chatting or reading, before dressing for dinner with the rest of the family. Charlotte's tea room was a happy noisy place.

Charlotte's other favourite room was Mama's blue room, called so because of its colour. It was there Mama took tea with her visitors, and rested in the afternoon warmth. It sat on the far side of the house, away from the bustle and noise. Set to get the sun all day, it had two of the many large bookcases in it, along with comfortable chairs, rugs and cushions, so a reader could be contented all year round. Charlotte's innovation for the room had been a large bay window jutting out over the garden on the eastern side. She asked Papa to put in a window seat, and add bookcases up the walls. With heavy velvet drapes to pull across, the window seat was the perfect morning hideaway. It warmed quickly in winter, and had everything Charlotte or Mama wanted, warmth, books, and a view of the gardens.

The house was full of noise then, children laughing and screaming, Mrs Wallace the housekeeper and her helpers calling to each other or shouting at the boys for treading dirt across newly scrubbed floors and on half a dozen occasions, allowing the hens, and a litter of piglets, to escape and run riot through the kitchen.

She remembered Papa organising a romantic dinner for Mama on the veranda, playing songs on the gramophone, and dancing with her as the meal grew cold. The boys, eating in the kitchen, made retching sounds, until Mrs Wallace sent them out to eat in the barn with the other animals.

Was that why I never married, because I couldn't find anyone who could live up to Papa? Well, not after Peter died. My dear sweet Peter, Charlotte mused.

She was suddenly awake, but what had woken her? There was no noise outside, no shouts of children to waken her, but she felt more alert. She glanced at the shadows; it was about midday. Hunger gnawed at her belly, perhaps that was what had jolted her back into to consciousness. She wondered when she had last eaten, but realised she was far more thirsty than hungry. Maude wouldn't be back until late afternoon, too long to wait.

The bathroom was the nearest place for water. Charlotte was pleased Papa had built it so close to the bedrooms, but the walk there took her longer than she believed possible. She was terribly weak. She went from handhold to handhold; the bedside cabinet, the bedroom chair, the door-frame, and when there was nothing else, the wall. There were no towels hanging in the bathroom, and only a few old facecloths in the cupboard.

Maude must have put them all in the linen closet. I must remind her to put a new set in here every Monday. Perhaps she didn't, because I've been unwell. How long has it been? I've lost track of the days, but surely, I haven't been unaware of everything for a full week.

Charlotte didn't drink a lot—her body couldn't cope with

too much—and long before she wanted to, she put the glass back on the shelf. She washed the nasty little tablets down the sink, making sure they had fully disappeared, and decided she needed some food. Her journey to the kitchen was made in fits and starts; the same way she walked to the bathroom. Again, she was shocked at how long it took, and how weak she felt.

Charlotte didn't really take a lot of notice of her surroundings, her hunger and exhaustion meant she just concentrated getting to the kitchen. However, she did note that the two chairs in the passage were now old kitchen chairs, not the lovely tapestry seats she had covered in time for Mama's sixtieth birthday. They had taken a long time to embroider, but the delight on her mama's face had made it all worthwhile. And they had been so comfortable.

Maude must have shifted them. I'll ask her to put them back.

However, when she stepped into the kitchen, everything else was wiped from her mind. The huge kitchen table, the matching chairs, the oak dresser, the small round tea table and chairs, Mama's armchair, everything in fact, was gone.

My furniture! Where is it?

Nothing was left except shadows on the walls and floor. Shadows that told of pictures, chairs, cabinets and other pieces of furniture. She touched the dark area on the wall where the dresser had sat since before she was born. Gone, and everything in it. Her grandmother's crockery, brought over from Cornwall when her parents emigrated, the silver cutlery; a gift from Charlotte and her brothers in 1914, to her parents for their fiftieth wedding anniversary. Everything her papa and brothers had made, the presents given to her and her mama over the years, all her family had collected and valued for more than a century. Only the Aga stove, the sink bench, and the plate rack, still screwed to the wall above the sink, were left. The room, that seemed so small when bustling with people and full of furniture, was now so big, it echoed.

In shock, she wandered back into the passage, and then realised the long mat that graced the centre of it was gone. She was so used to walking on the wood to one side—a long-term family habit, to ensure the mat stayed in pristine condition—she hadn't noticed.

Her first thought was to get back to bed where she could think about everything, but again, her stomach gurgled, so she returned to the kitchen.

The fridge, the obvious place for food, was gone; even the bread bin had disappeared. The pantry, or rather the room Charlotte used to store jams, preserves and dried food was also stripped of everything. However, back behind the door, was the old cool-store, where initially meat was hung to cool, and milk was kept before they had a fridge. She hoped it had been overlooked. Sadly, that too was empty, but what of the sliding panel in the left-hand wall. Few knew about that.

It slid open, and there was a small but divine piece of cheese, wrapped in muslin, and sitting beside it, the box of jewellery, gifts Papa had given her over the years. She pushed the dark blue jewellery box to the back of the nook, and took a bite of cheese. *Not much,* she warned herself. *You've not eaten in days. Don't overdo it.*

After two bites, Charlotte resolutely put the cheese back into its muslin, and started back to her bedroom. As she reached the east passage to where the bedrooms were, she caught a glimpse of the lounge ahead. The tables, normally visible from the passage, were gone.

Moments later, she stared at the massive room, big enough to hold everyone they loved and more, but now empty.

Empty! Everything was gone, the side-tables, the lounge

suites, the piano, the large mats that covered the floor, the pictures, the lamps, the bits and bobs the family had collected over more than a century of life, all gone.

Overwhelmed, Charlotte returned to her bedroom, and climbed into bed. Tears welled, but she took a deep breath. *Think,* she told herself. *You can go to pieces later, once you've figured this out.*

When could it have happened? She had slept a lot lately, day and night. That wasn't normal, certainly not for her. Maude hadn't mentioned it when she came that morning. Could it have happened since she left? The facts ran through her mind, until exhausted and in shock, Charlotte slept.

She woke to the shouts of children, so it must be about four o'clock. Maude was due in about half an hour, and Charlotte suddenly knew what she needed to do. She now suspected the tablets she had been given. The new doctor Maude brought along was horrid, not like Doctor Amberg, who had been caring for her for over twenty years. That was a different problem, one she would think about later. Right now, she needed to figure out why she was taking the tablets, tablets that seemed to do nothing, but make her sleep.

Charlotte's companion Becky, had been with her since she left school, although they had been close since Becky was born. Together they had had a wonderful time, more friends than anything else. Then Becky left on her OE, and Charlotte's middle brother, Jonny, had suggested his grand-daughter, Maude take over. Initially, everything was fine, although Maude never stayed through the evenings or overnight, which was the original agreement. Becky had rung when she got to England, and every week after that, a terrible expense, Charlotte felt. Becky was now on a six-week cruise, and would then travel around Europe for six months. Charlotte had forbidden her to ring, telling her to keep her money to spend on herself.

Days after Becky's weekly calls stopped, Charlotte had a few moments when she felt faint while drinking her afternoon tea. Maude had called the doctor, and insisted on him visiting immediately. When he arrived, he was a stranger.

"Amberg moved to Wellington; sold me his surgery," he said, when Charlotte asked for her own doctor.

The new doctor—he didn't introduce himself—interrupted her every time she tried to speak, had taken her temperature, held her wrist for a few moments, said he would prescribe some tablets, and told her to rest. "I'll tell Maude what to do for you."

He didn't explain what was happening to her, what the tablets were for, nor how long she should take them. Henry Amberg always explained what he was doing and why, but this man seemed not to see her. He and Maude talked for quite a long time in the lounge. Maude returned as his car drove away, and gave Charlotte two tablets.

"You have to take them twice a day, and he'll see you later in the week."

That was the last thing Charlotte really remembered until today. *I've slept far too much, and I'm sure it's because I'm taking the tablets. Yes, I do feel faint, but that's due to a lack of food and water.*

She dozed until she heard Maude's car chug up the drive. *I've got to keep alert, but act sleepy, and somehow make sure I don't swallow those damn tablets.*

She closed her eyes, let her body slump in the bed, but tried not to doze. As was usual for family, Maude used the French doors that led straight into the lounge. They opened, slammed shut, and Maude's footsteps echoed as she walked down the main passage, and turned up towards the bedrooms.

The door opened.

"Time for your tablets."

Charlotte rolled over, and tried to push herself up.

"I don't want to take them anymore."

"Don't be tiresome. The doctor said you have to. Just open your mouth."

"I want to see a different doctor."

Maude pushed the tablets into her mouth.

"Can you get me a glass of water, please?" she asked as she flipped them under her tongue.

"Just swallow them," Maude snapped, and slapped Charlotte on the face.

Charlotte was taken aback, felt tears form. Had the tablets not been firmly under her tongue, she would have swallowed them. "Maude!"

Maude slapped her again. "Just lay down and shut up. I'm sick of you." She walked out of the room, and slammed the door. Charlotte quickly spat the pills into her hand. She had only just closed her hand and pulled it under the sheet when the door opened again.

Maude didn't even acknowledge her, but walked over to the French doors, snapped a padlock onto the bolts papa had put on them years earlier, when a prisoner had escaped from Mt Eden prison. The police had advised everyone lock exterior doors, and Papa did, but once the man was captured, the locks were ignored.

Now, not only were they used, but they were padlocked shut. The door would not open without a key.

Maude turned around to see her watching her. "Don't try leaving." She walked away, "Stupid old bitch," she said, under her breath.

As Maude stamped down the passage, Charlotte wondered if Maude knew she had gone to the kitchen. *Was the passage floor dusty? Did I leave footprints? And if I did, would Maude return unexpectedly to try to catch me? What would happen if she did? She hit me! How far would she go?*

As the sound of the car faded, Charlotte thought of what she had learned during Maude's visit. Maude hadn't mentioned the furniture, and she had come through the lounge. So, she knew what had happened to it. She had come straight to the bedroom, it seemed the tablets were important. The bolt was already on the door. All she had done was add a padlock, and lock it.

Charlotte turned over to study it, but as she did, she heard Maude's car chug back up the hill. *Now I do have to act. The tablets would have put me in a deep sleep, so I must put up with everything, and not respond normally—perhaps not respond at all.*

Maude didn't bring her car to the lounge door as usual. Instead, she came through the front door. Had she walked up the hill, she may have surprised Charlotte, although the front door always alerted Charlotte to visitors. It always squeaked loudly.

Thank goodness Papa never managed to fix that squeak. I didn't hear a key, so maybe the locks are just for my door.

Charlotte closed her eyes, tried to breathe as if she was deeply asleep, keeping her eyes still. She could hear Maude tiptoe across the floor. Then something hit her on the side of her face, and she was grabbed by the shoulders and hauled across the bed.

Don't respond! her brain screamed, as she hit the floor. She couldn't help but whimper, however she made herself settle immediately. *React later!* She tried not to tense as she waited for another blow.

"So, the tablets do work," Maude mused, "and now you have fallen out of bed. Stupid old bitch. That'll help explain the bruises when they eventually find you. Of course, I've told everyone what a difficult bitch you've become. Quite doolally." She laughed and walked around the bed. Charlotte wondered if she would continue the attack, but instead, she went again to the French door. Charlotte was facing away from the door, so she couldn't check what Maude was doing. After what felt like a long time, Maude walked out of the room, slamming the door behind her. Because the movement was so violent, the wooden latch didn't catch, and the door swung open again, but Maude continued through Papa's study, the shortcut to the front passage. The front door squeaked open and closed, but Charlotte lay still until she heard Maude's car freewheel down the hill and roar up the cul-de-sac.

Then she cried. For the pain that now wracked her body, the hunger, the loneliness, and the fear. She didn't move, she no longer had the energy.

If Maude comes back, you will never get away again, and she could return at any time.

The thought galvanised her into activity.

She opened her eyes, the room was dark. *It's almost night. Have I dithered about for so long?* She dragged herself to her knees, waited until her head stopped spinning, then using the bed to help her, gingerly got to her feet. She paused, leaning on the bed and glanced outside. The windows had been covered with a black substance. Charlotte wondered what and why. *I'll find out later. Right now, I need to escape.*

Initially, she returned to the bathroom, dropped the tablets down the drain, and had another small glass of water. Then she quickly used the toilet. As she walked towards the garden door, the quickest way to get outside, she realised she was barefooted and wearing a nightdress she had worn for possibly a week. She went back to her bedroom and turned the light switch. Nothing happened. *Blown bulb. Oh well, I've dressed in the dark before.* She opened her wardrobe, but even in the half-light, she could see it was empty. Her drawers were also empty. *My beautiful clothes! All gone!*

She had a moment of grief when she thought of the clothes she had carefully bought over the last fifty years. Tears prickled her eyes.

Back in the passage and down to her parent's bedroom. The door was open, and from the passage, she could see it too, was empty. But the telephone was still screwed to the wall. Charlotte grabbed the handset and dialled one-one-one. When she listened, there was no sound. No ring tone. She put the hand piece back on the cradle, lifted it again and held it to her ear. No dial tone. No phone. She replaced the handset back on the cradle. *It's been cut off.* The easy option was gone.

Her nightdress looked worse in the light, so she resolutely turned towards the staircase at the back of the house. Every door she passed was open, and the rooms, empty. However, there were places in this house few others knew of, secret places she had played in when she was a child. Papa loved the idea of his children having special secret places to find and explore, and these had remained, even after they had grown up.

When she pressed the wall panel beside the forth stair-tread, the sixth step slid out; a hidden drawer. The fragrance of sandalwood and lavender wafted up, and she lifted three layers of washed muslin, and pulled out an old linen shift. Called a kirtle, a shift, a petticoat and a nightgown over the years. It had been in the family for quite a few generations, handed down to Mama to wear on her wedding night. It had been worn occasionally when needed, but had long gone out of fashion. Now, it was the best thing, the only thing available.

In the back bathroom, Charlotte slipped out of her stained gown. She ran a bowl of water, and when it didn't run even to warm, she realised the power had been cut. No power, no hot water. The towels and face-clothes were missing, so she used the hem of her old nightgown as a wash cloth. Once in the clean gown, she immediately felt better. Back to the pantry for another bite of cheese.

The kitchen door was then the closest, but the bolt had also been padlocked, as was the door in the storage pantry which led to a basement. It was the same with the garden door and the courtyard door, and the windows Charlotte saw as she passed. She went straight to the front door. That could not have been padlocked, because Maude had used it.

The front door, however, was locked, not a padlock, it was one she had seen advertised in the newspaper. It needed a key to open it, even from the inside. Charlotte fiddled with it, but quickly realised it was fool-proof.

For a few moments, she felt beaten, and the tears came unbidden. "You will not be a blubbering idiot," she told herself. "Jowan Thompson did not bring his daughter up to surrender."

There were other ways out of the house, although Charlotte had not used them in years. They were the delights of an agile young girl, not a stiffening, creaky old lady. *Well, if only a girl can escape, then that is what I must be. I'll not remain in this house while Maude has control.*

It was getting dark now. Charlotte walked through the library—all the books were gone—and pulled the bookcase open. This secret passage was not secret at all, and most people assumed it only went to the playroom. But half way along, turning a wall sconce opened a panel in the wall giving access to a small space. Once inside, the panel had to shut before another could be opened to reveal a narrow staircase. It was pitch black in there, but Charlotte had done this many times before. Although now she held onto the wall as she descended the stairs, she didn't feel as frightened as she had earlier, when she had roamed the empty, echoing rooms.

The wall at the bottom of the stairs could be opened, one just had to know where to push it, and then Charlotte was in the storage basement. There was little in there, that amount of storage had been needed with a family of thirteen, and as each of them left, fewer things were brought down here.

Charlotte pulled open the storm shutter; a little light entered, but not much, it was almost dark outside. In the past, she had needed to clamber on to a sack of potatoes to climb up, but she was taller now, and she would only need to pull herself up. It took her longer than she thought it would, more because she had less arm strength, a problem of age. However, five minutes later, she stood on dirt, and breathed freedom.

Her hair was covered with cobwebs. She brushed them off her face, but could do little else to be rid of them. Her nightgown was dusty, and she brushed as much as she could off, but the rest would have to wait until she was safe.

She followed the path to the corner of the house, and peered around at the drive. Even though it was getting dark, the drive was visible to the whole neighbourhood. If one of them, and here she was thinking about Barbara Smith, saw her and rang Maude, she would be back where she started. Maude did seem to get on well with Barbara, although she had made several derogatory comments about Kevin Smith.

Car lights turned into the lane, and Charlotte panicked. She darted into the old wooden summerhouse, and even though the car didn't come up the drive, she decided to remain there until it was fully dark. Then she would make her way down through the orchard. That would keep her out of sight for most of the escape, until she reached the lower meadow. She settled down to wait.

She woke with a start, when car lights flashed across the summerhouse as the car reached the top of the drive. Charlotte panicked again. Why had she fallen asleep? The car, not Marge's, disappeared around the house, and stopped outside the front door. Two people walked to the door, and a minute later, had disappeared.

Charlotte stumbled across the drive as fast as she could, and down into the trees. It was a dark night, a crescent moon and stars shone, but under the trees, little light showed. Even so, Charlotte knew the white of her nightgown would make her visible, so she worked her way down the hill some distance, crawled under a bush and huddled there, wondering what she should do next.

There were two houses close by, Barbara and Kevin Smith, and Annie Romford. No, she wasn't a Romford now, she had married her young man. Anne was lovely, but Charlotte had no idea how she would act in an emergency. But the other house held Barbara Smith, and she would broadcast the story far and wide. Annie really was the best option, and certainly the nearest. Also, there was a gate in the fence. Everyone used it as a shortcut to get between the houses when they were first built. If it was unlocked, it would make it quicker, easier, and it would mean she didn't have to go out onto the street where the occupants of ten houses could see her easily.

Her decision made, Charlotte carefully walked down through the orchard, trying not to make any noise. It was a slow journey. Her hair kept getting caught up on branches she couldn't see, she slipped several times. While she occasionally caught herself, more often she fell; her knees were soon grazed and bloodied, and her back hurt. She slipped against a tree trunk, hitting her cheek, it was swollen and bleeding. Her feet suffered; it was far too long since she had run barefooted between the trees. She stubbed her toes on deadfall, stood on sharp twigs and other prickly debris.

Eventually, she came to the edge of the trees. She was opposite the empty section between Annie, and Kevin and

Barbara Smith, but slightly closer to the Smiths. If she had been sure Kevin would answer the door, she would have gone there, but she knew Barbara would most likely ring Maude. Then she'd tell the whole neighbourhood.

So, Charlotte skirted along the edge of the trees, until she was as close to number twenty-seven as possible. She was shivering violently, unsure if it was nerves or cold.

She began her walk over the open area, feeling terribly vulnerable in the open. When she heard a car start-up, she froze. *Listen first,* she chided herself. Yes, it was coming down the hill, moving very slowly, and the lights would still pick her up before she could get to safety.

Charlotte darted over to a straggly bush, crawled under it, and curled up as small as she could. She could hear her heart beating loudly—surely the whole neighbourhood could hear it—she breathed deeply, trying to calm herself down. *Get a grip, girl. You faced a mob of angry tribesmen in Algeria easily enough. Breathe. But the tribesmen had turned and walked away, whereas Maude had hit her.* It was the first time someone had hit her with intent. That was more frightening than facing the tribesmen.

Breathe! Don't panic!

The car travelled in first gear, and a light from it flashed across the areas either side of the drive. They were searching for her. She semi-closed her eyes, knowing they could reflect the light if it hit her. She wouldn't shut them tight as she wished too, she needed to know what was happening around her. If they saw her, she still had a small chance of escape, so she needed as much warning as she could get.

The car stopped, the passenger got out and shone the torch over the field. It lingered here and there; Charlotte's heart was in her mouth as it paused on the bush she was hiding under. She tensed, ready to spring up and run towards safety. She mentally planned the race to the old gate in the fence, wondering if it was still there.

The light disappeared, the car door slammed, and the car slowly continued down the drive and out onto the lane.

Charlotte got to her feet and continued across the field as fast as she could, but the lights of the car washed over her again. The car had continued around the oak tree, and back up the drive.

They've seen me! She tried to move faster, praying the gate would still be there, and unlocked, so she could use it. She felt so weak.

The car turned onto the field; it had to use the tractor track, the rest of the ground would be too soft, and that would give her added seconds.

The car was opposite her when she reached the fence, and began to feel along it for the gate. Already she was thinking ahead. If the gate wasn't there, she would continue around the fence, past the Romford house, and get to Annie's front door—and she would scream and scream until someone heard her, even if it was Barbara Smith.

The car door slammed.

"Grab her!"

That was Maude.

"Stop, you stupid old woman. Stop!"

It's a man's voice, the doctor!

Charlotte found the gate. She felt around for the opening to the bolt, terrified it had been padlocked. Her fingers closed over the bolt, and she worried it lose. Suddenly, it opened, and she almost fell through it. She pushed it shut, slid the bolt back home; hunkered down to push the bolt at the bottom of gate shut too.

The second bolt had been her papa's idea, to stop his boys swarming in on the Romfords when they just wanted peace and quiet. Such a sensible idea, better than a padlock.

Charlotte shuffled to the back door, and knocked on it.

She didn't make nearly enough noise. She moved closer, stood on a shoe, bent and picked it up. The heel of the shoe made more noise than her knuckles could, and she was rewarded when a light went on. She kept knocking, until the lock was turned and the door opened.

Not Annie! The woman who stared out at her was much younger.

"Help me, please! I've been attacked, robbed." Charlotte's brain was working overtime. Yes, Annie had sold the house. A family, three children, and her husband had died.

"Come on in. Oh, you poor thing. You're safe now. You're Miss Thompson, aren't you? I'm Bella Rudd."

"They're following me. They were at the gate." Charlotte was startled at how scared she sounded.

Bella reached past her, locked and bolted the door. "I won't let anyone in. Come and sit down, oh my goodness, you're freezing. Have you come down the hill wearing only that?" Bella guided Charlotte over to a chair by the stove. "I'll just get you a wrap."

From a hook beside the door, she took a crocheted shawl and wrapped it around Charlotte's shoulders. Bella pushed the kettle onto the stove. They both jumped when someone knocked loudly on the front door.

"Don't let them in, please!"

"I won't. I'm going to call the poli—" The kitchen door opened.

Charlotte whimpered and clung to Bella.

"Mum, what's going on?"

"It's all right, dear. This is my daughter. Lara, stay with Miss Thompson, I'll see to the door. Make a cuppa when the kettle boils."

Lara pulled a kitchen chair beside Charlotte, and held her hands. "Mum will handle them. No one will get into this house unless she agrees."

They both listened, but most of what was said was indistinct, until: "I'm going to call the police. Now get off my doorstep. Get off my property!"

There was a loud protest from beyond the front door.

"Police, please." More protest from outside, and then Bella's conversation was again unclear. After a few minutes, she put the phone down. "I told you, get off my property. You are trespassing. Get off my property." She closed the door and returned to the kitchen.

"I think we need to call your doctor. Who do you go to?"

"That man out there came last time. I don't like him, but he's taken over from Doctor Amberg."

"Didn't you take Mellie to Doctor Amberg on Thursday, Mum?"

"Yes, I did. I'll ring him."

She went back to the phone, spoke briefly, waited, spoke again, hung the phone up, and came back into the kitchen.

"He's coming straight away. Now, a cuppa. Lara, get some cups." Bella took over the chair Lara vacated. "I know you would like a wash, Miss Thompson, but I think you should wait until you've seen the doctor and the police. In the meantime, we need to get you warm. How long have you been outside?"

"Please call me Charlotte. I escaped just before dark."

Bella glanced up at the clock. "Seven hours! No wonder you're cold. Put some more wood on the stove, Lara." She left the kitchen, and returned moments later with two blankets. She wrapped Charlotte's feet in one, and lay the other over her knees. Both were warm.

"Straight off the hot-water cylinder," Bella said. "I talked to the police again, and asked them not to come to the door, until Doctor Amberg arrives."

Lara placed a cup and saucer on the table, looked at Charlotte's shaking hands, and brought a coffee mug out of the cupboard. She poured half a cup. "Sugar?"

"Yes, a heaped teaspoon, I think," Bella said, as Charlotte declined. "You're in shock," she added.

Charlotte sipped the tea, wondering how long it had been since she'd had a cuppa. More than a week, although she had only a loose grasp of the last few days. She jumped visibly when there was a loud knock at the front door.

"Don't worry, Charlotte, only the doctor and the police will get in."

Ben opened the kitchen door. "Mum, the car on the lawn has its lights on," Ben rubbed his eyes in the bright light.

"Is it a police car?"

"No, it's that blue zephyr, the one that almost hit me last week. The guy was driving like a maniac."

"Thank you, Ben. Go back to bed, please."

"Awwww, Mum. I'm awake now. I'll never get back to sleep. Anyway, Lara's up."

"That's Ben, my brother. Never one to be left out if there's something going on."

Ben and Lara looked very similar. Charlotte found herself smiling. "No one could ever mistake you two for anything other than brother and sister."

"That's 'cause we're twins," said Ben, matter-of-factly. "You're the mad old—" He stopped, his hand over his mouth, looking mortified.

"Ben!"

"Sorry, Mum. Sorry, ma'am. It's just that's what all the kids—" He stopped again. Bella looked furious.

"It's all right, Ben. I know some of the children call me a crazy old bat. I caught a few of them breaking branches in the orchard, and told them off. They were so rude, I talked to their parents." She studied Ben. "I've never seen either of you in the orchard."

"We don't trespass, Miss Thom—"

"Call me Charlotte, please."

Ben was still bright red. "Sorry, Miss Charlotte. Darleen Smith said everyone knew you were mad. But you seem okay. Well a bit hippyish, but-then-lots-of-people-are." He finished in a hurry and sighed deeply. "Maybe I should've gone back to bed."

There was another knock on the door; Bella went to see who it was. Moments later, she returned with a policeman, policewoman and Doctor Amberg.

"Sergeant Tim Williams, and this is Constable Amber Hunt." He turned to Bella. The couple who were trying to get into the house, left as we drove in. Do you know them?"

"He's a dark-haired guy, he drives a blue 1972 Zephyr with a black roof, and the number plate is FY5682," said Ben, as Bella shook her head.

The Sergeant's eyebrows rose a fraction. "That's very precise, young man. Are you sure?"

Ben looked affronted.

"He's very good with numbers," said Bella. "I've never known him to be wrong with them, and he knows more about cars than school work. Now can we concentrate on Miss Charlotte?"

Doctor Amberg had already taken over the chair beside Charlotte and was taking her pulse. He quickly finished the rest of his examination, and agreed Charlotte could give a statement to the police.

There was a moment of silence after Charlotte had finished speaking.

"I'll need to radio it in. Get them to contact Auckland in

case they've gone there. They could have changed cars, of course. Did your niece have access to one, Miss Charlotte?" Sergeant Williams asked.

"She drove a manky green beetle," Ben said. "1969, rego EZ1943. Miss Charlotte had a car too. It's really old, but nice. A red 1935 Humber Vogue. It used to have a really old number plate, but last time I saw it—that was three or four days ago—it had LR1212, which is fairly new. I didn't look at the driver," Ben said.

The sergeant patted him on the back, and went out to his car.

"We'll have to interview you all again," said Constable Hunt. "Probably in the morning. We'll call to let you know. If you can think of anything else, Miss, let us know."

"I'd like to know how they got the furniture away," Bella said.

"It would have needed a big truck if it went in one load," Doctor Amberg said. "Some of the pieces would be too big for just two people to lift."

"I'm surprised Barbara Smith hasn't been around to tell everyone about it. She would have seen something, she always does. Could the furniture have gone some other way?" Bella asked.

"Oh, Mr and Mrs Smith separated last week," Lara said. "Darleen missed school. She told the teacher her parents had split up, and they were living under a tree. Joleen had already told everyone they were staying with her nana. Darleen was annoyed; she hadn't done her homework, and got into trouble again. They're back together now, though."

"Mrs Smith will be furious when she realises that leaving her husband for a week, meant she missed such a huge story." Ben laughed.

Doctor Amberg stood. "Well if you've all finished, it's time I called an ambulance. Charlotte, I'm going to put you in hospital to ensure there are no other problems."

"No! I will not go to hospital."

"You can't go home, there's nothing there, and I don't want you to be left alone. Until I can get you a nurse, there is no other choice."

"I'm not sick, just a little tired, dehydrated and rather hungry. I'll go to a hotel."

"You could stay here," Bella said. "I have a spare room. I'm home all day, and I'd love your company."

Doctor Amberg nodded. "Very well, I'll agree to that, but I'll be back in the morning to check on you, and unless you have improved a lot, I will send you to hospital."

Charlotte was woken just before 7.00a.m., by Bella's door bell. A long, loud insistent ring.

Bella opened the door, and someone rushed past her. "Wha'? Ben!"

The front door closed and Charlotte's bedroom door opened. Bella entered. "I'm so sorry. It was only Ben. He has never done that before; I didn't even know he was out. He's on the phone right now, but I'll be having some serious words with him when he's finished. In the meantime, can I get you a cup of tea, or would you prefer to sleep?"

Charlotte decided she would get up and drink her tea in the kitchen.

Wearing the nightdress and dressing-gown Bella lent her, she sat beside the stove with a rug over her knees, as Bella cooked baked beans, poached eggs and toast. Charlotte asked for a poached egg, no toast.

As Bella was dishing up, Lara came down stairs carrying a smaller version of Bella, and introduced Mellie. "I thought we were all sleeping in, Mum," she said.

"I thought so too. You can go back to bed later if you wish. When I've sorted Ben out, I'll ring the school and tell them you won't be in."

Ten minutes later, Ben swaggered into the kitchen. "You are looking at totally awesome! ME!" He pointed to himself with all fingers.

"Benjamin Rudd! Why did you leave the house without telling me? How did you get outside? I thought you wanted a sleep in. If you have so much energy, perhaps you should go to school today."

"Oh, Mum! I couldn't sleep, and I couldn't get my book because it was in Miss Charlotte's room, so I went for a walk. I climbed down the fire escape, because I didn't want to upset anyone by leaving the front door unlocked. But it was all brilliant, because guess what?"

Ben looked expectantly from Bella to Lara. Neither responded.

"Okay, I'll tell you then. I walked over to the park, through the trees to the small carpark. There was a man getting into Miss Charlotte's car. He drove away, and I raced after him. Got to the road just in time to see him turn towards Auckland. So, I sprinted home—I bet I broke the four-minute mile record—and because I had the stitch, I rang the bell instead of using the fire-escape. I just talked to the police, got ta talk to the guy who was here last night, and he said he would let his mates down the line know, and he's sure they will pick him up before he reaches Auckland, and he promised to let me know what happens."

"Oh, well done, Ben," said Charlotte, after a long moment as everyone took in Ben's story. "You deserve a medal."

Bella nodded. "Yes, well done. But, do not climb down the fire escape. That's to use only when we practice, in case of an emergency, or when we do have a fire. Going for a walk, is not a good reason. Now, the police may not tell you what happens, although they will tell Miss Charlotte."

"But, he said he would tell me! It might be my tip-off that solves the case."

"Well, we'll see. But don't expect too much."

"If they don't tell you, Ben, I will," Charlotte said. "Now, eat some breakfast. You must be hungry after all that excitement."

They shared a quiet breakfast, broken at 09.15a.m. by Barbara Smith ringing the front door bell. When Bella answered, Barbara tried to push her way in, but Bella had wedged her foot behind the door, to ensure it could not open far. Barbara had seen Ben race home 'soon after dawn', as she put it. She put that and the late night Police visit together, and jumped to her own conclusions. Bella neither confirmed nor denied; Barbara would spin her own story no matter what was said.

Bella finally managed to shut and lock the door, when Lara took pity on her, and called out that Mellie needed her. Bella entered the kitchen to Mellie's outraged denials.

The police returned soon after 1.00p.m. Bella answered the door to let them in, Barbara Smith was standing on the footpath beside Bella's letterbox, watching and shaking her head.

"If you need any help, Bella, just call. I'll be there in a jiffy. It must be so hard, you a solo mum with a son who's running wild."

Bella closed the door firmly, locked it, and led the police into the kitchen. Lara had already put the kettle on, and was setting out the cups.

Everyone settled into chairs around the table, waiting expectantly.

"Well," Sergeant Williams began. "We've been checking out a few leads, but Ben gave us the best one so far. Your car was apprehended about eighty kilometres away. The driver, a Mr Bruce McKay was unknown to us. Do you recognise the name, Miss Thompson?"

Charlotte rolled her eyes. "It's Charlotte, and no, the name means nothing."

"He claimed he bought it legitimately, from a Charlotte Thompson. We believe he was conned. He is furious he's been involved in something illegal. He's cooperating as much as he can. Your car is in the police workshop. We will return it when the paperwork has been sorted out. So, well done, Ben."

"Now, we've a lead on your furniture," said Constable Hunt. "Realising that most of the furniture was antique, I knew it was unlikely they could attempt to sell the items in Emory, because advertising would be an issue. We rang several antique shops and auction houses in Auckland. None had any of the items, but one auctioneer had been offered pieces that sounded similar to the stolen furniture, with a hint of much more to come. They refused to buy sight unseen, but agreed to give a quick decision on sight. They wouldn't commit themselves, but said if all was true to description, it would have been a gold mine. They mentioned the seller had asked for advice on other possible buyers for vintage items, such as clothing and crockery etc."

"When will the stuff be there, Sarge?" Ben asked.

Tim laughed. "Not so fast, young Benjamin. Let Amber finish the story."

"Because the auctioneer was expecting everything in one load, we thought it may be taken down by a removal company. So, we rang around, and hit the jackpot. One of the companies has a large house-load of goods fitting the description of your things, Charlotte—they are waiting for the destination to be confirmed."

"Wouldn't the confirmation be done by phone?" Bella asked.

"Generally, yes, but the company has asked them to sign the confirmation personally, especially as it's such a valuable load, and they wanted the consignor to cover any loss or breakage."

"When will that happen, Constable? Lara asked.

"On Wednesday."

"Wow!" Ben's face was shining with excitement. "That's tomorrow. So, can I be with you when you meet the truck in Auckland, Sarge? I'll be able to tell Miss Charlotte all about it, because obviously, she can't be there."

"We will allow you to be there at the end, Ben, but you're not thinking at all like a policeman," Tim said.

"Why would they let the truck go through to Auckland," said Lara, "when it's still here in Emory?"

"Oh! I didn't think of that." Ben's face fell. "But that's even better. What time do you want me ready, Sarge?"

"We'll be with the truck when the paperwork is signed. I'm hoping your clothes will be there too, Ma'am," Tim said. "We—"

"Not Ma'am, please. It makes me sound like the queen," interrupted Charlotte. "So, you will arrest them then? What about my furniture? How long will you hold it? As welcoming as Bella is, I can't stay here until it's gone through court. I have nothing, not even a change of clothes. I doubt my wearable clothes will be there, although I never thought of the older items as being vintage."

"Let's first see if it is your furniture, Miss. If it is, it will need to be itemised, and to that end, it must go into storage." Tim looked meaningfully at Amber.

"Miss Thompson, our storage area is too small to hold such an excessive load, and we were wondering if we would be able to store it in your house. It's one of the few places we know that's big enough."

"Of course, that's an ideal resolution to your problem," Charlotte said, with a straight face.

"So, what time do you want me at the truck yard?" Ben asked.

"Well, no. I want you to be my final destination, point man, Ben. It'll be your responsibility to move the smaller items from itemisation area to end storage area," Tim said with a smile.

Charlotte, Bella and Lara kept straight faces with difficulty, but laughed when Ben realised what he had volunteered for.

"You want me to help unpack the truck?" He sounded horrified.

Amber patted him on the back. "Sometimes a policeman's work is quite mundane and tedious. But Miss Charlotte can't do it. Tim will be there too, and quite a few other policemen. We will need you there, Miss. We'll ensure there is a comfortable chair for you."

"I'll come with you too, Miss Charlotte," said Bella, "I doubt Doctor Amberg will agree otherwise."

Six weeks later, Sergeant Timothy Williams, and Constable Amber Hunt called to bring Charlotte up to date.

Bella was with her, having become her companion until something else could be organised. They were both enjoying themselves.

"Well, Miss Charlotte," said Tim, "it's all over except sentencing. We've kept you in the dark, because there has been a lot of negotiating between the police prosecutor and the two lawyers involved. When we arrested Maude and her accomplice, Warren Marshall, they both rushed to blame each other, but it was soon apparent they were equally guilty. Maude has been charged with, kidnapping, assault, theft as a servant, robbery, forgery, and conspiracy to commit murder. Warren Marshall, has been charged with impersonating a doctor, illegal procurement of drugs, assault, theft, burglary, and conspiracy to commit murder. Both pleaded guilty. They realised if it got into the newspapers, along with photos of you, the public would turn against them. That could make the judge consider a harsher sentence. Maude asked to have her name withheld, she claimed it would hurt her family, and may affect you adversely. The police prosecutor objected; her surname is not the same as yours. She will be named in tomorrow afternoon's newspaper, and I suspect some of the story will be on the TV news on Thursday."

"In the meantime, Miss Charlotte, how are you managing here?" Amber asked. "No nightmares?"

"I'm doing remarkably well. I'm planning a trip to England. Maude's third cousin, my grand-niece Becky, who used to be my companion, will meet me at Heathrow, and we'll tour England and Europe together. It'll be exciting. Well, at my age, I didn't think I'd leave Emory again. But I'm convinced if I can come through Maude's ministrations, I can do anything."

10

by Derin Attwood

Bella saw John Marshal for the first time at precisely 10.15a.m. on a Tuesday morning, early in July.

She was drinking a well-deserved cup of tea in her sunroom, when a taxi stopped at the beginning of the cul-de-sac arch. Not actually outside Smith's at number 23, nor the empty section between Smith's and her, but sort of in the middle.

He wore a blue tee shirt under a jacket that even to Bella's untrained eye, was designer. He wore boat shoes, with no socks. The only unfashionable thing about him was his beard. It was longer than had been favoured since the sixties, and looked a little straggly. It looked as if it belonged to a much older man. His eyes, and much of his face were hidden behind large sunglasses.

John, although she didn't know his name then, hauled a large knapsack out of the taxi, and tossed it over his shoulder. He stared at the big oak tree that stood in the centre of the turning circle. Then he strolled casually along the footpath, past the empty section, past Bella's house, past George Romford's, and at each house, he paused for just a moment, and stared, before carrying on.

When he got to the path into 28A, he looked in the letterbox, walked up the footpath, tried the front door, and then he and his knapsack disappeared around the back.

Bella took a sip of her briefly forgotten tea.

Shortly after, he came back around the house—minus the knapsack—and strode purposefully down the footpath towards Emory Road.

Once he walked past the tree, he was lost from Bella's sight. She finished her tea, curiosity swirling through her mind. However, with a household to run single-handed, the list of things to be done squeezed their way to the front of her mind, and she returned to her chores.

She next saw John on her door step at 3.17p.m.

"Mrs Rudd?"

"Yes."

"Young Mr Young told me you take in boarders in occasionally. Do you have any vacancies?"

Bella looked at him carefully as she thought of the two spare rooms, one downstairs, piled with clean laundry, and the attic, piled with unsorted books waiting to be shelved.

"You'd better come in," she said, untying her apron as she opened the door wider. "I wasn't expecting anyone, so I'll show you two rooms. I'll tidy them while you're collecting your bag. If you want one of them, that is," she added.

John chose the attic. "Let me put the books in the bookcase, Mrs Rudd. Give me a chance to look at what you have. Books are one of my passions."

"Call me Bella, not Mrs Rudd. I'll put the kettle on while you get your bag. Leave the door ajar when you go out, easier for when you return. I'll find you a spare key. And make yourself at home."

When John returned, Bella was in the pantry buttering some scones and the kettle was just beginning to boil on the old Aga. Bella came out of the pantry to see John pour a little hot water into the teapot, swirl it around and tip it down the sink. She watched with approval as he measured out two spoons of tea and poured boiling water over them. As he turned and picked up the tea cosy, he saw her and smiled.

"You did say I should make myself at home, and when I'm there, I help out. I'd be doing this for my mum. You keep things," he paused. "Well, the places are obvious. Shall I get the cups?" Without waiting for her answer, he opened the cupboard above the ceramic tea and sugar containers and took out two tea cups, saucers and side-plates.

Bella sat down. "Now tell me why you left your bag at 28B."

He laughed. "So you were watching. You're good. Most people just have to touch the curtains. It's a dead giveaway. Well, I was going to move in there. The landlord was supposed to leave the key either in the letterbox or on the kitchen bench. No key, no kitchen bench for that matter. The unit has been gutted. I went down to see if anything had been left for me at the shop, or alternatively, if Steve Young knew what was going on. Surprisingly, he knew no more than I did. On top o' that, Railways lost the rest of my luggage, not that there's much coming, but I don't even have a sleeping bag. Without you, I'd have to go to a hotel." He paused. "I looked at your books. Do you have children?"

Bella smiled at the swift change of subject "Well first, where do you work, and what time do you need breakfast in the morning?" she asked.

"Oh, yes," John smiled, and looked a little sheepish. "I'll fit my meals around you. I'm an investigative reporter. I'm taking some holidays I'm owed. I might run off a few minor articles for a magazine or two, but really, I just want to rest; do some sightseeing. And read a lot of books."

Bella told him about fourteen-year-old twins, Lara and Ben, and five-year-old Amelia, who everyone called Mellie.

John fitted in well, and Bella appreciated that he was no trouble. He paid his board on time, helped prepare meals and babysat occasionally so she could go shopping.

When he'd been there for just under three weeks, he bought a second-hand Cortina Mark III, and did some local sight-seeing. Occasionally he went to Auckland for a day. Mostly, he read and wandered around the town. On the third weekend he spent with them, he brought back fish and chips for the children, and when Mellie had her sixth birthday, he bought her a book about fairies and a dress to match.

He seemed to get as much pleasure watching the children dig into the cake, as they did eating it.

Lara and Ben each received a book a few weeks later.

The months passed and it felt as if John had always been with them. He spent Christmas in Auckland, but watched 1984 become 1985 with Bella, Lara and Ben. Mellie, for all her attempts not to, had fallen asleep on the couch at about ten o'clock.

Through the summer, John took them all to the beach, to look at a nearby forest, and some sightseeing around the district.

Then suddenly the days were quiet again as school started, although the evenings and weekends didn't change.

One Saturday morning, Bella realised she was sitting in an empty house. Lara and Ben had gone to a school camp, and Mellie was staying with a friend.

Bella felt at a loose end as she wandered around collecting odds and ends to put away. Ben's socks, Lara's handkerchiefs, three of Mellie's books, two of Lara's, Ben's maths book and a folder of typed pages.

She opened the folder and began to read, trying to figure out who had left their homework out, Lara or Ben.

While reading, she made a cuppa and took it into the sun room.

The subject was not something she would have thought either child would write about, but after a few pages, Bella felt it more likely belonged to Lara. She had written, *or more likely copied*, Bella thought, an early Victorian bodice-ripper. It was well written, about a girl, Sarah, a live-in scullery maid up at 'the big house', who was raped by the young master. When it became apparent that she was pregnant, he denied all knowledge; she was beaten and thrown out on her ear.

While wondering what to do, she was approached by the youngest son, Robert—destined against his will to be a priest, because that's what fourth sons in this family did—who asked Sarah to marry him. His family disowned him, so the couple left England and travelled to New Zealand, a small country as far from away from England as it was possible to go.

Bella now realised it wasn't a copy of an already written

book, because on the boat, Robert and Sarah befriended a young family man called Henry Thompson. When they arrived in New Zealand, the two families stayed together, travelled north and settled in a little village called Emory.

Bella stared at the pages, confused. If this was Lara's work, she needed to talk to her. If not, then whose? One of Lara's friends, perhaps. Either way, the writer had talent.

As Bella adjusted the folder, a pile of hand-written pages fell onto the floor. When she picked them up, she realised they were rough notes to continue the story.

As she put them back in order, two sentences jumped out at her. One contained her name. '…unit didn't work out, so I'm staying with Bella Rudd at number twenty-seven. Much better for my plans'.

Beyond that, the notes were just lists of ideas, some addresses, and phone numbers.

It was written by John.

"I'm home, Bella," John called, as he walked in at 2.45p.m. "Do you want a cup…" He paused at the door of the kitchen.

Bella sat opposite him, her arms folded across her chest, the folder on the table with the loose pages fanned out around it.

"Ahh. I had a feeling I'd left it beside the phone."

"I thought it was Lara's. Had I known it was yours, I wouldn't have read it. I always look at Lara and Ben's schoolwork, I like to know what they're learning. I realised it was yours only when I saw the hand-written notes. I wouldn't have read further, but you wrote about me, and I want to know what's going on?"

"Yes, you do have a right to know, but it's not about your family, Bella. It's more to do with your neighbour."

"Mr Romford?"

"Let me tell you the story. I was born here. Literally here, in this house. The story written there is true. Robert and Sarah were my great-grandparents. They teamed up with Henry Thompson to buy the land. They built two houses, up the hill for the Thompsons, and next door for Robert and Sarah. Together, they broke in the land. The boy, their only son, Charles, was my grandfather. He married and had three children, George, William and Anna, and that part of the story is why I'm here. This house was built for Charles, but the family moved between the two homes as needs arose. Anna, my mum, was the youngest. My dad died just before I was born. She needed a house, so I grew up here. She took in boarders, by the way."

Bella was relieved John was being honest with her, and that her first impression of him as a decent man was not wrong. She pushed the kettle onto the heat. "We may as well be comfortable while you tell me the rest of it."

They took the tea into the sun room, and John continued.

"By the time George was born, the rift in England had passed. So in 1925, George was sent over to boarding school with his cousins. At 12, he was big for his age, and very bright. Holidays were spent with his uncle and aunt. Of course, the other boys talked about the exciting war years, army adventures they'd heard from older brothers, uncles and friends, that generally had little to do with reality. As boys do, they played their own war games. George turned out to be a good tactician. He was a great storyteller, and at school, an excellent scholar. He joined the Army Corps at school, becoming an officer before going on to study at Oxford. He wrote long letters to young brother William, when he was old enough to read and dream. When George came home in March 1936, he had a lot to tell young William. Life in England sounded much more appealing than boring old Emory."

"So, George is the old man next door?" Bella asked.

John nodded. "William followed George's footsteps to boarding school in October 1937. He too was bright, and big for his age. When war was declared in 39, he stayed on in England and in 1940 at age 14, lied about his age and signed on. He didn't tell his parents, but George, an investigative reporter in America at the time, picked up something mentioned in a letter. He raced over to England to retrieve him. He used the Old Boy network and discovered William had been sent to France. George and another reporter got permission from the war office to go over there. On the way to the base, the car they were in was hit by a run-away army truck. A drunk driver.

"George was badly hurt, and it was some weeks before he regained consciousness. When he woke up, an orderly told him his brother had been to see him, and would see him at home.

"George's eyesight was seriously damaged, and he had to learn to walk again. After an extended period of convalescing, he made his way back to Emory. William wasn't there; Nan broke the news, he was missing in action. George blamed himself. He continued physiotherapy to help his leg. An operation gave him more sight, but he only went through it so he could return to France to find William. Then William's dog-tags and personal property arrived."

"Didn't they send a telegram?" Bella asked.

"That got lost somehow. There was a very nice letter from his commanding officer. Despite his youth, William had been a good soldier, but the biggest impression he made was from his stories about his big brother. He painted George as a World War One hero, bragged about him to his mates in the trenches and tried to imitate him. George felt so guilty he had a breakdown and never left the house again."

"Didn't you say William visited him in hospital?" Bella asked.

"That's what George had been told, and it worried me for a long time," John said. "I finally figured it was a priest from his old school. After the war, a few of his friends visited, but George refused to see them. Nan never asked any questions; she just sent them away."

"It's so sad, but why are you here?" Bella asked.

"Do you know who owns the land behind these houses?"

Bella was thrown by the change in direction. She frowned as she thought. "What? Well, Charlotte Thompson, and I guess the Council owns the park."

"You'd think so. However, a paper road goes between George and the units. It originally accessed two farms beyond Thompson's. Those farms are now owned by the A. Huntington Corporation called AHC. They also own the three farms south and west of Thompson's hill."

"John, this is very interesting, but it doesn't explain why you're here? Why not stay next door?" Bella went red as she realised she sounded quite aggressive. "Sorry."

John closed his eyes briefly. "No, no, I'm sorry. I'm getting ahead of myself. No one stays with George. He couldn't cope. Did you know he hasn't left the house since 1946? There were no problems while Nan and Grandad were alive, but they died in 1960. The family lawyer, Griz Murtle handles everything for George. He's a family friend. You'll have noticed George doesn't have a letterbox. Mail goes to Griz, and he pays the bills from the family trust."

"I never thought about it, I don't often see the mail being delivered. I've seen Danny and Steve Young deliver Mr Romford's groceries."

"Meals. They are left on the veranda at dusk. George takes them in during the night. Griz sees George once, maybe twice a year, and there are no other visitors, ever. Griz only goes there when he really needs to, and even that is fraught."

John refilled his tea cup, drank, and continued.

"Griz keeps in touch with Mum by phone. When she's overseas, I try to get here to see him a couple of times a year. Griz rang me a few months ago. Someone slipped a letter into George's food box. Danny Young noticed, and handed it to Griz the next day. The letter came from AHC. They offered to buy the house and section at its current valuation plus $5,000 dollars. Griz contacted them, asked some questions, but got stonewalled, so he called me."

"Wow, $5,000 extra. That's a massive amount. Most people would jump at it. But why would this corporation offer so much more than the house is worth?" Bella asked.

"That was the big question, and I checked it out. The house valuation hasn't changed for quite a long time, and the next valuations aren't scheduled until 1987. So it's really worth a lot more than is stated on the present valuation, but even then, 5,000 is far higher than I would expect."

"Why haven't valuations been redone?"

"There is a major change coming up for Emory, and valuations will be affected by it. I've heard all sorts of whispers, a sanitation complex, an airport, a prison, a new Police Station, or a huge shopping centre. Something is definite, and it will put Emory on the map, but it is being kept very secret. Four towns are vying for it, Emory being one of them. The others are non-starters, well, that's what I hear. I doubt it's sanitation, because the Council has looked at Morning Point for it, and that's too close to the Estuary for almost everything suggested. Anyway, Morning Point has a lot of different land owners. A judge lives there, a couple of lawyers, doctors, and most of the Councillors. Big houses and newly built; there would be strong objections. The other area is south-west of here. It has one new owner, and he could name his price, but the sale would be easier. And of course, whatever is built will attract all sorts of other businesses to the area. Emory will become a very important city in New Zealand."

Bella nodded. "So George's house and land will be worth a lot more than has even been offered. But how did you find out all of this?"

"I'm good at picking up whispers. That's what a lot of investigative reporting is all about. As of this moment, the information is not in the public records. I'm sure the Council have discussed it behind closed doors, and the minutes have been sealed. There's nothing in the library records, I checked the day I got here. As it turned out, I already had a piece of the puzzle, although I didn't realise until I was unpacking that evening. I visited here briefly last year, and I thought I might try to do a feature on the Public Library. They were renovating, but returning it to its original 1890 floor plan. I had photos of it before anything was done, and wanted more while they were replacing the walls to the map-room. I took a couple of photos from the balcony looking down onto the map-tables. There were two men there, comparing maps. One map was marked out as if the planning decisions were already made."

John glanced up at the darkening sky. "Dinner time. What say I make it? Give you a break."

"I was going to throw together some leftovers."

"I can do that while you sip a glass of wine. I have a bottle in my room." He checked Bella's fridge and pantry. "What about a pizza. Any preferences?"

Bella shrugged. "I've never had one," she said.

"Oh, you are in for a treat. My speciality."

She watched, amazed, as he put it together. She ate more of it than she should have, it was so delicious. The wine suited it perfectly. After they'd eaten, they moved into the lounge. John lit a fire, although it wasn't cold, and then refilled their glasses.

"Mmm, this is nice," said Bella. "It's a long time since I had an evening like this."

"Why not? You deserve it."

She shrugged. "With three children—I don't get much opportunity. Too tired after they're settled, I guess, and no reason to. It's different with an another adult here."

"Don't answer if you don't want to," said John, "but can I ask where Mr Rudd is?"

"Arthur died in a car accident. A couple of stupid boys in a stolen car."

"What happened to them?"

"Their father paid a huge amount to the owner of the stolen car and he withdrew his complaint. The police charged them, but they couldn't prove who was driving. Good lawyers, I guess. Well you know what it's like. The boys were sent to boarding school, but they were expelled within six months. They're still getting into trouble."

"What did you get?"

"I didn't want a bar of their money. Arthur had a good life insurance of course, but that wasn't the point. I wanted them in jail. It wasn't going to happen, everyone advised me to take what they offered, otherwise they'd get away with it. So there's a very generous university fund for each of the children. There was a payment to me too. My lawyer has invested it. I hated accepting, but I had to be sensible."

When did it happen?"

"Just over four years ago. Mellie doesn't remember him, which breaks my heart. It was hard on the twins, especially Lara. She was very close to him, and Ben is now at an age where he really needs his dad."

"I'm sorry, I shouldn't have asked."

Bella smiled mischievously. "It's not a secret. You'd have found out if you had done your job."

"Touché." John laughed. "Can't say I wasn't tempted, but I owed you the privacy. You really didn't have to tell me, you know. You can ask me any embarrassing question you like."

"Where do you get such good wine?"

"Well that's hardly embarrassing. Auckland, but Brown's in North Street are stocking them for me now."

"Tell me why the corporation is so important? Did they buy the land with knowledge or was it a fluke? I didn't realise they weren't owned by the men farming them."

"Five farms are involved. Huntington Corp have already paid the farmers. They stay on the land and farm it as before. All outgoings are covered by the corporation. The farmers did very well out of it. The only provision on them was they did not tell anyone about the sale."

"So how did you find out about it?"

"My granddad grew up here. I grew up here. Farmers like to reminisce over a few whiskeys, especially when it's provided by the grandson of an old mate. I pass through with a few bottles every couple of years. They pass on the local news."

Bella nodded. "I still don't get it. From a single offer, some farm sales, and a photo of a map, you decide the farmland would become some big business in Emory."

"It's always the little things that confirm it. Take the units. The landlord bought them to make money, but he has no tenants. Rates, and insurance still have to be paid. I rented 28B months before I got here. I paid the rent regularly, but when I arrived—no key, it had been gutted. 28A is the same. The landlord returned all of my money. He added ten percent when I started asking questions. He said he didn't realise he hadn't asked me to stop the payments. Thing is, I received a receipt every fortnight, signed by him. Steve Young said it must of happened in July last year."

"Who by?" Bella asked.

"The landlord said louts from Auckland had done it, and the police hadn't found them. It didn't ring true, so I checked it out. There was no complaint to the police, and that in itself is a clue. Most information is easy to find, so when something is hidden, it's a signal that not all is as it should be. The last rates payment was made in cash, and that also is unusual for a business. Personally I think the corporation now owns the units, and the previous owner got to strip everything out of them."

"Yes, definitely weird. Why did Mr Murtle need you here?"

"George wouldn't let Griz in the house, and just before I came up, his food box was left on the doorstep for a few days. That rarely happens. Last time was when some kids put fireworks through the mail slot in the front door. Another time a dog got into his yard. The owner knocked, George didn't answer the door, the dog was barking, and the owner called the police. Danny Young saw them turn into the street; sent Steve down here while he called Griz. Not a big thing for you or me, but not so easy for a man who is terrified of noise, people, and change."

Bella nodded. "That's sad. So what does Griz normally do?"

"He calls Mum. She'd stay here for a while, but this time she can't because she's in England. So I came."

"And that's why you took the attic, so you can watch him. How long do you plan to stay on the off chance something happens?"

"As long as is necessary, but I think it is coming to a head."

John sighed deeply. "George's routine has changed. Maybe you noticed."

"Ben mentioned something about George occasionally staying outside all night," Bella said.

"Yes. He marches up and down and digs holes."

"Any idea why he does it?"

"After Nan died, George got pneumonia. He was very sick, we thought he'd die. The night marches started after that. Mum thought he was searching for William or protecting him. The digging? Well I think he's digging a fox-hole. He'd do it all night, and then sleep through the day. This time though, I think it's worse. I've heard him marching up and down during the day too. Inside the house."

"It's so sad. How can we help him?"

"Normally mum would go in. She looks like nan did when George was young. She reassures him and he calms down."

"Don't you want to tell her? Maybe she should come back," Bella said softly.

"She knows. Griz rang her. But she can't get away. This time, I have to deal with it."

"Will he accept you?"

"I dunno. I don't want to make it worse, so at the moment I'm just watching. You made a comment a while back about my beard. I normally go for a John Oates moustache myself, but granddad had a full beard. I thought maybe it'd help if I looked a bit like him. It needs to be longer and stragglier. Greyer too. Then Griz and I will force an entry if necessary. I just don't want to rush it; he might come right. I'm worried I'll time it wrong, or make him worse."

"Well, if there's anything I can do to help..."

John laughed. "You could help me streak it grey when the time comes. And put up with it until I can shave."

"Shaving would be a shame. I like a man with a beard. Reminds me of my dad."

John grimaced, leaned over and added a little more wine to Bella's glass. "I wasn't really trying for a fatherly image. Not with you, anyway." He leaned forwards and gently kissed her lips, encouraged when she didn't pull away. He sat beside her on the couch, and put his arm around her shoulder. She leaned her head back, and together they watched the flames in the fireplace.

"You know, something's not quite right."

John glanced down and raised an eyebrow. "Really?"

"Demolishing the units would provide a good wide drive to the farms, and maybe getting Mr Romford's would allow them to make it into a road. But are you sure?'

John nodded. "If this becomes the business access, it'll need to be much wider than that even. The empty section between you and Smith's belongs to Miss Thompson. She'd never voluntarily sell but her farm will go up for sale when she dies."

"So, why have I not had an offer?"

"I was wondering that, and I don't know. I need to find out who owns the corporation. So far, I've traced it to a Wellington firm. That's a subsidiary of a company in Washington, which is split between two others, one in Mexico, the other Puerto Rico. Those two are wholly owned by a conglomerate based in The Cayman Islands. Then I hit a dead end. I think the're all just paper companies. I have a couple of American friends working on it. It's a waiting game, but all of the secrecy implies some doubtful doings. Charlotte Thompson won't last forever. She must be almost ninety years old, and even if she has another ten years, it'd not change any overall timetable. The land will be sold when she dies, or is forced into care. As I see it, you're the only anomaly."

Bella nodded. "Maybe George is a bigger problem. I mean, they must know they can't deal with him now. Any negotiation has to go through Griz. Maybe the biggest worry for them is how soon before the Council drops the bomb on us all. That there'll be an airport. I mean, what if another town gets it? Then the corporation will lose out completely."

"Perhaps the corporation knows something."

"Then you have to ask what connection the corporation has with the Council."

"And that's the telling question, Bella," said John, "because normally a Council would do a compulsory purchase order on each of the properties. That would cause problems right now, because the rates haven't been reassessed for so long. Unless it's handled very carefully, there'd be court cases, which could be enough to derail the whole plan. If there was only one owner, that person could negotiate a much higher price, if they guarantee a straightforward sale. Either way, the houses would be worth much more than they are valued at now. But with a bigger amount of land, the corporation can pretty much name their own price. They're sitting on a gold mine."

John kissed Bella again, and suddenly the land problems seemed irrelevant.

"Hiya, smelly Mellie," Ben said, as he climbed into the back seat beside her. "Blar-de-blar-blar-blar is coming on the next bus," he added.

Mellie punched him on the arm, and he fell back on the seat, groaning and clutching his shoulder.

"Ben, you're asking for trouble."

He went red. "Yeah sorry, Mum. I know. They'll both get their own back. Sorry, Mellie. Did you have a good time with your friend?"

Mellie nodded happily, and started to tell him about her weekend.

"Why are you on different buses?" Bella asked, as Mellie ran out of breath.

"Because weirdo Graig Hoshnal and the girls wanted to go to look at the flower gardens on the way home, and the sensible brigade wanted to see the shipwreck. Two buses, obvious solution. And here they come. Come on Mellie, let's go get Blar-de-blar's bag."

Lara climbed in beside Bella as Ben and a giggling Mellie waited for the bags to be unloaded.

"Did you have a good time, Mum?" she asked.

"Nice and restful."

"Did you and John get it together while we were away?"

"What! What does that mean?" Bella asked, somewhat taken aback.

"Well, it's obvious he's mad keen on you, and it's time you found a nice boyfriend, dated and stopped relying on us for company. It's been far too long."

"Lara, I do not need romantic advice from a fourteen-year-old. John's a boarder, and other than that, I know little about him. I mean, he could be married."

"Mum, you're blushing. Anyway, there's no wife or children."

"How do you know?"

"I asked him, of course. How else would I know? Anyway, I hope you didn't waste the weekend. It wasn't easy to get us all out of your hair at the same time. You cling on to Mellie as if she's a chastity belt."

"Lara!"

"Mum! Muuu-uum!"

"Shush, Ben. Mellie has a temperature, don't wake her up."
Bella glanced down at Mellie's flushed face, and changed the
damp cloth on her forehead for a fresh one. She pointed
out to the landing, pleased when Ben walked out of her
bedroom without arguing.

She rubbed Mellie's back until she settled, then pulled on
a light robe and followed Ben into the hall.

She put her hand on his forehead and checked his
temperature. He was warm, but then they all were. As usual,
February, March and April had been scorching, but the
cooler weeks in May, suggesting an early winter, had given
way to an unseasonably hot muggy June. The air hadn't
cooled since the sun set.

"What's—?"

"He's doing it again, Mum. All that thudding and
stomping. It's louder than ever, and it keeps me awake. He
keeps slapping his spade handle with the flat of his hand, as
if he's presenting arms. He hasn't stopped since dusk."

Bella sighed. George had been so quiet over the last few
months.

"It's been every night this week, Mum. It's too hot to
shut the window and anyway, I can still hear him. And he
stinks."

"All right, Ben. I'll talk to John in the morning. He will
have to do something. But nothing can be done tonight. In
the meantime, go and sleep in the lounge."

"Muummm! It's even hotter down there," Ben said.

"Turn the fan on. That's the fan, not TV. Go to sleep, or
you will be straight back into your room."

"I can hear him too, Mum," Lara said, appearing at the
door to her bedroom. "Ben's right, he's getting noisier, and
the heat doesn't help."

"Well she can't come into the lounge. The couch won't fit

both of us," Ben insisted.

"Go into my bed, Lara. Put the fan on, and put a light rug over Mellie. Don't wake her up."

"That's not fair," Ben whined. "She always gets the best deal. Why couldn't I have your bed?"

"Because you're using the couch and you refused to share. Now go before I change my mind."

Lara paused by the bedroom door. "What about you, Mum?"

Bella shook her head. "I can't sleep anyway. I might as well catch up on some embroidery or read. Now off you go."

The door clicked shut and Bella heard the whir of the fan as it started up. She closed her eyes and massaged her neck. The headache that had been threatening all day was now a reality.

In the bathroom, she rummaged through the cupboard for some aspirin. *It must be bad if I'm considering these horrid powdery things*, she thought.

The cold tap gave warm water, even when she ran it over her wrist for a while. With a full glass, she wandered into Ben's room and pushed the window wide, searching for a breath of air.

Ben's bedroom window looked over the southern side of George's house.

Along with no letterbox, George had no electricity and no phone. The one securely bolted gate in the eight-foot-high fence to the back yard, gave George privacy from the street. The yard was similarly fenced on all sides. He had no garden, and now there was no longer a lawn on the south side.

George had been digging in it every night, no matter the weather, and if he wasn't digging, he marched.

He was down there now, digging the ground over. The soil, drying in the unseasonable heat, was mounded up on the far side of what should have been a garden.

That old army surplus greatcoat would stink, but Ben couldn't smell him from up here, thought Bella. He probably caught a whiff of his own socks. I must suggest John buy George a new greatcoat though.

Normally George was just a shadowy figure in the garden. Tonight the combination of a full moon and clear sky meant he was more visible than usual.

Bella glanced around her own garden. The grass, thick and green was neatly cut, compliments of that nice man, Gareth, from down the road. She had fruit trees, a gazebo, and a garden shed next to the garage. Such different yards.

She glanced again at George.

He arranged his spade neatly beside his fork and rake on the ground beside the front fence. Then he marched back to the foxhole, turned his back on it, and raised his right hand in a sort of salute.

Bella's eyes widened when she realised he was holding a pistol. She took a breath to call out, but too late. He put the gun under his chin and pulled the trigger.

It seemed to take forever. His head distorted, and his body propelled backwards, falling into the hole he had dug.

He dug a grave! He took time to dig his own grave, and then she was running for the phone.

Her bedroom door opened.

"What was that, Mum?"

"Nothing, Lara. Go back into my room and stay there. Look after Mellie."

She raced upstairs and knocked on John's door. She didn't wait for an answer, but ran back down to pick up the phone. She could hear the low drone of the television in the lounge. For once, she was thankful Ben had disobeyed her. The noise would have helped muffle the sound of the gunshot.

It seemed to take an eternity to dial one-one-one. She

wished she had updated to a touch phone.

"Police and ambulance," she said to the operator, and to John's questioning look, as he reached the bottom of the stairs. She gave her name and address. "My neighbour—an accident with a gun." She listened. "No, he's not holding the gun. He's not conscious." She paused again and answered the questions they asked.

John was already racing back to his room.

Bella answered more questions, and as John sprinted back past her, she sat the phone on the cradle, grabbed a torch and followed him out of the house. Lights were showing further down the street, but there was no outcry. The tall, solid fence would have muffled the sound of the gun. In all honesty, the gun shot had, to her memory, been little more than a pop. The sight of George's head distorting as the bullet discharged would stay with her forever.

John was at George's front door, trying to get his key into the lock.

Bella's torch lit up the scene, and close inspection showed dried plaster of Paris bulging through the key hole.

John sagged against the door. "I messed up. I really messed up."

Bella put her arms around him, and he buried his head in her neck. "You couldn't fix him. No one could." She pulled away, shaking him slightly. "John, the police will be here soon. We need Griz. I'll ring him."

He took a deep breath. "Emergency services may not let you. They generally hold the line open until the police tell them they're not needed."

"I'll get him, but don't do anything silly. Don't climb the fence, you'll contaminate the scene."

His voice broke as he spoke. "I'll wait until the police and ambulance arrive." Then on second thoughts, he grabbed her arm as she turned away. "Bella, did Arthur have a chainsaw or even a hand saw? It'll be easier for the police to cut a section from the wall. It'll be better access than breaking a window."

"In the small shed in the back yard." She handed him the torch and ran back to her house.

Just as she reached her front step, Bella's stomach rebelled. She fell to her knees and vomited. By good luck more than management, only a small amount hit the path, the rest in the garden. She took a deep breath, wiped her mouth on the back of her hand, and struggled to breathe. Finally, she stood, climbed the front steps and opened the front door.

"Here's Mum now." Lara handed the phone over. "It was making a funny noise, Mum, so I picked it up." She wrinkled her nose. "I'll get you a facecloth."

Bella nodded. "Hello." She gave the operator a brief update, and then asked them to put her through to Griz's phone. She explained who he was, and why he was needed.

Moments later, she heard the phone ringing, and after ten long rings, a very groggy Griz answered.

"There's a problem with George Romford. John wants you here now."

"I'll be there in five." Griz thumped the phone down, there was a click, and the emergency operator was back. "Is there anything else you need?"

"I don't think so. I can hear the sirens now, so I'll go and see if I can help."

Lara handed her a damp cloth. "I'll take your dressing gown. It stinks." Bella washed her face and took the robe Lara held out, a gift from her grandmother.

Bella was tying it up when John looked in the front door. He carried the chainsaw and a can of petrol.

An ambulance followed the police car as it swung into the street, its red and blue lights flashing through the bare oak tree branches, although the siren was now silent.

Bella told them what she'd seen. John explained the problem of entry and handed over the chainsaw.

Senior Sergeant Bill Tennant, who was in charge, listened and agreed it would be the easiest way to enter the yard. Bella's closest neighbour, Barbara Smith, arrived wearing a dressing gown, and close behind, her daughter Darlene, who wore a very skimpy nightie that showed her advanced pregnancy.

Barbara Smith looked different, her hair in curlers with a thick net over them.

She looks like Nora Batty from Last of The Summer Wine. I wonder which of the local men lusts over her from afar. Bella had to suppress a giggle. *Oh dear, I'm probably in shock.*

The scream of the chainsaw echoed in the still night air, and the number of neighbours standing by the oak tree swelled. Torchlight shone beyond the tree, showing more people on their way.

Peter Mansell, a neighbour from number 8, approached the police, his offer of help echoed by Herbert Croft.

"Best thing you can all do is go home and look after your families. Nothing'll happen here for a long time yet. You'll hear all about it soon enough," said a policeman, who looked as if he still went to school during the day.

"It's a sign of getting old," Bella said to herself. Peter and Herbert withdrew to the tree, but went no farther. Steven Young walked up to the policeman. "Excuse me, Constable. Mrs Rudd will need these; I can't imagine she'll find time to go shopping today." He thrust a large box of groceries into the constable's arms. "Can you take it? It'll be too heavy for her."

Barbara Smith bustled forward, swept past the men and put

her arm around Bella's shoulder. "Come with me, dear. I'll get you a cuppa. You'll rest better at my place. So shocking. Such a tragedy, but you'll be able to tell me all about it. Best get it off your chest. I'll come back and collect the children too."

"Mrs? Um, Bella, isn't it?" interrupted an older policeman, striding swiftly towards her. "I need you over here, Mam." He took Bella's elbow. "Best you go home, Madam," he said to Barbara Smith. "Nothing's going to happen for a long time."

"There's always a nosey neighbour wanting to get the first whisper of a story," he said to Bella, as he directed her towards her house. They caught up with the Constable.

He glanced into the box. "Oh, that's nice. Steve has put a bottle of whiskey in there too. It'll come in handy. Now you'd best get inside, get a hot drink and put a shot o' that whiskey in it. I imagine next door's been rather a shock for you. Don't talk to your family, well not until sarge has taken statements from everyone. And don't talk to your neighbours at all. As nice as they may be, some o' them'll pass it on before you've finished telling it, and before you know it, they'll have embroidered it like hell." His nose wrinkled at the odour of vomit. "Who was that?" he asked.

"Me, I'm afraid."

He nodded. "Constable, when you have finished being a grocery boy, get a bucket of water and wash that away. Mrs Rudd doesn't need that at her front door. There's a watering can around the side o' the house by the tap. Then you can stand here by the steps and keep the neighbours away."

Just then, a car sped up Bella's drive and screeched to a halt. The door opened before the car had fully stopped. A man jumped out and came over to them.

"You must be Bella," he said. "I'm Grizwald Murtle, of Murtle, Murtle and Frazer."

Daybreak saw them sitting at the kitchen table, tea cooling in the teapot. They could still hear the noise of the police next door, and occasionally the flashing lights on top of the black and white Ford Falcons reflected on the white tiles above the kitchen bench.

The murmur of the neighbours came and went in the distance. All had returned home at some stage through the early hours, but only to dress, bring food, rugs and deck chairs. They ate breakfast together under the tree, and it took on the air of a picnic, although not as boisterous as those the neighbourhood had had in the past.

The day heated up. Bella's doors and windows were open as usual, trying to catch a tiny breath of wind.

Just after eleven o'clock, a piercing scream brought Bella to her feet. John, Lara and Ben raced for the front door and returned a minute later.

"Tommy Dawes took all the boys up the tree. Probably trying to look over the fence," Ben said. "That Indian kid, Abhi, fell out. His mum over-reacted a bit. I'm surprised she allowed Abhi up there at all. She doesn't like him climbing the tree."

"Darlene Smith gave him a hard time. Nasty girl, that," John said.

"And yet Jolene's so nice," Lara said. "But Herbert Croft is there. He won't let Darlene get away with it."

John nodded. "He'll help Abhi's mum to accept that it's not the end of the world if he breaks his arm. Falling out of trees is what boys do. It's a rite of passage. Anyway, I've shut the front windows and door. That'll keep out the noise."

"I haven't seen Darlene on the school bus lately," Ben said.

"Does pregnancy get you off school?"

"Pregnant!" John said. "She's only, what, thirteen?"

Lara shook her head. "Fourteen. Jolene told me about it a few weeks back when we were studying. Her dad's worried cause she's, oh, I'll tell you the rest some other time."

Bella sat with a large rug around her shoulders. Lara had said she had been shivering. Everything seemed to come through a thick fog. Someone put a mug of tea in her hands. She remembered thinking it was a comfort, whereas a tea cup wouldn't have been. It seemed only moments later when John remarked that it was cold and took it off her.

He hunkered down in front of her, holding another mug of tea. "Bella, you need to drink this. You're in shock. Believe me, it'll help." He guided the mug to her lips, and deftly removed it when, having taken a mouthful, she coughed violently.

"What's in it?" she gasped.

"Just a wee dram of whiskey, love," said Griz. "Help warm you up. The police will want to have a chat soon. You and John at least. It'll be cut and dried."

The police interviews were brief. The children were questioned, and when it was obvious they heard little and saw nothing, they were sent off to get dressed, and then out into the back yard to kick a ball around.

"Just don't climb on the fence, or look through it. And if anyone tries to talk to you, come back in straight away. Or call me and I'll come and see them off," Sergeant Williams said.

Bella's interview was next, and again, mercifully short. Then she too was released. She gladly headed up to shower and dress while John and Griz were interviewed. Sergeant Williams gave the usual warnings about not talking to any of the neighbours, and suggested they have a hearty breakfast. "You'll feel much better with some bacon and eggs inside you."

When Bella returned to the kitchen twenty minutes later, she was hit by an air of suppressed excitement from everyone there.

Lara pushed a very thick handmade envelope towards her. "It was on the ground just this side of the fence. We think it came from George, Mr Romford."

Mrs Bella Rudd was inscribed in copperplate handwriting on the front.

Bella picked it up. "Oh, should I ...?"

"Bella, don't ask any question I may have to answer," said Griz. "Just open the envelope."

She picked up the letter knife, slipped it into a corner of the thick handmade envelope, slit it open, and carefully shook the contents. A second envelope and a folded sheet of paper onto the table. She picked the paper up first.

Mrs Bella Rudd.

I apologise for the upset that is going on next door. You have been a good neighbour, and I have no wish to impose on your life any longer than is necessary.

Please tell young John I was aware of what he was trying to do. As much as he resembled my Da, I wasn't fooled, nor with his Ma and her attempts to look like his Nan. It's nice that they cared enough to try, but the world has been hostile to me for a long time.

Assure them that the contents of the envelope, which was posted through my mail slot is a guarantee that there is nothing wee Annie, John nor Griz could do. They couldn't stop progress, and I personally don't see the point in carrying on. The modern world has now become all too much for me.

Of course you will already know about the changes coming in the street. I imagine the same documents will have been pushed through your mail slot.

I wish you and your children well, and remain, yours respectfully and somewhat unhappily,

George Charles Robert Jonathon Romford

Bella glanced up at John. "Why didn't he write to you, rather than me? He knew you were here."

"It's the nature of the man, Bella. Look at that letter. It says a lot without saying anything," Griz said. John nodded in agreement.

"It tells me he planned to kill himself," said Bella.

John put his arm around her. "You could get someone else to open the other envelope. Maybe your own lawyer."

Bella took a deep breath. "It'd take a month to get an appointment, and I couldn't stand the wait." She picked up the paperknife again, slit the next envelope open, and shook the contents onto the table.

"Yet another envelope, and a document." She opened the document first.

Order for Compulsory Land Purchase

"Oh dear, no wonder he didn't see the point in carrying on." Bella felt as distraught as she sounded.

"Wait a minute," John leaned over, and grabbed the tip of the page, laying it out on the table. He scanned the document. "This isn't right. I'm sure it's..."

Then he rushed out of the room, and returned a few moments later with a large satchel, through which he began to search.

A full minute passed before he pulled out a large piece of thick paper, folded in the same manner as the purchase order sitting on the table. He smoothed his out, and began comparing the two.

"It's not bad," he said, "but the one given to Uncle George is a fake. You didn't get one, did you, Bella?"

She shook her head. "The amount offered for it is unbelievably low. This was deliberately designed to put pressure on him."

"Pressure for what?" Ben asked.

Lara leaned over, and looked at the document. "Who'd do this? I mean the Council would have told him it was fake, wouldn't they?"

"Only if he went in and asked," Griz said.

Bella glanced up at her two older children. "This is important, Lara and Ben. As with Mr Romford's death, this isn't to be mentioned to anyone else. It is still an ongoing police investigation."

"Well I didn't get to see anything until the police arrived with their sirens and lights blaring," Ben grumbled. "Then Lara made me stay in the kitchen. Even the neighbours saw more than I did."

"And it was best that way," said Griz. "You have the delight of knowing things none of your friends know, without having anything emblazoned on your over-active mind. You'll just have to keep mum for a while. You can tell your mates the police have told you not to say anything. And they would tell you that, if you had seen anything. Your mates'll think you were eye-witness to the whole thing. Before you know it, they'll have you battling assassins to try to save old Mr Romford, or they'll paint him as a spy who you outed, and stopped from passing information on to the dreaded enemy."

"Bella, I need to make some phone calls," said John. "I know you've said I can, but these'll cost a lot. I want to call Mum in England, I need to ring a reporter in Christchurch, but I also want to check some things with my friends in Washington. I'll pay for the calls of course, but your bill will be a shock this month."

Two hours passed before John returned to the kitchen. He held two notepads and a number of extra pages of foolscap.

"Mum sends her love, Griz. Said she wouldn't be back for the funeral, but then we expected that."

Griz nodded.

"Griz, we need Senior Sergeant Tennant here, I want to talk about what happened next door and why. It would be better if the invitation came from you. This, I think, is a bigger crime than we realised."

Senior Sergeant Bill Tennant was a practical man. He listened to the story first, and then looked at the documents John handed over.

"Yes, well it does look as if this corporation has attempted to drive Mr Romford out of the property, and has in fact hounded him to his death. Is there any possibility someone else pulled the trigger?"

Bella shook her head. "George did it, no question. What about conspiracy?"

"I doubt we can go there either. It comes down to intent, and even a third rate lawyer could argue his way out of that one. Who would we charge? We don't know who owns the Huntington Corporations."

"Ahh, but now I do," said John. "One Councillor Anthony Hunt."

"What!" Bella exclaimed. She looked shocked.

"Tony?" Griz echoed.

Both Bella and Griz sounded equally horrified.

Senior Sergeant Tennant looked from one to the other. "I think I need to know more. Mrs Rudd, you first."

"Oh, well, nothing really. Just a shock hearing the name. His sons drove the car that killed my husband. About four years ago, they ran him down on a pedestrian crossing."

"Oh, of course, Rudd. Allan—no Arthur it was, wasn't it? Yes, nasty! Stolen car, wasn't it. Turned up at Morning Point. The boys got off, didn't they?"

Bella nodded.

"And you, Griz?"

"Well, I never knew about Bella's husband, but Tony and his brother Mark were driving the car that killed George's parents. There was a question about who actually was driving. They both denied it, then wouldn't talk further. The steering wheel had been wiped down, but not well. Both boys' prints were there. The boys said Charles and Miriam were on the wrong side of the road. But it really looked as if the cars had been moved around after the accident. A water tower at the side of the road had emptied over the accident scene. The water washed away most of the evidence. Tony and Mark said it had been intact when they left to get help." Griz shook his head. "They walked past the Police Station to get to their father's office. Tony Sr made them take a bath and burned their clothing. He said he was in shock, but hours past before he called the Police. Because of the water, there was little evidence left. No charges were laid."

"What year? I'll look it up."

"1960," said Griz. "Bella's history perhaps explains why she wasn't offered the same deal for the land as everyone else."

"What? Wait, what's that about? What history?" Bill asked.

John explained about the new development, what offers had been made, who had accepted and the money involved. "I guess the fake compulsory purchase order was the next step. With Bella, maybe Tony was miffed at already having paid out over her husband. Mean attitude though."

"And funny too," said Bill Tennant. He glanced up and saw the enquiring looks and shook his head. "I need to make some enquiries. Don't talk about this to anyone. I will say, the future has a way of throwing surprises at us. It'll take time, but don't panic. Yes, lots of surprises." He took a deep breath. "Now, I've been working all night, so I'm going back to the station. Then home to sleep. I'll be in to see you tomorrow. I would suggest you all eat while you have the chance. Celebrate life. Your neighbours will be over all too soon to get the story. Put a note on the door saying you're sleeping. It may not keep Mrs Smith at bay, but it's worth a try. Griz, don't drive until you've slept. I'm sure there's a spare bed here for you."

The day passed quietly, until 4:30p.m. Then Mrs Smith could no longer contain her curiosity, nor her desire to be invited to everyone else's home to pass on the gossip. Griz sent her away with nothing.

"Oh, you know what she's like. She'll just make something up and pretend you told her," Ben said.

The order to attend the Coroner's Court in Auckland came two months later. It was really just a formality. The Coroner guided Bella carefully through her evidence. Nothing was mentioned about the letter and documents she had shown Senior Sergeant Tennant.

The verdict was given as, 'Suicide while the Balance of his Mind was Disturbed'. With that, the coroner thanked Bella for her bravery, apologised that her life had been so impacted, and suggested she put it behind her as quickly as possible.

A small notice appeared on page twelve of The Auckland Times. Days later, someone from the Emory News rang for a comment. Bella was out, and Mellie, who answered the phone, told the reporter about her new doll, until John took over the phone, and reamed the reporter out for speaking to a child without parental permission.

A half-inch comment appeared a week later. It said nothing that wasn't already known.

Life began to return to normal. Bella was no longer asked what had happened; few people knew she had witnessed George's death.

She now wondered how long it would be before John packed up and left. He had taken her out to dinner once since the Coroner's Court met, and taken the whole family to Auckland for an extended weekend.

He organised a tour of the Tip Top ice cream factory, Cook Street Market, Rainbow's End and the Zoo. The children loved it, but Bella felt listless. She knew it was just a reaction to seeing George's death, and not knowing what the future held, but she couldn't shake the feeling off.

When they arrived home on Tuesday evening, Mrs Smith grabbed Bella's arm before she had reached her front door.

"I collected your mail, dear," Barbara said, handing her three letters. "Well, I realised you weren't coming home. I'm glad I did, because that mailman is just too rough with them. He left them hanging so far out of the letterbox, they would've blown all over the neighbourhood had I not rescued them."

The three letters she handed Bella had been opened. One from Griz for John, an official one from Kevin Burke the local Member of Parliament, and one from Lara's teacher.

"Oh, and your phone has been ringing off the hook," said Mrs Smith. "You really should get one of those new answerphones like I have. It's just so useful." She paused. "You'll have a letter from that ghastly MP. He's calling a meeting." She shuddered theatrically. "I shan't be bothered going, nothing he says could be of the slightest interest to me."

She showed her teeth, Bella assumed it was a smile.

"I do hope everything is all right with your Lara. My Darlene said the teachers want to talk to you about her. I thought she looked a bit peaky. Do you think she was more involved with next door, and hasn't said?"

Bella smiled sweetly as she gritted her teeth. "She's been studying hard. She's applying to attend Oxford University. She has big plans for her life, not quite like your Darlene." She had the guilty pleasure of seeing Mrs Smith's smile fade before Bella firmly closed the door on her. She felt a bit guilty about her final comment, but Barbara Smith did have a knack of rubbing her up the wrong way, and she was fuming about the mail, even though she had nothing to hide.

She read her letters while John rang Griz. "Kevin Burke has invited us to a private meeting of the Oak Tree Lane home owners," she said. "It's in the Council Conference Hall on Wednesday."

"Griz just told me. He'll be there too."

The ten o'clock meeting was well attended. Bella, Lara, and John had seats in the third row from the front, next to June and Peter Mansell.

Kevin Burke, the MP was there with Richard Prebble, Minister of Transport, the Mayor, and two Councillors. They sat at a table at the top of the room, with a large map of the area on the screen behind them.

"Do you notice who isn't here?" asked John.

Bella glanced around. "Barbara Smith is missing, and the claimed landlord of the units. But look, there's Charlotte Thompson. I offered her a lift, but she decided to driver herself. My, she is such a strong woman. Bill Tennant is here too. I wonder why."

"And so is our dear Councillor Tony Hunt." John paused. "He isn't at the top table. Hmm, that says a lot."

The mayor stood, cleared his throat and began. "Within three weeks, you will all be receiving new valuation papers. You will be pleasantly pleased with the figures. Along with them though, you will receive notice that your land is being rezoned as commercial. It means that over the next few years, all of your homes will be purchased under Compulsory Purchase Orders."

"Oh, my goodness," gasped June Mansell. "We've just got the house and garden right."

"Well, we'll have to start afresh." Peter Mansell looked positively pleased.

Bella stared around at the shocked look on the faces of her

neighbours. Some looked shaken, others horrified. She felt relief.

Richard Prebble took over. "The new business is Emory Airport." He waited for the buzz of speculation to die down. "It'll be a large national airport, huge for the area. The land around it, including Oak Tree Lane will be taken over for the road approach and some of the associated businesses. Before anyone asks, the oak tree will remain. At Miss Charlotte Thompson's insistence, there is a protection order on it, and the road will be designed to give it a very wide berth."

"Look at the smug look on Anthony Hunt's face," whispered Bella. "He must be quids in."

Kevin Burke took over again. "The airport will sit from Thompson's Hill in the south, and up to the northern tip of Granger's Flats. Access will be through Thomson's Hill."

The map behind them changed to a close-up of the street and the land around, with a large section shaded red.

There was a long moment of silence, and then John grabbed Bella's hand. "They went northwest instead of south. Look at Tony Hunt's face. His farms aren't included. All he has are the units and Smith's. It's almost as if someone has purposefully cut the corporation out."

He leaned over and pressed Griz's arm. "On purpose?"

Griz chuckled. "I'm sure I couldn't say, but look at the smile on Bill Tennant's face."

After another twenty minutes of talk, and five or six questions from the floor, everyone was offered a cup of mediocre tea, some stale iced buns and Sally Lunn while they chatted.

"So we'll have to move, Mum," said Lara. "Do you mind?"

Bella shrugged. "I guess not, but it is the only home Mellie has ever known, and I like Emory."

"There will be other houses for sale, Mum," Lara said.

"You'll all be fine," said John. "It'll be nice for you all to have a new start away from George. I was planning to buy a house, and I was hoping you'd all move in with me, Bella. It'd make it easier when we get married."

Bella stared at him in shock.

"Will you?"

"Honestly, John, that's the most unromantic proposal I have ever heard," Lara said loudly. "Of course she'll marry you."

Everyone turned and stared, and they were swamped, as their friends and neighbours rushed up to congratulate, hug and shake hands.

Bill Tennant was last in line. He grasped John's hand and slapped his shoulder. "Well, there's an early wedding present for you both." He indicated the far side of the room.

Two policemen were there, placing handcuffs on Tony Hunt's wrists.

"Evidently there were some very dicey dealings when he was Mayor. The investigation has been going for quite a long time. A different department, of course, and I wasn't told until I asked specific questions. A new inquiry into the two car accidents has given a few interesting titbits, and IRD is investigating Tony and the Huntington Corporation. They're very unhappy it seems. Mind you, John, it might not be enough of a reward if young Bella here doesn't say yes to your proposal."

John turned and took her hands. "Please set a date."

Bella smiled. "I will if you trim your beard. What about the last day of the year? December 31st, 1985."

He leaned forward and kissed her gently on the lips. "Under the oak tree so everyone can celebrate with us?"

She nodded, and gazed around at her neighbours. "Emory will never be the same, will it?"

About the Authors

Derin Attwood

Derin Attwood began writing seriously in 2006, although she has always loved spinning stories for others. Her short stories were subsequently accepted in a number of magazines, and on various Flash Fiction websites. She had an Honourable Mention in NZWC 2010 Annual Short Story Competition for her story 'Towards Freedom'.

In 2008 she began a short story, which grew and grew, and eventually became The Caves of Kirym, published in 2012. It was followed by The Fortress of Faltryn, The Trail to Churnyg, The Sands of Valythia and The Burl of Meglinor. These make up the early books of her fantasy series, The Token Bearers. The series is continuing. The Fortress of Faltryn was short-listed for the Sir Julius Vogel Award in 2014.

Writing chapters for Emory was a step out of Attwood's comfort zone, mainly because she couldn't branch into her usual fantasy solutions of adding a fleet of dragons, or whizz off to another planet. However, it was an interesting experience, and she proved to herself she could do it.

She lives in Whangarei, with her adoring husband, who has always encouraged her to write.

Robert Burt

Rob Burt, seventy years old, hails from Whanganui. He has four adult children and four mokopuna (grandchildren).

He is a retired social worker with over thirty years of practice to his name, mostly done in Auckland.

He travelled extensively in the 1990s and spent significant amounts of time in South Asia and the Middle East. It was his experiences during numerous trips to India that inspired the idea for his story.

Burt settled in Whangarei in the middle of 2015. Although he dabbled in writing over the years, albeit in an undisciplined way, he was able, over the last twelve months to find the time to develop his craft.

Alison Davie

Made in Scotland, she moved to New Zealand 20 years ago after she left the British Army. Having been attached to the UN, she served in Bosnia in 1994—95, and was awarded the UN Peacekeeping Medal.

Once in New Zealand, as well as working as a Registered Nurse, she obtained a Bachelor of Performing and Screen Arts Degree. Her graduating short film 'Danny Alexander' was accepted into the Ivy Film Festival in New York in 2006 as well as other festivals. She wrote for the TV medical drama, Shortland Street before becoming an independent film-maker. She has spent the last two and a half years writing and directing a documentary called 'Crazy Happy, for which she won Best Writer of a Feature at the Toronto Alternative Film Festival.'

"It has been great fun being part of this anthology and having the support of the others in the group."

She is currently working on her own novel, as well as continuing her script writing.

Teresa Herleth

Always full of creative energy and ideas it took Teresa a while to value her joy of writing enough to give it more attention.

After a magical trip to the USA in 2013 the seed of writing stories was planted. That same year she joined a writing group which ultimately lead to this project.

In June 2015 Teresa packed up her idyllic beach-side life and moved to London to make writing her priority. She currently has people working on the illustrations for three different stories and is working on a children's chapter book about a group of friends who must creatively save their soil city.

Kamala Jackson

Kamala Jackson was born in India and lived there with her expatriate parents. This early experience has influenced much of her writing. Her NZ home was in Takapuna, and she went to Auckland University.

Her OE lasted seven years. Her early writing included a short story published in Air New Zealand's inflight magazine; four stories broadcast on National Radio; prose and verse included in the anthology, *the new gramophone room,* published by Auckland University Press; and a novella accepted by a literary journal that folded before publication, someone's idea of a joke?

Her energies then went into bookselling. In 2009, she wrote a 100,000-word novel for the AUT Master of Creative Writing degree, for which she was awarded an A. She spent some years looking after her elderly husband. In 2016, she started writing flash fiction. Her entry was longlisted in the National Flash Fiction Competition 2016, judged by Elizabeth Smither and James Norcliffe.

Clare Matravers

Although Clare Matravers was born in Te Aroha, she spent most of her childhood in Whangarei before moving to Hamilton to study, and live for many years. After a two-year stint in Taupo, she moved back to Whangarei to look after her elderly mother.

Being a care-giver has given Clare plenty of time to write. She completed her first novel 'Ripples in the Water' in 2015, and the sequel The Truth Will Out in 2017. She won third prize in the Whangarei Public Library Flash Fiction competition in 2016, and fourth prize in 2017.

The social science degree and research diploma she gained from Waikato University have helped her with characterisation, research and writing skills.

Anna Williams.

Anna began writing stories during primary school, and when she was around ten years old, had two stories published in the N.Z. Herald.

In 2010, she completed some papers in Northtec's Diploma of Applied Writing and also submitted articles for the 'BabyTalk' column in Savvy magazine. In 2014, her first book Simply Parenting was published. Over the next two years she has been shortlisted in the Whangarei Library Flash Fiction competition, being placed third and fourth consecutively. She has also just had her first children's book, Remember the Moon published.

Writing Emory in collaboration with the other members of the Pen-Ultimate group has been a whole new challenge for her, but a lot of fun as well.

Anna lives in Whangarei with her husband, has a son and daughter and two grandchildren.

Acknowledgement

We wholeheartedly thank Derin for getting our group together, for masterminding and leading the Emory project, and hosting our meetings with tea and coffee for two years. Our special thanks to her husband Ron, for accepting our regular, noisy incursions into his space with generosity and good humour.

If you have enjoyed Emory, please leave a review on the website of the seller you purchased it from. Good reviews are the life blood of independently-published authors, so please take a few moments to let others know what you thought of the book.

Thank you for reading.

www.wordlypress.com

www.ingramcontent.com/pod-product-compliance
Lightning Source LLC
Chambersburg PA
CBHW051333250626
47155CB00007B/2576